WI

Collecting Sins

COLLECTING SINS

A NOVEL

STEVEN SOBEL

SANTA
MONICA
PRESS

This book is a work of fiction. All of the names, characters, places, and incidents
portrayed in this novel are either products of the author's imagination or are
used fictitiously, and any resemblance to actual events, locales, or persons,
living or dead, is entirely coincidental.

All books published by Santa Monica Press LLC are available at special
quantity discounts when purchased in bulk by corporations, organizations,
or groups. Please call our special sales department at 1-800-784-9553.

Published by:
Santa Monica Press LLC
P.O. Box 1076
Santa Monica, CA 90406-1076
1-800-784-9553
www.santamonicapress.com

Printed in the United States

Book design by Ken Niles/Ad Infinitum Design
Cover illustration by David Mellon

Sobel, Steven, 1954–
            Collecting Sins / by Steven Sobel.
                  p.   cm.
            ISBN 1-891661-04-3
      PS3569.023C65 1998
      813'. 54–dc21   98–54322
                                    CIP

10 9 8 7 6 5 4 3 2 1

For Susan

CHAPTER ⊙NE

Graham and I went into the sewers one early summer afternoon because Graham was short on sins for his next confession. Graham's family had recently become Catholic and we were constantly sinning so that Graham would have a supply for his confession each week. We eased ourselves through the curb opening, then slid feet first on our stomachs and elbows through the first pipe that led into the larger pipe. The smell of the molding leaves along the bottom of the pipe was familiar by then, and I almost liked the smell. It was cool and moist in the sewers compared to the dry heat outside.

Actually, I'm not really the type who would spend that much time in the sewers. I shouldn't say this, but I'd rather be traveling the world's oceans on giant ships and small working boats and crossing the continents on jets and trains and horseback and by foot along old cobblestone roads and narrow mountain paths. I'd rather be sitting comfortably drinking wine in small cafes in Paris, having heated discussions in French about philosophy with someone brilliant. I'd rather be climbing the Himalayas. I'd rather be loving beautiful women, deeply and passionately, and them loving me. I'd rather be finding a cure for cancer. Things like that. I'd rather be committing some incredible kindness that would make people pause and remember for all of their lives. It's just that Graham got on this religious kick where he had to do certain things, like collect sins every week for confession, and we were friends from the time we were little kids.

In fact, we were born within two months of each other although, in our fifteen years, life had already treated us a little differently. Graham had grown up taller and thinner than me and with thick blonde hair and a scar on his forehead below a big cowlick. I had brown hair and a scar on my back, from my father—nothing too big.

I lowered myself into the larger pipe and stood straddling the few inches of water that ran along the bottom. Graham followed me in and we stood silent for half a minute. "No whispers from the dead," Graham said, finally.

"None for me, either," I answered. We lived in a housing development where some company had carved up part of the open valley and made it into little rectangles with houses. Ours was the richer section of the development because the houses and rectangles were bigger than the rest and there were Buicks and Chryslers parked in our driveways instead of Chevys and Fords. Anyway, Graham had watched a program on television about how some of the houses in our area had been built on ancient burial grounds of the Indians that used to live around here and we figured the sewers were just deep enough that they probably went right through where those Indians lay buried in the ground. It wasn't right that they built houses and sewers on sacred ground and so we stood in silent respect whenever we first came into the sewers. That seemed appropriate, especially given that it was religion that brought us into the sewers in the first place.

In our pockets we carried books of matches and long white candles that we had broken into pieces. We each lit a candle. Both candles together illuminated only about ten feet each direction, but that was as much as we needed to see. There was only pipe in both directions. In the distance we could see specks of light where there were manholes leading to the streets above or side pipes leading to curb openings.

We always walked the same direction because a few yards the other way the pipe narrowed about eight inches. It was like a larger pipe fitted over the end of a smaller one and we figured that smaller and smaller pipes were fitted into each other in that direction. We walked slowly, straddling the water and bowing our heads a few inches below the ceiling of the pipe. Along the walls were occasional names and dates and a few incomprehensible messages. There were a lot of different dates. One said August 17, 1863, so I couldn't trust any of them. Most were written in different colors of spray paint in a sloppy squared-off handwriting. I wondered who had written all of these messages, because we never saw any signs of other people in the sewers. There were also a few words written by holding a burning candle up close to the wall of the pipe, which were written by Graham and me.

The pipe we were walking through was surprisingly clean. Except for the water constantly running along the bottom, we rarely saw anything else. In the six or eight times that we had been down in the sewers we had seen only leaves, a small branch or two, a few pieces of paper, a folded wet newspaper that we thought at first was a cat, and two dead rats in different places.

After ten minutes we passed a pipe about five feet square that connected into our pipe. We had passed that connection a few times before, but had never explored it because that pipe was smaller than the one we were in, and it seemed to be headed back in the general direction from where we had come. We didn't figure to get anywhere if we kept heading back. Quite a while later we reached another five foot square pipe. This one connected on the left side instead of the right. A trickle of water dripped out of one corner of the square pipe a few inches into the pipe that we were walking through.

"Let's sit down a minute," I said. I was getting a little sore from the way we were bending and walking.

We sat next to each other on the ledge of the square pipe. "I need a new candle, anyway," Graham said. We had each lit new candles after our first candles burned down, but Graham's second candle was now less than an inch long. We melted the bottoms of our candles and stuck them behind us on the floor of the square pipe. The candles made our shadows jump around on the walls of the pipes in front of us and to our sides. I started to think about how long we had been in the sewers and how far we were from the opening where we had entered and it made me nervous. We had passed a few smaller pipes connecting to the large pipe and looking through those pipes I could see light at their far ends. I assumed that the pipes led to curb openings, but the smaller pipes were so long that the far ends seemed to be only a few inches across, and I wasn't about to take any chance of getting stuck by dragging myself headfirst through a pipe that might be getting smaller and smaller.

Graham said, "Somebody was saying that these pipes end up at some river and then the ocean. All the water runs through these pipes and ends up at the river. Maybe we can get there. The water's flowing the way we're walking so we must be going the right way."

"What river does it go to?" I asked.

"I don't know, but it has to go someplace."

"Maybe the river's miles from here. I don't even know of any river where this thing might lead. It could take us days to get to a river."

Graham sneezed twice, loudly. "Who knows," he answered. "Maybe this is a shortcut."

Graham's candle on the floor behind us had burned out and mine was only a wick in a small pool of melted wax. The flame was flickering spasmodically. I lit a new candle from the flickering one and stood up. "Well, let's get going," I said. Graham stood up and lit his candle from mine. He suggested, "Maybe we won't go all the way to the river today. We can always come back with food and things."

"That's a good idea," I agreed. We walked on and left the little pool of my old candle burning feebly, the flame flickering.

We walked a long while in silence until I said, "You know, Graham, it's a lot easier for girls to belong to things than for guys. Especially pretty girls. They don't have to do anything. Even if they're ugly, but especially if they're pretty. They just have to be there and they belong."

"What?" Graham asked. "What are you talking about?"

I told Graham about a little shop called "East" that Jackson had taken me to. Jackson was a friend of mine who had moved from Connecticut to our neighborhood a couple of months before. I liked him almost right away, although Graham didn't care for him at all. Jackson was seventeen and had thick, shoulder length brown hair that he parted in the middle. He was incredibly thin, all the way down to his face and his long, curved nose, and he was over six feet tall. He always wore old, torn blue jeans and long-sleeved shirts rolled up to his elbows. So far I had never seen him wearing shoes and his feet were bony and calloused.

"East" was a converted old house hidden among a lot of other stores along a main street. From the street you couldn't even tell it was there. To get to the front door you had to walk along a narrow walkway of cracked cement, through overgrown shrubs and up three steps to an old wooden porch. Inside incense burned constantly and there were posters all over the walls with poems about love and peace, and pictures of rock bands and distorted, colorful pictures that I couldn't figure out. In glass cases around the rooms were strings of beads and other necklaces, pipes in a hundred different sizes and shapes and clips and other things that I wasn't sure what they were for.

Jackson walked slowly around the place, looking casually through the cases. I wandered through the house, which had only a few rooms, and found a small room with very thickly padded black carpets, black walls, and posters covering almost every inch of the walls and ceilings. The smell of incense was even stronger in the room. On each wall were thin tubular lights that made parts of the posters glow and also made certain white clothes, like underwear, glow. I knew that because there was a girl sitting against the wall with her legs out in front of her, crossed at the ankles. She shifted the way she was sitting and her skirt pulled up so that I could see a small, glowing upside down triangle of her white underpants. There was music blaring into the room and every once in a while a light would start blinking on and off so fast that if you watched someone moving it looked as though they were moving in slow motion. I recognized the music playing, but I didn't know the name of it or the name of the group that played it.

Another girl was sitting next to the first one. The girls looked about my age, or maybe a little older. I sat in the corner of the room, away from them. The girl whose underwear I had seen was sort of cute and I wished that I could talk to her. But I just sat there on the thick black carpet. The air was overly saturated with the smell of incense and the music was so loud that I wouldn't have been able to hear myself if I had anything to say. I listened to the music and looked around the room at the posters and the girls. I envied the girls because they were comfortable sitting there and I wished like anything that I was sitting across the small room with my arm around the cute one, maybe kissing her, and later walking hand-in-hand and talking about peace and love.

Of course I didn't tell Graham all of that. In fact, I didn't tell him very much and he still didn't understand what I had been talking about. He just asked, "How come you're hanging out with Jackson? He's a skinny, greasy hippie."

"He's not greasy. And what do you have against hippies? They're into peace and free love and everything. You should come with us to 'East,' you'd like it. There's something really cool about that place."

"Ben, you have to deal with real life, with reality. People like Jackson don't deal with reality."

I just shook my head. Graham was obviously way too influenced by his parents. I was there when his father had said almost exactly that same thing. It was bad enough that Graham was caught up in this religious thing—not that I have anything against religion—but to be quoting his own father was too much. I didn't know how to get any of that across to him so I just said, "What's worse is that you want to belong even more because the girls are there. It just doesn't seem fair."

Graham laughed loudly and his laugh echoed through the pipe. "You're going crazy, Ben! What're you talking about?"

I noticed that my candle had burned very low. "I'm not crazy, Graham. But hold on a minute—I have to light a new candle." I melted the bottom of the candle stub I was carrying and stuck the soft wax onto the pipe a couple of inches above the water level. That was what Graham and I always did when our candles burned so low that we could no longer hold them. We would look back for a while and see the weird shapes moving around in the pipe, getting wilder for a minute before disappearing, as the flame burned smoothly at first, then flickered, searching for something else to burn just before dying out. After I had secured the stub I reached into my pocket for a new candle. "Damn!" I said and I felt one of those panics that shoot through you. I patted all of my pockets. I didn't like the idea of being down here without any light.

"What is it?" Graham asked.

"Damn!" I repeated. "I only have one short candle left!"

Graham searched his pockets. "I've only got two," he said. "How did that happen?" He patted each of his pockets again. "I had more than ten when we started."

"We must've walked for miles," I answered. I leaned down and blew out the flame on the candle I had just stuck to the pipe and I peeled the small remaining piece of candle from where I had attached it to the pipe. "Let's just use one candle at a time on our way back," I suggested.

"Good idea. Let's use mine for now." Graham stepped past me so he could lead the way back. "Jesus, Ben! I don't want to get caught down here in the dark. Remember that time we blew out our candles, how black it was? You could feel death."

"Shut up, Graham. We can always go out through one of those other openings along the way if we have to."

Graham started walking pretty fast, moving awkwardly, hunched over and stepping on either side of the water, but the candle kept blowing out because he was moving too fast. We tried walking without any lit candles, but that only lasted a short while. It was so dark without the candlelight that, except for the wet squishing of Graham's sneaker and its echo, I couldn't tell if Graham was right next to me or gone altogether. It was a spooky feeling—I didn't seem to be going anyplace in the dark, and I had to hold both hands out and rub them along the pipe to keep balanced as I walked. As much as I strained and focused my eyes I couldn't see anything and I figured it must be like that to be blind.

"I think we should try a manhole, if we find one before we get to another pipe," I suggested.

There were no openings for a while, but when the last of our candles burned out we were just a few feet from a manhole. Looking up we could see sunlight coming in beams through the holes in the thick metal manhole cover that was at street level. Graham climbed the iron steps that were cemented into the wall of the pipe, up the four feet that led to the cover. I heard Graham knocking against metal with his hand and then I heard him curse.

"What is it?" I asked. I tried to look up through the pipe, but Graham's body filled so much of the pipe that only a few thin rays of light got through.

"This thing weighs a ton. We'll never budge it."

I climbed up the steps after Graham came down and I tried to lift the metal manhole cover, but I couldn't move it even a fraction of an inch. When I was back down next to Graham he suggested, "Maybe we should go up there and yell or something. Someone might hear us and open it up. There's no way we can lift it."

"Go ahead," I said. "But I don't think anyone's going to hear you. That metal is too thick and the manhole's probably right in the middle of the street."

Graham climbed back up the steps and started yelling. He yelled for a minute or so, then stopped to see if anyone had heard him. When no one answered he started up again. After five minutes of yelling and stopping Graham finally climbed back down the stairs. "No one's going to hear us," he said.

We had to walk slowly in the dark, but it wasn't too bad because it was soon clear that there was actually some light ahead. When we got there the light was coming from one of the smaller pipes that led to a curb opening. About an inch of water was running along the bottom of that pipe into the pipe we were walking through.

We looked into the smaller pipe and Graham said, "No wonder there wasn't very much light coming out of this thing—it's a mile long!" The far end of the pipe looked like it was only four or five inches across.

"I don't know if I want to go in there," I said.

"Well, I'm going," Graham said. "I don't think I can take it down here anymore. Besides, we can always come back if we have to." Graham lifted himself into the pipe, which was too narrow even to crawl through on our hands and knees, and he started moving through the pipe, using his elbows to drag his body along. Graham's legs disappeared after him into the pipe, blocking out almost all of the small amount of light that had been coming through. I heard his muffled voice say something, but I couldn't understand what it was.

I cursed to myself as I hoisted my shoulders into the pipe. At least Graham would get stuck and I could always slide backwards. I dragged myself through the pipe on my elbows, trying to keep my chest and shoulders off the bottom of the pipe, but it didn't take long for my pants and the bottom of my shirt to become soaked. I was surprised at how cold the water felt, especially when it soaked through my pants. But it didn't bother me, I just kept my head down and tried to keep up with Graham, who was splashing ahead furiously. Soon my elbows were wet and sore and the rest of my shirt was wet from my own splashing. I looked up occasionally, hoping to see the opening at the other end, but all I could see was the trickle of light that found its way past Graham. I couldn't look back because the pipe was too narrow for me to turn. As I continued to crawl I started to get real nervous. I was closed into a narrow tube, buried under tons of dirt and cement, where I might be trapped and never found. And the pipe seemed to go on forever. After a while I could feel the skin wearing off of my elbows on the pipe, so I started dragging myself using the sides of my forearms, until they hurt worse than my elbows and I had to switch back to my elbows. But I didn't even care much about that, because I just wanted to get the hell out of that pipe. And I think that Graham did also, because he was moving along like crazy and not saying a word.

Finally there was more light and Graham crawled out through the end of the pipe and I had just a few feet left to go. It was then that I started to notice how much my arms really hurt. I crawled out of the pipe into one of those cement cubicles like the one that was at the entrance where we always came down to the sewers, and Graham was sitting on a pile of leaves, his back against the side wall of the cubicle. He was holding his arms out away from his body and blowing on his right elbow. My arms hurt all the way from my fingers to my shoulders. I sat next to Graham and started blowing on my arms, but it didn't help anything. The skin was worn away to where both our elbows and forearms were raw. Blood was beading up in a few places on my arms and Graham was dripping blood from one of his arms.

"We shouldn't have crawled so fast," I said.

"I know, but I couldn't help it. I just had to get out of there."

"Yeah, I know. So, let's get out of here. I want to get something for my arms." Like the other cubicle, this was cement on all sides, and the only openings were the pipe that we had just crawled out of and a narrow opening to the street that ran the length of the cubicle and was at the top of one of the walls.

"You know, we're lucky," Graham said. "I forgot all about it, but this thing doesn't even have any bars on it." Most of the curb entrances were covered by heavy metal grillwork. The one near our homes had been knocked loose by an automobile accident and never repaired.

The ceiling of the cubicle was low so I walked hunched over to the opening, where I felt a sort of shudder that froze my body for a second. I moved all along the opening, then my body froze again. I looked around the cubicle and took a deep breath, which I let out slowly. I didn't notice my arms hurting very much, just a dull throbbing. "We can't get out of here," I said. "It's not big enough."

"What? What do you mean?" Graham hurried over to the opening and tried fitting his head through. I got a short panicky feeling when it occurred to me that Graham's head might be smaller than mine and that he might get out and I would be left inside alone. But I felt better when I saw that Graham couldn't fit his head even halfway through the opening. I looked out to the street, hoping to see someone, or to at least figure out where we were. All I could see was some vacant land with overgrown bushes and a few trees across a narrow street.

"I told you," I said. But Graham kept trying to squeeze his

head through different places until he finally pushed too hard and hurt his head. I was still looking around outside, hoping that someone would walk by.

"Where the hell are we?" Graham asked.

"I don't know. There's nobody out there."

Graham started yelling, "Hey! Anybody out there!" Pretty soon we were both yelling and sticking our arms out through the opening and waving them around. But nobody answered us and no cars drove by, and after a while my arms got tired so I pulled them back in. Then my voice got tired so I shut up and just sat looking out at the street. Graham kept yelling and waving his arms for a few more minutes until he finally gave up also.

"There's nobody out there," I said and we both sat down.

"I didn't see one car drive by," Graham answered. "Maybe everyone died while we were walking around down there. I saw a movie once where that happened, except that the people in the movie were underwater instead of in the sewers."

I hadn't seen that movie, but it had also occurred to me that everyone might be dead, although it might only be that no one ever came to this little spot where we were sitting. "Well, if that's true," I said, "we're never going to get out of this place unless we go back to where we came in."

"My arms can't take it. And we don't have any candles left."

"I know, but even if somebody sees us down here, I don't know how they're going to get us out. You think they're going to tear up the street just to get us out? They'd have to rip up some of the cement to make a hole big enough for us to get through."

We were silent for a couple of minutes, just resting I guess. Then Graham said, "Let's try yelling again. Just once more. Maybe everyone isn't dead and there's someone close enough to hear us, now." I didn't think it would do any good so I didn't have the heart for it. I was worn out and I figured I should save my energy for getting back through the sewers. But Graham started yelling and waving his arms again.

"Ben! There's somebody out there!" I looked out and saw three guys a little older than Graham and me walking toward us from across the street. One of the guys was very heavy and had stringy black hair covering his ears. His stomach hung over his jeans and his face was wide and sagged into a huge dropping chin.

When they got up close to us the heavy guy asked, "What're you doing in there?"

Graham answered, "We're stuck. We can't get out."

The three guys stepped even closer and squatted to get a better look at us. One of the other guys, just a normal looking kid, asked, "How'd you get in there?"

"Through a pipe down here," I answered. "But we can't fit through this opening. It's not wide enough."

"That's right," Graham continued. "Could you call the fire department to get us out. They got a dog out once."

The second guy asked, "Why don't you try squeezing out?"

"We did already."

"They can't get through there," the heavy guy laughed. "And we don't want them around here anyway, do we?"

"*I* don't," said the third guy, who had a pimply, weasel face.

"Me, neither," said the second guy. "Maybe if they were dogs or something."

"What do you mean?" Graham asked. He couldn't believe that these guys weren't going to help us. He didn't know anything about the real world. "We're not going to hang around here," he continued, with a sort of whining, begging in his voice, that I didn't like at all. "Just let us out of here and we'll leave and go home. Our arms are cut and we have to take care of them."

"Let's see your arms," the heavy guy said. Graham and I held up our arms and he leaned closer.

"That's nothing. I think you should go back the way you came. We don't want you around here."

"That's right."

"Yeah, go on back how you came," said the weasel guy.

Then the fat guy choked up a big wad of mucus. Graham started to say something when the guy leaned forward and hocked the snot through the opening and it landed on the side of Graham's face.

The second guy said, "Alright! Nice shot!" The weasel started choking up some of his own snot.

Graham wiped his face with his hand and then rubbed his hand in the leaves that were under our feet. He yelled, "You fat slug! Disgusting fat slug!" I started yelling, "Fat slug!" and then I started with "Slimy weasel!" and Graham picked up on that also. The three guys started spitting like crazy, but Graham and I were already leaning up against the back wall so they couldn't reach us with the spit, except maybe once in a while on our feet or the bottom of our legs.

It didn't take long, though, for the guys to run out of snot and just have water spit left, which didn't travel very far and got them frustrated. The weasel said, "I can't spit no more. I'm going to get some rocks," and I could hear him run across the street.

The fat guy said to us, "Don't you two go anywhere. You just stay right where you are." He and the second guy ran across the street after the weasel.

Graham looked at me with his eyes open wide. "We'd better get out of here," he said.

"You're not kidding." It didn't occur to me at the time, but I can sure see why we can't manage to come up with a world of love and peace and all that, which is what we're all working for. There are just too many people like those guys. I looked back at the pipe that we had to crawl through and I cursed under my breath.

"I'm sliding on my stomach and I'm sliding slowly," Graham said. "My arms are wiped out."

I followed Graham into the pipe except that I went in feet first instead of head first. By the time I was most of the way into the pipe the three guys were back and throwing rocks. I managed to get all the way into the pipe without getting hit, although a rock ricocheted off the back wall of the cubicle and came pretty close to my head. I could hear the guys yelling and throwing rocks after I was a long ways down the pipe.

My elbows and forearms were too sore for me to put any pressure on them, so I lay flat on my stomach. My clothes had started to dry while we were in the cubicle, but they soaked up the water again as soon as I lay down. I used the palms of my hands, pushing against the sides of the pipe to slide backwards through the pipe. It was easy to move because the pipe was slightly downhill and there was a layer of slime growing along the bottom where the water ran and my body moved easily over the slime. It didn't take long, though, for my shirt to hike up to my chest and the slime to get all over my stomach and up inside my shirt.

When we were back in the larger pipe, Graham started cursing about the slime under his shirt. I was shaking a little and my teeth were chattering because my clothes were soaking and it was cool in the pipes. I noticed for the first time that there was a gentle breeze blowing against us. In the distance we could see another faint light and we walked in silence until we reached a small pipe connecting a few feet inside one of the large square pipes that connected with the pipe we were walking through. There were two little craters of wax on the floor of the square pipe where Graham and I had left the stubs of our candles, either earlier today or on a different day. It seemed a long time ago that we left the candles at that spot, whatever day it had been. Graham walked into the square pipe and looked into the smaller round one. He said immediately, "Forget it. This one's longer than the last one. My arms can't take it—they're killing me." I looked through the pipe and agreed with Graham. My arms didn't hurt as much as they had, but they still ached. "Let's keep going," Graham said. "Eventually we'll get back to where we came in. And don't forget, there'll probably be metal bars that keep us from getting out, even if we crawl through one of these other pipes."

There was a faint light deeper inside the square pipe and I said, "Why don't we check out the light down this pipe. If it's a real short pipe it'll be worth a try."

"Forget it . . ."

"Just a minute," I interrupted, and I stepped back to the large round pipe we had been walking through. The square pipe had a lower overhead than the round one, but it was easier to walk in because all the water ran along one edge so you didn't have to walk bowlegged to straddle the water and your ankles didn't get sore from bending to the round walls. I stared down the round pipe in the direction we were going to walk, waiting until I was sure that my eyes had adjusted to the dark.

"What're you doing?" Graham asked.

"If we keep going through the round pipe, there's no light in sight. We're going to be walking in total darkness."

"So? At least we know that there's a way out up there if we just keep walking."

"Well, I'm going to check out this square pipe. It's easy to walk in here and it'll just take a couple of minutes." I hoped that Graham wouldn't go back to the round pipe by himself.

"Alright," Graham agreed.

As we got closer to the light we could tell that it was coming from above. "It's a manhole," I said. "Let's forget it."

"Wait! There's something in there!" Graham said, excited. "Look, there's something on the floor." We were walking a little bent because the pipe was so low, and I slowed as I squinted to see what was ahead of us. Graham said again, "There's something there!"

I saw what Graham was talking about. "It looks like a pile of something. It's probably a branch," I said.

Graham was walking a little faster and he was a few feet ahead of me. Suddenly he stopped. "It's a body!" he said.

I felt my body freeze up a bit, but I said, "Bullshit!" I squeezed past Graham, staring ahead, trying to make out what it was. A few scattered rays of light from the manhole above were shining right on it, and it was beginning to look like a pile of something. "It's a pile of clothes," I said.

Graham was walking behind me now. "I'm telling you, it's a body!"

"Bullshit," I said again, but I was walking slowly. The light must have gotten better or something because suddenly I could tell that it *was* a body. It was a woman lying on her side, facing away from us.

"It's a woman!" Graham whispered loudly. "She's wearing a dress!" He stopped walking again and whispered, "Let's get out of here! She's dead!"

"How do you know?" I asked.

"She's dead! Let's go! We'll tell someone when we get out."

I kept walking and whispered back, "Come on." I was walking very slowly and I could hear Graham following behind me. I stepped up to about eight feet from the woman, and then I stopped. She was lying directly under the manhole. Her dress was brownish or black, one of those mini-skirts, and it was pulled up on one side. She was wearing black nylons and I thought that I could see the bottom of one side of her underpants, which looked brown or black, also. She wasn't exactly lying on her side, but her legs were mostly stretched out and her shoulders and head were bunched up against the wall with her head facing away from us.

"Who is she?" Graham whispered.

"How should I know?" The woman didn't move so I leaned forward and said, "Miss?" She still didn't move so I slowly stepped closer, repeating "Miss?" about ten times.

"It's a body!" Graham said loudly. He was still following a few inches behind me.

I got to within a foot of the woman and I leaned toward her. I still could not see her face. "Miss?" I said. My muscles were tightened up all over my body and my breathing was shallow and fast. I leaned over further and touched her shoulder. "Miss?" I looked along her body and down at her legs. I could see the tops of her nylons that were hooked with little knobs onto some straps that hung down from somewhere under her dress. I tapped her on the shoulder.

"What does she feel like?" Graham whispered. He was leaning over my shoulder, pressing against me.

"I don't know." I could smell a powdery, flowery perfume when I touched her.

"Is she dead? She's dead, isn't she?"

"I don't know." I gently took hold of the woman's shoulder to shake her a little, and her body rolled toward me. I jumped back and hit my head on the ceiling of the pipe. Then I froze. The woman's face was turned toward me, her eyes slightly open, as though she was trying to see me but just couldn't. Graham started screaming and running back through the pipe. The woman lay on her back, her shoulders flat on the bottom of the pipe, her legs bent over each other and her head and neck bent up against the wall. She didn't move at all. I glanced down and saw the tops of her nylons, then I looked back at her face. Her hair was long and black and a comb hung in her hair where it was wet and matted from the water in the pipe. It looked like there was a little spit at the corner of her mouth, and her eyes had closed all the way.

Behind me I could hear Graham running and screaming, but I couldn't move. I yelled, "Graham!" after a few moments, but after the echo and reverberations of my own voice died away all I could make out were muffled screams and the echo of Graham still running through the pipe. I reached out slowly and touched the woman's cheek, which was softer than I expected. In the dim light she had a youngish face, but a worried face, wrinkled around the eyes and lined around the mouth. Or maybe it was a face lined and wrinkled from always smiling.

After touching her I was sure that she wasn't dead, but I couldn't tell for sure that she was alive. I got down on both knees and leaned my ear next to her mouth. I couldn't tell if I heard anything or not, so I put my ear lightly against her chest to listen for her heart. I was holding my breath, but my own heart was pounding so hard that I couldn't tell whether or not I heard anything there, either. I leaned back on my knees and I didn't know what to do. Graham had stopped screaming, but I could still hear the faint echo of him running through the pipe. He seemed to be a long way from me already. I sat for another minute, looking at the woman, and I noticed that I was still shivering from being wet. I considered opening the woman's dress so I could listen better for her heart, but I couldn't decide what to do. Then I heard Graham scream. I heard sort of a thump echo through the pipe followed by Graham's scream echoing. It wasn't a yelling scream like before but a scream from pain.

I turned and ran until I reached the end of the square pipe. I called to Graham who was now screaming, "Ben! Help! I'm hurt!"

I glanced back down the square pipe, but the woman was

already hidden in the darkness. I wasn't sure what to do. I didn't want to leave the woman lying back there, but Graham was obviously hurt. Finally I stepped into the round pipe and called, "I'm coming, Graham! I'm coming!" My voice echoed dully and unclearly in the dark pipe. I walked as quickly as I could through the darkness for a minute and then I started running, bent over and stepping on either side of the water at the bottom of the pipe and trailing my fingertips along the pipe to help me keep my balance. Graham had stopped calling me and all I could hear was my own running and hard breathing.

After a short while Graham said, "Ben, I'm here!" and he was just a few feet ahead of me.

I stopped and answered, "I can't see you, Graham."

"I'm right here. I broke my ankle."

"Graham? What did you say?" I was walking slowly, reaching my hand out through the complete darkness. As I stepped forward the water seemed to be rising in the pipe because my feet were getting wet. "The water's rising!" I said, and then I felt the top of Graham's head with my hand. He was sitting on the bottom of the pipe, damming the water with his body.

Graham grabbed my hand. "Ben, I broke my ankle. I slipped back there." He spoke with pain in his voice.

"How do you know it's broken?"

"It is. It's killing me. I can hardly walk."

I squatted and put my hand on Graham's shoulder. It was so dark that even up this close I couldn't see Graham. "Why did you run?" I asked.

"I don't know. Did you see that lady's face? She's stone dead. Goddamn it—I broke my ankle!" Graham was still breathing hard and I could hear a hint of whining in his voice.

"I don't think she's dead. Her eyes were open, a little. I touched her face and she was warm . . ."

"You touched her? She probably has some wild disease! Which hand did you touch her with?"

"What kind of disease?" I asked.

"I don't know. Maybe VD or TB or something. Why else

would she be lying down here? If she was alive she would've gotten up and left the way she came in. Or at least she could've said something to us. I didn't see any blood gushing out of her. She's got to have some disease." Graham was breathing hard as he spoke. "Help me up, Ben. We've got to get out of here."

I helped Graham stand and as he gingerly took a step on his bad foot he strung out a list of curse words that would fit nicely on his list of sins. Finally he said, "It's broken, Ben, I know it," but he managed to walk, limping pretty badly, stepping in the water with his bad foot. The pipe was too narrow for me to stand beside Graham to help him walk so I followed a couple of paces behind.

"I can drag you through the pipe," I offered.

"No, it's okay. I just have to go slow."

"I didn't see any blood, either," I said. "But I don't think she has to be dead. And she didn't look like she had any disease to me. I touched her, Graham."

"Maybe she has leprosy or malaria," Graham suggested.

"Nobody has leprosy or malaria," I answered. "I wonder how she got in here."

"Maybe she got down the way we did and she's been wandering around for days until she got that disease and died. Maybe everybody outside got the disease and died."

"I don't think she's dead," I answered. Graham watched too much television.

"Or maybe she had the disease so bad she didn't know what she was doing and she accidentally crawled down here and died. Maybe we'll come down with the disease before we get out of here and the same thing will happen to us. Maybe you got it touching her and you've already given it to me. I'll tell you, though, she's dead. You could tell that a mile off."

I was angry that I had left the woman behind. I was thinking that Graham was so stupid that it would probably qualify for a sin he could confess. I said, "Aren't dead people supposed to be cold and stiff? She wasn't stiff at all; in fact she rolled right over. And she didn't feel cold to *me*. Maybe someone threw her down the manhole. It was right over her head."

"She's dead, man."

"We should've saved her."

"I broke my foot, Ben. We should get out of here."

It took quite a while to walk through the pipes, what with Graham limping along at a snail's pace. It was an eerie feeling to be underground and walking away from a woman who lay dead or unconscious someplace behind us in the total darkness.

After a while there were a lot of manholes and connecting smaller pipes that gave us a little light, and as we got close we started to recognize the different pipes and felt more comfortable. I had to crawl through the smaller pipe first and lean back into the larger pipe to pull Graham through. He was hurting all over his body. When we finally got up to the street I couldn't believe that we had actually made it out of the sewers, and I also couldn't believe how bad Graham looked. He might have just come out of a coal mine or a battle in Vietnam or something. His arms were cut up a lot worse than mine were, and his ankle was swelled up and hanging over his sneaker.

As we made our way home, it occurred to me that if the woman *was* dead, maybe her spirit was wandering through the pipes with the spirits of the dead Indians. I said to Graham, "If that woman's dead, her spirit might have been with us down there."

"Don't be stupid," Graham answered. "She's dead, but her spirit can't be down there. That's sacred Indian burial grounds. The dead Indians got buried with special ceremonies when they were Braves that got killed in battle or lived to be a hundred or something. You can't compare that to a dead woman in the sewers."

"A spirit's a spirit, Graham. It's just religion that makes up the ceremonies."

"A spirit *isn't* a spirit, Ben. That's the whole point of religion. If you ever understand religion, you'll understand that." I just shook my head in silence. Graham was getting ridiculous about the religion stuff, using it to justify every crazy thought he had.

CHAPTER TWO

I got Graham to his house and ran home to tell my mother about the woman so we could call the police or something to save her. Unfortunately we were in for a typical night at my house. It was already time for dinner when I walked into the kitchen and my mother looked over at me with that sad, disgusted look she was real good at. She sat on a small stool watching television and I knew that she had been glancing every once in a while at the clock and then out the window, on the lookout for my father, Ben Sr. She looked me up and down and asked, "Where have *you* been?"

I sort of hated to create more problems for my mother—she seemed so tired all the time, anyway—but there wasn't any choice. I tried not to sound too excited. "We have to call the police or something. Graham and I found a woman in the sewers. Graham thinks she's dead, but I think she's alive."

My sister, Marla, sat at the window watching for Ben Sr. "What?" she asked, sarcastically. "You were in the *sewers?*"

My mother waived her off. "What are you talking about, Ben?" She looked me up and down again.

"Yeah, we were in the sewers. Graham and I went down there—just to look around. We found this woman who was knocked out or something. She's still down there and we have to call the police."

My mother sighed. She glanced once more at the clock and then out the window. "Well, of course your father's not home yet. Let's eat and we'll call the police after dinner." She walked slowly over to the stove and put on some pork chops.

Just after we sat down, Ben Sr. got home. I looked out the window at the driveway when I heard his car drive up. "How is he?" Marla asked. My mother was eating, looking at her plate, and she didn't say anything.

"I'll tell you when he gets out of the car," I answered. I was getting quite good at telling when Ben Sr. was drunk, even from a distance. Sr. staggered out of the car. "He's wild!" I said.

My mother cursed. The only times I ever heard her curse was when Ben Sr. was drunk. She looked at Marla and me and said, "Why don't you two eat in the den."

"I'm going," Marla answered and she picked up her plate and a can of soda and left the kitchen. She always left the kitchen when Ben Sr. came home drunk. He hit her in the eye once when he was drunk. Of course he hit me a lot of times, but Marla was a girl and she still had a little scar on her face, just below her eye. I was quicker than Marla and lately I was getting quite good at staying out of Sr.'s way when he took a swing at me.

"You, too," my mother said. She had a tired look on her face, and I couldn't figure out whether she was trying to act severe or get sympathy from me.

"That's alright," I answered. I still had a lot on my mind about that woman who was down in the sewers, but these were the best scenes and I guess that I didn't want to miss them. Besides, I didn't really want to leave my mother alone with Ben Sr. when he was drunk. She could handle him fine . . . but just in case.

Ben Sr. came through the front door, yelling before he even got the door fully open. That was one of the things he did a lot when he was drunk. He was yelling something about dinner. My mother had already gotten up from the table and was walking quickly over to the stove.

"Yes, Benjamin," she said, gently. "I'm just finishing your chops." She tossed three raw pork chops onto a skillet. Ben Sr. staggered into the kitchen and my mother said, still gently, "Sit down, dear. It's just about ready."

Ben Sr. was carrying a briefcase and a newspaper, and he set both on the table as he sat down. My mother brought over his pork chops and dropped them onto his plate. The pork chops had been on the stove for only half a minute or so, and even from across the table I could tell that they were barely browned on the outside. My mother slowly lifted the briefcase and newspaper off the table, set them on a chair, then sat down and continued eating her dinner.

Ben Sr. was silent. He went right to work, slowly and intently trying to cut a piece off of one of his pork chops. Blood squeezed out onto the plate as he tried to cut. My mother was watching him as she ate and she had a slight grin on her face.

After a while, Ben Sr. gave up cutting the chop and he picked it up with his hands. He studied the pork chop closely. "Ssssraw," he said loudly, and he started to stand.

"It's not either," my mother returned, firmly. "It's exactly what the rest of us are eating. You look at mine." She looked at me for a moment without any expression on her face.

Ben Sr. slumped back into his chair. He ate all three pork chops. He ate with his hands and blood from the chops dripped down his arm and onto his plate as he ate.

I didn't know all the things my mother did to Ben Sr. when he was drunk. I wish I did know all of them. After dinner Sr. would usually go into their bedroom and either watch television or just pass out on the bed. Sometimes my mother would follow him into the bedroom, and sometimes I would follow her in. One time I heard banging coming from their bedroom and I ran back there and Ben Sr. was passed out on the bed. My mother was knocking his head against the head board . . . and hard! When I walked in she looked over at me, smashed Sr.'s head once more, extra hard, and said, "He'll wake up with a hell of a headache and maybe he won't drink so much next time." Then she took a half-full bottle of liquor which was on the table next to the bed, went into the bathroom with it and I heard the trickle as she emptied the rest of the bottle into the toilet. She flushed the toilet, walked back into the bedroom and threw the bottle onto the bed next to Sr. She said to me, "Maybe he'll think he drank all of that and it will shake him up a bit, but I doubt it." We both watched Ben Sr. for a few moments, lying on his back on the bed with his mouth open. My mother shook her head. For a second she looked sad and then she shrugged her shoulders. "Who would've thought . . . well, it could be worse." She looked at me intently and said, "Learn something here, Benny. You'll have a wife someday, so learn something." And after a moment she added, "And you'd better not mention this or we'll *all* pay."

I was sort of impressed. I was sad and all, but I was also sort of impressed. I didn't know that an average-looking housewife like my mother could be that resourceful. Of course that's the thing about life—you never have any idea what you don't know.

I was nervous all during dinner waiting for my mother to call the police. I didn't understand how she could just sit there eating while that woman lay in the sewers, except that I guess Ben Sr. could get pretty ornery. Fortunately, Sr. was even worse than usual and he passed out on his bed right after dinner. My mother called the police and they came and spent hours and left and he was passed out through all of it. When the police got to my house, Graham was still at the hospital because of his ankle. They were pretty nice cops in regular clothes and they took me out for a milkshake while we waited for some city engineers to find maps of the sewers. By the time Graham got home, two LAPD cops, a city engineer and a fireman were sitting in my living room and there was a fire truck and a regular cop car parked in the street in front of my house.

Graham came in on crutches and he had bandages wrapped around his ankle. I could tell that he was angry about missing all the excitement. I knew that he'd be especially upset when I told him later about the free milkshake the cops had bought me. The cops introduced themselves and Graham hobbled over and shook their hands. One of the cops said, "Looks like you did a little damage to your foot. Why don't you sit down."

Graham answered, "Yeah, I fell in the sewers. It's just a sprain, though."

Then they made Graham tell the story of what happened. They wanted to hear it from Graham in case I missed a point or two. He ran through the basic story and at the end of it he said, "We saw that it was definitely a body and Ben touched it and it

rolled over. It was a dead lady. We took one look at it and ran."
Graham left out a few of the details, like his screaming. I wondered if he did that because he was embarrassed or because he
considered it a lie and just wanted another sin. I guess it figured
to be a pretty good sin—lying to a cop doing an investigation
about a woman who might be dead.

One of the cops asked, "What did she look like?"

Graham answered, "It was kind of dark, so it wasn't too easy
to tell. She had dark hair and she was wearing a dress." They went
through a few other questions, but Graham couldn't say much
about those things, either. He acted as though he were right up
next to the woman and that it was the darkness that had kept him
from seeing more than he had. Then the city engineer showed
Graham a map of the sewers, the same one he had shown me, but
a copy without the lines I had drawn. It was amazing how many
sewers crisscrossed all over the place underground.

The city engineer said to Graham, "All these lines are drainage
pipes that flow underground. This legend, right here, tells you
the characteristics of any particular line. For example, this one
here has a diameter of thirty-two inches—it's a fine line. This
heavy line here . . . and over here, are larger pipes, sixty-four inches
in diameter. The dashed lines mean square pipes, and the sizes are
listed in the legend, same as the round ones, by how thick the
lines are."

Graham said, "Are you kidding? All those are sewers?" He
looked at me. "We could've been down there forever."

The city engineer said, "Actually, they're water drainage pipes.
The sewers are a different system. And that's why we have the
covers over the entrances, so that people won't get in there and
get lost or hurt . . ."

"Excuse me," one of the cops interrupted. "I hope you both
understand *how* dangerous it is down there. If there's any rain at
all those pipes fill up in minutes and you will drown. Sometimes
dogs get caught down there and they get scared and hungry and
mean. There are rats down there that could have rabies. Now, I want
you boys to promise me that you won't go back down there, ever."

He looked severely at each of us until we promised. Then he nodded to the city engineer who continued, "Now, this is where you started, at the corner around the block, and you were going in this direction. You were walking through the sixty-four inch pipes." The city engineer made an "X" with a red pen and drew a line leading away from the "X" along one of the thicker lines. Then he handed the pen to Graham. "You continue the line along the route you followed. Try to remember pipes that you passed and the entrances above your head."

"You mean the manholes?"

"Right. They're the circles you see along the drainage lines."

"You want me to draw it just to where the body is?"

"No, you draw it to the end of where you walked and then back. We want to know everywhere you went down there."

Graham took about five minutes to draw the line, stopping pretty often to think. I watched him draw the wrong route, but I didn't say anything. When he finished, the city engineer put my copy and Graham's copy of the map next to each other on the table. We all looked at both maps and the fireman, who hadn't said anything since he got there, said, "There seems to be some disagreement." Anyway, our lines were pretty different, so we went over it together a few times, but I couldn't convince Graham that he was wrong. Finally the fireman said that they would have to check both places and everything in between. I offered to take someone down there and show them the place, but the fireman said that they couldn't do that.

Graham and I rode in the back seat of a black and white cop car to a place under a freeway overpass, about a mile away. The two plain-clothed cops showed up a little later. Pretty soon there were trucks and cars all over the place—cop cars, a fire truck, regular cars and a couple of white and yellow trucks. The street was blocked off and people were hanging around to see what was happening. A guy took some pictures of us through the side and front windows of the cop car we were still sitting in. He used a wide camera with a flash. Graham covered his face with his hands and ducked his head every time the guy took a picture.

"Why are you doing that?" I asked Graham.

"People always do that," he answered. I didn't say anything. I just shook my head to myself.

We sat in the car for a long time while they checked the sewers in the area. A man we hadn't seen before asked us some more questions—like what the place smelled like and what the woman felt like and things like that. After we told him, he said the woman probably wasn't dead. I asked him whether she had a disease and he said that it didn't sound as though she had any disease that we should worry about.

They didn't find the woman, so everyone drove to another place. They let us out of the car and we stood around and followed them through the alleys and along a few streets. Just after they let us out of the car, a lady wearing a nice dress and a lot of make-up walked up to me and asked, "Are you the boys who found the woman?"

"Yes," I answered.

The lady said, "Wait here a minute, would you mind?" and she ran off calling, "Phil, over here."

Graham asked, "Who's that?"

"I don't know. Some crazy lady. She told me to wait here."

In a minute the lady was back and a man was following her. The man was carrying a big television camera on his shoulder. The lady walked up to us and said, "I'd like for you to tell us exactly what happened. We're from channel nine news. I under-stand that you two found a dead woman down in the drain . . ."

Graham interrupted her, waving his arms. "No comment," he said, "We have no comment at this time. Let's go, Ben." He pulled at my arm and then limped away on his crutches. I saw the lady look at the guy with the camera and shrug her shoulders. "Can *you* tell us what happened?" she asked me.

I looked over at Graham who was still limping away. I decided that Graham definitely watched too much television. I answered, "Sure, I'll tell you." The man faced the camera toward me and the woman held up a microphone and asked me some questions. I told her all about what had happened. After a couple of minutes,

Graham hobbled back and he interrupted one of my answers to say that my answer wasn't quite right, and then the lady was interviewing both of us.

It was getting toward sundown and they still hadn't found the woman. I kept telling people that I could show them where to look, but they kept saying that they couldn't let me down in the sewers again—there was too much liability. It was crazy. Graham and I went down there plenty of times alone without any liability at all. But now that they had the fire department and everyone else in town who could save us if we ran into trouble, there was liability.

It wasn't until way into the night that they gave up looking for the woman. It seemed as though we had walked ten miles while they checked through so many manholes that I lost count. I felt bad that they spent so much time and didn't find her. The plain-clothed cops even picked up dinner for Graham and me. But it was frustrating, because however much I tried, I couldn't convince them to let me go down in the sewers and show them the right spot. They said the woman must have gotten out by herself, but I was certain that she was still down there.

Once the police and fire department gave up on finding the woman everyone seemed to lose interest and disappeared pretty quickly. Just like that it was all over. I went home and lay under the tree in my front yard. I lay there for a long time, until my mother made me come in and go to bed.

Of course I couldn't sleep. I lay on my bed for just a couple of minutes and then I sat on the floor in my bedroom staring out the window into the night, listening to music. I kept picturing that woman lying in the sewers. I wondered who she was and how she got there. I remembered touching her cheek. And I just knew that she was still down there.

Eventually the late night settled into me and I started to relax. I watched the night sky through my window and got to thinking about the whole universe. Then I got to thinking that I wanted my life to be different. I wanted to be suntanned and grow my hair long. It was something I had been thinking about lately and it was because of this girl who went to my old junior high school.

I never actually talked to her or even learned her name. And I can't really describe the girl, except that there was something so nice about her. Something that made you take a deep breath and made your heart float up in your chest when you turned a corner and she was right there and maybe she glanced over at you. She was a couple of years older than I was, but she was about my height, and she was thin and she had long straight brown hair. I guess that she was the girl who I really wanted to meet at East or someplace like that. Maybe the woman in the sewers was once like that girl.

Every day after school, while I waited for the school bus that dropped me a few blocks from my house, I watched the girl and her boyfriend walk past me out of the school and down the street. They must have been poor because I think they lived near the school. The guy was one of those who's a step different from the rest; not better, necessarily, just different. Except to the girls that you really want, the ones that can strangle your insides because they're almost too good for anyone—those girls always seem to end up with guys like him. This guy was at least a full head taller than the girl and he had brownish-blonde hair down to his shoulders. One of his upper front teeth was only half as long as the other front tooth. He had an ugly, stupid-looking face that always seemed to be suntanned, if you really looked closely at his face, which you never did because all you saw was his long, thick hair and his sloppy, loose clothes. I never saw him after I left that school, but every day while I waited for my bus he walked past and he had his arm around that girl, sort of bent over her, and who knows what they talked about and how long they walked together and where they walked. Now if I saw them I'd say he probably took her somewhere to screw her brains out. And I'd figure he'd grow up so he couldn't read and he'd beat up that wonderful girl sometimes when he got drunk until she had kids and got old too fast. But when I used to watch the two of them walking around I didn't really know. I envied their intimacy and the romance of their lives. I thought it was love or something, and that's what I'll always think.

So I decided that I would grow my hair long and that I would go to the beach the next day to begin my suntan. And then, finally, deep in the night, I went back into the sewers. I wasn't too happy about it, but if I didn't go back to save the woman it would be a black mark against me always. I took everything I thought that I would need, including my camera with a flash, loaded with a new roll of film.

The fire department had bent the metal bars covering the opening back in place, but they hadn't yet attached the bars so I just pulled them away from the opening and bent them back into place once I was inside. I had to crawl very carefully through the small pipe because I was carrying my camera, but also because my arms were still raw from the day before. It was cool outside but I was sweating from nervousness, and when I got into the larger pipe the cool breeze in there gave me a chill from the sweat I had all over my body.

I stood silent in the larger pipe for half a minute, then said softly, almost to myself, "No whispers from the dead." I couldn't go on until I said that, which surprised me because I hadn't realized how superstitious I was.

I was nervous like I couldn't believe as I started walking through the dark tunnels. It was night so there was no outside light coming through the manholes or the sewer openings. When I was back in my room making all those decisions, I was calm and it seemed clear that everything would get better in my life. But the pipes were darker and lonelier than I expected. I used a flashlight because I was a little afraid of the weak, eerie, flickering candlelight. But the flashlight left complete darkness behind me and created a hazy, almost luminous tube ahead of me that seemed to have no beginning or end and pulled me forward.

I tried not to think about the woman, but she was all I could think about. Except for the hungry dogs and rats with rabies and flash floods that the cop had told me about. I was annoyed that he would scare me with all that stuff when he knew I'd have to come back down here if they couldn't find the woman. I walked for a long time, deeper and deeper into the pipes. For a time the manholes and connecting pipes were all familiar. I had walked through the sewers many times in my mind last night. As I continued, though, the sewers were different than I remembered them, and I realized that Graham and I had both given the police the wrong directions. I was getting more and more nervous, thinking about the woman and realizing how alone I was. Until finally I stopped walking for a moment, thinking that maybe I should go back. Actually I sort of froze. I turned the flashlight behind me, so that the darkness was ahead of me, and I almost went back home. But I punched myself on the side of the head to knock some sense into me and I continued. That seemed to calm me a little and then I started to look forward a little to finding the woman. It was something of a journey I was taking alone to save her. I would wake her up and help her walk through the pipes, or carry her or at least take pictures of her to show the police to convince them to go back after her. I was the only one who believed that she was still in the sewers and I was the only one who could save her.

I approached the second square pipe, where I was going to turn left, and I began to feel nervous again, just because I was so close. I stepped into the square pipe and took a few steps and then I noticed a smell. The sewers have a moldy smell that you don't notice after a while, but this was different. I shined my flashlight down the square pipe but I couldn't see anything. The light was absorbed in the empty distance. I started walking slowly through the square pipe and my heart began pounding so that it was hard for me to breath. After a while the smell became distinct. It was the woman's powdery perfume smell that had spread out through the whole pipe. I shined my flashlight down the pipe again and in the distance I could make out what looked like a pile of something, but which I knew was the woman. My heart started pounding even worse and I had to take deep breaths just to get oxygen into me. I remembered her eyes being slightly open and I couldn't help walking even more slowly. I called out a couple of times, but stopped myself when it occurred to me that I might attract some of those hungry dogs. There was no answer to my calls except for the dull echo of my own voice.

When I got up next to her the perfume smell was just about gone, and there was just a body smell, like someone had been sweating. It was as though her perfume had crept out away from the woman and through the pipe and left her to sweat. She wasn't lying quite the same way as when we left her yesterday. Her head was facing away from me and her body was mostly stretched out along the pipe. I noticed that her dress was down over the tops of her nylons. My heart had slowed a bit but it began to pound again, even harder because I knew that she was still alive. I called to her loudly a couple of times, despite the dogs and even though I was right next to her, and I nudged her gently with my hand, but she didn't move. I wasn't sure what to do to try to wake her up, so I set the flashlight on end on the bottom of the pipe, set up the flash on my camera and took a picture of her lying there. The pipe lit up for a split second, then resettled into the shadows that the flashlight threw. I leaned down on one knee and gently shook her shoulder. I shook it harder, saying, "Miss, miss, hello?" She felt soft, like yesterday, but up close she didn't have that flowery perfume smell anymore. It was the body smell. Finally I pulled her around so that she was lying flat along the bottom of the pipe, out of the water which was just a trickle along one corner of the pipe. Her head swung toward me as I moved her and I jumped back as little. Her mouth was open and her hair was matted across the side of her face. Her eyes were closed now. I stood up and took another picture.

I picked up the flashlight and shined it on the woman's face, which was as I remembered it, except that she looked older today. She almost looked like she was sleeping—except for the smell and the dirt and the hair matted on her face and the cement pipe all around. I shined the flashlight all along her body, down to the bottom of her short skirt, which I could now see was black. She also wore a black blouse with little pink and white flowers. I stared for a long time at her chest, but I couldn't tell if she was breathing. I set the flashlight back down and took another picture of her, from a different angle.

Then I did an incredibly stupid thing, although maybe it wasn't completely my fault. It started when I leaned down to listen for the woman's breath. I couldn't hear anything so I moved down to listen for her heart. I held my breath and listened real close, but I couldn't tell for sure if there was a heartbeat or not. I thought there was, but I just wasn't sure. So I unbuttoned the woman's blouse to make it easier for me to listen. She was wearing a black bra which was sort of hard to get off. I reached under her to try to undo the bra, but I wasn't sure how to go about that, so finally I just pulled the bra higher up on her chest. Her breasts, which were pretty big, sort of spilled out and hung over her sides when they were released. I wasn't really planning to look at the woman, just to listen better to her heart. But as soon as I got her bra off, I noticed them immediately—little gold earrings on her nipples! I leaned down and listened again for the woman's heartbeat, but by now my own heart was pounding much too loud for me to be sure if I heard anything coming from her, although I still thought that I heard something.

Anyway, I sat there for a long time, thinking, just looking at the woman, especially at those thin little gold hoops on her nipples. I got to wondering if they were clip-on type rings or if they went all the way through. Finally I had to find out. Her nipples were big with little bumps and when I touched one of them to look more closely at the ring, the nipple sort of scrunched up and stood out. I pulled lightly on the ring, but it didn't come off. I turned the ring and it moved through a little hole that went right through her nipple! I checked the ring on the other nipple and it was the same way. I couldn't believe it. I knew that girls pierced their ears and wore earrings there, but I didn't know they wore them on their nipples. And I didn't understand how I could be almost sixteen years old and not even know that. I lifted the woman's breasts to see if I could keep them on top of her, just to do it, but they were too soft and kept falling over her sides.

Then I had to feel her down below. It was wrong to do, and I thought about it for a long time before I did it. But after those rings in her nipples I just had to check. I was just going to feel around down there for a moment, then hook up her skirt again and try to drag her through the pipes. But of course she had to have little rings down there also, and I had to take a look at those as well. There were three of them, about the same size, but thicker than the ones on her nipples. Two of them went right through her lips down below, one on each side, and the third one went through the skin sort of at the top. I pulled gently on the rings in different directions and it made everything down there open up. I couldn't believe these rings even more than I couldn't believe the rings in her nipples. Not that there was anything wrong with it— in fact the rings were kind of nice. It was just that I couldn't believe all the things I didn't know about. Then I thought to check her ears and there were rings there, too, almost like the others, except a little bigger.

Once I had her clothes off I took a couple of pictures. Don't even think of asking me why because I don't know how I could let myself do it. She wasn't even all that attractive, once you got her clothes off. She had sort of a big, saggy belly with a scar. And then I couldn't get her goddamn clothes back on. It was impossible. I tried for a long time, holding her different ways and balancing her against the pipe and against me, but she just lay there and I was nervous and getting all sweaty and angry with myself. Finally I just sat back and relaxed for a couple of minutes, looking down the pipe, away from the woman, until I could calm down and I tried again to get her clothes on. I pulled and twisted the clothes and turned the woman different directions and, finally, after a long struggle I managed to get them on, but not so they looked right. Her nylons were crooked and baggy in places and her dress and blouse were twisted and uneven. I stepped back and shined the flashlight along her body and cursed myself.

I stood there for a while, still sweating and getting angrier and cursing myself some more. Until I realized that if I dragged the woman through the sewers no one would pay any attention to her clothes being a little messed up—everyone would figure they just got that way from being dragged. So I hung my camera around my neck, stuffed the flashlight in my back pocket and grabbed the woman under her arms and began to pull her through the pipe. I dragged her about five feet and realized that it was no use. She was much heavier than I expected and it was awkward trying to move her while bending in the low overhead. And I had a very long distance to go all the way back through the pipes. I set her gently back down on the floor of the pipe so that she was out of the water, and I left her.

The problem was that the film had pictures of her with her clothes on and without them on. Obviously I couldn't give the whole roll of film to the police because they'd know I took her clothes off, and I couldn't take the chance of trying to get the pictures developed so that I could give a few to the police. I realized all of that as I was walking through the pipe and it made me so angry that I hit myself in the head again, as hard as I could. I couldn't believe that I could be so stupid. And I had almost brought an extra roll of film with me, which would have solved everything.

I left the flashlight and candles under a pile of leaves at the opening of the smaller pipe. I was still agitated and I was still sweating. I walked back to my house to get another roll of film. I felt like running, but I was so irritated that I had to walk just to keep myself from going crazy. When I got home I put the old roll of film in my closet and put a new roll in my camera. I was so annoyed and angry with myself that I decided to relax on my front lawn before going back into the sewers. I still couldn't believe that I had been so stupid. I lay under the tree for a long while, cursing myself until finally I realized that I was only human, like everyone, and a while after that I relaxed a little.

I just lay there for a long time, a couple of hours. The summer night lightened into dawn all around me. I rolled onto my back and looked up into the tree, which was so thick with leaves and branches that not a single one of the stars whose light had carried through the centuries could find its way through. At first I was planning to go right back into the sewers, as soon as I calmed down. And then I couldn't imagine going back down there and I started to think that maybe I wouldn't go back. The woman lying in that stuffy dark pipe seemed almost like a dream or a scene out of a movie. No one else even thought that woman existed. I wondered vaguely if they could get fingerprints off of people's bodies.

I fell asleep under the tree and didn't wake until mid-morning. My mother was leaning over me, shaking me gently. "What? What?" I asked as I awoke.

"Ben, are you okay? What are you doing out here? You didn't sleep out here all night, did you?"

I looked around for a few moments until I realized where I was. "No . . . no, I just got up early and I must've fallen back asleep." The events of last night were slowly coming back to me.

"What is this? Your camera?"

"Yeah . . ." I answered and everything rushed back into my mind. "I . . . I got up early to take some pictures . . . of the early morning."

My mother smiled at me. "That's just like you, Ben. That's nice. I just don't want you to worry about yesterday evening. Everyone makes mistakes. You did the right thing by telling us what you thought you found in those drainage pipes. Now come into the house and I'll make you some breakfast." She looked so sincere and I wondered how she could've gotten stuck with my father.

I ate a quick breakfast, just to get up my strength because I hadn't slept much, and I ran down the street. That woman lay in the sewers while I slept.

As I approached the corner where I would get into the sewers I slowed to a walk. A large city truck was parked by the entrance and orange cones blocked off part of the street. When I got up close my heart dropped. They were fixing the goddamn metal grid that covered the entrance! I walked right up to where I could see two men bending the metal into place and putting new cement to hold it in. I watched for a few minutes, then walked around the block. When I came back they were still there so I walked around two blocks and then three blocks and they just wouldn't leave. I knew that there were no other entrances I could get into because Graham and I had spent a lot of time looking for them. I figured my best chance would be to pull the metal out from the wet cement, if only those guys would finish. So I walked around five blocks and then six blocks and then I ate lunch and finally at eight blocks they were gone. It was already mid-afternoon.

I was exhausted by then, and not really in the slightest mood to go back into the sewers. I was working on momentum in the morning, but that was pretty much gone. I decided to stop at Graham's. It only seemed fair since he had found the woman with me.

Graham's mother let me in, but she wasn't very friendly to me. Graham was watching television in the family room. His ankle was covered by ace bandages and he lay on the couch with his leg propped up on some pillows. A pair of crutches was leaning against the wall next to the couch.

"How's the ankle doing?" I asked.

"Not bad. I told you it was just a sprain."

I walked over and sat next to Graham on the couch. "I'm going back for her," I told him.

I expected Graham to get a little excited, but he just glanced away from the television for a moment and answered, "She's not there anymore. They looked everywhere and she wasn't there."

I couldn't tell Graham how I had gone into the sewers after the woman the night before, but I wanted him to help me go back for her. "I thought you said she was dead. How could she have gotten out?"

Graham sighed loudly. "Look, Ben, I can't even hang out with you anymore."

"What?"

"That's right. My parents think you're a bad influence. They're sending me to camp in a few days, after my ankle gets a little better."

"*I'm* a bad influence?" I asked, and I couldn't believe it. "If it wasn't for your sins, we never would've gone into the sewers!"

"It was still your idea." I shook my head and Graham continued, "It was a great idea, don't get me wrong. And when I get back from camp everything will be back to normal."

"What about the woman?" I asked.

"What about her? There must've been twenty people looking for her last night, and they couldn't find her."

"But she might still be there. She might be dying right now because we're not getting her."

Graham sighed again and pointed to his foot. "I can't even walk."

I could tell that Graham wasn't at all interested in the woman, and I was a little angry at him because of it, but I said, "I know. I just wanted to tell you I was going back down. I mean, we found her together so you have the right to know." It was my responsibility to get her and that was fine.

"Yeah. Thanks for telling me, but you're wasting your time."

I stood up and my first thought was to give Graham our secret pinky handshake, but he had already given up on the woman in the sewers, so I walked away before he could offer me the handshake.

"Let me know what happens," Graham said, and I just stared at him, sitting there watching some stupid television show while the world carried on around him. I couldn't believe that he just didn't care. The woman was *our* responsibility—any idiot would know that. And I was angry that Graham's parents blamed me for Graham going into the sewers. But it didn't matter.

I walked back to my house to pick up some extra supplies, including a hammer and chisel in case I had to chip away the new cement. I put everything in a small backpack I carried over my shoulder and then I walked down the street toward the opening in the curb where I would go back into the sewers after the woman. I walked slowly, remembering what I had done with the woman the night before. I felt pretty bad that I hadn't been able to control myself. I wondered a little if there was something terribly wrong with me. But more than that I was annoyed that I had gone to sleep and left the woman for so long. Maybe she had died by now. I jumped when I felt a tap on my shoulder. I turned around to see Jackson. "Hey, Ben," he said. "You're walking like your mind's in another dimension."

"I am?" I answered. "I guess maybe it is. I'm going back into the sewers after a woman we found the other night."

"Yeah, I heard something about that. You actually found a woman in the sewers? You're kidding?"

We reached the corner where the sewer entrance was and I

paused. I had to get back down there to save the woman, but I just walked past the opening and told Jackson the whole story. I guess maybe I was a little relieved that I had an excuse to put off going back into the pipes. Of course I might have been better off just going back down there and not walking any further with Jackson. I didn't know that we would run into Connie and that Jackson would get me started with her and that it would end up, well, I guess like a lot of things in life. Something that had good parts and pretty bad parts but that I was happy I did when it was all over and I looked back at it.

Connie was in her front yard watering her vegetables. She worked in her garden every day, but it didn't seem to me that she had all that much success with it. Her vegetables were a scraggly bunch, crammed together in a small plot below her living room window.

When I saw Connie I left Jackson on the sidewalk and I walked silently up behind her. She was wearing her overalls, standing and looking down at the plants and the top of her head came up to the bottom of my chin. I stuck a twig in the loose brown curls on her head. Without looking around she said, "Hi, Ben."

"How did you know it was me?" I asked.

Connie turned around and answered, "I don't know." She looked into my eyes so that I felt uncomfortable and I had to look away. Jackson walked over and I introduced him.

Jackson asked, "You're growing vegetables? That's cool. That's real cool. Maybe you'll let me taste them when they get ripe." I glanced at Jackson because I couldn't believe he would seriously eat anything that looked like these vegetables.

"Sure I will. I don't use any pesticides so they don't look like the ones in the stores, but they'll be delicious. In fact, one of the ears of corn is ripe already." Connie pulled a scrawny little ear of corn out of her pocket and handed it to me. "See, Ben?"

I took the ear of corn and Jackson and I examined it. "Are you sure it's ripe?" I asked.

"I'm pretty sure," Connie answered. She leaned over and peeled the sheath away from the corn, supporting the corn by holding onto my hand. She pointed to a brown kernel and said,

"That's a bee sting, which means that the corn is ripe." She was still holding onto my hand. It figured that a bee would sting Connie's corn and turn it brown. We talked a little more about Connie's vegetables and she invited us both over next week to eat a salad with her, and then Jackson and I left.

As we walked away, Jackson asked, "Is she your girlfriend or something?"

"No."

"She likes you."

"I know she does. She's sort of ugly."

"She is a little bit ugly, but so what."

"And she has cancer . . ."

"What?" Jackson stopped walking. "She has cancer?"

"That's right. Everybody knows about it. It's some kind of slow cancer that you can't do anything about.

Jackson stared at me for a long time without saying anything. "That's terrible," he said, finally. "But she looks fine."

"Yeah, I know. You'd never think she had it."

"And she seems so happy and everything."

"That's just how she is."

"Well, you can tell she really likes you," Jackson said again. "It's maybe not that often that someone really likes you."

"I know, but she's not my girlfriend or anything. I mean, I felt her boobs once . . ."

"What? What do you mean you felt her boobs once? How did you do that?" I explained how one night a few months ago, Connie and I were playing cards for a long time and just started kissing, and how after a while I just reached under her shirt and there were her boobs. When I finished Jackson asked, "How did you just start kissing?"

I thought for a minute, then answered, "I don't know. We just did."

Jackson shook his head. "And that was it? You didn't even care for her?" Jackson was getting angry and I didn't understand why.

"I cared a little bit for her."

"You just used her."

"I didn't *use* her . . ."

"Well, you didn't even like her. You just felt her up and walked away from her. Don't you think you should at least *care* for someone before you put your hands on her?" Jackson was getting angrier.

"She's sort of ugly . . ."

"Jesus Christ!" Jackson was screaming all of a sudden and I was happy that we were already down the block from Connie. "She wasn't too ugly for you to put your hands on her . . ."

"Take it easy," I interrupted. "I *did* like her, even if she is a little ugly. But she has cancer, I told you that."

Jackson started walking again and I followed next to him. He was calmed down, but he didn't say anything for a while. "I'm sorry," he said, finally. "It's just a thing with me. I guess I'm a little uncool that way."

"What do you mean?"

"Never mind," Jackson answered. I watched his face, hoping to figure out what he was talking about, but he was staring down the street, thinking about something else. I looked closely at Jackson, maybe for the first time, and I realized that he was actually a pretty ugly guy. He walked a little hunched and I figured that even with his long hair and lack of respect for society, he wasn't the type that girls would go for. After a while he looked back at me and said, "You should still like her, Ben, even with cancer."

I didn't know why Jackson would say that or even what to answer, but I said, "You think so? Why?"

"If you had cancer what would you be doing? What would you want out of life?"

"I guess I'd . . ."

"You'd want to live every minute. You'd want to love. You'd want to experience everything before you died. You wouldn't want a single p minute in your life."

"A p minute?"

"That's right."

"What's a p minute?"

"It's a pussy minute, a potential minute . . . a wasted minute.

A minute you could be out . . ."

"Finding pussy?" I interrupted, and then I was a little sorry I said that because I thought Jackson might yell at me.

But instead he stared off down the street again and answered, "Yeah, maybe. Maybe that's right." I didn't know what Jackson was talking about, but then he said, "I had a friend in Connecticut who used to hate p minutes. Just hated them. He called them pussy minutes." Jackson laughed for just a second, thinking about his friend. "He was a very smart guy, but he never even had a girlfriend. He used to say that if he could spend all those wasted minutes chasing pussy, then he'd be knee deep in it. He used to say 'Think of all the pussy minutes you could add up in a year and tell me you couldn't get some good pussy with all that time.'" I could understand that, and it made sense to me, but Jackson added, "Of course, that's kind of a disrespectful way to look at women, and the world. I think of them as potential minutes, potentially anything. But I call them p minutes out of respect for John, who thought of the idea." I liked pussy minutes better, myself, but I didn't say anything. I figured I could think about it later to decide if it was really that disrespectful. Then Jackson looked back at me and said, "Anyway, don't you think Connie wants the same thing you would want if you had cancer? You should like her even if she has cancer. You should *love* her, if you do."

I wasn't really prepared to think about something like that on top of the woman being down in the sewers and all, but I answered, "Okay." Jackson was definitely a strange person.

I was thinking about the woman in the sewers again and I guess Jackson read my mind. "So you really think she's still down there?" he asked.

"I'm sure she is. I'm not *absolutely* sure, but I'm pretty sure."

"Even after all those people the other night were looking for her and couldn't find her? How could they not find her?"

"I don't know. They just couldn't figure out the place. I don't know how."

Jackson said, "Well, then, we have to go back down there and make sure. We *have* to."

I already knew that, but I wasn't sure I wanted Jackson to be involved in this. I liked him and all, but I hadn't known him that long and I didn't feel that he had the history yet to be going down in the sewers after this woman. And I was a little concerned about how upset he got at me about Connie, especially considering how the woman's clothes were pretty messed up down there. Meanwhile I was a bit worried about being down there alone with the woman again. I didn't know if I could trust myself and it could turn into a goddamn nightmare—who knows what stupid thing I might do.

After giving it a little thought I said to Jackson, "You're right—let's do it now." Besides not trusting myself I decided that it would be better if we both found the woman with her clothes messed up and Jackson could tell everyone that her clothes were that way when we found her. I wasn't even sure I remembered what condition the clothes were in. Jackson and I would probably have to move the woman and that would explain my fingerprints on her body.

"Let's go," Jackson said. "We should get some flashlights or something, shouldn't we? Isn't it dark down there?"

"There's a flashlight and some candles down there and I have everything else in this bag, including my camera. I, uh . . . Graham and I left a flashlight and candles down there last night."

"What's the camera for?"

"In case we can't carry her. I thought I'd be going myself and if I couldn't carry her I wanted to get pictures to give to the police—so they'd believe she was down there."

Jackson didn't ask anything more about the sewers, which surprised me at the time. Of course now I know that the sewers didn't make any difference, they just happened to be there. It was the woman that mattered to Jackson.

The cement was almost dry so we had to use the hammer and chisel to loosen the metal grillwork covering the entrance. Fortunately the repairmen hadn't done a very good job and it took us only a few minutes. I chipped at the new cement and Jackson pulled on the metal until the grill pulled out. I wondered how it could possibly have taken those men so long to do such a bad repair.

Jackson laughed when we first got into the sewers and I told him about the Indian graves, but after thinking about it for a few moments he said, "No, that's cool. I have to take it back—I respect that." He stood silent and repeated after me, "No whispers from the dead."

Jackson didn't do all that well in the sewers. He didn't like sliding on his stomach through the first pipe and he was tall so it was hard for him to walk through the larger pipe. He walked for a while straddling the water at the bottom of the pipe, but it was too awkward for him and so he finally ended up walking in the water, splashing along in his bare feet. He didn't say anything about it, but I could tell that he was uncomfortable being underground.

We found the woman where I had left her; she didn't seem to have moved at all. We stood next to her, and Jackson shined the flashlight along her body. "Damn!" he said and he handed the flashlight to me and we both got down on our knees. I was surprised that her clothes weren't as messed up as I had expected. Jackson put his first and second fingers under the woman's neck for a few seconds and said, "She's alive!" Then he pulled opened one of her eyelids and said, "Shine the light in her eye." Jackson looked into the woman's eye and said, "I think she's okay."

"How do you know? What are you doing?"

Jackson answered, "I could feel her pulse in her neck and when the light shined in her eye her pupil got dilated—it got smaller. That means she's okay."

"How do you know all that?" I asked, amazed.

"My old man taught me. He's a doctor." Jackson had taken the flashlight back from me and he shined it slowly along the woman's body again. "I wonder if we should move her. She could have a broken neck." Jackson sat with the light shining on the woman's face, staring at her. "She's kind of pretty, isn't she," he said.

"Yeah, she is. Maybe she's a little too heavy."

Jackson glanced along her body. "It's kind of hard to say, but maybe you're right. I wonder how she got down here."

"There's a manhole over there. I think someone threw her down through the manhole."

We both looked up at the small beams of light that came through the holes in the manhole cover, which was a couple of yards further into the square pipe. "Why don't we climb out there?" Jackson asked.

"We can't open those things. Graham and I tried." Jackson had to try himself and I held the flashlight while he climbed to the manhole and struggled with the cover. I could hear him grunting as he pushed against the heavy metal.

"I think we should carry her out," I said. "They might not believe us, even if you've seen her too."

"We'll have pictures."

"Yeah, but they could say those are pictures of any woman. The police and the fire department and everyone else in Los Angeles spent half the night looking, and they couldn't find her. I don't think they'll believe us."

Jackson sat down with his back against the pipe and I sat next to him. "We should save the batteries," I said and I turned off the flashlight. I lit a candle and melted it to the floor of the pipe. The candlelight danced and sent our three shadows shifting around the pipe.

"This is really eerie," Jackson said. "But it's cool in a way." He seemed to be thinking about something else.

"They're not going to believe us," I said again. The more I thought about it the more I was convinced that even with the pictures no one would believe us. "They think what they want to think." I told Jackson about a telephone call that Graham and I had made. We used to make these telephone calls now and then, probably so Graham could use them for confession. An old lady answered the phone.

"Hello," I said, deepening my voice. "This is George Larkins from the Comet Soap Company. We're doing a survey and would like to know whether you use Comet Soap."

"Oh, yes," the old lady said. "I do use Comet. Yes, I do."

"We're happy to hear that," I said. "Do you use it on your dishes?"

"Yes, I do."

"On your clothes?"

"Yes, on my dishes *and* my clothes."

"What about your furniture?"

"I use it on my furniture, too."

"You use it on your furniture?" I asked. The lady was going to say she used it on everything.

"Yes, I do," she answered.

"What about your face and your floor?"

"Oh, yes, I use it for those, too."

"What about your vagina?" I asked. "Do you use it on your vagina?"

"Yes, for china, too."

"Your *vagina!*"

"Yes, I do use it on my china."

"Not your china, your *vagina! Va – gina!*"

"Yes, yes, I *do* use it on my china—on everything!"

I hung up on her after that. Graham had been listening on another telephone and he thought that the lady didn't know what a vagina was.

Jackson laughed when I told him the story. He said, "Graham thought she didn't know what a vagina was? You shouldn't waste your time with guys like him, Ben. Those are all p minutes you spend with them."

I answered, "I was just trying to say that people hear what they want to hear and see what they want to see. That was the point . . ."

"I know," Jackson interrupted. "You're right that we have to take this woman out of here. We can't take the chance that they won't believe us. And maybe next time they'll fix that metal covering so that we'll need a jackhammer to break it away." But neither of us moved and after another minute Jackson said again, "This is really eerie." He looked over at the woman. "And she's just lying there . . ."

"These are pussy minutes," I said.

"No, they're not pussy minutes . . . p minutes. We're here to save this woman and we're gathering our physical and emotional strength to carry her out. And we're also absorbing the experience of this place for a little while—that's fair. This isn't your usual experience."

"It sure isn't," I answered, and then I realized what Jackson was saying and that he was right. He had a different way, a good way I thought, of looking at things and I was beginning to understand it.

A half minute later Jackson sighed loudly. "Let's go," he said and he stood up and stepped over to the woman.

It took us a couple of minutes to figure out how to carry her, but finally Jackson carried the woman under her armpits, walking backwards while I carried her rear end across both of my arms. We turned on the flashlight and laid it on top of her chest, between her breasts so it wouldn't roll off. It was awkward, but we managed to carry her to where the square pipe connected with the large round pipe. Jackson had told me that she was alive and I wondered what it would be like to carry a dead person.

We paused at the end of the square pipe to figure out how to carry on. We were already tired from our short walk. Behind us, in the square pipe, our candle still held tightly to the bottom of the pipe, its light holding pretty steady. "This is going to be a bitch," Jackson said, lowering to his knees and supporting the woman's head against his chest.

"You're not kidding."

We had more of a problem carrying the woman in the round pipe. Jackson walked backwards, splashing through the water, still holding the woman under her armpits, but I had to walk behind, holding onto her feet. It was difficult because Jackson and I were both bending over in the low pipe, trying to carry the woman, her body sagging at her hips, her rear end pulling down, and she was heavier than you would think. I was also splashing in the water, struggling to keep the woman's butt from dragging in the water. Pretty soon, though, we were so tired that we had to set her down, and there was no place to rest her but in the water at the bottom of the pipe. When we set her down she made a dam and the water collected on my side. We'd carry her a little ways, then set her down and rest. Her clothes soaked up more water each time we set her down and she got heavier and heavier. We were both sweating and cursing and our muscles tired and then burned. But we carried on: it was something we had to do and we both knew it, and so we sweated more and cursed louder and our muscles burned more and our backs ached. We stopped when we had to, but we carried on.

Finally we reached the smaller pipe where we had first entered the sewers and I couldn't believe that we had made it. I climbed through the pipe to the cubicle, turned around and crawled back in head first. Jackson lifted the woman into the smaller pipe and I dragged her through, holding onto her hands. When I took hold of her hand I felt a ring on one of her fingers that I hadn't noticed before and I thought that there must be a million other things I didn't know about this woman. It was difficult to move backwards through the pipe, which was sloped downwards, holding onto the woman with both of my hands. I sort of scooted with my feet and my knees and my elbows, which were still sore from when Graham and I first found the woman. But Jackson pushed from the other side and with the slime on the bottom of the pipe I managed to pull her through. I pulled her out of the pipe into the cubicle and held her under her armpits the way Jackson had carried her. Jackson came through the pipe a few moments later and when he was in the cubicle he looked at the woman for a few moments and then at me and he smiled and sort of nodded his head and said, "We did something real, Ben. We did something that matters. Let's get her to a doctor."

We had a much tougher time squeezing the woman through the opening out to the street. Jackson got out first and I tried lifting her through, but she was too heavy so Jackson climbed back into the cubicle and I got outside. Jackson managed to slip her through with me pulling on the outside, but we scratched her face on the street as we put her head through the opening, and I felt pretty bad about that. Jackson carried the woman in his arms to my house. He was tired and struggled with her, but he wouldn't let me help. She just lay there, peaceful and unmoving in his arms, a few drops of water dripping occasionally from her clothes, and Jackson walked as though he were carrying some sort of a prize. We had been in the sewers for hours and it was already the late afternoon of another hot summer day. Somehow those hours merged a little with the hours I had spent down there during the past couple of days and it seemed that I had spent one hell of a long day in the sewers. The world around me was familiar and different. I was exhausted, but I felt good.

An ambulance came to my house and a few minutes later the police arrived. I was hoping the police would be the same ones who had spent all the time with Graham and me after we first found the woman, but these were different police who hadn't heard anything about last night, and weren't much interested when I tried explaining to them how all those people had searched for hours through the sewers and given up while the woman still lay down there. A doctor checked the woman and told us that she was alive but needed to get to a hospital and then a couple of attendants lifted her onto a stretcher and carried her out. Jackson and I followed the stretcher outside and watched the attendants lift the woman into the back of the ambulance. We watched the ambulance drive away and when it turned the corner out of sight we looked at each other and Jackson nodded his head. I held out my hand and Jackson shook it gently. "We'll have to get high some time and think about this," he said softly, so that none of the people around us could hear.

CHAPTER THREE

The next morning I put on a pair of cut-off corduroy pants and a t-shirt, and out of the linen closet I took the largest towel I could find. I folded the towel lengthwise into thirds and rolled it up so that I could carry it easily under my arm. I saw someone at the beach do that once. Then I walked over the freeway on-ramp, leaned against the wooden post with the sign that said no bicycles or pedestrians past that point, and I put out my thumb. I had been delayed by one day because it took so long to get the woman out of the sewers, but I was ready to start my new life. I was going to get suntanned and grow my hair long.

The beach was about twenty miles from my house. To get there I had to take the freeway maybe ten miles through the hills and out of the valley and then another ten miles or so down any of a number of streets. I stood leaning against a sign post and a few cars passed before one stopped. It was a silver Lincoln Continental. The electric window on the passenger side rolled down and the driver looked over and asked, "Where are you going?"

I looked into the car and answered, "To the beach."

"That's what I figured. Get in—I'll take you part way." The driver was a guy about fifty or sixty years old, and very fat. "I'm going to put the window up," he said after I got into the car. "When you get this old and this fat, you need air conditioning on days like this."

I wasn't sure if I was supposed to laugh at that or what, so I just said, "Yeah, it's pretty hot already."

The man had some classical music playing on his radio and we just drove for a while, listening to the music and not saying anything, except that the man said, "This is Chopin. I played the piano as a child and I always wanted to play this piece."

"Did you ever play it?" I asked.

"Never did." It *was* beautiful music and I thought that some day I would learn all about great classical music and be able to identify music like this that came on the radio. After a while the man asked, "Are you just bumming around these days?"

"I'm on summer vacation," I answered.

"How old are you?"

"I'll be sixteen pretty soon."

"Well, that's what I'd do," he said. "If I were sixteen I'd just hitchhike to the beach. Do it while you can—before it's too late. It gets too late too fast." He sighed and said again, "That's what I'd do if I were your age." He seemed like a nice old guy, and I felt a little bad that he wasn't sixteen so he could do what he wanted. I thanked him when he let me off and he said, "Enjoy yourself."

"I will," I answered, although I thought that was funny. I always think it's funny when people tell you to do something that you can't do—something that just happens or not.

It was early summer, but hot already. I stepped out of the car and the sun was scorching down on me. I leaned my head back and I could feel my face and arms getting tanned already. It was a good feeling, a feeling of freedom, to be standing in cut-off pants while people in suits drove by and tall buildings in the distance hummed with inside activity like painted-over ant farms.

After ten minutes or so I got a ride in a beat-up old convertible sports car. The driver was about twenty years old and he had long greasy black hair that was parted in the middle of his head. He didn't say much, but he sang off-key with every song that played on the radio. We drove past the one and two-story office buildings that lined the street. Along the way we had to stop at a crosswalk and wait for a bent old woman with a cane and a big black handbag to slowly cross the street. A song was playing on the radio, and I watched the old woman walk exactly in time to the beat of the song, all the way across the street, while the guy next to me was looking around and singing off-key, oblivious.

The guy took me to the end of the street where I crossed to

the park overlooking the highway and the beach and I stood for a long time looking out over the ocean, which seemed to stretch forever into the distance. Then I walked down to the beach and lay in the sun, feeling the hot rays soaking into my skin, making me tan. I lay there for a couple of hours, thinking about the happenings of the past couple of days and about the adventure I wanted in my life. I felt pretty good about having saved the woman, but I wanted that to be only the beginning of many great things that I would do. Only I couldn't figure out how to go about making those other things happen. And for some crazy reason I also couldn't seem to get the woman from the sewers off my mind.

I got restless and walked along the beach and it didn't make me any less restless so I decided to leave the beach. I stopped at the light waiting to cross the highway and a couple of kids my age were sitting on the ground putting their shoes on. I stood there thinking about the woman and the night before. It was the only thing I could think about. It was those goddamn gold rings she had all over her body. With the toes of my right foot I tore off a piece of the ice plant that grew from cracks in the asphalt, and I ground the ice plant into sticky mush. Then I did a thing that was a little crazy, although I'm not sorry I did it. In fact, I'm happy I did it.

The kids finished putting on their shoes and one of them said to his friend, "Barry, I forgot all about that! You see the wall running up along the incline?" Across the highway was a 300 foot cliff that stretched for miles both directions. The incline was a two lane street and a sidewalk built onto the side of the cliff so you could walk or drive a quarter mile from the highway up 300 feet to the top of the cliff. The incline was supported by huge cement pillars that reached from the underside of the incline to the ground at the bottom of the cliff. "Rich was down here about a month ago and some guy tried to walk all the way up the incline on that wall. The guy made it, I think he said, up to the fourth cement thing and then he fell off."

Barry asked, "You mean those cement supports holding up the road?"

"Yeah, I think so."

We counted to the fourth pillar, which was less than halfway up the incline. Barry said, "That's about a hundred foot fall. Did Rich actually *see* the guy fall?"

"Yeah! He said you couldn't miss it. The guy let out some wild scream that you could hear a mile away, and you could even hear him hit the ground. He demolished half his body."

The crazy part came next. We crossed the highway and Barry was saying to his friend, "Well, I'm sure someone could do it, if he was lucky enough. But it would be crazy just to try. I bet the wind as it comes off the cliff is enough to knock you off."

The first kid ran ahead to the sidewalk on the incline and turned toward Barry and me. "I think I'll give it a try," he said and he jumped up on the wall.

Barry said, "Go ahead, Mike. I'll give you ten bucks if you make it farther than that guy who fell off."

Mike answered, "Okay," and he walked about five feet along the top of the wall before jumping off onto the sidewalk. "Forget it," he said.

I said, "What's the matter?"

Mike looked at me for a moment or two. "You do it," he answered, and we were both still kidding.

"I will. Here, hold these for me." I handed my towel, shirt and shoes to Mike and I jumped up on the wall. I stood for a few seconds, just being up there and adjusting my balance to the shape of the top of the wall, which was a little over a foot wide and raised to a slight peak in the middle. The top of the wall felt rough and sun-warmed to my bare feet.

Barry said, "I'll give *you* the ten bucks."

"Okay," I answered, and I started walking, and then I changed my mind and said, "Never mind, you keep your ten bucks." I watched my feet as I stepped slow, careful steps on either side of the small peak. After I had walked only ten feet or so I was already beginning to feel comfortable walking up there. I glanced back and saw Mike and Barry talking as they followed behind me on the sidewalk, ignoring me because none of us thought I was serious, and I just kept walking. A few people passed me on the sidewalk. Some looked up at me and some ignored me as they walked by. But further up the sidewalk they all stopped at least once to look over the wall, and most of the people looked back at me after they looked over the wall. I guess I was enjoying the fact that people were getting interested in what I was doing. I wondered how much danger they thought I would be in if I kept walking.

At first Mike and Barry didn't have a thought that I would try walking all the way up on the top of the wall, and neither did I. After a while, though, I could tell that they were beginning to consider the idea, and about that time I think that *I* was beginning to consider the idea, myself. And then it wasn't long before they were afraid that I would try it, and maybe I was becoming a little afraid of that, too. Actually, they weren't afraid that I would *try* it, they were afraid that I might *make* it. Of course, at that point it wasn't much of a fear because they wanted more to see me try the walk and fall, or get a good part of the way and give up the walk and be a coward. But I didn't blame them for what they felt—they were just human, like we all are.

It hadn't taken long, but I was already almost at that point where I would *have* to keep walking. On my right the ground was slowly dropping away. The highway was now over thirty feet below me, though the fall would be only about six feet before I would hit the side of the cliff and then roll. On my left was the sidewalk, just three and a half feet below my feet, but in a sense it had been dropping away faster than the ground on my right.

It didn't bother me that I was in that position. In fact, I was beginning to enjoy it. It was a chance to feel that I was accomplishing something for a change, and a chance to separate myself from Mike and Barry and all the people like them. Not that there was anything wrong with either of those guys. It was just that I didn't want to be kept down to their level anymore. It wasn't such a bad level, but it was less than I *could* be, even less than they could be, if they only knew it, though there was no way to tell them. It's the kind of thing you learn by yourself.

I felt the sun warm on my back and shoulders. A gentle breeze blowing in from the ocean carried the briny ocean smells over the highway and the beach crowds and up to me. The wall was really not difficult to balance on, and up to now there was sloping ground less than ten feet below me; sort of a safety ledge that would stop my fall and let me roll the rest of the way down. And I wasn't going to get more than a few bruises, at most a broken arm or so, if I rolled down a hill.

Up ahead I could see where the ground to my right became steeper and steeper and finally disappeared under the road, and for a span of about twenty feet there was nothing to break my fifty foot fall to the highway, if it happened. I knew that below that stretch were the first two cement supports. I walked steadily, watching my feet, and I didn't think that I would be bothered when I reached the area where the ground dropped away. But as soon as the side of the cliff disappeared under the incline and there was just empty space below me, my body seemed suddenly to have outside forces working on it, overpowering what I wanted to do. Though I wanted to walk casually and undisturbed over this dangerous area, my body leaned to the left and slowed my pace. I kept walking and I tried to straighten up and increase my walking pace, but I couldn't do it, until there was once again ground below me to my right and then, even though the ground was at least twelve feet down, my body relaxed and I was able to walk normally again. I wondered how much I had been leaning away from the fall, and I decided that it probably was not much because Mike or Barry would have said something if they had noticed me leaning.

A man walked up alongside me and asked where I was going. He was mocking me and he had an obnoxious smile on his face. For a second I felt a little foolish standing up on the wall with possible death awaiting me on the side of the wall away from this guy, but I glanced again at his fat face and his fungus-covered brown teeth and I answered, "To an opera."

"By way of the hospital or the morgue?" he asked and he laughed. But I was already looking the other way and not paying him any attention. When I didn't answer he slowed a little and waited for Mike and Barry. He wanted to see what was going to happen. Mike or Barry said something to me, but I wasn't paying attention to them, either. By now, none of that really mattered. It was something more that mattered, and I was struggling a little, wondering what it was and feeling that it was just beyond my grasp. I noticed that people were starting to collect behind me and along the wall ahead of me.

I looked down at the highway and across the highway to the summer houses and parking lots that lay between the highway and the beach. It was a new perspective for me—a perspective that no one on the incline, or on the beach, or the highway, or in the city that spread out beyond the top of the cliff could share. I suddenly felt exhilarated and began to actually look forward to when I would stand above the maximum fall, alone, in a position inaccessible to any of them.

The ground to my right disappeared again under the incline and I looked down eighty feet to the bottom of the cliff. I couldn't help shuddering slightly and I felt my body lean toward the road again. I was surprised that the wall was becoming more difficult to balance on and that my steps were beginning to feel insecure. I had to watch very carefully in front of my feet as I made each step. The top of the wall was exactly the same shape here as it had been all along, but it seemed narrower and the way my body was leaning made it even tougher for me to balance. I tried to straighten up and relax, but I just could not force my body to straighten past a certain point.

As I looked down I could imagine myself falling—the five second fall through space never occupied by anyone, followed by a sharp pain when I hit the ground. And if I lived past the fall, my body would be bruised and scratched as I bounced and rolled the rest of the way down the hill into the sharp, dry chaparral at the bottom of the cliff. I looked up and ten feet ahead there was ground again about six feet below the wall. The ground was steeply sloped and the roll down the side of the cliff would be much longer, but it didn't seem dangerous as long as I didn't have to fall a long distance before hitting the ground. I watched my steps along the wall, but glanced up every few steps to make sure that I was getting closer to where there was ground below me. I managed to increase my speed a little until I walked that ten feet.

I was surprised at how tight my muscles were becoming. My shoulders and left side were beginning to ache. Still, I felt pretty good. I no longer had the exhilaration I felt earlier, but I felt good, and I couldn't figure that out. I had a couple of minutes ahead of me before the ground dropped away again. At that point it was a long stretch to walk with a long fall, but I would pass the fourth support halfway through the stretch. And after that I could jump onto the sidewalk.

In the distance was the crowded highway at the bottom of the cliff where the highway split into the freeway and a small road to the pier. Cars were moving slowly both directions along the length of the pier and people, insect size, were walking in and out of the shops on one side of the pier or looking over the railing into the ocean on the other side. The small marina between the end of the pier and the breakwater contained its usual number of small boats rocking gently on the chops in the water. I could picture the children sitting along the edge of the pier with their fishing lines in the water and their small buckets empty or full or partly full of the small perch and bass they had caught.

As the ground to my right dropped away again, I glanced back. A large number of people had collected on the sidewalk behind me. I heard a few people talking, but I could not hear what they were saying. Ahead of me were more people standing at the top of the cliff, at the end of the incline where the wall leveled out and ran along the edge of the top of cliff. They were a lot of the people who had passed me on the sidewalk. I guess they expected me to try walking all the way up the wall. I wondered what the people behind me were talking about and I decided that they must be talking about me. But then it crossed my mind that they might be talking about something that had nothing to do with me. Their minds might be on a television show from the night before, or what they were going to wear to a party the next weekend, or some other bullshit thing, and that I was just an incidental diversion to them. Unless I fell over the cliff and then they would talk about me to everyone they knew and probably remember me for the rest of their lives. Especially if I died or got paralyzed—then they'd even be interviewed on television and tell everyone how I looked when I hit the ground. They'd remember me and tell their children and grandchildren. Anyway, I didn't care what they were thinking.

The ground dropped away and my body pulled hard to the left. Sweat was beading on my forehead and on the back of my neck. I couldn't help glancing down and I estimated the fall to be about a hundred and twenty-five feet. I remembered that I was not far from the fourth support under the road, and I also remembered that it was about this point that the other guy had fallen off. I started to think about what I would do if I fell. If I just lost my footing I might be able to grab the wall on my way down. But if I fell outward because I lost my balance, or because someone pushed me—I couldn't help looking back when that thought occurred to me. I could imagine someone jokingly grabbing my leg and accidentally pushing me off. But there was no one closer to me on the sidewalk than about ten feet. If I fell outward there would be nothing to grab onto—not for a long ways down. I was getting these crazy thoughts about whether there was a best way to land if I did fall: on my feet, my butt, or maybe my head. I thought about landing on my feet or my butt and being paralyzed for the rest of my life. I didn't know whether I would prefer to be alive and paralyzed or dead. I was sure to die if I landed on my head. Life would carry on everywhere, and I would be gone. I even wondered whether I would be thinking and trying to make that decision while I was falling through the air.

The breeze suddenly picked up to a wind blowing along the cliff, and I felt a chill down my back as the wind pushed me off balance. My right foot lifted off the wall and I had to swing my arms sharply to regain my balance. Someone behind me said, "He's falling!" He sounded pretty excited about it and that made me sort of angry. I felt like turning around and saying, "Screw you," and jumping onto the sidewalk. But I didn't say anything and I kept walking.

The wind continued to blow and I felt my body contorting to adjust. My body was already leaning toward the road and the wind was pushing hard enough now that unless I leaned to my right, away from the road and toward the cliff, I would be pushed by the wind onto the sidewalk. It was an uncomfortable adjustment to make; my mind and my body leaning both directions, different directions, at the same time. I kept telling myself that I was almost at the fourth support. I picked a spot up ahead, a place where there was a chip out of the top of the wall that I could keep glancing up at, and I set that as my destination. The fourth support was under the incline so I couldn't see it, but I was sure that the spot I had picked was past the support.

Then I got to thinking that if I quit at the place with the chip I would be quitting at the toughest part of the walk up to that point. I could tell Mike and Barry that I had made it past the fourth support, further than the guy who fell off, but I didn't want to have to tell them anything. And now there were over twenty people walking behind me, and at the top of the ramp was another group of people, and when I looked down at the highway for the first time thinking about something other than falling, I saw that there were a number of people standing along the sidewalk on the other side of the highway looking up at me. And probably none of them knew anything about the guy who fell off. They would just see me quit at the toughest spot.

It frightened me, a little. Earlier, lower down the wall, I was thinking, kidding myself, that falling onto the sidewalk would be as bad as falling over the cliff. Now I was really beginning to feel that way. It was me, I know, but it was also all the people standing around, making me into something that I wasn't and that they weren't either. Something that nobody was until somebody got stuck in the position of proving that he was. Meanwhile, I stepped on the chip on the top of the wall and then past the chip. When I stepped on the chip I could feel it under my left foot, and I hesitated for a second. But I kept walking. And once I stepped past the chip I looked up to see how far it was to where the wall leveled out along the park at the top of the cliff. And I stopped thinking about jumping down onto the sidewalk.

My steps were becoming slower and more careful. I glanced to my right again, and just then the wind increased and I had to stop walking. I stood there and felt my body shaking. I tried to tell myself to relax, but my body continued shaking and swaying slightly, all on its own. I glanced down the cliff again. A piece of paper floated in the wind, suspended a few feet off the cliff. And below the paper was air—*only* air all the way to the bottom of the cliff. I looked ahead and saw that I had over forty feet to walk before there was ground below me to my right. And further along the wall, after the ground disappeared again, was the last stretch—probably a hundred feet where the fall would reach three hundred feet.

I tried to start walking again, but I had the feeling that if I lifted one of my feet the other, alone, would not be able to support me. I got a picture in my mind of falling off the wall and down the side of the cliff and having all kinds of regrets on the way down. I remembered reading about this great chess player who said, "There's always a way out." I liked that saying and I used to believe in it. But now I realized that it wasn't quite true. Once you were over the cliff there was no way out. So while I was walking along the wall I added a little to that saying, "There's always a way out if you don't end up over the cliff." I looked around at the people behind me and ahead of me and on the highway below me. And I told myself that I had already made it nearly to the top; that another hundred and fifty or so feet of walking over a big fall and I would be the only person that any of these people had ever seen, or ever would see, walk all the way up the incline on the wall. Not that it made any difference what any of those people saw.

I started walking again, very slowly and deliberately. I kept telling myself that the wall was as easy to balance on up here as it had been at the bottom of the incline, and that I could not let the pressure get to me. But my body stayed very tight and my walk felt forced and unnatural. The wind picked up and decreased in small bursts for a short time and I shuddered as I felt how awkwardly I was adjusting to the wind changes. I knew that a big change in the wind would cause me to fall, and I felt a slight panic with that realization. I seemed to suddenly perspire even more and I glanced up to see how far it was to where the ground to my right began again. I judged it to be about fifteen feet and in a semi-panic I increased my speed. The increased speed made my walk very unbalanced, but I stared ahead and lost thought of anything but each step followed by the next step for fifteen feet. The wind and the people and the stiffness in my body were forgotten—only the wall and the fifteen feet ahead of me remained in my mind.

Once the ground was below me my entire body relaxed. My body no longer leaned away from the fall so the strain of leaning and fighting the wind was gone and I straightened up. My left side ached much worse than before and now my right side hurt, also. My shoulders remained stiff and the pain had moved halfway down my back and up my neck. I walked slowly and leaned my head from side to side to relax.

I glanced behind and ahead of me on the ramp and down at the highway. The people were still watching. A small crowd was now standing on the highway below, looking up, and the number of people behind me had increased a lot, although I didn't know exactly how many people were there because I couldn't let myself turn around to look. All that I could do was casually glance back. I realized suddenly that no one had walked past me for quite a while. As I kept walking with the safety of ground below me on both sides I started to get this feeling of aloofness and superiority. And then I wasn't sure whether that feeling was fading to a feeling of isolation, or whether the isolation came with the aloofness and superiority, but just took longer to notice. And all this happened pretty fast because the ground to my right was already getting narrow. Just a few feet ahead it disappeared under me leaving empty space and a fall of probably two hundred and fifty feet.

I walked along the top of the wall until just before the ground disappeared altogether, and then I stopped. I glanced for a moment out at the ocean—that remained unchanged—and I realized that my body was shaking. It was a strange kind of shaking; it seemed that my individual muscles and nerves, the little parts of me that I knew were there but that usually kept working without reminding me of their existence—*they* were the parts of me that were shaking. The last stretch was ahead. It was a hundred or so feet and it was worse than all of the walk behind me. Even though I had stopped walking, nobody walked past me or even said anything to me. That's how tough the walk ahead of me was. Nobody wanted to take a chance on doing something that would make me decide not to try to finish the walk. The wind was blowing strongly up against the cliff ahead of me—I could feel it already and see the dirt and brush blowing up along the cliff.

I started walking. Two little kids ran up behind me and leaned over the wall to get a better look at the cliff ahead of me. I heard one of them say, "That guy sure must have a lot of guts. I can't hardly look down from up here . . . But wouldn't it be neat if he falls?"

Anyway, I walked all the way across that last span. My body was shaking and leaning and generally not helping very much, but I made it. There was a long string of people along the sidewalk on the other side of the highway and there were a lot of people who were leaning over the wall, then watching me for a bit, and then leaning over the wall again. I was worried that people could see that I was shaking and leaning and it wasn't until I got almost to the end that I realized that few people would notice and no one would care. Because they weren't even watching me. They were watching a show and I just happened to be in it. They were hoping I would fall and thinking about how they would feel if they were walking along the top of the wall. But that's okay, I was still the one who walked all the way up the wall.

And as I walked across that last stretch, I kept thinking that I didn't want to end up dead at the bottom of the cliff where all those people would come over and look at me. I guess it was because I got to thinking about the woman in the sewers, although I don't know how I got to thinking about her during that last stretch because I had pretty much forgotten all about her during the rest of the walk.

When I got to within about twenty feet of the top of the cliff, the end of my walk, I heard someone behind me say, "Damn! . . . He's going to make it all the way!" As I approached the end I felt pretty good. In fact, I felt great. I reached the top of the cliff and I hesitated before jumping off the wall. I wanted to hold onto that accomplishment, the excitement and fear, the independence. I was fifteen and I had another real accomplishment in my life. It wasn't finding a cure for cancer or anything, but it was *my* accomplishment. I glanced out at the ocean, fixing my gaze for just a second on a single sailboat in the distance, and then I jumped down onto the sidewalk. As I hit the ground I could feel the difference. I wasn't the same kid who had climbed up onto the top of the wall earlier. I just knew I wasn't—I could feel it.

The people who had been standing at the top of the incline had stepped back from the wall as I approached and now they just stood there, looking at me. Mike stepped up to me and hit me on the arm with his fist. "Nice goin'!" he said. Barry hit me on the other arm and said, "What a stud!" I was a little surprised that they were so friendly because I really didn't know either of them. The guy who had spoken to me earlier said, "Nice goin', buddy."

I stood there for a few minutes looking first at Mike and then at the guy and then around at the other people who were watching me or already wandering away, and finally I answered, "Yeah, I guess so." Those were pussy minutes that I stood there, although I didn't realize it at the time. "Well, see you guys," I said and I walked away. I had my life to carry on with.

When I got home that afternoon I lay around for most of the rest of the day, just thinking. I lay on my back under the tree in my front yard and the little breeze was there that was always there. Under my arms and head I could sense that almost imperceptible movement of green, moist individual blades of grass trying to disentangle themselves, bent under the weight of my body. I was thinking about different things. I was thinking about my walk up the incline and about the woman being carried away on a stretcher and wondering if they had gotten her to wake up yet. I was thinking about that girl in my old junior high school and her boyfriend. I was also thinking a little about Moscow, wondering what kind of a day they were having there. Sometimes I would look in the newspaper to see what the temperature in Moscow was the day before, and I would think that there was probably a kid, my age, maybe even born on the same day that I was born, who walks along streets that I've never heard of and that I'll probably never see. He or she is probably a Communist, but I couldn't care less about that. During the winter I would think that there was snow on those streets. As I lay there I was thinking that if that Russian kid ever lay down on grass under a tree in summertime, then there are things that we both know. Maybe I notice more than he or she does, or maybe I don't, but there's something in the both of us that makes us share some of the feelings about what we notice. It's like a full moon on a warm summer night. How many people throughout the world and throughout history have leaned back and looked up at that same moon and if they were in love or something thought how great it was to be alive, and if they were lonely or something thought how small they were in comparison to the universe.

Altogether I was restless and impatient and exhilarated from the past few days, but still sort of bored because I knew that there was a whole world out there and despite the woman in the sewers and the incline and getting tan and growing my hair long I still didn't know how to get at it.

Graham interrupted my thoughts when I noticed him limping slowly toward me across the lawn. "You don't need your crutches anymore," I said.

"I got rid of them. But you found her!" he said enthusiastically, but a little sadly, as he approached. "I wish I could've gone with you!" He sat next to me and I sat up with my back against the tree.

"Yeah, it doesn't seem quite right that Jackson found her with me, although he is a pretty good guy."

"He's just some skinny hippie. It should've been me."

"He's a good guy," I repeated. "You didn't even think the woman was still down there. Jackson just took my word for it and went down with me."

"Yeah, well, if it wasn't for my foot I would've gone down. You didn't even ask me to go—I might've gone even with my foot!"

I figured Graham was just adding to his list of sins by lying so outrageously. I answered, "You couldn't have made it and you'd never have been able to help carry her out. What did your parents say, now that we saved someone's life?"

Graham shrugged his shoulders. "Nothing really."

"Yeah—why should they? But I think my mother was a little proud of me for doing that."

"What about Ben Sr.?"

"I'll see tonight. If he's drunk I'm staying away. I promised him I'd stay out of the sewers."

I told Graham some of the details of our finding the woman and then Graham shook his head and said, "Well, I've decided something. I'm going to give up on religion for now."

"Why is that?" I asked. But I knew Graham was getting pretty frustrated with the whole business because he was wasting so much time finding the right sins to confess.

"It's a lot of things," Graham answered. "I mean, I don't have any problem with sinning in general—that's fine—in fact, you can get me out there and I'll sin with the best of them. But it gets to be kind of a burden to collect sins *every* week for confession, having to pick and choose as you go. You have to remember not to break windows for sins because there are too many broken windows at the church, or you can't sin with girls because one of the priests is eighty years old and you might get him and then kill him with your confession . . ."

"What sin did you ever do with a girl that would kill a priest?" I asked. "What sin did you ever do with a girl, period?"

"Maybe none, yet. But I very well might. I might at this camp—in fact I'm planning to. Just believe me, Ben, this religion is a burden."

"I thought religion was *supposed* to be a burden, Graham. If it's not a burden, what is it?"

"Well, I might get back into religion if the old priest dies or something. I'm still keeping my list of sins, though."

"You are? Why?" I hadn't mentioned yet to Graham that I was also collecting sins.

"Because sins last. They're as good ten years from now as they are today. In fact, sins can last forever. You can carry them as long as you want. I used to think that you had to confess a sin the first week you committed it, but the whole thing works just the same whenever you confess a sin. Someday I'll probably get back into it and I'll have all these sins saved up."

"Makes sense to me, Graham," I said, although I was getting more convinced every day that Graham was crazy.

"Anyway, I've got to go pack for camp. I'm leaving tomorrow. Keep it cool," Graham said as he left and he offered me our secret pinky shake. I hesitated, then shook with him. I was too old for that stuff, but it was still there.

I wasn't in the mood to take a chance with Ben Sr. so I ate dinner early and left the house before he got home. I took my camera with me. I sometimes carried my camera because, in some ways, I'm an artist always searching for those great pictures that last just a second. I wandered around the neighborhood, not really expecting to find any good pictures, but just wandering. The day slipped to sunset and then to night. It was getting late, long past dark, when I walked past Connie's house and I was surprised that Connie was sitting alone on her front lawn. "What are you doing out here?" I asked.

"Just enjoying the night," she answered and I could understand her wanting to sit outside on a warm beautiful night like tonight instead of spending pussy minutes watching television. "What are *you* doing out here?" she asked.

"The same," I answered, and I sat next to Connie on her lawn. We talked a little, then lay on our backs next to each other and looked together into the night sky. We talked some more about nothing, and I could tell that Connie was very happy that I was there. I thought a lot about what Jackson had said about

Connie and I wondered how Connie could be so happy all the time, and I couldn't get it off my mind that even though she looked fine she had cancer and was dying.

We went for a walk a little later and Connie took hold of my hand. It felt nice to hold her hand and we walked for a long time, mostly without talking. When we got back to Connie's house it was pretty late. Connie dropped my hand and stepped around in front of me. She looked into my eyes and smiled and said, "Thanks for stopping by. It was nice talking and walking around and everything."

I couldn't really help it, but I put my arms around her and we held each other very tightly for a long time, and then I kissed Connie and she held me even tighter, until her mother called through a window from the house, "Connie? Where have you been? We've been looking everywhere for you."

Connie called back, "Sorry, Mom. We just went for a walk. I'll be in in a minute." To me she whispered, "See you later?" and she took my hand for a second.

"Sure," I answered.

I didn't go home, but walked around some more. I had only spent a little time with Connie and I was already thinking that I didn't know if I wanted to be in love with someone who was dying.

I walked for a very long time until it was so late that it was that peaceful time of the late night. There were no other people around; no cars making noise and spewing poisonous gases at you; no people sitting in their dens watching television. In the distance I could see an occasional set of headlights moving along the highway as they climbed up over the hills. And somehow I didn't mind those few cars on their late night undertakings, out of synchrony with everyone else.

I thought about the list of sins I was keeping. I was a little annoyed that Graham had gotten me started, not because I was keeping the list of sins—that was fine—but because it wasn't my own idea. Actually, I decided that I needed to have four lists. I guess I could have had two or three or twenty lists, if I wanted, but I settled on four. You have to settle on something. The first was for great things that I did, and that list had walking up the wall and saving the woman in the sewers. That was the real list, the one that had to be full if you lived a full life. Later I decided that I should have a super great list in case I ever cured cancer or something, but I also figured that list would likely be blank for a while. One or two things on that list during a whole life would be incredible. The second list was good things, things that were fun or exciting or helped people or helped peace, but things that any person might do. I was going to put on that list things like exploring the sewers with Graham, having all the commotion with the police trying to find the woman in the sewers and walking around with Connie and kissing her. The third list was typical sins. That was the toughest list because I wasn't Catholic or religious so I wasn't sure how to decide what was a sin. I had to look at everything I did and decide in each case if it was a sin. I figured taking the clothes off the woman in the sewers and taking pictures of her were sins. Those were my only sins since I started the list. It seemed a little strange that the same thing could be on more than one list, like saving the woman was on list one and taking off her clothes in the process was on list three. But that's just how it is in life, I guess. My last list was mortal sins. That was a term I got from Graham and it sounded pretty serious. Typical sins were sins where you could understand how it would happen. It might be stupid or a little mean or thoughtless, but you could understand how some guy down in the sewers alone with a woman might want to see what she looks like and might be stupid enough to take her clothes off and take pictures of her, for example. Mortal sins you couldn't understand. So far I didn't have any-thing on that list and I wasn't expecting to have any. But I figured it was important to keep that list, just to keep tabs on myself. When I started the lists I considered adding all of my past sins, but I knew I'd never remember them all and it just wasn't the same if the list wasn't complete. I sort of wished I had thought of collecting my sins when I was five or six or seven or whenever you can figure out what's a sin. Then I could have a collection of a whole lifetime of sins. Actually, I guess that any way you looked at it I would some day have a lifetime collection of sins, only it would be nice to have them all in a long list. But it was too late for that so all I could do was try to keep it complete from here on out.

I was exhausted but I kept walking. I walked into the hills and saw a coyote standing in the street with his back toward me. When I saw him I stopped, and at that moment he glanced back at me, not moving except to turn his head to look at me. We just stood there for a minute or so, neither of us moving, and then he ran off down the street and further up into the hills. I walked over to where he had been standing, and from that spot I could look out over the thousands of houses strewn at the base of the hills and as far as I could see. It seemed to me that night had turned to early morning and at any moment it would be daytime. I could almost feel the earth rolling over to get this part of it under the sun. I was thinking that out below me in one or two or a few of those houses, but in at least one of them, was some special girl, some unique girl, and that at any time I might meet her. There were so many houses. Connie's house was down there and I tried to figure out exactly where it was. I wondered whether the coyote had been looking out over the houses before I scared him off.

CHAPTER FOUR

I hitchhiked to the beach the next day, then a couple of days later and then a couple of days after that. I was getting tan and my hair was getting longer, even if you couldn't really notice it yet. Connie was in another city at some special hospital where they were checking her out. She called to tell me she was leaving, but I didn't get a chance to see her before she left, which was fine because as the days went by I wasn't all that sure how I felt about her. That first night we walked around and for a couple of days afterward I thought it was love, maybe, but then I wasn't sure because who really knows what that is, anyway?

I quit the beach before lunch, but I didn't feel like going home so I decided to try to hitchhike up the coast and through the canyon. I walked across the beach and the parking lot to the highway and I waited for a break in the traffic so that I could cross. About twenty feet on the other side of the highway was the base of the cliff. As I stood waiting I noticed about two-thirds up the cliff a little bluff with a tree growing on it, and a person sitting under the tree. It seemed like a nice place to sit and I thought that I might try sitting there myself sometime.

I got a ride up the Coast Highway to the canyon and after standing for only a minute or so at the entrance to the canyon I got another ride. The driver was a middle-aged man who didn't say anything until we got to a little town about midway through the canyon. It was actually only a few stores, a post office and a gasoline station—maybe not enough to be a real town. As we approached the town the man said, "I suppose you want to get out here."

"Why do you say that?" I asked.

"You kids always want to get out here. I just can't figure you out."

"Yeah, anywhere is fine," I answered.

I walked around to the different stores in the town. I found a place called "The Fifth Quatrain," which was a lot like "East," where Jackson had taken me. It was a converted house with beads and necklaces and all kinds of odd pipes and other things in glass counters, posters all over the walls, incense burning and one of those blacklight rooms where it was almost dark but certain things glowed. I was hoping to meet a girl in the store, but there was no one interesting there. I bought some incense on long sticks and rolled them up in my towel. After a while I didn't know what else to do in the little town so I went home.

That afternoon Jackson stopped by my house and he was more excited than I had ever seen him. "She's okay and she wants to see us!" he said.

"Who is?" I asked, thinking that he might be talking about Connie.

"The woman we found in the sewers. Victoria. She's fine and she wants to see us. She called me this morning."

"That's her name? Victoria?" I had never thought about what the woman's name might be. "How did she sound?"

"She sounded nice—real nice. She's in the hospital but we can go see her there. She wants to see us because we saved her. She asked the cops and they gave her our names." It had also never occurred to me that I would see the woman when she recovered, even after Jackson and I saved her. I guess because of the way I messed up the first time I went back into the pipes after her.

Jackson drove us to the hospital in his mother's station wagon. He drove pretty fast with the radio turned up loud and he constantly changed the stations to find music he liked. Out of nowhere he said, "I'll be eighteen next month."

"Yeah? That's pretty old," I answered.

"I could get drafted."

"That's true." I never thought about getting drafted. "You could go to Canada or something. That's what everybody does so they don't end up in Vietnam."

"Some people do. I guess I'll wait and see what happens." We discovered that Jackson's birthday was two days after mine. Jackson asked, "Have you ever been stoned?"

"You mean with marijuana?"

"Yeah."

"No, I haven't."

"Well, that's something we should do for your birthday. You'll be what, sixteen?"

"That's right."

"That's too old to never be stoned."

"Really? How old were *you* when you started smoking marijuana?" I asked.

Jackson shook his head. "I'm not your usual case. Everything in my life is stunted. I just got stoned for the first time about six months ago."

"What do you mean everything is stunted?"

"It just is. I hooked into the wrong philosophy in life, at least in parts of it."

"I thought your philosophy was for, like, peace and love and all that."

"It is. It is for peace and love and all that. But then there's your philosophy on girls and smoking pot and taking chances with your life and all of that."

"So, what's your philosophy about that stuff? You smoke pot, you grow your hair long, you don't care about the Establishment. What's wrong with that philosophy?"

"Nothing. It's only that I just started smoking pot six months ago. You're not even sixteen yet and I'll bet most of your friends are already smoking pot . . ."

"No, they're not."

"They probably are and you just don't know it because you're not plugged in well enough. I never knew it. It was the same thing with girls. I thought they were all virgins at my old high school, and now I'm finally finding out that *I* was the only virgin. They were all having sex when their parents weren't home and in cars and in the woods and . . . I don't know. It never crossed my mind that the kind of girls I'd be interested in would be doing that." Jackson shrugged his shoulders. "I just didn't know. I was too stupid." There was a trace of anger in Jackson's voice. "So I missed out."

"What did you miss out? You're not that old."

"It's still different to be eighteen, graduated from high school and to be fifteen or fourteen or whatever and just starting high school or still in the middle of high school. It's a different experience."

"Kids aren't doing that who are fourteen and fifteen, are they?"

"A lot more than you think. Do you know that I just slept with a girl for the first time last week?"

"You did? Who was she?"

"Lisa Boothe. Do you know her? She goes to your high school. She's sixteen."

"I think I know who she is, maybe."

"She's my girlfriend. See, she's only sixteen and she's already, well . . ." Jackson trailed off and he didn't say anything more for a while. I couldn't believe everyone was doing everything Jackson was saying. I didn't personally know anyone who smoked marijuana, although I knew of older kids who did. And then I remembered the gold rings that the woman in the sewers was wearing and I figured that maybe Jackson was right, that I just wasn't plugged in well enough to know what was going on. It was kind of disappointing. I thought about the girls I knew and I wondered which ones were having sex and who they were having sex with.

We got to the hospital and Jackson bought some flowers in a shop downstairs and asked at an information desk where we could find Victoria. When we got to her room I was anxious to see her and a little nervous. I wondered if she had any sense of what had happened that night when I was alone with her. Jackson knocked on her door and a woman answered, "Come in."

She was sitting up in bed watching television. I recognized her immediately, even though her light brown hair was tied behind her head and she wasn't wearing any make-up. She looked younger and gentler than I remembered her. I thought she must have been twenty-five or thirty years old. A bottle hung from a rack on the side of the bed and a tube ran from the bottom of the bottle to her left wrist. When we stepped in the room Jackson said, "Hi. I'm Jackson and this is Ben." We walked over to the bed and Jackson handed the flowers to the woman.

"I'm Vickie," she answered and held out her right hand to Jackson and then to me. "Thanks for coming. I just wanted to meet the boys who saved me. How did you happen to be down there, anyway?"

"I was down there with a friend of mine," I answered. I noticed that her earrings were off of her ears and I couldn't help glancing along her body under the sheets, wondering if she was still wearing the other rings. "He's Catholic and had to collect sins every week for confession. He didn't want to go in without any-thing to confess, so we went into the sewers to get some sins . . ."

Jackson interrupted me. "You've got to be kidding. Who was collecting sins? Graham?"

"He was before, but not anymore. He gave up on religion since then."

Jackson shook his head and Vickie laughed. "Well, whatever the reason, I'm glad you *were* down there."

"How did *you* get down there?" Jackson asked Vickie. I was wondering the same thing. There were a couple of small bruises on Vickie's face and the scratch we had made dragging her out of the cubicle, and a bruise on her arm, but otherwise she seemed like a usual person, just sitting there in bed, watching television. I tried to remember her lying in the sewers, but it didn't seem that it could have been her who I had seen down there. Then I noticed a couple of gold rings on the table by her bed, but I was certain that they were her earrings and not any of the other rings because they were pretty large. I scanned the table intently, and the other counters around the room, but there was no sign of the other rings. I looked again at Vickie's body stretched out under the sheets and I pictured the little rings, and I remembered feeling her, and I felt a little bad about it, although it was done and so that was that.

"I'm not really sure," Vickie answered. "I went out to dinner with a man . . . I had just met. We went to dinner and then we were driving and . . . and that's about all I can remember, until I woke up here. Now they can't find the man and I don't know what happened. But if it wasn't for you two, I'd probably still be down there—dead!" Vickie shivered.

"But you were unconscious or something," I said. "How did they wake you up? We carried you all the way through the sewers and you didn't wake up."

"Someone must have hit me. The doctors told me I had bleeding in my head that they stopped with some medicine and by putting a little tube in my head to drain it out." Vickie turned and showed us a three inch square patch at the back of her head that had been shaved. "I must have been hit pretty hard because I have some nasty bruises on my head and neck. The doctors said I was lucky to recover so well. A lot of people don't ever get better from something like this." She shivered again. "I don't even like to think about it. But I'd like to give you two some kind of reward . . ."

Jackson held up his hands and interrupted, "No! We couldn't take any kind of reward. We're just glad we could help."

We talked for a long time and it turned out that I liked Vickie a lot. I told her about how Graham and I ran out of candles and then found her in the sewers and how the police couldn't find where she was so Jackson and I went back in after her. She was very interested and asked me all kinds of questions about the sewers and the police and everything, like I was telling her about a movie or something. I was surprised that she didn't seem to be that upset for someone who had ended up in the sewers.

Before we left Vickie said, "I do want to give you two boys something for saving me. Not many people would've gone back after . . ."

"No," Jackson interrupted.

"I know you don't want money, but maybe something . . . more special." She paused and sort of smiled and leaned up a little in her bed, and I could see that it hurt her to sit up. She looked at each of us and asked with her voice real low, "You two can keep something between us, can't you?"

"Of course," we both answered.

"You two look like healthy young guys. What if I . . . what if each of you could spend a night with me?" She looked at me and then at Jackson and she was still smiling. She leaned back and asked, "What do you think?"

I glanced over at Jackson and I could see that he was as stunned as I was. His eyes were open wide.

"No . . ." I started to say because I was certain that Jackson was going to say it, but Jackson interrupted,

"You don't have to do that," he said, gently. "I mean . . ."

"But I'd like to," Vickie said. "It's probably not what you expected, but wouldn't you like it?"

"Sure, but . . ." Jackson answered, still talking more softly and gently than I was used to hearing him talk.

"Then let's do it. You did something *really* special for me. Let me do something for you." She had been talking to Jackson but she looked over at me. I was more than ready to agree, but I was waiting for Jackson. I glanced over at him again to make sure he wasn't changing his mind and his eyes were still open wide.

"Well," Jackson began and he looked at me briefly and then around the room. "What if . . . suppose it was sort of an IOU that . . ."

"Of course," Vickie answered. "We couldn't do it here!" She looked around the room, smiling. "After I get out."

"I mean . . . what if I didn't want to do it for a long time, maybe a month . . . or a year, or *ten* years, would that be okay?"

Vickie looked pretty puzzled and I didn't have any idea what Jackson was saying, but Vickie said, "Sure, why not?"

"Like an IOU that we could use any time, even though we probably never would use it."

Vickie looked at me but I didn't make any expression at all that might make her think I had any idea what Jackson was talking about. I was planning to use my IOU, or whatever it was. "Sure," she said, smiling again. "Anytime you want it."

Then Jackson made Vickie write it on a little sheet of paper. I don't know how he did it, exactly, but Vickie thought it was pretty funny and she went along with it. There was a small pad of paper on the table next to the bed and Vickie wrote, "I owe you Ben" and "I owe you Jackson" on each of two little sheets of paper and she signed them "Vickie." It was important to Jackson that Vickie write our names on the papers. Altogether I thought that Jackson had gone insane.

Finally we left. Vickie said, "Well, thanks again. Thanks for coming by and for everything. You two are incredible." She kissed each of us and hugged us before we left, and it felt nice to be hugged by her, and I couldn't help thinking about cashing in that IOU.

Jackson said again, "We're probably never going to use these, you know," and he held up his IOU, which he still held in his hand.

"Well, I hope you do," Vickie said, smiling.

And that was it, except that as I was watching Vickie talk and as she hugged me I decided that I had to tell her what really happened in the sewers. I had to tell her about feeling her and taking her clothes off and all of that. It was something she had to know. I knew that she would be angry with me, but maybe she would understand. Or at least, since I had saved her life, she would offset the other things I did against saving her and she wouldn't hate me but just wouldn't like me anymore and we would carry on with our lives. Or maybe she would just cancel the IOU. But I had to tell her.

As we walked out of the hospital Jackson carefully folded his IOU and put it in his wallet. I folded my IOU and put it in my back pocket because I didn't carry a wallet. I asked, "Why did you have to get these little notes and everything if you're not even going to use yours?"

"I don't know, exactly. It's just nice to have. It's nice to know that it's there . . . that *she's* there if I ever need her. If I had maybe twenty, or *fifty* of these, from women in cities all over the world that I could just drop in and see and they would make love with me . . ." That seemed like a great idea to me, only it sounded a bit strange coming from Jackson.

I said, "Well, I don't know how likely you are to find fifty women in sewers all over the world . . ."

"Not just from sewers, but from all different things. Women whose lives you save, women who just love you, women who . . . I don't know, all different things. Anyway, that's that. Time to move on to the next thing." Jackson patted his back pocket where he had returned his wallet.

"What next thing?" I asked.

"The next thing in life. The next adventure. That's what life is—a series of adventures with dead space in between. You can't sit thinking or making too much out of one adventure—you have to move on to the next one."

"I thought you said we were going to get stoned sometime and talk about saving Vickie. You said that when they took her in the ambulance, remember?"

"Unless you're stoned, of course," Jackson answered. "When you're stoned you re-experience your thoughts and the things you do because you see them differently. Otherwise, unless you're stoned, sitting and dwelling on something that happened is pussy minute city . . . *p* minute city."

I was already taking different routes to the beach, just for variation, but I seemed to be hitchhiking through the canyon most of the time. Younger people lived in the canyon, mostly, people in their late teens and twenties, although there were occasional older men with grey beards and women with long grey hair. They drove beat-up old cars and vans that had barely enough power to creak up and down and around the curves through the canyon, and they all dressed shabby, with old, torn clothes, like Jackson. The men all had long hair and a lot of the women let their hair grow under their armpits.

There was something going on with those people that I could feel, but I couldn't quite reach. It was a little of what Jackson was hooked into, although Jackson must have picked more of the wrong philosophy for his life because he was living at home instead of in the canyon or in some place like the canyon, and he had only slept with a girl for the first time last week when there were all those women out in the canyon and all over who believed just like Jackson in free love and all of that.

One day I woke up very early and left for the beach before the sun even came up, because I was awake and just to do it. I was chilly wearing only shorts and a t-shirt and I walked quickly to a different freeway on-ramp where I thought it was more likely I would find some cars at that time of the morning. When I approached the on-ramp it was just getting to be dawn and the street lights had turned off. I stood for a while across the main boulevard from the on-ramp. The only movement was my breathing and the occasional changing of the traffic signal. After a couple of minutes a car drove past me. It was an old car driven by an old man who stopped in front of me and waited a long time at a red light. He glanced over at me, probably wondering what the hell I was doing dressed like that, carrying a towel. I felt like calling to him to ask why he was waiting at the red light when there wasn't another car anywhere in sight, but he was an old man and I didn't say anything.

After the old man drove away I walked diagonally across the intersection, not paying any attention to the traffic signals. I liked the feeling of being the only person on the street. I stood in the middle of the intersection for a minute, looking both directions down the street. There were traffic signals at about every block and the street was a straight line as far as I could see. I thought that I should take a picture of that sometime. The artistic part of taking the picture would be getting the right combinations of red, green and yellow lights. Actually, it was crazy how all the lights kept changing even though there were no cars around to bother with them. I was thinking that I could write a science fiction story about how all the people died off and the traffic signals kept changing anyway.

I stood at the on-ramp for a long time and not a single car turned, although a number of cars drove past me along the boulevard.

I was shivering a little from the cold and finally I walked home and went back to bed.

It was still early when I left for the beach a second time that day. I decided to hitchhike through the canyon. I got a ride to the entrance to the canyon and waited a few minutes until a young guy with short hair stopped for me in a small convertible sports car. The top was down on the car and there were people in the two front seats and in the small space behind the seats, but the driver told me that I could sit on the trunk of the car and hold on if I wanted to. Of course I did, and he sped through the canyon while I was stretched out across the back of the car, holding on and bracing myself around each turn. It was great fun, but I had these little pangs in my heart, or someplace, as we sped around grinding old cars or passed people standing or walking along the road, living their gentle, peaceful lives. I barely had room in my head for hanging onto the car and trying to anticipate the way my body would be thrown as we went around the next turn, but I had the feeling that I was moving further away from what was going on—separating myself from it as we sped through the canyon in the fancy sports car, driven by the guy with short hair who probably wasn't even aware of the people he was passing.

I left the beach after only a short while and hitchhiked back through the canyon. I stopped in the town and walked to the Fifth Quatrain. I liked to sit in the black light room, smelling the incense and listening to the loud music and watching the people and imagining that I lived in the canyon and belonged to what everyone around me belonged to. I sat in the black light room for a while, then wandered all through the small store and out the open back door. A girl sat on a wooden box in the shade of a gnarly, ancient tree, just a couple of yards from the door. She was about nineteen or twenty and one of her breasts was out—a full, veiny breast, and a tiny baby was sucking away at it. I was looking at her breast and the baby for a while and when I looked up the girl was smiling at me. She said, "It's beautiful, isn't it?"

I wasn't sure what she meant, and I was a little embarrassed that she was looking at me looking at her breast, so I just said, "Yeah, it is," and I walked back into the store. After a minute I realized that she was talking about the baby and the whole business of feeding the baby with her breast and everything, and I wanted to go back to tell her that it really was beautiful, but I didn't know quite how to do it. I left the little town and as I climbed into the car that stopped for me I felt that I was just passing through the canyon, and passing through is nothing but passing through.

When I got home there was a letter from Graham in the mail. Graham's ankle was much better but he didn't like the camp at all. He had thought a little more about Jackson and me saving Vickie and he was pretty disturbed. Graham didn't care much for Jackson and didn't think it was fair that Jackson should help save a woman that Graham and I had found. I figured Graham would be a hell of a lot more upset when he found out about the IOUs we got from Vickie.

It was a religious camp that Graham was at and I guess they put a lot of stock in confession or something because Graham was back to using up his collected sins at confession. He had no self-control and had already used up his accumulated sins during his first confessions. He wanted me to throw eggs at his house while he was at camp, as a protest against his parents sending him away and trying to break up our friendship, and as a sin that he could use in confession. Graham figured that if he suggested the eggs he would have a sin for each egg that I threw. I was to throw the eggs and report to him in my letters how many I had thrown. I decided not to throw the eggs but to tell Graham I was throwing cartons of them, and when Graham came home I would tell him that he had been confessing to sins that had never been committed. I was sure that making a false confession was a sin in itself, so Graham would have a storehouse of sins that he could use whenever he needed them.

I went back to the hospital to tell Vickie what had happened in the sewers. Somehow I had to make it right with her. I had been thinking lately how most of the people all over the world are basically scum—well, maybe not scum exactly, but pretty low and nothing special. Every once in a while you get a Mozart or a person like that, but in the meantime all the other people are running around cheating on this little thing or that little thing, stealing a little or a lot or lying or all kinds of other things. I didn't want to be just one more of those people.

I got to the hospital but before I reached Vickie's room I changed my mind about telling her and left the hospital without even seeing her. I didn't know how I could tell Vickie and it almost didn't seem right to ruin her faith in people that way. She got thrown into the sewers by one person, at least she could believe that Jackson and I were good people. Besides, it was almost like collecting on the IOU in advance. I didn't ever have to collect on the IOU she had given me.

Connie got home and I stopped to see her in the evening. She was a little happy to see me, but she seemed unhappy overall. We sat in her den with her parents, who just sat there looking at Connie, and made me feel very uncomfortable. Connie's father, who was very thin and bald except for a grey fringe around the edge and seemed too old to be her father, asked me a couple of questions about school. Her mother was nice looking and much younger than her father and she asked me about my family. They were just trying to be polite and it made me more uncomfortable. After a while I suggested to Connie that we go for a walk. Connie's mother said she didn't think Connie felt like going for a walk because Connie was tired from their trip, but Connie stood and said to me, "I think I'd like to go for a walk," and she walked out of the room without saying anything to her mother.

Outside it was a warm, wonderful summer night. Connie took my hand and held it tightly, and she walked very close to me. "How was your trip?" I asked, not really wanting to talk about it.

"Not good," Connie answered. That was the first time I had ever heard sadness in Connie's voice. I just stared ahead, not knowing what to say, and Connie continued, "This was supposed to be one of those places with all the super doctors and all the new breakthroughs and everything, but they can't do anything for me."

Connie and I had never before spoken of her sickness. I asked, "What's wrong with you?"

"You know I'm sick, don't you?" Connie looked over at me, I could feel her looking over, but I kept walking, staring straight ahead.

"I heard something about it."

"I have cancer." She said it as though she were talking about someone else, except that I could feel a trace of anger in her voice. "It's this kind that slowly takes over your whole body—they say 'slowly,' but it's really pretty fast, and there's nothing they can do about it. And then when it gets to a certain point it starts to take over a lot faster. You get really sick and . . . it's terrible." Connie didn't say anything more and I didn't know what to say.

"Maybe they'll find a cure pretty soon," I suggested. "They're always coming up with new cures."

"Maybe they will. But they better do it fast. They're trying all these new experimental drugs and everything, but the drugs aren't safe and none of them work anyway." We continued walking slowly, not talking, both of us looking straight ahead and away from each other. Connie was sniffing a little and I thought maybe she was crying, but I didn't know what to say to her or what to do. We walked a couple of blocks and Connie said, "I was thinking about you when I was gone," and I could hear her hiding the tears in her voice and she was holding my hand very tightly. I didn't answer and she said, "You got tan while I was gone."

"Yeah, a little. I've been at the beach a lot." I was getting this feeling in me that I wanted to hold Connie and tell her that everything would be alright, although I had no idea if it would be and somehow I knew that it would be terrible. "I thought a lot about you, also," I said, and I stopped walking and pulled Connie around in front of me. She was looking away, but she slowly looked up at me with tears in her eyes and this "I'm sorry" expression on her face and out of nowhere it was breaking my goddamn heart and out of nowhere I said, "I think I love you, Connie," and then she was holding onto me and crying and saying, "Please love me, Ben," and "I don't want to die," and other things that I couldn't deal with until I was crying, too.

CHAPTER FIVE

After a while I got to be quite good at hitchhiking. It's not what you'd call an art, exactly, like taking pictures or drawing, but you can be artistic *at* it. Being good at hitchhiking wasn't a style of holding out my thumb, but the way I looked and the way I talked to people. I didn't realize that at first, even though I should have seen it on my first ride with that fat old man who wanted me to have a good time and who was a little happier just knowing that there were kids around who could hang out at the beach.

My favorite time to leave for the beach on weekdays was between eight and nine o'clock in the morning, which was when everyone was driving to work. There were four or five streets that led to the beach from the freeway and I took any ride that would drop me off at one of those streets. After I got off the freeway I took any ride, no matter how far it was going, so long as it was going generally toward the beach. Those were my only rules because the real adventure of life is never knowing exactly where you're going to end up.

I was very tan and my hair had already grown down below the bottoms of my ears. People liked to give me a ride. They liked it more as I got more tan and as my hair grew longer, except for the occasional guy who drove by and leaned over and made an obscene gesture at me or yelled to me that I should cut my hair and go get a job. A lot of times I got rides from men trying to figure out their kids by talking to me. They tried to joke about it, but they asked me serious questions. I answered the best I could, but the answers sometimes weren't too good and I would think up better answers a couple of hours later when I couldn't help going over the conversations in my head.

It was already mid-July, a Saturday morning. I left early for the beach and after a lot more rides than it usually took me to get to the beach I ended up probably five miles from where I usually hung around, so I took off my shirt and walked along the wet sand. A couple of inches of foamy water ran regularly up over my feet and then back out to sea, erasing my footsteps even as I walked. We were into the heat of the summer, but in the morning at the beach it was only warm, not yet hot. A number of people were already laying and walking along the beach, but few compared to the millions that I knew would be there in the afternoon. In the distance, to the south, white sailboats floated and tossed lightly on the ocean, scattered over a small area, a few drifting away from the rest.

Later in the day I walked up to The Grille to buy some lunch. The Grille's real name, in worn red lettering on the outside wall, was The Beach Cafe. After the word "Cafe," someone had written, in white spray paint, "And Grille." That was years ago because even those words were wearing away of their own, as everything does down by the beach. Now everyone just called the place "The Grille" and you never heard anyone mention "The Beach Cafe." I sometimes wondered if the person who wrote those words in spray paint ever did anything that was more enduring or that affected more people than that two-word spray paint inspiration on the wall at Santa Monica Beach.

Inside The Grille you had to stand in line to buy hamburgers and french fries and you could sit with your food on benches at thick wooden tables covered with salt and smears of ketchup and carved with inscriptions. There was a juke box and once in a while it would be turned up extra loud and a few people would dance on the table tops. There was a girl who I often saw at the beach who sometimes danced on the table tops. She was probably a couple of years older than I and she was very pretty. She had long blonde hair, a very nice body with big breasts and a deep tan. I never talked to her, but I liked to watch her dance and even walk around.

The week before, the girl was dancing on a table top with

some other girl who I hadn't seen before and her breasts were bouncing around in the green bikini top that she always wore. I noticed that as she danced a white crescent began forming below her bikini top where her right breast was slipping out. The crescent got bigger as she danced until she pulled her top back into place. But she kept dancing and after a while the white crescent reappeared, and then she swung her arms and jumped and twisted and her entire right breast and half of her left breast slipped out of her top before she brought her arms together over her chest and covered herself. A couple of guys yelled remarks to her, but she just stepped onto a bench and then onto the floor and ran into the bathroom in the back. She didn't come back for a long time and when she did return those same guys made more remarks. But the girl just lifted her chin up and walked out of The Grille and after a minute the girl she had been dancing with followed her out. I was annoyed at those guys who made the remarks because after what they did the girl would probably never dance on the tables again and that ruined it for those of us who just like to watch her dance. I saw that girl a couple of times after that and I always thought how nice and white her breasts looked compared to her tan. I wanted to tell her that, and to tell her to forget about what those other guys had said, but I had no idea how to go about it. I sometimes wondered if I would ever meet a girl like her, and I figured that I wouldn't. Even when I got older I probably wouldn't be her type.

After I got my food I sat down at a table where a kid about my age was holding a deck of cards and talking across the table to a couple of girls. In the midst of all the barefoot people wearing bathing suits, shorts and occasionally t-shirts, he was wearing a long sleeved black shirt, blue jeans and black boots. A black cowboy hat with a snake skin band around it lay near him on the table. He started setting the cards out in rows in front of him, still talking to the girls, but paying close attention to the cards. He was telling them that he could tell a person's future with his cards, but that he didn't like to do it anymore. The girls were about my age also and they kept asking him to tell them their futures.

Finally the kid said, "It's personal. I just don't like to do it anymore." He had laid out the entire deck, some of the cards covering or overlapping other cards. Certain of the cards had been cut in half. He studied the cards for a few moments, then looked up at the girls and repeated, "I'm sorry—it's personal." He sounded sincere, even to me.

One of the girls, who was kind of cute with long dark hair asked, "What's so personal? You just can't do it."

The guy pursed his lips and turned toward the wall, away from the girls. His hands were flat on the table. After a few moments he started picking up the cards, slowly, one by one, with his right hand and setting them carefully, face up, in his left hand. He turned some of the cards around as he set them in his hand.

The other girl asked, "So, are you going to tell us our futures, or not?" She was very skinny, almost bony, with reddish hair that frizzed out and her voice was high pitched and irritating.

Without looking up and still watching the cards as he picked them up, the guy answered, "How do you know you have a future?"

The skinny girl asked a little sarcastically, "What do you mean by that?"

The guy picked a card off the table, held it up for a second, then set it on the table to his right. The card was the top half of the ace of spades. He picked up the few other cards remaining on the table in front of him and he looked directly at the girls, intently. "That card," he said without making any motion toward the half an ace, "is death."

I was eating my cheeseburger, but the way he said it made me hesitate; it almost made me believe him, for just half a second. The girls looked at each other and one of the girls said, "That card is death?" I wanted to ask what happened to the other half of the card.

The guy picked up the half-ace and carefully slid it into the deck. He asked, "Do you know The Ridge?" The girls didn't know it. "It's up at The Bay. I was up there six months ago and someone wanted me to tell his future. We were sitting in a place like this, next to a big street. He was twenty years old. So I told his future and the ace came up. Then I did it again and the ace came up again. I did it four times and the ace came up four times. You know what happened?"

The pretty girl asked, "What happened?"

The other girl said, "He died, right?"

"That's right. About a half hour later he was hit by a truck, killed instantly, right outside where I was talking to him. I saw the whole thing. I was standing on the sidewalk and I saw the truck coming as he stepped into the street. In fact, I might've saved him if it wasn't for my leg. I just couldn't get there in time." He gazed out the window, slowly shaking his head. I glanced down at his leg and saw a cane with a carved handle leaning against the bench beside him. "Of course," he continued, and he looked back at the girls, "it was fate. It was in the cards, and you can't change that. It was everything working up to that point— everything that happened to him and everything that happened to me." He was talking intensely now, and the girls were listening just as intensely. He sighed when he finished talking, as though he had some great knowledge or burden.

There was already sympathy in the girls' eyes and one of them asked, "What happened to your leg?"

The guy answered, "Do you know how rare rhinos are in Eastern Borneo?"

Both girls answered, "No."

"They're rare, especially in the Senai Peninsula, where I was stomped. I tossed a little girl out of his path, but I couldn't move myself fast enough. It's all connected—that girl in Borneo and the man up at The Bay . . ." I left after that. I can handle only so much bullshit. I might otherwise be curious to hear the story, but I couldn't stand the idea of those girls eating up everything he was saying. And they weren't bad-looking girls, either, although they were obviously pretty stupid if they were taking that guy so seriously. As I walked away from The Grille it occurred to me that the girls might just be bullshitting the guy and all of them playing out something they wanted to play out. That made me think of Jackson and how he complained about always being unplugged from what other people were doing. It suddenly seemed strange to me how people carried out their insignificant, intricate games with life the way it is and I wondered if maybe I didn't have a little of Jackson's problem.

When I was outside The Grille I stood and searched three-quarters of the way up the cliff that was across the highway for the flat top of the bluff that had the tree growing on it. I could make out the top half of the guy sitting under the tree. It was about a month since the first time I had noticed him there. I noticed him by accident a few times after that, and then it struck me that he seemed to always be up there and I started watching for him. For the past week or ten days he had been there any time that I thought to look for him. I looked up at him for a little while, but he didn't move, so I walked back out to the sand.

Connie was getting real sentimental with me. I guess that happens, but it made me sort of uncomfortable. And damn Jackson, he had something really wrong with the way he looked at life so that he was making me feel bad about things I had no business feeling bad about. I don't think he was trying to make me feel bad, but he was doing it.

Connie and I had been spending almost every evening together for the past couple of weeks, just walking around the neighborhood or sitting on her front lawn or on a low brick wall at the edge of her front yard. Connie couldn't stay out in the sun because of some medicine she was taking and I couldn't stand sitting around her house during the day, so I usually stopped by after dinner, when the late afternoon sun was dropping over the hills. These were the long days of summer and I felt bad for Connie. Tonight her parents were out at a party or something and Connie had promised to stay around the house, so we sat on the low brick wall, not saying much. It was probably nine o'clock, hot and muggy from clouds that had rushed in suddenly and rain that was due at any time. The sky was gray with a dull glow from the clouds. I kept looking up, waiting for that first drop of rain. Finally I felt a drop on my arm, and I raised my face and a couple more drops fell on me, one after the other. Around me the drops began coming down, still one at a time, kicking up the dust that you couldn't see but that lay on everything. I loved to wait for the rain and I loved that sour smell of dust and whatever else it was that was stirred by the very beginning of every rain. After a minute the raindrops became more frequent until we were on the verge of a heavy rain. Connie looked over at me with a strange, intense look in her eyes and said, "It's raining—let's go up to my room." Then she took hold of my hand and we ran into her house, just as the rain started to come down hard. We stood for a half minute at her front door, looking out at the falling rain.

I had never been in Connie's bedroom before. It was a typical girl's bedroom, the way I expected. She had a double bed with a couple of stuffed animals on the pillows and a yellow flower pattern bedspread. Her furniture was white and covered with a few dolls and little nicknacks that girls like to collect. On the wall was a copy of a painting of a young girl with a dog, and I couldn't really figure out how a picture like that would end up on someone's wall, until I remembered some of the things hanging in my own house. In a way it would have been nice if her room was filled with books or aquariums or a telescope or anything different like that, but the room was nice anyway. It smelled nice, too.

I sat on the edge of Connie's bed and looked around her bedroom until she stepped in front of me. I only had to look up a little to meet her eyes even though I was sitting on the bed. I hadn't noticed before the three tiny beauty marks below her left eye. And I also noticed that up this close she wasn't ugly like I thought, but actually kind of pretty. Her face looked soft and smooth, although sort of pale, and her hair hung in gentle curls to her shoulders. Connie asked, "Ben, do you remember when we were playing cards at my house a few months ago? You kissed me and . . ." she smiled and dipped her head sideways, referring to how I had felt her breasts.

"I remember," I answered.

"Why didn't you call me for a long time? And why haven't you touched me since we've been seeing each other every night?"

I didn't know how to answer, partly because I wasn't sure of the real answers. When we had kissed before maybe I hadn't cared much for her, or maybe I was afraid of her cancer, or something. Finally I answered, "It's Jackson's fault."

"Jackson's fault?" Connie looked at me doubtfully.

"That's right. When we . . . then, I just did what I felt like doing. I wanted to hold you and . . . touch you and everything. I felt like doing it. And then I was talking to Jackson and he's got this big thing about everybody having sex when they don't even care that much about each other and about how all the guys are just trying to feel up all the girls and there's no respect . . . that kind of thing. I think he's crazy, but he's actually a pretty smart guy. Maybe he's going to be a preacher or something, because he made me feel bad about that night."

"So that's why you didn't call me for two months? You didn't care anything for me?" Connie sounded offended and she pulled away from me.

"No!" I answered, immediately. "That's why I've only kissed you the past couple of weeks. I didn't call you because . . ."

"Because why?" Connie spoke softly and she stood with her head cocked.

It was difficult for me to answer. I took a deep breath. I wanted to tell Connie about how I was afraid of the cancer, but I couldn't make myself say it. I remembered how I couldn't tell Vickie what I had wanted to tell her and I thought that it might be a sin I should add to my list that I couldn't make myself say the things I wanted to say. Finally I said, "Maybe because I thought I was going to care for you a lot and . . . I don't know." It was pretty much a cowardly answer that didn't really say anything, but all of a sudden I could feel emotion choking up in me. I had to blink a number of times to fight back tears I could feel coming to my eyes. I was sort of shocked and couldn't understand why I was getting so emotional when I wasn't even sure that I meant what I was saying.

Connie said, "That's kind of strange about Jackson. I thought he was a hippie and they're into free love and everything."

"Yeah. Actually, Jackson thinks free love is good. It's just that . . ."

"Ben?" Connie interrupted me. "Would you make love to me tonight?" I opened my mouth to answer, but I couldn't say anything. I was stunned.

"What?" I asked, finally.

"Do you want to make love to me?"

"Sure," I answered, slowly. I was wondering why this was happening to me—I usually figured I wasn't likely to be this lucky in my life. I guess Connie could see in my face that I was stunned and she continued, "I *want* to, Ben."

"We'll do it here?"

"My parents won't be home for hours. They never get home from these things before midnight."

"I've never done this before," I said.

"I *hope* not," Connie said, smiling. "I haven't either, but we can figure it out. It'll be fun to figure it out." I had always thought that Connie was smart, but I couldn't believe how she had such an open approach to everything. I knew that she was going to make the night wonderful, and I was thinking that there couldn't be anyone better than Connie.

I wasn't too sure what I was supposed to do so I put my hands on Connie's waist and pulled her gently toward me, but she pushed me away and stepped back and took hold of my hands. "Not so fast," she said. "First we have to make a deal." She spoke very seriously.

"What kind of a deal?" I asked, concerned that she was so serious. I was prepared to make any deal she wanted, but I was afraid that she would say something that would put a shadow over everything.

"First, you have to love me."

"I do. Is that the deal?"

"Say it."

"I love you."

"Say it with my name."

"I love you, Connie. Is that the deal?"

"That's the first part. The next part has to do with the sun."

"The sun?" I asked, and then I agreed, "Okay, it's a deal."

"You can't agree if you don't know what it is. That's not a real deal. You have to understand what you're giving away so you don't ever give it to anyone else."

"Okay, what is it that I'm giving away?"

"Half the sun." I didn't say anything for a while. I wasn't sure if I could see a smile hidden in Connie's lips. "Not really half the sun," Connie continued. She was looking past me, thinking. "Because then you could give away the other half. You have to *share* the sun with me, so that it's both of ours and it takes both of us to give any of it away. Would you do that?"

"Okay, but how can I?"

"Because it's *your* sun, at least to me it is. You're at the beach all the time, and you're so tan. Even your hair is bleached out." Connie reached over and lightly touched my hair with both of her hands and then she touched me face. "You look so nice with that tan. I know it's kind of crazy, but sometimes I really do feel that it's your sun." Connie's face suddenly seemed even more pale.

"It's a deal," I said and then I couldn't help thinking that as long as we were making deals, maybe I should ask Connie for an IOU like I got from Vickie. I would be that much closer to the fifty IOUs that Jackson had mentioned. I asked, "Can I get a deal from you?"

"Of course. What's *your* deal?"

"Well . . ." I began, and I remembered Jackson asking Vickie to sign those IOUs and I thought that maybe I wouldn't ask Connie the right way and I would offend her or something and ruin everything for tonight. "Nothing."

"No," Connie said, and I was pretty pissed at myself for being greedy and starting this thing. It would be one huge black mark against me if I got Connie angry and she made me leave. "You have to tell me."

"I was . . . I was just thinking that I gave you the whole sun . . ."

"You shared the sun with me."

"Well, it's practically the same as giving you the whole thing because I can't do anything else with it. So I thought maybe you should agree that I could make love to you again after tonight. I mean, the whole sun for just one time . . ."

I looked at Connie carefully, watching for any hint that she was getting angry or anything, but she just smiled and said, "Okay."

"Okay? Can I have it in writing?"

"Sure," she answered and then she just stood there, holding my hands and smiling at me, I guess because neither of us quite knew what to do next. After a while I gently pulled her toward me until she was leaning up against me and then I kissed her. We kissed for a little while like that and Connie suggested, "Maybe we should get into bed." We kissed for a long time and I kissed Connie's face and her neck and gradually her breasts and her stomach as I took her clothes off, until I think I kissed almost her whole body. When I finally pulled off Connie's underpants I looked at her stretched out naked on the bed, smiling, a little embarrassed, and I couldn't actually believe this was happening to me. Connie helped me get my clothes off pretty quickly and then I couldn't believe it was over so fast. It was great and all, but you would think it might be just a bit better. It hurt Connie a little, but she didn't seem to mind. She wanted to kiss some more and be affectionate and then we did it a second time and it seemed better the second time.

I had forgotten about the IOU but Connie remembered and as I was getting ready to leave she asked, "So, what do you want this agreement to say?"

"How about just 'I owe you Ben,' and then sign it," I suggested.

Connie went to her desk and took out a small piece of stationary with flowers on it. She wrote the date and then "I owe you, Ben. Good any time. Connie."

On my way home later that night I thought how great it was that Connie and I had made love, and I wondered a little about how it might have been even better, it being the first time for us. Finally I figured that maybe it was right what people said that nothing is ever as good as you think it's going to be. Then I got to wondering about what it would be like with different women who I might meet over the years, until I started to feel a little bad thinking about that after being with Connie that night and her having cancer and all.

I couldn't figure out what list making love to Connie should go on. It was probably a sin on Graham's list, but definitely not on mine. At first it seemed like it should go on my list of great things. But as I kept thinking about it I decided to put it on my list of good things because I realized that all those people that you see walking around every day all over the place are doing the same thing, so it couldn't be a great thing. It was kind of hard to believe, but I knew it was true. And then I thought that maybe it could still be a great thing even if everyone was doing it. Maybe it was a great thing because it was with Connie and not some-body else. And then I remembered the girl at the beach whose breast popped out while she danced on the table and I wondered what list making love to her would be on if Connie was already on the list of great things. Finally I decided to leave making love to Connie on my list of good things, although I felt a little bad about the way I got to that decision. I stopped at a street lamp and looked at my IOU from Connie and I wondered whether I was ever really going to get to fifty of those. Then I was a little annoyed at myself because it was Jackson's idea to get the IOU from Vickie and then to get fifty of them, and here I was using someone else's idea again.

CHAPTER SIX

I don't exactly know how it started with Franny, it just did. I sometimes felt sort of bad about it, what with Connie being my girlfriend and having the cancer and all. In fact, I put it on my list of sins (although I also put it on my list of good things). But it happened and it wasn't such a bad thing, if you think of what happens in life. I met Franny by accident one day on my way to the beach. I left late for the beach that day so I stopped to have lunch in the town in the middle of the canyon at a little cafe called Nature's Way, where I liked to eat. They didn't serve any meat at Nature's Way, just different kinds of fruit and vegetable dishes, which never quite filled me up. After the first few times I ate there I generally ordered a salad because I sometimes felt a little sick when I left the place. The vegetable stews, without even considering the women who worked in the place, were way too scary to eat, although a lot of people did eat them. But I liked the atmosphere at Nature's Way. I could sit at one of the tables and almost imagine that I lived in the canyon and that the canyon was in a different part of the country or a different part of the world, far from here. Once in a while I might imagine that I was living with a girl I saw in the town, or maybe with two girls, and that we went around the country in a beat-up van to sit-ins and demonstrations because we were so dedicated to peace. I sometimes thought that Connie might get well and she and I could move to the canyon, or to a canyon somewhere else in the country. Connie was dedicated to peace, but I didn't think she was going to get well. She was already starting to seem sicker.

Franny worked in a clothing shop in the town and she ate at Nature's Way every day, although I had never seen her before. She

picked up some food at the counter and walked straight over to
where I was sitting, and she asked if she could sit down with me.
She said that she didn't like to eat alone. I think it was something
like, "Life is more real if you share every minute with someone—
even if it's with a stranger." Actually, that's the one thing that
makes me a little unsure if I really had a love affair with Franny.
She was always saying things like that—things that made me
feel sort of unimportant, like a random choice. Although I guess
that it could still qualify as a love affair even if you got into it
only because you happened to be sitting at a certain table at a
particular time.

Franny sat down before I could decide on something to
answer, and she said, "You look good with that tan. Are you a
surfer?" She looked for a few moments right into my eyes and I
don't know how she did it, but she sent something right into my
heart. That's the truth, even if it does sound a bit cornball. She
was just looking at me, and I didn't notice if she changed her
expression or what, but suddenly I got this feeling in my whole
body that pulled together and focused in my heart. It almost
made me catch my breath, just slightly.

"Not really," I answered. "I just hang around at the beach a lot."

"You look like a surfer. I'll bet that everyone asks if you surf."

"I guess a lot of people do."

"Maybe you should just say you *are* a surfer. Then everyone
would be happy because that's what you look like." She had a
small, very white, gentle face that looked even smaller because
her thick brown hair grew low on her forehead. Her nose was also
small and had the slightest hook to it, and when she smiled her
teeth were small and very white and perfectly lined up. Scattered
across her nose and cheeks were tiny, light freckles. She wore a
long baggy dress with a flower pattern all over it, that came down
below her knees. Her hair looked clean and soft and was tied in
a pony tail that hung halfway down her back.

We talked very easily for a while. It turned out that Franny
lived in the canyon with her sister and some other people. She
was a couple of years older than I was, but I lied about my age by

a couple of years. I told Franny that I didn't have a driver's license and that I hitchhiked everywhere because I didn't believe in driving cars. I told her that driving was too much an expression of modern technology carrying us past the early morning dew drops on individual blades of grass and the hope embodied in the faintest rustle of a breeze on a hot, stagnant day. I couldn't remember where I had heard that before, but I hoped that she hadn't heard it herself. I also told her that driving was a distraction to a student of the human condition, such as myself, and that compared to hitchhiking it eliminated much of the uncertainty and adventure in going from one place to another. Anyway, she bought all of it, even the part about my age. We talked until she was late for going back to work, and before she left she told me to stop by the clothing store sometime. I told her I would stop by. On my way home I started thinking about her and about our conversation and after a while I just couldn't stop thinking about her.

The Grille is a pretty greasy place. People track in sand with their sandals and bare feet and the suntan oil on their bodies smears on the benches and tables and walls and when they finish eating people usually leave the remnants of their lunches on the tables instead of throwing them in the trash cans. One of the guys who works behind the counter comes out every hour or so and cleans off a few tables, but most of the time people just push papers and cups down the tables or onto the floor or gather them up and toss them into a trash can to make enough room on a table to eat.

There were unusually few people in The Grille, even for a weekday. The guy was sitting at the next table, facing in my direction. I didn't notice him until another guy and a girl sat down at his table. Almost immediately the first guy awkwardly gathered together his food and left the table. Either he couldn't carry everything or he was so nervous that he forgot to pick it up, but he left his drink on the table. He was a puny-looking guy—small and scrawny with dark hair and glasses with thick black rims. He was wearing cut-off *slacks* and he was white like you get when you're never in the sun, except for a few moles and patches of red on his shoulders where he was getting sunburned.

As the puny guy was getting up from the table the second guy called out, "Hey, what're you doing?" The puny guy didn't look around, but just lowered his head a little and started moving faster, except that he was getting tangled up in the benches between the tables. The second guy jumped up and ran around in front of the puny guy. The second guy was scrawny also, but he was bigger than the puny guy.

The puny guy asked, "What?"

"I was talking to you."

"What? What do you want?" The puny guy was standing a little stooped and his head seemed bent even lower now.

"I want you to pick up that cup!" The scrawny guy spoke loudly and pointed to the cup that the puny guy had left on the table. "We have to eat here and I don't want your trash around." The puny guy looked stunned. His lips moved a bit but before he could say anything the scrawny guy grabbed his arm and pushed him backwards. "Now, pick up your trash!" The puny guy stumbled a little and he looked panicky when he almost dropped his food, but he managed to keep hold of everything, and when the other guy stepped toward him he lowered his head even further and walked back over to where he had been sitting. The puny guy crushed his bag of french fries into the cup and I could see the drink spill up into the bag of fries. He picked up the cup with the soggy fries and walked quickly out of The Grille, staring straight ahead.

The other guy walked around the table and sat down next to the girl. He shook his head and said, "God, I hate it when people do things like that." I guess maybe the puny guy might some day become a brain surgeon or a senator or something and marry a beautiful woman who was also a brain surgeon or something and the other guy might become a heroin addict on skid row. But I was still pretty disgusted. I mean, everybody wants to be a hero, but it's awfully pathetic if it's at the expense of a puny guy. I was reminded of the other day when I got a ride to the beach from a man who stopped for a few minutes to visit his mother who lived at one of those old age homes that happened to be along our way. While I waited in his car, I saw a beat-up old dog lying in the shade of a couple of trash cans. His fur was matted and I could see sores in places where his fur was very thin. There were flies all around the trash cans and a number were buzzing around and landing on the dog. The dog was bobbing his head and I thought it was because he was sick, until I realized that he had a fly in his mouth that he was chewing, spitting on the ground, then picking up and chewing again. He seemed to be taking great care to crush the fly between his canines, over and over. I figured that he was trying to get back at all those other flies that he couldn't catch through that one dead fly. I guess I could have done something for the puny guy, but I didn't.

I left The Grille and decided that maybe I should put it on my list of sins that I didn't help the puny guy. I looked across the highway and up the cliff. The Poet was there, as I expected him to be, sitting under the tree. Of course I didn't know at the time that he was a poet.

The beach was different today than I had ever seen it before. There were scattered white clouds in the sky and the ocean had brought in a strange current. Two sets of waves broke at one time instead of the usual single set. The second set was fifty or so yards outside the first break and the waves broke in sets of ten to twelve instead of the usual five to eight. The waves were much larger than usual, especially the outside set, and they got larger during each set as the set progressed. The sand a few yards off the shoreline where the waves were breaking was churned up and uneven, shallow in some spots and dropping off suddenly to deep holes in other spots. Few people went into the water. I looked out at the ocean and wondered what it was somewhere else in the world that had brought this strange tide.

I walked a long ways down the beach, then sat on the dry sand and stretched my legs so that my feet rested just above the point where the edge of the ocean sank into the sand after boiling and churning and running up the beach with each wave. The day was hot, but there was a mild breeze blowing in from the ocean and an occasional cloud floated between the sun and me. I sat and was reminded of Hawaii, where I had never been, and of long trips on small working boats on tropical seas, where I had also never been. I sat looking both directions down the beach and out to sea. People walked and ran past me, singly, in pairs, in groups. Some people walked past me one direction and later back the other direction. I thought of the people who I didn't know who had walked this same beach and were now dead or maybe in a hospital someplace, dying. I thought about Connie, who was at another clinic today, this one in Arizona, and Jackson, who was turning eighteen years old. And I thought about Franny. I couldn't get her off my mind. I didn't even know her but I wanted to spend time with her in the canyon. She was the person I imagined living with in the canyon and driving around the country with to sit-ins and all of that. I wanted to become part of what she was part of.

The water rushed up as high as my knees. It was rushing up fast and my impulse was to jump up so I wouldn't be sitting in the ocean. But the water lost its momentum, suddenly, when it reached dry sand and it barely reached my knees. After that, the water began to fall short of my feet and hours later I was ten or twelve feet above the ocean's best efforts. Finally I walked back to where I had left my towel on the beach below The Grille. I stood at the edge of the water for a couple of minutes before I picked up my towel. The sun was bright orange, just a foot above the horizon across the ocean from me.

When I reached the parking lot next to The Grille, I remembered the Poet. I looked up with a feeling on the verge of both triumph and sadness, certain that he would not be up on the bluff. But the Poet was still there, sitting under the tree as usual, and I almost couldn't believe it.

The parking lot, which was full every morning and early afternoon during the summer, was nearly empty now. I frequently got a ride by asking people who were driving out of the parking lot if they were going anywhere near where I lived and if they would give me a ride. But now there were few people left at the beach and no cars leaving, so I ran across the highway and started up the dirt path that led to the park at the top of the cliff. The path was narrow and steep and in many places I had to hold onto rocks or shrubs or exposed roots to keep from sliding backwards. I rested about halfway up the cliff, and I looked back down at the highway and the beach and out at the ocean. My face was emanating heat from my sunburn, in spite of the breeze.

Then I got an inspiration—I guess it was an inspiration. I searched for the tree where I could find the guy who was always sitting there. But the cliff was steep in front of me and the tree was blocked from my view. I climbed higher until I saw the top of the tree twenty yards away. Then I noticed a narrow, almost imperceptible path leading along the side of the cliff toward the bluff where the tree was. It was a path you would never notice unless you were looking for it. The Poet must have made the path by walking back and forth every day—assuming that he did leave that spot once in a while.

The path was narrow but easy to walk, and it led directly to the little bluff where the tree grew. The bluff was about fifteen feet square and level, with the tree and a few small shrubs growing on it. I don't know what kind the tree was, but it was small with sparse round leaves. The guy was sitting under the tree and looking out to sea. He didn't seem to notice that I had walked up behind him.

I stood for a few moments trying to figure something to say to get the guy's attention, but before I could think of anything he looked around at me and said, "I was wondering if you were ever going to come up here." The Poet was not quite what I had expected him to be. He had blonde hair, thinning in the front, that grew down over his ears and a heavy brown and blonde beard and moustache, and he looked to be in his late twenties. He sat cross-legged, wearing a pair of blue jeans and no shirt or shoes. He had a dark tan, but a tough tan—a worker's tan rather than a leisure tan. "What do you mean?" I asked and I stepped a few feet closer to him. I noticed a pad of unlined paper and a pencil on the ground next to him.

"I've been watching you down there. I've seen you look up at me just about every day. I was wondering whether you'd ever decide to come up here. I didn't think you would." He turned away from me so that he was looking out to sea again, and he asked, "Well, what do you want?"

I didn't have an answer to his question, and I didn't say anything. But he didn't say anything more or look back at me, so finally I said, "I don't know what I want. I just thought I'd stop by. I guess I just curious to know what you were doing up here all day."

"Why?"

"What do you mean?"

"Why do you want to know?"

I didn't answer for a few seconds, and then I said, "I guess that I just have a desire to learn more about the human condition." I don't know why I said it—it was another inspiration I guess. Anyway, it worked on the Poet. He turned back around and looked at me for a while, with a crack of a smile on his face and without saying anything, as though he were deciding whether I was serious or trying to make a fool out of him. I kept my face as still as possible and finally he picked up the pad that was on the ground next to him and tore out a sheet of paper.

"Here," he said and he handed me the sheet of paper. As I took the paper he said, "Don't read it now, read it another time."

"Okay," I answered. "Does this tell me what you do up here all the time?"

"No, but I'll tell you. I write poetry. That's a poem I gave you."

"Oh yeah?" I wasn't sure what else to say so I looked at the paper and asked, "Can I fold it up and put it in my pocket?"

"It's just a poem."

"So why do you sit right here? I mean, you could sit at different places or something."

"I sit here because of the poem-tree." He watched me closely while he spoke and I acted as though it were pretty serious stuff.

"The poem-tree?" I asked.

"That's it." He still had that crack of a smile across his face.

"This tree here?" I asked. I wasn't sure if he meant a real tree or something else.

"See any other trees around here?"

"No . . . but what makes it a poem-tree?"

"That's hard to say. What makes a poem a poem?" I didn't have an answer to a crazy question like that so I didn't say anything. He continued, "It just seems that you can sit under certain trees and write poetry. Or *I* can."

I was starting to wonder whether he was trying to make a fool out of *me*. I said, "People write poetry all over the place."

"That's true."

"So what does this tree have to do with your writing poetry?"

"It has a lot to do with it. When I find a poem-tree I can write poetry, otherwise I can't."

"And this tree here is one? A poem-tree?"

"I said it was. It's not a great poem-tree, but a pretty good one. Some poem-trees are better than others and I write poetry under the better trees. Some trees dry up fast and some last a long time, longer than I have patience for."

"So what do you do then? You just look around . . ."

"I search. I search for poem-trees and I write poetry. If I ever find the ultimate poem-tree, I'll write the ultimate poetry." The Poet turned away and I followed his gaze to a beautiful sunset over the Pacific Ocean. Only the upper edge of the sun rested far out at sea. A myriad subtly different red-orange tones stretched across the sky, encircling and absorbing the few clouds and skipping unevenly over the ocean. It was nearly dark. Many of the cars on the highway below had their headlights on and it was later than traffic rush hour so the cars moved quickly.

"Well," I said, "thanks for the poem. I'll read it later." I climbed the rest of the way up the cliff. As I reached the top I looked out over the ocean again. I was thinking, "He's a crazy man, but maybe not all that crazy." I remembered that it was Jackson's birthday and that I had promised to celebrate with him.

It took a while for me to get rides home, the way it was always harder to get rides after dark than during the day. I think that people close out part of the world after dark, or maybe they're just more afraid. I was standing under a street lamp with my thumb out, thinking about the Poet. I didn't know if he was a lost soul or a sap or a wise man or what. I was leaning against the street lamp and there was a wire mesh trash container a few feet away. The container was filled to the top and a few pieces of trash were strewn next to it on the ground, including a single shoe, a white high-heeled shoe. I looked all around for the other shoe, but I couldn't find it, and I wondered how that shoe ended up there alone. I took out the sheet of paper and read the poem written on it. A couple of lines and scattered words had been crossed through and rewritten. The first line of the poem was underlined, but I didn't know if it was the title or what. This was the poem:

> <u>The sun settles into another</u>
> Tomorrow, somewhere in the world
> Far out at sea. Sunset
> Over the Pacific Ocean.
> The sea reflects infinite
> Arrangements of red-orange
> And unsettles the wind.
> Parting cries of tired gulls evaporate.
>
> The wind after a scathing
> Summer day against a sunburnt face —
> I walk the beach at sunset.
> Foamy water runs regularly up
> Over my feet and back,
> Erasing my footsteps even as I walk.
>
> Delivering bottled milk
> A young man not yet fully awake
> On cobblestone streets across
> The world catches the first rays
> Of sunrise in the corner of his eye.

I read the poem and didn't know whether it was a good poem or a bad one. I turned the paper over and saw that there was another poem on the other side, and I wondered whether the Poet had intended to give me two poems, because he had only mentioned a single poem. I read the other poem:

> Toward sundown a solitary man sat
> On the flat surface of a large boulder,
> Part of a small jetty into the sea.
>
> Fine spray carried by a chilly offshore
> Breeze from crashing waves, settled, drop by drop,
> To a thin layer, moistening his shirt,
> And beading tiny seas on face and arms.
>
> The goddamn world around was catching him
> Up again.
>   Careless manipulation
> Of/by—he does not know—the world around.
>
> His so trite wandering soul, his heart, his
> Terrified dream, bit by bit by ever
> The tiniest bit losing hope of time --
> A day, a single moment of mindless
> Comfort and wistful loneliestness of
> Open roads; a gentle gentle heart-pull
> Of one lighted house on dark and quiet
> Narrow roads.
>   Memories of days past and
> Other days, that must be, have to be out
>
> there,
>
> Somewhere.

I read the second poem twice, and I liked it more than the first poem. I wondered again whether the Poet had intended to give me both poems, and I thought that maybe I should take the

poems back to him. Instead, I crumbled the poems into a ball
and tossed them onto the overfull trash container, but they rolled
off the trash onto the ground. I left the poems there for a minute,
then picked them up and uncrumpled them. I flattened the
sheets of paper, then folded the poems and put them in my back
pocket. After all, they were poetry that someone had given me. I
wasn't sure why, and I had to think about it, but it seemed that it
might qualify for my list of good things that the Poet had given
me his poems.

When I finally got home I quickly changed my clothes and
ran over to Jackson's house. Jackson was in his bedroom as usual,
lying on his back on his bed, listening to "The Eve of
Destruction," loud, the way he always seemed to be. Jackson
looked over at me as I walked into the room and I could tell that
he was happy to see me. He got up from his bed and turned
down the music and I said, "Happy birthday, old man."

"Thanks," he answered.

"Sorry I'm late. It took a long time to get back from the beach."

"Why do you say you're late? You're not late for anything."

I looked around Jackson's room at all the posters and the
poems and the quotations he had copied and tacked to his walls.
I asked, "How come you're always listening to that same song
whenever I come over?"

"Because that's my song. Come on." Jackson walked past me
out of his bedroom and I followed him out the back door of his
house through the back yard. As we walked through the yard
Jackson turned to me and asked, "Are you ready?"

"Ready for what?"

"Ready to get stoned."

"Yeah, I guess so," I answered. Jackson had mentioned a number
of times that for my birthday he was going to have me smoke
some marijuana, but I was never sure that he was serious. I
followed Jackson into the garage and we climbed a narrow ladder
up to a small attic, where I had never been before. Outside it was
dark and the only light inside was from a single bulb that hung
from a wire in the middle of the room. The walls were steeply

slanted and there were boxes and old furniture piled all around and collecting dust. In the center of the room was a small area that had been cleared away and there were two low chairs on either side of a small table. "This is great," I said. "Why didn't you ever show me this before?"

"This is a stoning room. They would've been p minutes for me to take you here before." Jackson took a metal box about a foot square from the piles of junk. It was an old box with an advertisement painted on it. "Have a seat," Jackson said and he motioned to the chairs. Then he closed a door that covered the opening we had climbed through and he set the box on the small table. Inside the box were some candles, matches, cigarette papers in a small packet, a pipe and a little baggie of what looked like crushed up green, dried leaves. Jackson handed the baggie to me and said, "Smell this."

I tentatively opened the baggie, which was a plastic bag just like those my mother used to put my lunch in when I was a kid, and smelled the pungent, dusty smelling contents. "Is this going to get me stoned?" I asked.

Jackson laughed. "No, you have to smoke it. You can't get stoned just by smelling it." He laughed again. "It would be nice if you could." Jackson had set three thick, partly burned down candles on the table and he lit them, and then he turned off the overhead light. The candles threw a lot of light that made shadows dance, and I was reminded of Vickie in the sewers.

I asked, "Do you remember the woman we saved from the sewers—Victoria?"

"Of course! We have to talk about her. But first, give me the stuff." Jackson held his hand toward me and I handed him the marijuana. He set the baggie on the table and took out a pinch of marijuana between his thumb and forefinger, which he crumbled into a piece of cigarette paper he held in his other hand. He took out another two pinches and skillfully rolled the marijuana into the paper. He licked the edge of the paper, sealed the narrow cigarette and twisted both ends. He held up the finished product, "Voilà," he said.

"Where'd you learn to do that so well? Do you smoke a lot of this?"

"A pretty fair amount." Jackson lit the cigarette and took a long drag, making the end glow and causing the cigarette to burn down quickly. He held his breath for about ten seconds, then blew out a cloud of smoke. "Here." He held the marijuana out to me. I sucked in deeply and coughed out a cloud of smoke. I coughed for a while before I could talk.

"That burns my lungs . . ."

"You'll get used to it." We smoked the entire cigarette and then Jackson leaned back on the chair. "Feel anything?" he asked.

"I'm not sure. Do you? What does it feel like?"

"You'll know. Just wait a minute. I'm already stoned because I've got it in my blood."

Suddenly I felt a slight chill run down my back, and I was stoned. I didn't realize it at first—I thought it was just a chill. But I looked at Jackson and at the table between us and then at a pile of boxes beyond Jackson and I noticed that I could only focus on one thing at a time. I looked all around, staring at one thing after another. It was an odd feeling, like I was in a dream or something. I guess Jackson was watching me and he said, "You're stoned!" and he started laughing. I started laughing also, for no reason. "Let's do another," Jackson said, and he began to roll another cigarette. We talked about nothing and laughed a lot while we passed the second cigarette back and forth. When the cigarettes burned low, Jackson hooked the half-inch butts to a little clip so that he wouldn't burn his fingers and he breathed in the smoke through his nose. "This is the best part," he said. "All the resin's collected here." We talked and laughed a while longer and then I got to thinking about Vickie and I wanted to talk about her with Jackson.

But before I could figure out what I wanted to talk about Jackson said, "I was just thinking about Victoria. That was awfully cool how we saved her."

"I was thinking about her, too."

"What I can't figure out is why she gave us those IOUs." Even in the candlelight I could see that Jackson had a very serious expression on his face. "I keep thinking about that and it doesn't quite make sense."

"Why? We saved her, didn't we? I thought you were going to get fifty of those."

"Just think about it. If you had a girlfriend and she told you how she screwed someone—no, two guys—because they saved her life, what would you think? Don't you think she should be screwing guys because she loves them, not as a reward or anything?"

I thought about it for a few moments. It had seemed a little strange to me at first, but right now I couldn't think of why, maybe because I was stoned. I hesitated before answering, because I knew this was a touchy subject for Jackson, but he seemed pretty mellow being stoned. "I don't think it's so strange. It's her body. It's something she has, so she should be able to do whatever she wants with it . . ."

"But then it loses its value, its significance . . ."

"Maybe it *gains* value. What could be better than saving someone's life? Maybe she thinks we did something so great for her that she wants to give us what's the most important thing to her." "Maybe," Jackson said, thoughtfully.

He didn't say anything more so I asked, "Are you going to use your IOU from Vickie or just save it?"

Jackson answered, "I'm not sure. You wouldn't have taken another kind of reward, would you? Like money? So why would you take this reward."

"Then why get the IOUs?" I asked. "You could go through your whole life and get fifty of those and never use them and what would they be worth? And what if she gets stuck in the sewers again and dies and you never get a chance to use your IOU? That would be a big waste."

Jackson nodded his head slowly. His hair had fallen forward and covered much of his face. He didn't say anything and I figured he must be extremely stoned. Then I realized that I was very hungry and when I told Jackson he said, "You've got the munchies—me, too. Let's go get a burger."

Jackson drove us in his mother's station wagon to a little

hamburger stand called "Betty's Burgers." It was a greasy place that was always open. Inside was a small area where people waited in line to order and there were two or three tables outside, but most people took their food to go or ate in their cars. We walked into Betty's and except for the couple of people behind the counter there was only an old man and an old woman. The man stood ordering food with his back to Jackson and me but the woman watched us as we walked toward her. She looked about fifty and she wore heavy make-up with bright red lipstick and heavy red rouge on her cheeks and her clothes were brightly colored and worn and seemed to me not to match each other. Her dress was cut low across her large chest. She looked very strange to me and I thought that it must have been because of the marijuana. I couldn't help staring at her and I felt like laughing, although I stopped myself. The man in line took his food and walked past us out the door. I expected the old woman to follow him, but she turned slightly and stood where she was. Jackson asked me what I wanted to eat and he stepped up to order the food. I stood a few feet behind him, very stoned, staring past him and watching the cook clean the grill with a metal brush. A few moments later I felt something brush by my arm and it sent a little shiver through me. I looked around and there was only the old woman standing a couple of feet from me. It happened again and then once again, and a wave of panic rushed through me. I thought that the marijuana was making me go crazy. I had visions of myself going crazy in Betty's and the police coming and my parents having to get me out of jail. I could even picture Ben Sr. picking me up at the police station, staggering in, drunk and yelling at me while all the police stood and watched. Then Jackson turned toward me. He looked at me for a moment and then past me and I turned to where he was looking and the old woman was walking slowly away. Jackson stepped up to me and nodded toward the old woman and asked, "What'd she want?"

"What do you mean?"

"What was she doing to your arm?"

I was relieved that it must have been the woman brushing by

my arm and that I wasn't going crazy. "I don't know," I answered.

We took our food out to Jackson's car and sat in the front seat to eat. We were both starving and we laughed when we took the food from the bags and saw how much food we had ordered. A minute later the woman walked out of Betty's. She looked around for a few moments and then started walking toward us. "Uh oh," Jackson said. "I'll bet she was trying to pickpocket you or something and she's coming for food. What should we give her?"

"I'm starving! We better give her a couple of dollars," I answered, and we both laughed.

The woman walked directly toward us and stood two or three feet away from the car, outside Jackson's door. She just stood there, looking around and Jackson and I continued eating. After a minute she stepped over to Jackson's window, which was rolled down, and she wrapped her arms across her chest and said, "It's so cold out here."

Jackson looked at me and we laughed and he turned back to the old woman and said, "It's warm out there. It's summertime. Do you want a couple of dollars for food?"

The woman mumbled, "A couple dollars?" and then she leaned down and stuck the top part of her body through Jackson's window so that she was leaning between Jackson and the steering wheel. When she leaned down the top of her dress hung open and I could see the top half of her breasts, which were pretty big. She turned so that her breasts pushed into Jackson's face and she said, "It's okay, you can touch them." Jackson and I had both started to laugh when the woman first leaned into the car, but now we just looked at each other. Jackson was sort of cramped in there, with the woman leaning right in front of him, and keeping him from eating. The woman just stood there, leaning into the car and staring past me. I considered putting my hand into her dress, but Jackson beat me to it. He shrugged his shoulders and reached his hand up and inside the dress. The woman leaned a little lower so that Jackson could reach in more easily and I could see Jackson hold one breast and then the other under her dress. The woman leaned her face over and brushed against Jackson's face and then gently pulled Jackson's hand away from her. She leaned back so that her face was just outside Jackson's window and she said, "A couple dollars and I could get some food and come back." Jackson took a five dollar bill out of his pocket and gave it to the woman. "You just wait for me," she said and she walked quickly back into Betty's.

"Jesus Christ!" I said as the woman walked away. "What did they feel like?"

"Pretty good," Jackson said. "She looks old. I thought they'd be mush, but they felt pretty good."

"What are you going to do?"

"I don't know." Jackson started eating again, but suddenly we both started laughing so that Jackson spit up some of his food. We calmed down and Jackson started eating again and a little later he said, "I don't know, but you have to catch up somehow."

"Catch up with what?" I asked.

"I'm eighteen today," Jackson answered.

"I know that. So?"

Jackson shook his head. "I had this girlfriend a couple of years ago, when I was sixteen, back at my old school. I didn't sleep with her, but I should have. I passed up my chances because I didn't even know they were chances. I couldn't imagine that she would sleep with me?—I don't even know that I wanted her to sleep with me. We were sixteen and I figured she *had* to be a virgin, and I wanted it that way. I couldn't imagine that she wasn't a virgin. She was cute and smart . . . she was just a nice person. And then when I found out about her we got into a big fight and broke up before I could sleep with her."

"What did you find out about her?" I asked.

"Just that she started having sex when she was fourteen. *Fourteen*! Can you imagine that? Well, I'm sure *you* can. But I couldn't. She wasn't a dumb, ugly girl that didn't have anything else going for her. Anyway, she was smoking pot one day, a warm summer day, and drinking a little wine with some friends. It had rained the night before. They were all in a little loft in some beat-up little guesthouse over a garage at some kid's house whose parents weren't home. It was back in Rhode Island, in some little town no one ever heard of. They were all getting high and listening to music—The New Riders of the Purple Sage. Have you ever heard of them?"

"Of course I've heard of them," I answered.

"Well, they were all listening to the New Riders, getting high, laughing. And Teri—that was my girlfriend's name—she liked this kid who was older, who was sixteen, and he was one of the kids there smoking pot." Jackson paused and looked out the window toward Betty's. I didn't know what he was thinking, but I was amazed at how much detail Jackson knew about that day, especially when he wasn't there. I wondered whether he remembered it the way it had really happened.

Jackson looked back at me. "So, she and this kid—his name was Vinny—they started kissing, and eventually they ended up in bed in the house. The parents were gone until late that night, or until the next day . . . I can't remember.

"That was when she was fourteen. I won't go over the details of the others, but by the time *I* met her, when she was sixteen, she already had six other boyfriends that she slept with. Just one boyfriend after another, and she slept with every one of them. Except me, of course. Some of the boyfriends she saw for a long time, like five or six months, and some for just a little while.

"And you know what else? A couple of the guys she slept with she didn't even *want* to sleep with. They sort of pushed her into it and she went along. Can you imagine that?" Before I could answer Jackson continued, "And you know Lisa Boothe, my girlfriend?"

"Yeah," I answered and I noticed the old woman walk out of Betty's carrying a paper bag. "She's coming back," I added.

Jackson looked over at the woman who was walking toward the car and he said quickly, "I shouldn't tell you this, but she already slept with three other guys before me. She's sixteen and . . ." The woman walked up to Jackson and asked, "Should I get in the front seat?"

Jackson answered, "Why don't you get in the back and you can eat there." The woman got into the back seat and took her food out of the bag. She flattened the bag on her lap and began to eat voraciously, as though she hadn't eaten for a few days. Jackson and I both turned around and watched her eat. She ate intently, without even looking up at us. I was still stoned, but less than before, and everything seemed to be less of a dream and more of a sleepy reality. We watched the woman eat all of her food and neither of us said anything. I was thinking about what Jackson had told me about his girlfriends and I wondered whether he was really thinking of having sex with this woman. She seemed pretty old. I felt sort of sorry for him, although I *was* a little curious about how this woman looked naked. I thought about Connie and realized that I shouldn't even have thought about putting my hand down the woman's dress. And then I thought for a moment about Franny, and figured that if I could be thinking so much about Franny maybe it wouldn't have been so bad if I *had* put my hand down the woman's dress. Finally the woman finished eating and I took all of our trash to a trash can a few feet from the car.

After she finished eating, the woman smiled a wild, crazy-looking smile at me and leaned forward and put her hand on Jackson's face for just a second. "Where to, Honey?" she asked.

"I don't know," Jackson answered. He started the car's engine and drove us away from Betty's Burgers.

"What are we going to do?" I asked Jackson. I glanced back at the woman, who sat silently, staring out the window.

"I don't know. Are you interested in anything?"

"I don't think so," I answered.

After a couple of minutes we were close to our houses and Jackson asked again, "You sure you're not interested?"

I *was* a little interested, but I couldn't even imagine how it would work with both Jackson and me, and there was Connie who had cancer and I couldn't do this to her. "I don't think so. What are you going to do?"

"I'm not sure, but I think I'll let you off here." Jackson pulled to the side of the road and stopped the car. "You can walk from here. It's just a couple of blocks."

"That's fine," I answered. "Just tell me what happens."

"I will. First I have to decide what to do." When I opened the door and the overhead light in the car turned on I looked back at the woman. She continued to stare out the window, as though she hadn't even heard that we were talking about her. I closed the door and as Jackson drove away I could see the woman lean forward in her seat.

It still wasn't very late and I was afraid I would run into Ben Sr. if I went into my house, so I walked around the neighborhood. I felt a little high still, but pretty much back to normal. I walked past Connie's house and thought about Connie in some hospital in Arizona. I thought that I would tell her about smoking the marijuana and I knew that she would want to smoke some. I walked past Jackson's house and the station wagon was already parked in the garage. A faint light shone in the small window above the garage, and I wondered whether Jackson was up there with the woman from Betty's Burgers.

I guess I was still more stoned than I thought because I got this crazy idea of getting my camera and trying to sneak up to the room above Jackson's garage and surprising Jackson and the woman from Betty's, if they were up there. I could take a couple of pictures and embarrass Jackson with them for the rest of his life.

I had to creep carefully through my own house to get my camera and avoid Ben Sr. And then I didn't want Jackson's parents to see me walk into the garage and ask me what I was doing, so I decided to go around to the back door of Jackson's garage. The only way to get to the back door without being seen was to go part way around the block and through the Kuchers' backyard.

The Kuchers' house was on the corner and I climbed the low cement block wall into their backyard. I had to cross the yard, slip along part of their house and under a couple of windows, and then I would climb a wooden fence and run about ten feet to the back door to Jackson's garage. Once I was in the Kuchers' yard there were bushes and trees I could hide behind most of the way, and soon I was up against their house. I was a little out of breath from climbing and running and as I stood with my back against the house scanning the yard to be certain that no one was watching me, I almost laughed at how ridiculous it was that I was doing this. I walked with my back against the house, ducking under the first window, which was dark, to the second window about twenty feet along the house that was lit with that blue television light. As I approached the second window I thought that I would crawl quietly under the window and around a small bush that grew there, but at the last moment I decided that I had to glance through the window, just to see what was inside. I ducked and moved under the window, then slowly lifted my head above the sill and looked in the room. The curtains were pulled open so I could see most of the room, except for a small part that was blocked by a branch that grew up from the bush. A fan set on a table near the window was blowing into the room, turning from side to side, and the television was playing a commercial where two dogs were talking to each other with foreign accents. The only light in the room came from the television, so it took me a moment to notice Mrs. Kucher lying on her back on a couch across the room. She was partly blocked by the branch and a pile of books on a coffee table in front of the couch. The moment I saw her I dropped to my knees and froze. I didn't think she had seen me, but I wasn't sure, so I sat ready to run if she came to the window. I stayed there for at least five minutes without moving. I had only caught a glimpse, and it was pretty much blocked by the bush, but I thought that Mrs. Kucher was wearing some kind of a short nightgown and that she was lying with her legs apart, watching the television. It was sort of killing me to sit there because I just had to take another look. Finally I moved over a little and lifted my head to the corner of the window where my view would be clear of the shrub.

Mrs. Kucher was still lying on her back on the couch. She lay with her knees bent and apart with the bottom of her feet together. Her nightgown was pulled up to her waist and although I was looking at her from the side I could see that she wasn't wearing any underwear. She looked like she was watching television, but her right hand was between her legs, moving slowly from side to side. It looked like the fingers of her right hand were sort of curled into a fist and her thumb was sticking out into the air as her hand moved back and forth. I watched for a short while, sometimes seeing clearer than other times as the room brightened or darkened, changing with the scenes on the television. I felt a little bad about watching her like this and nervous that she would look over and see me, and I remembered the woman in the sewers and that I was on my way to sneak up on Jackson and I thought that maybe I was becoming a pervert or something. My heart was pounding, but I decided that I should leave, that I *had* to leave, so I slipped away through the Kuchers' yard until I got back to the cement block wall. And then I couldn't go any further. I sat crouched by the wall for a few minutes, fighting myself to stay or leave. I kept wanting to go back just to get another look at Mrs. Kucher and to see what she was doing. Finally I realized that I was only human and there was no way I was going to leave and I ran back over to the window.

By the time I looked back through the window my heart was pounding like crazy. I lifted my head slowly until I could see in the room again. Mrs. Kucher lay the same way as before, except a little lower on the couch and with her legs farther apart so that her right leg was up against the back of the couch and her left knee hung over the edge of the couch. She was still watching television and she still moved her hand like before, except faster than before. She stopped moving after a little bit, then started again, then stopped, and she kept stopping and starting like that for a long time. I stood there watching and I just couldn't make myself leave.

After a while I got used to her moving and stopping periods, except that her moving periods started to get longer. That's when I started taking the pictures. I felt bad about it, but I could always throw away the film, and in a way it was fate that I had the camera with me, and you can't argue with fate. Then, after a very long time of moving her hand without stopping, her hand started to pick up even more speed and her thumb stuck way out and her arm started to move a lot with her hand. Pretty soon they were moving so fast and regularly that it almost looked like a machine was at work. I couldn't believe that Mrs. Kucher had that much strength and coordination. She lay with her head back on a pillow against the arm of the couch and she seemed to still be watching television, but I couldn't tell for sure. After a few seconds her legs opened wider and her body sort of stiffened and bent forward a little and her head arched back a little and turned slowly toward me and I could see that her eyes were closed. She had a look on her face like she was in pain. Meanwhile, her hand was still moving back and forth at an amazingly constant speed. Then her hand slowed and suddenly she stopped and she brought her legs together and crossed them at the ankles and brought her fingers up to her mouth. She continued to watch television as though nothing had happened. I watched for another five minutes or so, but she just lay there watching television.

I walked home slowly, feeling a little shaky and still trying to catch my breath. I forgot all about taking the pictures of Jackson with that woman from Betty's. I couldn't believe everything that was happening to me. It seemed that there must be all *kinds* of things going on that you'd never know about or even *guess* unless you just happened onto them. I put watching Mrs. Kucher on both my sin list and my list of good things, and I put taking the pictures on my sin list.

I think that's when I decided that I would cash in my IOU with Vickie. I didn't care if Jackson got mad. It was chance or fate or whatever that I saved Vickie and got the IOU and I didn't know how I was ever going to discover all those things going on in the world if I didn't take advantage of opportunities like the IOU.

CHAPTER SEVEN

It was a hot and hazy morning a couple of weeks later and I had not hitchhiked back through the canyon since I met Franny. I couldn't stop thinking about seeing Franny again, but each day I decided I wasn't ready yet. Each day I decided that I had to think about it some more. I had to figure out the things that I would say and the way I would act. See, the thing with Franny was more than just Franny. It was maybe the chance to belong to something important that was happening, to be part of whatever it was that was going on with the people in the canyon and the other people like them around the country. Meanwhile there was real life with Connie and I couldn't say how exactly, but I knew that I was getting a little crazy from her.

I sat on a street corner waiting for a ride and all around the world was drawn in. The road didn't stretch as far as I could see, but dissolved with the buildings and the trees into the haze. The sky didn't open into the universe, but was muddled and limited. On a hot sunny day you can lie in the sun and enjoy the sun's rays soaking into your skin, or you can lie in the shade and appreciate that you're out of the hot sun. Today I sat on the curb, my feet in the gutter, and I couldn't lift my face to the sun because I could only estimate where the sun was hidden beyond the haze. Instead, I watched some ants crawling through a crack in the asphalt and I tried to count the number of different colors of small pieces of broken glass scattered on the street. Finally I started spitting on the ants to see what they would do, but they didn't do anything interesting.

On my way back from the beach that afternoon I stopped at the store where Franny worked. The store was pretty much the way I expected it to be—small, everything inside sort of beat-up and old looking. The clothes were old and old-fashioned and they were hung on racks all over the place. On the walls were a couple of small mirrors and pictures of old advertisements for clothes. There were no customers and Franny sat on a chair looking out the window. She must have been somewhere else in her mind because I walked past her outside the window and she didn't even notice me. When I walked into the store she looked over at me and said, "Hi. Can I help you with something?"

I said, "Hi Franny." I was a little surprised that she didn't seem to remember me. I guess I expected that she had been thinking about me all the time since we met and that she would jump up and be happy to see me. But after a couple of seconds, before I said anything else, she remembered me.

"Oh, hi," she said. "We met at lunch last week—or the week before. You're the surfer . . . who's not really a surfer."

"Yeah, I guess so."

"Are you looking for some clothes?"

"No, I just thought I'd stop by and say 'hi' to you." She smiled so I felt better. "I would've stopped back sooner, but I've been pretty busy."

"I'm glad you stopped by," she said. She was looking into my eyes again, but I had to look away because it got me nervous.

We talked for a long time—a few hours. But I couldn't tell for certain whether she was happy to talk to me or just happy to have someone to talk to. A person or two came into the store every half-hour or so, and I sat on a chair looking out the window, waiting for Franny to finish helping them. The few people who came into the store were average people off the street, wearing average clothes. A middle-aged lady wearing a lot of make-up walked around the store for a few minutes, making loud comments about how crummy all the clothes were. On the way out of the store she said loudly to Franny, "I don't know how anyone would be seen dead wearing this stuff."

After the woman left Franny laughed softly and said, "Some of the people who come in here are funny. In fact, most of them are. They just come around here looking for something different to do for an afternoon. They want to see how we live and they think this place is amusing. They don't believe in the things the people who live here believe in. Most of them don't believe in anything."

"What about you? What do you believe in?" I asked.

"What about you?" she answered, and that was all I could ever get her to say about what she believed in. She was from Philadelphia and she had moved out to the canyon nine months earlier to live with her sister, Sheryl, who had been living in the canyon for about five years, and before that had been to demonstrations and protests around the country. Franny had graduated from high school the year before. She was pretty smart and had skipped a year and a half of elementary school so she was young when she graduated high school. She got accepted to a lot of good colleges and she almost went to the University of Pennsylvania, but at the last minute she decided not to go.

"Why is that?" I asked.

"I don't know exactly. I just felt that I was missing out on something. My sister was always so involved in everything. She's ten years older than I am. I sat at home with my parents and watched her running around the country and getting involved. She was even arrested once."

"For what?"

"A protest. A civil rights protest. They all linked arms and the police dragged them to the wagons and put them all in jail." Franny was staring out the window again.

"I know what you mean," I said, and I thought that I really did.

Franny glanced over at me and cocked her head, but then she just smiled like she didn't really believe me. I wanted pretty badly to tell her it was the truth, but before I could figure out how she asked, "Didn't you say you're a student of human nature? Or no—it was a student of the human condition, wasn't it?" She was still smiling.

I wasn't sure if she was laughing at me or not, so I said, "Who's not?"

"But most people don't say they are. You must be different from most people. I think you also said you don't believe in driving cars."

"Yeah, I guess I said that." I was a little surprised that Franny remembered a lot of what I had told her the first time we talked.

"So, why are you a student of the human condition?"

Franny was looking at me, waiting for an answer. She seemed to be interested in me, but she also seemed like a person who could lose interest easily, and I didn't want her to lose interest in me. Only I wasn't sure that I knew the answer to her question. Finally I answered, "You'll just have to get to know me to find out."

Franny shrugged her shoulders. "Okay," she answered and she told me to stop by her sister's house on Friday night. She invited me to come early for dinner with her sister and some of her sister's friends, and I told her that I would come.

When I was back on the canyon road I couldn't believe that for the first time ever I had taken Ben Sr.'s advice. It was only because I didn't know what else to do, but it still scared me a little. Ben Sr. was supposedly a ladies' man when he was younger—that's what he always said, anyway, and my mother went along with him, although that didn't mean anything. He was only a little drunk one evening and he was in a good, talkative mood, so he decided to teach me about women. He leaned across his desk toward me and said, "Son, if you're ever with a girl and your pants are down—and they're not supposed to be down—." He paused and winked at me. "Always take the high road. Always the high road. Do you understand me?"

"Sure," I answered, but he continued anyway.

"Let's say you dish out your bullshit and the plate's too high and she catches you, don't back down, don't try to explain it, just say, 'If you knew me better, you'd understand.' And leave it at that. Remember that. It's advice from your father."

It wasn't just that I took his advice that scared me, it was that he had hit the nail right on the head, to use his expression, and I worried about what other similarities there might be between him and me that I would discover as I got older.

I went to visit Vickie the next afternoon. Fortunately Jackson had made sure to get her address when we got the IOUs, and she didn't actually live that far from my house. She lived in a typical old apartment building in an average part of town, just like I expected. I got there in the late afternoon. Vickie's apartment was on the second floor and I climbed the stairs and walked right over and knocked on the door. I was sort of moving along on momentum—I guess ever since I took the pictures of Mrs. Kucher the other night—and not even thinking about what I was doing, until Vickie answered the door, and then it all struck me and I couldn't believe I was there. Vickie didn't recognize me right away, and then she smiled and sort of tilted her head and said, "Hi, Ben. How are you? What brings you here?"

All of a sudden I felt bad about coming to collect the IOU, until I remembered that you only live once and if you want to have any kind of a life you have to get out there and take your chances. "I want to collect on the IOU," I said.

Vickie looked at me a little funny and I was getting ready to tell her how it wasn't my fault that she had made the offer and then signed the IOU, and how I was a normal kid and what did she expect if she gave me the IOU. But I didn't have to say anything because she smiled and shrugged her shoulders a little and asked me to come into her apartment.

The apartment felt warm and comfortable and I liked being there. Vickie wore a pair of faded jeans that fit her pretty tight and a loose long sleeved shirt with little flowers and designs sewed onto it. "How about something to drink?" she asked.

"No thanks," I answered and I watched her walk across the room. I couldn't believe that I was going to see her pretty soon with her clothes off. I wondered if she would be wearing those little gold rings, or maybe some different jewelry.

"Well, we're going to have to make this kind of quick because I have another appointment pretty soon, but have a seat and I'll be right back." Vickie walked out of the room and I sat on the couch. It seemed strange to me that Vickie was so matter of fact about the IOU, but I figured that maybe she just looked at it like a debt or something and was honor bound to pay, or maybe she was so grateful about my saving her that she really wanted to do this for me.

I looked around the room for just a minute or two and Vickie was already back. Only she was now wearing a long, black, see-through negligé. I was a little stunned. I tried to look through the negligé for the little gold rings, but the negligé wasn't that see-through. "What do you think?" Vickie asked.

"It's . . . you look very nice," I answered slowly.

"Why don't you come into the bedroom." I followed Vickie through a short hallway past the bathroom to her bedroom, which was small but very frilly and lacy. A large bed against the far wall took up much of the room. Vickie sat on the bed and asked me to sit next to her, and I did. She didn't say anything else but started taking off my clothes until I was completely naked, and then she scooted to the top of the bed and pulled me along by my hand. I was trying to get a look at her, hoping to see those gold rings, but she didn't take off her clothes and she actually kept herself pretty covered up. She pulled me on top of her and her negligé sort of rode up with me, but I couldn't see her down below because I was already on top of her. I managed to feel one of her breasts through the negligé, but there was no ring, and I couldn't feel any holes or any sign of where Vickie might put the rings. And then it was over pretty quickly and Vickie managed to squirm away from me so that I still couldn't see anything and she walked quickly into the bathroom.

I wanted to stay and talk to Vickie or something, but as soon as I got dressed she gently pushed me out of her apartment. She kissed me on the cheek as I left and thanked me again for saving her. I walked all the way home, stunned because I had blown my IOU and I wasn't an inch closer to finding out anything about those gold rings. I wondered for a moment if there might be some way I could buy Jackson's IOU, but decided that I didn't want to chance mentioning anything about that to Jackson.

Connie called me late Thursday night when she got back into

town from another clinic. "What did they say?" I asked.

"The usual," Connie answered, and I didn't know what that meant because she never really told me what the doctors said. "But there's something I have to talk to you about. Something important. My parents are going out of town tomorrow afternoon, so you can come over and I'll make you dinner and we can have all night together."

"What do you have to talk to me about?" I asked. "I might be busy." Tomorrow night was Friday when I was supposed to see Franny.

"I have to see you—I can't talk to you about it over the phone, Ben. Please, it's *very* important. What do you have to do? Can't you get out of it?"

"Yeah, I'll get out of it," I answered.

I left the beach in the late afternoon and it was early evening when I got to Connie's house. I had stayed all day at the beach to get my tan as dark as possible for Connie, and as I walked toward her house I could feel my body emanating heat from the sun's rays that had soaked all day into me.

Connie was waiting for me and she kissed and hugged me as soon as I stepped into her house. She had made dinner for us— lasagna that her mother taught her how to make and garlic bread and vegetables so that the kitchen was a mess, but the dinner was nice. Connie didn't eat that much, but I ate a lot. It was almost like we were married or something. We had some wine with dinner that Connie found in her parents' liquor closet. She said her parents wouldn't miss it and I understood why—the wine tasted terrible and neither of us could drink more than a few sips. We made love on the living room floor and then in Connie's bed, and it was great. I looked closely at Connie's nipples when I kissed them, checking for little holes, but I didn't see any. Connie had pierced ears and always wore earrings, so I thought maybe she had rings for her nipples that she just didn't wear when we were together.

I asked her, "You know, someone was telling me that women wear earrings in their nipples."

"Who told you that?" she asked, with total disbelief in her voice.

"It was someone I met at the beach . . ."

"A girl?" Connie interrupted.

"No! A guy. Someone I was just talking to while I was eating lunch. He was talking about buying some jewelry for a present for his girlfriend. Some earrings, but for her nipples and her . . . her lips down between her legs. He said they were regular pierced-type rings and she wore them in both places."

Connie laughed. "You mean she had her nipples pierced? And her labias? That isn't true. You're making that up."

"No, I'm not. That's what he said."

Connie shook her head. "I don't believe anyone would do that. It would hurt too much. And where would you go to get them pierced? You can't just go to a department store and have them pierce your labias!" Connie laughed loudly. "You're just kidding me."

"That's what he said," I answered, and I was a little confused because Connie had never heard of women wearing rings like that, and she was right. Where would you get that done?

Afterwards we sat in the den and watched television until almost midnight. We sat next to each other on the couch and I had my arm around Connie and she was leaning into me. Then Connie turned off the television and sat up and turned toward me on the couch. "I have something important we have to talk about," she said.

I had been wondering all day what was so important, but had forgotten all about it for the past few hours. "Go ahead," I said.

Connie took my hand and looked into my eyes. "I love you, Ben," she said. "You know that don't you?"

"Is that what's so important that you have to tell me?" I asked, joking. It was like a scene out of some movie and I knew that there was something serious she was going to tell me. My heart started to pound and I silently sucked in my breath.

"No, it's not. But you know that, don't you?"

"Yes, I do."

"And you love me, don't you, Ben?"

"Of course I do," I answered, and I really did.

"More than anything?" she asked, shaking her head slightly and looking intently at me.

"Uh-huh," I answered. I knew that Connie wanted me to say more, but I couldn't. I was afraid of what was coming.

Connie sighed. "I have two things to tell you. One is kind of good, but the other is kind of bad . . ."

"They told you some bad news at the clinic yesterday," I interrupted.

Connie ignored me and continued talking. I got the feeling that she had memorized a little speech that she was working through. "The good is that I'm pregnant and the bad is that I'm going to die." She blurted it all out at once and immediately held her hand up over my mouth. "Don't say anything. Let me say everything I have to say and then you can say what you want.

"When I was at the doctor yesterday he told me that I was pregnant. It just showed up in the blood tests. He didn't tell my parents—he left that up to me to decide how to tell them. I was a little upset at first, but I've been thinking and I'm happy about it. The other thing is that I'm going to die. It's definite. There's nothing they can do for me. They have these experimental drugs that I could try that don't have any real success rate, but they make you real sick. I was going to do it so they could learn and maybe help the next person who gets sick like I am, but if I have a baby I can't do any of that . . ."

"How do you know it won't work?" I interrupted.

"It won't work, Ben, believe me. We've been to everyone. I might live a year, but that's it. They might discover something by then, you never know. But they don't have anything now that works. It just gets you sick so that your last days are worse than death. Believe me, Ben, I've thought a lot about it. But let me just finish, okay?

"Anyway, I called the doctor this morning and he said that the cancer shouldn't go to the baby. I could have a perfectly normal baby. But I'd only do it if you want the baby, Ben. It would be *our* baby. I might be gone, but we'd have a baby. The baby would be our love carrying on in the world. And you could tell the baby about me when it gets older. And my parents would have a grandchild. My mother's going to be in the nuthouse from this whole thing—I'm all she has."

Connie told me all of that and she was smiling the whole time. I couldn't keep the tears out of my eyes and she said, "Ben, try not to feel bad. It is what it is. Isn't that what *you* say? In the Middle Ages people who lived to their twenties were old people." She took both of my hands in hers. "What we can't change we can't change. I might not be that old when I die, but I've lived these years already and they've been pretty good and now I've loved someone and I'll have had a baby. Maybe they'll find a cure and I'll be fine—they discover new things every day. But if they don't find a cure I want the rest of this time to be good. I want to be happy."

"Wouldn't you like to travel around the world or something?" I asked.

Connie shook her head. "Well, I guess I would, but that won't happen. I'd rather be here with you than traveling around with my parents. My mother would be sad the whole time—it wouldn't be that great. If I get better, you and I will travel around the world, together." All I could do was stare at Connie. I didn't feel quite worthy of being part of this. "You *do* want me to have this baby, don't you?" she asked

"Of course I do," I answered. There was nothing else I could answer.

When I finally left Connie's house it was already early morning, probably four o'clock. I hadn't slept at all at Connie's, but it felt good to be walking outside. It was cool and dark and quiet. I couldn't help thinking about Franny, and I imagined her sleeping peacefully somewhere in the canyon. And I couldn't help thinking about Vickie. I imagined her sleeping in her frilly bed, in her negligé. I planned to walk a while and get home before my parents got up so Ben Sr. wouldn't kill me for being out all night. Around me was the calm of early morning, but all the things about Connie were running through my head. I was walking slowly, enjoying the solitude of the early morning, when my heart started to pound, for no reason at all. And then I felt like I was short of breath. I stopped walking and thought about what I had just been doing, wondering whether I had been running or walking for a long time to get me out of breath. I looked at my arms and felt my forehead, but I wasn't sweating. A wave of panic rushed though me, which only made things worse, so that my heart pounded harder and I felt lightheaded. Then I started to shiver, and I thought maybe it was the cold, but I knew that it couldn't be the cold. I tried to think of what to do, but there was nothing to do. I sat down on someone's front lawn a couple of feet from where I stood, waiting to see if I was having a heart attack or a stroke or something, waiting for my life to disappear, if that was what was to be. I lay back on the lawn and closed my eyes, and I thought about the good things in life. I thought about the beach and standing at the street corners holding my thumb out with the hot sun beating on my face. I thought about the calm and quiet of the early mornings and the dew drops on the grass. I thought about Connie, about how she let me hold her and how her whole body was available to me, the way you think it'll never happen. I could see her little face looking up at me, her eyes smiling and happy.

After a while I wasn't shivering anymore and my heart slowed down until it was thumping hard, but slowly, as though hesitating between each pump. I realized that I wasn't going to die or anything and I stood up and looked around. Everything was the same around me and I was the same. I started walking slowly and pretty soon I was okay, except that I was still a little shook up. I couldn't believe that something like that could happen to me. It was like a miniature nervous breakdown or something. I decided that it might have happened because I felt bad cashing in my IOU and still thinking about Vickie and Franny after spending the night with Connie, but I wasn't sure. Maybe it was just Connie.

I hadn't seen Jackson for a while and I was surprised when he stopped by my house because I always stopped over to see him. It was early evening and he wanted me to go with him to have a hamburger at Betty's Burgers. He drove us in his mother's station wagon and on the way he asked, "So, what's new with you?"

"Heavy things," I answered. I had been wanting to talk to Jackson about Connie and I was also curious about what had happened with the woman from Betty's Burgers.

"Me, too," he said. "I'm drafted."

"What? You're drafted?"

"That's right. I'm leaving tomorrow and by next week I'll be a GI. Me! Can you believe it?"

"What are you going to do?" I asked. I knew that Jackson was for peace and everything and there was the war in Vietnam going on. "Are you going to Canada or something?"

Jackson looked over at me and snickered. "I can't do that. I don't want to die, I don't want to kill anybody, I don't want to go to war, but I can't run away. I just can't. And believe me, I've thought a lot about it. I couldn't live with myself if I ran away." He laughed loudly, "They're gonna shave my head!"

"How did they draft you so fast?" I asked.

"I don't know. I've been eighteen for a month. I have to go to Tennessee by next week, so I'm going to leave tomorrow and visit some relatives we have out there. It's funny—my father's a little scared that I might be going to war, but I think he's finally proud of me because I'm going to be a soldier. He's proud of me for something I had nothing to do with."

After we ate we went to Jackson's stoning room and quickly smoked two marijuana cigarettes that Jackson had waiting there for us. We sat across the little table from each other while we smoked and outside it slipped into night's darkness. Jackson held the stub of the second cigarette in his clip, lit the little stub and breathed in through his nose the smoke that wafted up. "Let's go," he said, and he stood.

"Where are we going?" I asked.

"Just for a walk." We were both very stoned and we walked a long ways without saying much. At first I was a little worried that I would have another one of those attacks, but nothing happened. After we had walked for a while I remembered again about the woman at Betty's Burgers and when I asked Jackson he smiled at me and said, "It was interesting—definitely interesting. Her body was okay, even if she was on the old side and she sure learned a few tricks in her day."

"Like what?" I asked.

Jackson laughed. "Things with her mouth and the way she moved. I'll tell you more about it some other time. Right now I want to say good-bye to Lisa. She broke up with me, but I thought I'd say good-bye." I was curious to find out a little more about the woman, but I figured I'd have to wait until Jackson felt like telling me.

Lisa's mother sent us around the side of the garage to the back yard where Lisa and her girlfriend were sitting and talking on the back porch. Lisa didn't seem too excited about seeing Jackson. She looked over at him and then said something to her girlfriend and they both laughed. Jackson told Lisa he was drafted and leaving tomorrow and all she said was, "Good luck." It seemed that she hardly knew Jackson and I wondered whether being stoned affected the way I saw things.

Jackson asked, "Well, don't I get a good-bye, good luck kiss or something? I'm going to war." Lisa exchanged looks with her friend and they laughed. "Never mind," Jackson said. "It might be over between us, but it was still a part of our lives."

"A small part, fortunately," Lisa said and she made a face and looked over at her friend again.

I didn't like Lisa or her friend and I couldn't believe that Jackson would have Lisa as his girlfriend, unless she was just one more way for him to catch up. "Let's go," I said. Jackson looked at Lisa for a few seconds more, sighed and walked out of the yard along the garage the way we had come in. A door was open on the side of the garage and a light in the garage was on. Jackson stopped at the door and leaned inside. He looked back at me and then around and then he stepped into the garage. A few moments later he came back out carrying a large watermelon.

"What're you going to do with that?" I asked.

"Just follow me," Jackson said and he walked quickly away from the house and down the street, carrying the watermelon. I followed Jackson a couple of blocks until he sat down on a curb under a street light and I sat down next to him.

"Why did you take the watermelon?" I asked. I was very surprised that Jackson would steal something.

"It's just a watermelon—they can afford it." Jackson broke open the watermelon on the curb and handed half of it to me. He said, "Someone once told me that there's nothing tastes as good as a stolen watermelon. Let's find out if it's true." We used our hands to break off pieces of the watermelon and we spit the black seeds into the street. Jackson was right—it was the best watermelon I had ever tasted.

We ate in silence for a few minutes and Jackson shook his head and said, "You wouldn't believe Lisa and I made love together. It's something we'll have for our whole lives—something we shared. But you just wouldn't believe it."

I was pretty stoned still, but I couldn't see what was such a big deal to Jackson. He sat there eating his watermelon, still shaking his head. "Why is that such a big thing?" I asked. "I mean, everybody does it. Look along the streets at all the people walking around—all the great-looking people and all the incredibly ugly and grotesque people walking around, and they're all doing it. Just exactly what you're doing. You can meet someone while you're eating a hamburger and half an hour later you're doing it to her. Even the animals are all doing it. What's so special?"

Jackson looked over at me, spacing a little. "You're right, Ben, but you're wrong. Maybe you're mostly right. Maybe I'm just jealous."

I decided to tell Jackson about how I had cashed in my IOU with Vickie. I figured that he'd be pretty upset with me, but since he was leaving for the army the next day it only seemed right that I tell him.

"Yeah, I know," he answered after I told him.

"How did you know?" I asked.

"I cashed in my IOU also . . . yesterday. I decided that Vickie might move away while I was gone, or I might get killed in the war, and my IOU would just be a worthless piece of paper. I guess you sort of convinced me when we talked about it before."

I was a little shocked that Jackson had used his IOU, and it bothered me, although I didn't know why. "How was it?" I asked.

"It was fine."

"Mine was kind of quick . . . I mean Vickie didn't even really take her clothes off all the way. I didn't get that much of a chance to look at her with her clothes off. What about you?" I was curious about whether Jackson got to see the little rings.

"Yeah, that's about the same with me. She wore a black negligé that was pretty sexy . . ."

"Did you feel her boobs?"

"A little."

"When I felt them I could only feel them through the negligé and it seemed like there was a . . . I don't know, something on one of the nipples. Did you feel that?" For some reason I wanted to know for sure if Jackson knew about the rings, but I couldn't tell him about them because he might mention it to Vickie sometime and she would know I saw them down in the sewers.

Jackson shrugged his shoulders. "Maybe they were just hard or something. The nipples get hard and stick out, you know."

"Maybe that's it." I had wanted to talk to Jackson some more about Vickie and about Connie and the baby and everything that was going on with me. I wanted to tell someone, and Jackson was the person I most wanted to tell. But somehow the business with Vickie and his using his IOU took the edge off of it and so I didn't say anything.

We finished the watermelon and shook hands and I wished Jackson good luck and told him to write. He thanked me for sharing the watermelon and said he was happy to have me as a friend. I watched him walk away, slowly, and I figured someday we would get stoned together again and talk about everything.

CHAPTER EIGHT

I sat at the edge of the wet sand at the beach looking out at the ocean, the way I liked to do, sometimes for hours. Around me I could feel the summer winding down. People still came to the beach, but the intensity was gone. It seemed that everyone was waiting for the fall and the winter, passively enjoying these last hot days, knowing that they were only the remnants of summer. School was to start in two weeks and school was the end of summer. It was Friday and I stayed late at the beach to get my tan as dark as possible. I was going to see Franny that night. I had stopped to see her earlier in the week, even after everything with Connie. I wanted to apologize for not making it to Franny's sister's house the Friday night before. I told Franny an emergency came up Friday night when a friend overdosed on LSD. She didn't seem surprised and invited me to come by after dinner the coming Friday night. At first I wasn't going to go, what with everything happening with Connie, but then I changed my mind. I felt a little bad about it, but I wanted at least one chance to meet some of the other people in the canyon and to spend an evening with them in one of their little shack houses.

I was impatient trying to get rides home from the beach in the late afternoon and then I couldn't eat much at dinner. I kept thinking that Connie would call or stop by and I didn't know what I would say to her. During dinner my sister was belching at me like a wild woman trying to irritate me, but I was too distracted to care.

After dinner I took a shower and dried my hair with a blow dryer. I wasn't sure what I should wear, except that I didn't have that much of a selection, anyway. I wore a pair of white corduroy pants, a light blue short sleeve button down shirt, and a pair of thongs. On my way out of the house I slipped into my parents' bathroom and put on some aftershave lotion from a bottle that my father got as a present and never used. I just put a little on my neck, but after I was halfway down my street I got worried that Franny might think it was too middle class or suburban or something, or just wouldn't like the smell, so I went back to my house and scrubbed my neck to get the smell off.

It was a beautiful warm night and I didn't mind that it took a long time for me to get rides. Franny knew that I would be hitch-hiking and at the whim of circumstance so I might be late, and I liked the anticipation. I left before dark, but by the time I was dropped off in the middle of the canyon it had already been dark for a while. I had never been to Sheryl's house before, but Franny had given me directions. The house was about a quarter mile outside the canyon town, across a small stream from the canyon road, beyond a narrow wood and rope walkway over the stream.

I knew basically where Franny's house was from passing through the canyon, but at night the canyon seemed different and there were very few lights along the canyon road. By the time I saw the bridge in the car's headlights and asked the driver to stop, we were a long ways past the bridge. I stepped out of the car and watched it drive away and disappear around a curve in the road and I stood in the darkness of the canyon. I could make out a few dim lights in the distance and I could hear a number of dogs barking, some of them pretty close to me. I stood motionless on the shoulder of the road until my eyes got used to the dark and then I walked back toward Franny's. I felt as though I was in the wilderness and I couldn't help getting a little scared. I tried to keep my walking pace slow and even, but little by little it got faster as I walked.

I reached a narrow walkway that crossed a small stream beside the canyon road. I was still a little scared from being alone on a dark canyon road, but I was also getting nervous about seeing Franny again and about meeting her sister and anybody else who might be there. The house was across the walkway and about fifty yards up a slight incline. A bulb hanging over the middle of the walkway threw weak yellow light and another bulb was lit on the small front porch of the house. I could see flickering light behind curtains in one of the windows in the house and as I watched a light went on behind a window on the other side of the house. I was thinking about how often I had driven through the canyon looking at these little houses, wondering at all different times about what went on inside of them, and now I was going to get a chance to share a bit of it.

The walkway over the creek was a little bridge about twenty feet across that was supported overhead by heavy ropes attached to the tops of poles driven into the ground on both sides of the creek. The bottom of the walkway was made of wooden slats tied together with heavy rope and there were rope handrails along both sides. I stepped onto the bridge and it creaked and swayed, but I kept walking. The light overhead was too weak for me to see the creek below, but I knew that at this time of year it would be just a trickle.

After a few steps onto the bridge I got a very strange feeling. I suddenly wasn't scared or nervous any longer. Being out on that little bridge over a trickle of a creek on a warm summer night, just a few minutes from I didn't know what, but something exciting and new, was like being transported into a movie or a book or something. I decided that it would go on my list of good things, because it made me certain that exciting, unexpected, good things could happen in life, and that made life wonderful. It was a peaceful feeling. I felt like stopping right there on the bridge to save the feeling, but I didn't let myself. I knew that if I stopped I would lose the feeling, or lessen it, which would be the same thing. The extra time I stood there would be pussy minutes. I walked slowly across the bridge and up to the front porch. There were four steps up the front porch and I jumped to the top step. As I knocked on the door I had a momentary doubt that I might be at the wrong house, but Franny opened the door almost immediately.

"You made it," she said and she looked beautiful. I wanted to grab her and kiss her, but I didn't do anything. It shocked me a little that I felt that way with Connie back at her house, pregnant and dying and all. "Come on in," Franny said.

I stepped into a hallway that was narrow and dark and smelled of old wood. There was also a strong smell of marijuana. People were talking and laughing in another room. Franny closed the door behind me and the hallway was almost completely dark. She was standing close to me and she said, "I thought you weren't going to make it, again." I could smell marijuana on her breath.

"Sorry. It just took a long time to get rides tonight."

"That's right—you don't drive." I followed Franny into the small living room with the flickering light, which it turned out was from a couple of candles on a low table in the middle of the room, and I was reminded a little of Jackson's stoning room. Six people were sitting on the floor and Franny introduced me to them, although I forgot their names immediately, except for Franny's sister, Sheryl's. There were four guys and two girls and they were all much older than I was. I didn't think that I had seen any of them before. I wanted to get a better look at Sheryl, but it was too dark. Franny and I sat next to each other on a thin rug on the old wooden floor, leaning back against a couch. We were all sitting around the little rectangular coffee table with candles on it. Everyone had stopped talking as Franny introduced me, but they were all talking again. There was a little clear plastic bag of marijuana and one of those misshapen, crazy looking pipes on the table. Franny leaned over and picked up the pipe.

"You smoke, don't you?" she asked.

"Oh, sure," I answered, and I was thankful to Jackson. I thought that I would tell him about this when he came back.

Franny tried to light the pipe with a match, but it wouldn't catch and she said, "It's out." She picked up the bag of marijuana and an ashtray. "Here, smell this," she said and she handed me the marijuana. I wondered if everyone wanted you to smell their marijuana. Franny was emptying the pipe into the ashtray and she said, "Go ahead, smell it." I opened the little plastic bag, which was another one of those lunch bags, and I lifted it to my face. Jackson hadn't told me if there was anything special in the way you smelled this stuff so I glanced at Franny to see her reaction, in case I didn't understand what I was supposed to be doing. But she was tapping the bowl of the pipe on the ashtray and looking at me, waiting for me to say something. So I smelled the marijuana. It had a sweet and musty smell, like Jackson's marijuana, although it might have smelled a little sweeter. I didn't know if it smelled good or bad, for marijuana. "It smells good," I said.

Franny smiled. "It *is* good." She took the bag of marijuana from me and filled the pipe. With her thumb and forefinger she carefully lifted some of the marijuana from the bag, dropped it into the pipe bowl and packed it down. She did that three times. I was watching Franny but I was also still trying to get a good look at her sister, who was sitting on the floor at the far end of the table. With the unsteady candlelight I could see only a distorted, shadowy face on her.

"Here." Franny held the pipe out to me. "You've got some catching up to do."

"Go ahead," I said. Then after a second I added, "I'm a gentleman." I had never smoked a pipe before.

"Okay, you light." Franny handed me a book of matches. On the outside of the matchbook was an outline of a face and the question, "Can you draw this?" I lit the pipe for Franny and I read on the inside of the cover, in the flickering candlelight and the short-lived flame on the match, that I could be an artist if I could draw that face. Franny sucked in deeply and the burning marijuana glowed in the pipe bowl, and then she coughed out a big cloud of smoke. "It's good, but it's raspy," she said and her eyes were watery. "Here." She handed the pipe to me.

I took the pipe and sucked in gently. The marijuana glowed just a little and Franny said, "Take a good hit." So I sucked in as deeply as I could and I saw the marijuana burn and glow brightly for a couple of seconds. Then I coughed out twice the smoke that Franny had coughed out, and I kept coughing. My lungs felt like they were burning.

When I didn't stop coughing Franny said, "I'll get you something to drink." She rested her hand on my arm as she stood up. After she left the room I managed to stop coughing. The other people were talking among themselves and laughing all together every once in a while, not paying any attention to me. Someone had put a record on the stereo. I tried to listen to the conversation, but I was half listening to the music and half thinking about Franny, so I picked up only occasional words. I wondered if I was high from the marijuana, but I wasn't sure. I looked around the room and everything was a little hazy from the smoke, and shadows were dancing around the walls from the flickering flames of the candles.

Franny came back with a bag of potato chips and a bottle of wine. The wine was the kind that comes in a bottle with a round bottom and a screw-on top. "Munchies time," Franny said as she sat down next to me. "And here's something for your coughing." She set the bottle and a glass on the floor. I poured half a glass of wine and took a mouthful. I didn't like the taste of the wine at all, but I forced myself to swallow it. Franny was already eating the potato chips and she picked up the pipe and held it out to me. "I'll light it for you," she said. I finished the bowl and two more. Franny was eating the potato chips and drinking from my glass of wine.

Suddenly I knew I was high. I turned my head to the side and I got that same chill down my back. I stood up to go to the bathroom and my legs didn't seem to be giving me much support. I leaned over to ask Franny where I could find the bathroom and I stumbled over her legs. We both laughed for a while and then Franny put her arm around my neck and leaned to about two inches from my face. "Are you stoned or something?" she asked and we started laughing again. I liked how it felt to be laughing with Franny and to have her arm around me. I stood up again and walked to the bathroom, feeling all the time that I was falling forward.

I found the bathroom, turned on the light and locked the door behind me. A small mirror on a medicine cabinet hung on the wall over the sink. I looked at myself in the mirror for a long time. My eyes were bloodshot, but otherwise I didn't look any different from usual. I felt much higher than I had felt when I smoked either of the times with Jackson. I turned and took a step to the toilet and unzipped my pants. I stood for a long time but I couldn't get anything to happen. I had to go pretty badly, but I couldn't convince myself to let go. Finally I decided to sit on the toilet and try. As I sat on the toilet I noticed as I had when I smoked with Jackson that I could only focus straight ahead, except that now it seemed to be worse than I remembered it before. If I wanted to look to the right or left I had to turn my head because my eyes didn't want to move by themselves. They were stuck staring ahead. I moved my head around from side to side so I could look around the bathroom. It seemed small and very dirty. The tile around the sink was cracked and stained and the toilet was stained. I noticed a straight line on the floor that was a seam where two pieces of linoleum had been laid down. I wondered if I could walk a straight line and then I realized that I still had not managed to pee. I got it into my head that I didn't want to be sitting down, so I stood up again. After a minute of standing there I finally managed to go and it was a big relief to me. The thought had crossed my mind that I might never pee again, and I wondered what would be the final result of that. I figured they could put a tube in my side and it could leak out through the tube.

I flushed the toilet and very carefully zipped up my pants. I had a vision of catching myself in the zipper. On the way out of the bathroom I tried to walk the seam in the linoleum and I was very surprised that I kept falling off of it. I put one foot in front of the other on the line of the seam, concentrating on the line, and the floor on both sides of the line seemed to fall away. Each time I lifted my foot to take a step I fell off the line before I could get the foot back in front of my other foot. I remembered my walk up the wall and I laughed out loud. Then I remembered Franny and I gave up on the seam and left the bathroom.

Franny and I smoked some more and drank a few glasses of wine because our throats were so sore. We talked and laughed and then we just sat there listening to music. Franny wanted to listen to certain music, and while it was playing she leaned back

with her eyes closed, tapping her feet against each other. I tried
to close my eyes and lean back also, but everything was spinning
under my eyelids so I had to keep my eyes open. I had not heard
most of the music before and even though I liked it I was more
interested in looking around the room and at the other people.
Three of the guys were sitting and staring into space and a guy
and Sheryl were talking intently to each other. I couldn't figure
out where the other girl was, and for some reason it was important
to me to know, so I decided to go look for her. Franny lay with
her eyes closed, oblivious to me, so I left her without saying anything
and I searched through the house, which was only two bedrooms,
the bathroom, a kitchen and the living room. I couldn't find the
other girl anywhere in the house but I looked out a window in
one of the bedrooms and saw the girl sitting on the little bridge
over the creek. I could only make out her silhouette under the
dim light over the bridge. It looked as though her legs were
drawn up and her arms were hung over a rope that ran the length
of the bridge. I watched her for a little while, but she was motionless.
I considered going out to talk to her, but decided to go back into
the living room.

    Franny was smoking from the pipe again. She handed the
pipe to me as I sat down. I was a little afraid to smoke more
because I didn't like the feeling of spinning when I closed my
eyes, but I helped Franny finish the bowl. Then Franny put on
more music that I had heard before but that I didn't know too
well. When she sat down she leaned her back up against my
shoulder and closed her eyes. I looked down at her face and even
in the dim and flickering light I could see her eyes moving under
her eyelids. I was starting to notice the warmth of her body soaking
through my shoulder.

    Before the record was over the other people left the room.
They didn't say anything to Franny or me when they left. When
the record ended Franny said, "I just want to hear the other side,"
and she turned the record over. But instead of coming back to
where I was sitting, she lay on her back on the floor with her head
about a foot from one of the speakers. She crossed her hands on

her stomach and closed her eyes and stretched her feet out toward me. Her head moved a little once in a while and I heard her making a moaning sound as one of the songs was beginning.

I wasn't thinking about anything in particular. My mind was popping from one thing to another. I found myself staring at things and then wondering how long I had been staring. I started thinking about Mrs. Kucher and the photos I had taken of her. I had stopped by her window a number of times since that first night, but there was never anything to watch. I was thinking that it was a good thing that there was never anything else to watch because a person could get crazy with that stuff. Then I was thinking about Connie, but only for a moment because I couldn't think about her. I didn't have any idea what was going to happen tonight, but at some point I had decided that I wouldn't think about Connie anymore until I left. It was too exciting, too important, this night. I might never have another night like this and if I was a low-life I would live with it and deal with it tomorrow. I found myself staring at Franny. I got this strong feeling that I should crawl over to her on my hands and knees and kiss her, but I didn't do anything. I watched her for a while and suddenly it was as though Franny had left the room and I looked around the room and I felt alone. I felt left behind and I got angry with myself. I got determined to crawl over and grab Franny and kiss her. I decided to count to ten and then do it, and when I got to three I changed the count to twenty, but I promised myself that at twenty I would start crawling. When I reached twenty I sucked in my breath and leaned up on my knees. I crawled across the floor until I was just a few inches from Franny, but she didn't move, so I leaned over and kissed her lightly on the lips. She smiled but still didn't open her eyes or move otherwise. So I kissed her gently all over her face and then kissed her again on her lips, this time deeply. She opened her mouth, but lay still. I kissed her a few more times, but she still lay there. I sat back and watched her for a few moments, and I wasn't sure if I should be angry or what. Finally I put my hand on her stomach, and when she still didn't move I inched my hand under her shirt. She lay motionless, even after I reached her breasts. I pulled her shirt up and began kissing her breasts and she still she lay there. As soon as I had her shirt up I looked for rings in her nipples, and then for holes when I kissed her nipples, but there weren't any. I noticed for the first time that she wore a half dozen necklaces made of beads and silver and leather cords tied in knots. For a while I thought maybe she was asleep or passed out, except that once in a while she would say "Mmmmm." I just kept going and before long I had her pants off and her shirt up over her breasts, and all the while she just lay there. Then I didn't know what to do. Franny was lying naked in the middle of the living room, not moving or saying a word, and I was sure that someone would walk in at any time. I sat back, trying to figure out what to do next, just looking at Franny. She was skinnier than I had expected, even a little bony, and her breasts were sort of small and far apart. She didn't shave her legs and she was pretty hairy—probably hairier than I was. I kept thinking that I should say something, but I didn't know what to say. I sat there for at least a minute and Franny finally moved—she slowly pulled up her knees and opened her legs as wide as she could, right in the middle of the living room, still not opening her eyes. I couldn't believe it! But it made me nervous that she was lying there like that and I looked over at the door to the living room. I wanted to go see where everyone else was, but didn't think I should leave at that point.

Actually, I was going a little . . . *very* crazy. I was focusing on different parts of Franny's body, one at a time, because I couldn't seem to get the whole thing in focus at once, worrying all the time that someone would walk into the living room and see Franny like that. Then I remembered that I was in one of those little shack houses in the canyon where people believed in peace and free love and everything, and I got angry at myself for being such a prude or something. I had thought that Franny wasn't really into the free love and all, but I didn't know everything. Then the record ended and Franny opened her eyes and sat up, pulling her legs together. She looked over at me and asked, "What happened to you? I thought I lost you there."

"No, I, uh, just thought maybe someone would come in or something."

"Everybody's left except Sheryl and Marty, and they're in bed for the night." There was a soft hissing and skipping sound from the needle covering empty ground at the end of the record and Franny stood and walked across the room to turn off the stereo. There was a click as she turned it off and then there was silence. I stood up also and I felt very high and my legs were unsteady. Although she was standing across the room from me, I could still see Franny in my mind lying on the floor with her legs apart, and I couldn't believe that I had just sat there. I wondered if there was any way to make up for passing that opportunity, and I realized that there wasn't. No matter what happened, that would be a black mark against me always, because that's how it is with life. I decided that I needed another list for my black marks. I thought about Connie for a moment but immediately put her out of my mind. I was trying to think of what I should say to Franny, but I couldn't think of anything. I figured that Franny would probably ask me to leave or something, but instead she said from across the room, right out loud, "Let's make love." It was great—Franny standing almost naked across the room in that little shack house, in the middle of the night, both of us stoned, asking me—no, telling me!—to make love to her. For a moment I thought that everything was fine, and it was, except that of course it didn't erase that black mark, because nothing could. The candle sent dancing shadows across Franny's face and all I could tell was that she was smiling. She walked to the door of the living room and paused before walking out of the room. I hadn't said anything and Franny said, "If you heard me, then come on along. Otherwise I'll see you around."

I probably don't have to mention that I followed her, although maybe I shouldn't have. Loyalty is important. But there's always a little more to consider. Franny led me into her bedroom, which was the room from which I had seen the girl sitting on the bridge and hour or two before. I walked a few feet into the room and stood watching Franny light a candle on a small table beside her bed. Her shirt had dropped back down and covered her to her waist and she lifted the shirt over her head and tossed it on her bed, which was under the window. She looked out the window and said, "Moon's up." Then she turned back to me and said, "Make yourself comfortable. I'll be back in a minute," and she walked past me and out of the room.

Besides the bed there were a few pictures on the walls and a small desk with a chair across from the bed and some clothes lying in different places around the room. I pulled the chair out from the desk and sat down. I noticed that I was still focusing on only one thing at a time. I tried to remember whether I had been able to focus on both of Franny's breasts at once or just one at a time. I leaned over and looked out the window at the bridge. It lay silent and alone in the pale light of the single lightbulb and the moon. The fog was just beginning to creep into the canyon. I looked up at the moon, closely, and remembered that it was not out when I arrived earlier. I sat back on the chair and looked at Franny's bed. I pictured Franny sleeping there and waking up and I pictured her lying naked on the bed.

When Franny got back into the room she walked past me, trailing her hand gently along my cheek, then she sat on the bed and leaned her back against the wall. We sat in silence for a few moments, because I didn't know what to say, until Franny asked me to take all my clothes off. She made me turn on the overhead light for a little while so that she could see my tan. I had to stand in the middle of the room and turn around a couple of times for her. It was pretty embarrassing, but at that point I guess I was basically going to do whatever she told me to do. Then we made love, and it was a lot different from the way it was with Connie. For Connie it was all emotions and for Franny it seemed like it was mostly physical. She told me things to do to her and she seemed to have a lot of requests.

I kept remembering the little gold rings on the woman in the sewers and I wanted to ask Franny about them. I figured that she would know, if anyone would. But I just couldn't seem to get the topic into discussion. At some point I asked Franny about the music she had been listening to while she was lying on the living room floor. She said, "I listened to that album a lot when I went away to summer school at this college a couple of years ago. And I knew someone there who played the guitar and sang some of those songs. It just reminds me of that summer when I listen to that album." I couldn't get her to tell me anything more than that.

When I woke up the next morning Franny was dressing. Her hair was wet and combed back. "Good morning," I said.

"Good morning," she answered, smiling. "Did you sleep okay?"

"Fine. How about you?"

"Just fine. I'm late and I'm headed off to work. You know where the shower is and you can make yourself some breakfast. Maybe you'll come by sometime next week?"

"Sure, but . . ."

"See you," Franny interrupted and she blew me a kiss and walked out of the room, but came right back. "Oh . . . next weekend we're going up north to someplace near Santa Barbara to visit a friend of my sister's. We're driving up on Friday night and spending the night, maybe Saturday night. Wanna' come?"

"Sure . . ."

"Good. Come by next Friday afternoon. See you."

A few moments later I heard Franny close the front door. I was a little surprised that she seemed so casual and unaffectionate to me after the night before but still wanted me to go away with her. I wondered how I could talk my parents into letting me go away for a whole weekend.

I took a shower and then I called Franny's name a few times to find out who was around. When no one answered I looked into each of the few rooms and saw that no one else was in the house. I went into the kitchen to see what kind of breakfast I could find. The kitchen was old, but it seemed clean and there was only one dirty cup in the sink. I found a bag of mixed grains, nuts and raisins and a box of cereal in a cabinet, and a bag of bread in a drawer. I put two pieces of bread in the toaster and then I looked through the refrigerator for some butter and jelly.

I found butter and two kinds of jam, but it all looked as though it had been around for quite a while and I didn't trust any of it, so I ended up throwing out the toast as soon as it popped out of the toaster. I hid the toast under some other garbage in a bag under the sink so that no one would get upset about my wasting food when there were children starving all over the world.

I thought about calling my mother to let her know that I wasn't kidnapped or murdered or something, but there was no telephone so I decided that I would hitchhike home, then maybe go back to the beach. I figured I'd be in some big trouble for staying out all night, but there are some things you just have to do if you ever get the chance.

Since I was alone in the house I was getting an urge to look through Franny's bedroom and maybe her sister's bedroom also, just to see if there was anything interesting. I tried to ignore the urge because it didn't seem like the kind of thing to do now that I was becoming a part of all of this, with the attitude of peace and love and everything. But at the last minute, when I was about to walk out the front door, I changed my mind and went back into Franny's bedroom.

I was a little nervous that Franny or her sister might return and see what I was doing, but the house was so small I figured I'd hear anyone who came in. I looked through Franny's bedroom very thoroughly but there was nothing of any interest. The only thing that I even bothered to look at closely was a small, thin rectangular piece of cardboard with plastic bubbles and numbers on it and small white pills inside the bubbles. I found that inside the desk. You pushed the pills out through the back of the cardboard, although I didn't push any out. I thought of eating one, or at least taking one with me, but I didn't know whether they were vitamins, LSD or some special medicine that Franny needed. I decided not to take any of the pills because I didn't want to cause Franny to have an epileptic seizure or something because she didn't have all of her pills. There wasn't even a bra anyplace so that I could find out what size Franny's breasts were. They were definitely smaller than Connie's and Vickie's, but I wanted to know exactly what size they were. At that time I had been thinking that I wanted to get to the point where I could tell the size of a woman's breasts just by looking at them or feeling them, the way a bird expert can see a bird fly by and say what the bird is or an art expert can look at a picture and figure out who the artist was that painted the picture, and I needed to get some background for comparison purposes.

I was surprised at how little there was in Franny's bedroom. In the desk was nothing but a couple of completely uninteresting letters from her mother. I even checked between the mattresses and under the bed and for any secret hiding places. Finally I figured that Franny didn't keep anything interesting in her bedroom because she had only been out here for nine months, or maybe because her sister was so nosey that Franny didn't want to take a chance on leaving anything personal around, or maybe Franny's hiding place was so good that I couldn't find it.

I walked into Franny's sister's bedroom, but before I could open even one drawer I heard someone laugh and I looked out the window and saw two women walking toward the back of the house. I walked quickly out of the room and then out of the house, locking the door behind me. I was a little annoyed because the bedroom was cluttered and full and I was sure that it would be interesting to look through. After I walked down the hill and across the bridge I glanced back and saw the women walking past the house. For a second I was tempted to go back and see if there was an open window I could climb through to get back into the house. If someone saw me I could say that I forgot something. But I decided against it—I was out already and so it was time to move on in life. I figured that I'd probably get another chance sometime, anyway.

I jogged across the canyon road and stuck out my thumb. It was still at least an hour before noon and the day was already hot. I stood hitchhiking in a patch of sunlight between shadows cast by trees that grew along the canyon road. It occurred to me that Franny's house had been cool even though it had no air conditioning. I looked over and saw that the house was surrounded by old, beautiful trees. The house and the trees and the canyon hillside in the distance behind it could have been on a postcard or something, if you didn't get too close to the house to see how beat-up it was.

And then I looked around and suddenly it struck me that it was already the last day of August, and I couldn't believe it. I was suntanned and my hair was long and sun bleached and I was a regular at the beach and at The Grille and with my thumb out at the street corners along the way to the beach, and I was standing on this road in the canyon after smoking pot and spending the whole night with Franny. Summer was about to end, only I wasn't ready for summer to end, I just wasn't ready. Normally I like time and life to carry on and the seasons to change. But now there was too much happening in my life, what with getting so tan and growing my hair long and Connie and the baby and the possibilities with Franny and spending all this time hitchhiking and Jackson going off to war. Only there was nothing I could do to hold back time and I knew that the days would just keep coming, each one just a little shorter than the last.

Chapter Nine

Later that afternoon I sat with Connie on the front porch of her house. I was a little afraid that when I saw Connie I would have an attack or something because of my conscience and the night before with Franny, but nothing happened. Connie just kissed me and was happy to see me and that was it. I wondered why I had that first attack, because it obviously had nothing to do with my conscience or anything like that. I figured maybe it was what I ate for dinner or something. Connie and I sat without talking and I couldn't help thinking about Franny and wondering what I should be feeling about everything. I considered being honest with Connie and telling her about Franny and trying to explain that life was complicated and always carried on and that it wasn't so much Franny as it was my chasing after life, or whatever it was that I wanted to explain to her. I looked over at Connie and her eyes were a little glazed and she was staring at something I couldn't see. It seemed to me that she was starting to look sick. She wasn't taking the medicine anymore that kept her out of the sun, but she still looked too pale. I thought about how great truth is supposed to be, but looking at Connie I decided that it wasn't for me. I did what I did and I would suffer for it or not. Connie's reality was what Connie saw, so why make her unhappy just to get something off my chest.

Then Graham called out, "Hey, you bums!" I hadn't seen Graham walking down the street and didn't even know that he was back from camp. He ran up to the porch and held out his hand. Out of habit we did our secret handshake. I was happy to see Graham. He was pretty tan and his hair was longer than it had ever been, although still much shorter than mine. "What are you, a hippie?" he asked me, and laughed.

"A little bit," I answered.

Graham said, "I've got to go do something for my mother, but I'll catch you later. I have a lot to tell you."

When I saw Graham the next morning we were both happy to see each other. Graham's parents had forgotten that he wasn't allowed to see me anymore and we decided to go to the beach. We hitchhiked together the way I had hitchhiked all summer. Somehow, though, I guess it wasn't exactly the same between us because I wasn't ready to take Graham through the canyon and share that with him.

Graham's leg was completely healed and he wasn't going to confession anymore, although he was still keeping a list of sins for the future. Graham wanted to know what had happened to the woman in the sewers. He was still annoyed that Jackson had gone back with me to find her when Graham should have been the one who was with me. I told Graham about the IOUs from Vickie. I told him how Vickie had offered Jackson and me each a night with her and how Jackson had asked for an IOU instead. I told him how Jackson wanted to get those IOUs from fifty different woman.

"That is total, *total* bullshit," Graham said after I told him. "You're just trying to make me feel bad because I hurt my ankle and couldn't go back down with you to save her."

"I swear it," I answered and I raised my right hand. "I have the IOU at home even though I already . . . " I stopped myself from telling Graham that I had already cashed in the IOU, although I wasn't sure why. "I'll show it to you. I completely swear it."

"Damn!" Graham said and he stomped his foot and spun around. "But you didn't use the IOU, yet?"

"Uhhh . . . no, I didn't."

"Why not?"

"I don't know. I have to talk to Jackson some more about it."

We had lunch at The Grille. We sat at one of the wooden tables inside and I told Graham, "This is a nice place to hang around. Sometimes it gets pretty wild," and I told him about the people who danced on the tables and about the girl whose breast popped out of her bikini top.

Graham said, "It seems pretty good. At camp a bunch of us always went to Oscar's Red Barn. We knew Oscar. He's a cool guy. That place gets so wild its incredible. Oscar always has to buy new chairs after a wild night." I couldn't help laughing and remembering how Graham always lied about feeling Mary Ellen's breasts, also.

We didn't stay too long at the beach, and when we left we ran across the highway and climbed the path up to the park. While we were waiting for enough of a break in the traffic so that we could cross the highway, I glanced up at the bluff, looking for the Poet. I didn't see him up there. I hadn't seen him since that late afternoon about a month before when I spoke with him, although I still expected to see him whenever I looked up at the side of the cliff.

I climbed the path ahead of Graham and stopped at the point where I could cut across to the Poet's spot on the bluff. I stood for half a minute until Graham climbed up past me and asked, "What're you doing?" He stood with his lower foot on a thick root that grew out of the side of the cliff into the path and he looked down at me. The sun behind us was bright and the ground was hot and dusty.

Finally I answered, "Nothing, just thinking."

On our way home Graham put his hand on my shoulder and said, "Ben, I have to tell you something. I'm in love."

"With who?"

"With a girl I met at camp. Her name is Janie and she's beautiful. I felt her boobs at least twenty times and the day before I left she let me feel down her pants. I swear it!" Graham was excited and animated as he spoke.

"So you're really in love?"

"I am. And she lives just a couple of miles from us! I *am* in love, and you'll see why when you meet her."

"Well, I am, too," I said, and it was a relief to say it to someone.

"With who, Connie?" Graham asked, smiling.

"That's right," I said. "How did you know?"

"I just figured." Suddenly Graham got serious and asked, "Doesn't she have cancer?"

"Yeah, she does, and she's going to die."

"How do you know?"

"She told me." I paused, but I wanted to tell Graham. "And there's other stuff I have to tell you. But you can't tell anyone. What I'm telling you is only between us. It's so secret I'll have to kill you if you tell anyone."

"I wouldn't tell anyone. I swear it," Graham answered. "But this is heavy stuff."

"It's worse," I said. "I've been . . . making love to Connie . . ."

"You've been *screwing* Connie?"

"That's right."

Graham spun on his heels and then got real serious again. "And she's going to die?" he asked, almost in a whisper, and I could see that he understood.

"That's right. And you know what else is worse?"

"Worse?"

"Yes, worse. Connie's pregnant." I couldn't believe that I was talking about all of this like it was just the weather or something.

Graham's mouth dropped open. "Jesus, Ben, that's heavy, heavy, *heavy* stuff."

"I know," I answered, and then I couldn't help getting tears in my eyes, but just for a few moments.

Graham put his arm around my shoulder and said, "Jesus, Ben."

I almost told Graham at that point about Franny and about what had happened with Vickie down in the sewers, but I held myself back. "Sorry," I said. "I haven't told anyone else about this and I don't know what to do. Connie's parents don't even know she's pregnant and she wants to have the baby."

Friday was approaching and I hadn't yet mentioned to my parents that I wanted to go away with Franny for the weekend. I wasn't exactly sure how to go about asking them. I considered telling Ben Sr. the truth—how I had taken his advice the other night and how it had worked with Franny, and how I was going to have these great life experiences, and all of that. But I gave up on that idea. Never mind that I'd have to catch Ben Sr. in a pretty rare mood to get a sympathetic ear from him. I just couldn't tell him or my mother anything about Franny because of Connie.

Finally I asked my mother if I could go camping for the weekend with some friends. I told her it was a Boy Scout sort of thing.

"But you don't belong to the Boy Scouts," she said, looking at me doubtfully.

"I'm thinking of joining the Boy Scouts. Going camping would be a good way to find out more about them." When my mother didn't say anything or even change her expression, I added, "Okay, I just thought it would be a good thing to put on my college applications. I know I'd have to cut my hair and everything, but I'll be applying to college in a couple of years and I just thought I should start thinking about it now. I'm thinking I might want to become a doctor or something."

"When did you start thinking that?" my mother asked, suddenly very interested.

"I guess it was after Jackson and I saved Vickie—that woman in the sewers." I had thought out this whole discussion. I knew that I was setting myself up for problems because my mother would keep bringing up the topic and would start bugging me more about doing my homework so I could get into a good college, but I figured this weekend would be worth it.

"Well, Ben, I'm happy that you're finally growing up. That sounds like a wonderful idea. Just check with your father . . ."

"Why don't you just let me go. He probably won't care and we can just tell him you said it was okay."

My mother looked at me sideways with that frown she liked to get. "You had better ask your father."

"He'll probably be so drunk all weekend he won't even notice if I'm gone."

My mother shook her head and then sort of sighed and finally got that stern look of hers, only a little different from usual. "Don't even *say* that about your father." She paused for a while, staring past me. I figured she was thinking of some reason why I shouldn't say that, and having a pretty tough time of it. When she finally spoke it was even more gently than usual, "I know what you think about your father, Ben, and it's a shame. You have to understand him. He's . . . he's a poet at heart. He really is." I couldn't believe my mother was saying this stuff, especially about Ben Sr., and I guess she could see the doubt on my face because she stopped talking and nodded her head slowly. "He really is. I guess it's just that life is harder than you think it will be and your father hasn't been able to accept that very well." I could understand that Ben Sr. maybe couldn't handle life very well, but the business about him being a poet at heart was way too ridiculous for me to believe. I could just imagine him sitting under the poem tree, and all the empty bottles that would be strewn everywhere. It was something that didn't lie anywhere in the entire universe of possibility, but I just shrugged my shoulders. "Maybe you'll understand someday," my mother said. "In the meantime, if you want to go, you ask him." I was a little disappointed in my mother. She was in that middle ground of stupidity. She was stupid enough to believe me, but not stupid enough to let me go without getting Ben Sr. involved.

Of course Ben Sr. wouldn't let me go. It wasn't his style to ever be cooperative. I tried the business about wanting to be a doctor and all he could say was, "The Boy Scouts are crap to colleges. Just cut your hair and study and get good grades. That's what colleges care about."

So I figured I would just go with Franny anyway and take the consequences. If I didn't go it would be a major black mark against me and, anyway, there are some things you just have to do.

It was Connie who made the real problem. She called Thursday evening and absolutely *had* to see me Friday night. Her parents were going out again, and she had something else important to talk to me about. I had been afraid of that call, but even with a few days to think about it I couldn't come up with an excuse that would work, especially if Connie called my parents. I hung up the telephone with Connie and I was pretty disturbed. I couldn't pass up this weekend with Franny, but I didn't know what to do about Connie. There had to be an answer out there, only I didn't come up with it. The whole thing got me feeling pretty distressed, but I figured I deserved it for being such a low-life by seeing Franny when Connie was my girlfriend. Finally I decided to hitchhike down to see Franny tonight. Maybe they had changed their plans and were leaving late Friday night or Saturday morning or something.

On the way I stopped to see Vickie. It seemed like I was stopping to see her quite a bit since I cashed in that IOU. When she answered the door she was wearing kind of a nice dress like she was going out. She looked pretty. "Ben, what are you doing here?"

"I just thought I'd stop by and see how you're doing."

Vickie smiled sort of a half-smile. "I'm still fine. Same as a couple of days ago. Only I'm going out pretty soon."

"I thought so. You look nice."

"Thanks. See you later, Ben. I have to finish getting ready."

"Okay, see you later," I said and Vickie closed her door. I walked away, feeling like an idiot and wondering why I even bothered to stop to see Vickie.

I didn't have much better luck with Franny. It was hard to get rides at night and it took me hours to get to her sister's house, and Franny wasn't even there. Sheryl answered the door and didn't recognize me at first. I explained to her who I was and finally she said, "Oh, that's right, I remember you now. You're one of Fran's friends. She isn't here tonight. I'm not sure when she'll be back."

"Do you know where I can find her, just to talk to her?"

Sheryl shook her head. "I can't really keep track of her."

"Franny said you were going up north tomorrow and she asked me to come along. I just wanted to find out about that."

"Sure, you can come. There's plenty of room in the van. We're going up to visit a friend of mine, up past Santa Barbara. We're leaving about four tomorrow and coming back Sunday sometime."

"You're definitely leaving at four o'clock?" I asked.

"That's the plan."

"Hmmm. I might not be able to leave then. Maybe I could come up and meet you or something?"

Sheryl shrugged her shoulders. "Sure, why not? Come on in and I can give you directions." She wrote out the address and telephone number of where they were going and directions on how to get there. She seemed like such an average, normal person, except that the long dress she wore was a little tattered. I couldn't imagine her being arrested for protesting and I wondered if she believed in free love and was really dedicated to peace and everything. "It's about a two to three hour drive," she said as she handed the instructions to me. "Maybe we'll see you up there."

"And you'll tell Franny that I came by tonight and that if I'm not here by four tomorrow I'll meet you up there either tomorrow night or maybe Saturday morning."

"I'll tell her."

Four o'clock came and went the next day and I was at the beach. I sat on the wet sand looking out to sea and I pictured Franny and Sheryl and whoever else was going with them piling into an old van and driving up the coast, maybe smoking marijuana, maybe talking about peace, and who knows what else. I had spoken to Connie already today and she was counting on seeing me that night. There was just no way out of it.

Connie was to call me after her parents left and that was about seven o'clock. She hadn't made any dinner for us this time so we decided to walk to Betty's Burgers. Connie seemed pretty weak and had to stop and rest a few times along the way. I felt especially bad because all I could think about was going to see Franny.

"What happened?" I asked as we walked. "What did you want to talk about?"

Connie held my hand tightly. "I wanted to talk about the baby. I know I won't be around to watch the baby grow up, but there's so much I want to tell her . . . or him." I didn't like this kind of conversation at all, and I particularly wasn't in the mood for it tonight. But there wasn't anything I could do.

"You can tell me and I'll tell the baby," I suggested because I had no idea what else to say.

"No, because you won't remember everything exactly the way I'd want to say it, and you wouldn't know when to tell about the different things I want to say." Connie looked at me earnestly, "You'd be great at telling things to the baby—you'd be wonderful, but I'd like more of myself to be there. So I'm going to write letters, as many as I can, and you'll give the letters to our child as she or he grows up. And I'd like you to help me a little to decide what would be appropriate to say at what age. Would you do that?"

"Sure."

"And you'll promise to guard the letters and make certain to give them to our child at the right times?"

"Of course I will," I answered, and I wondered where I could keep the letters so my sister wouldn't find them and they wouldn't get lost. "Is that what you wanted to talk about?"

"Yes." Connie squeezed my hand. "And I wanted to be with you. I always want to be with you."

I felt miserable. I was definitely not worthy of Connie's love and I just couldn't seem to get myself inspired about this whole relationship the way she was.

We ate dinner at Betty's and Connie didn't eat that much. We walked slowly back to her house, holding hands. It was a warm beautiful night and as we walked I looked up into the sky. I couldn't help wondering about Franny. When we got to Connie's house it was only about eight thirty, but her parents were already there. Connie saw their car in the driveway. "Uh-oh," she said. "I wasn't supposed to leave the house."

Apparently Connie's mother didn't feel well so they came home early. But she was well enough to yell at Connie for five minutes about how they were so worried and couldn't trust her and all of the usual stuff. And she was plenty well enough to give me the evil eye the whole time. Finally Connie turned to me, a little embarrassed, and said, "I'll see you later, Ben."

I was relieved to be out of there and I walked slowly toward my house, trying to decide what to do. It was early enough that I might be able to hitchhike up north to Franny, but I decided not to do it. I wasn't really up for hitchhiking all that distance right now, and I was thinking that maybe I wouldn't see Franny anymore at all. I guess because I was feeling pretty bad about how sick Connie was and how much of a low-life I was. I decided to visit Vickie instead, just to tell her that I knew I was a jerk for stopping to see her all the time and that I wouldn't bother her anymore.

I had a little speech ready to tell Vickie as soon as I saw her. I would make my speech, smile, and walk away. I knocked on the door a number of times before Vickie finally answered. She looked a little disheveled, with her hair messy and hanging straight down and she wasn't wearing any make-up. Vickie stared at me for a few moments like she didn't recognize me, and then, before I could get started on my speech, she said, "You're back again? . . . Well, why don't you come on in," and she swung the door open for me and walked a little unsteady across the room. She was wearing only a shabby pink bathrobe.

"Are you okay?" I asked.

"Sure. You wanna drink?" Then I realized—Vickie was drunk, and I couldn't believe it. I should have known immediately, what with all my experience with Ben Sr. and all, but I would never have imagined Vickie sitting around by herself getting drunk.

I looked around the living room, which was lit by the overhead light in the small adjacent kitchen. "Are you sure there's nothing wrong?" I asked again.

Vickie looked over at me with an odd half-smile on her face, and then she smiled more broadly. "Nothing's wrong." She sat on the couch that was across the room and picked up her drink from the coffee table next to the couch. "What brings you around?" she asked.

I walked slowly across the room toward her. I decided to put my speech on hold for a bit. "I don't know. I was just in the neighborhood so I thought I'd stop by and see how you're doing."

"I'm still doing fine. You wanna sit here next to me?" She patted the couch next to her.

"Sure," I answered. I sat right next to her and she immediately leaned her head against my shoulder. "Everything's really okay?" I asked again, but she didn't answer. It was uncomfortable the way Vickie was leaning against me, but I didn't want to disturb anything, so after a few moments I put my arm around her. I thought she would be angry, but she just snuggled into me. She held a glass like you usually drank water from and it was about half full of what looked like scotch to me. She sipped on it pretty often and I could smell the alcohol on her breath. She didn't say anything at all. I was surprised that Vickie was so mellow because Ben Sr. always got angry when he was drunk.

We sat there in total silence for a long time, and I had no idea what to do. Vickie's warmth was soaking into me. The little speech I had prepared for her was long gone and of course I was thinking of those little gold rings. I wondered if she was wearing them now and I kept thinking that if only I could open her robe a little and take a look at her nipples. After a while I thought that maybe I could just reach over and open her robe and she would let me, and then I thought that maybe I should kiss her first and in a little while she would let me open her robe. But time was going by and I wasn't doing anything and I remembered the black mark I got when I couldn't decide what to do when Franny lay naked on the floor in her sister's house.

Finally I reached my hand over and slowly worked it into Vickie's robe. All the while I watched Vickie's face, but she didn't say anything, until I had my hand on her breast and she said, "You're a persistent little thing, aren't you?"

"I guess so," I answered and I reached in further, until I could feel her nipple, and the ring was in it! My heart about stopped. I felt her nipple and the ring gently for a few moments and asked, "What's this?"

Vickie sat up and my hand pulled out of her robe. "It's a nipple ring," she answered.

"Can I see it?" I asked.

"No."

"Please? I really want to see it. Please?" I couldn't believe that I was begging, but it seemed that lately I was finding out all kinds of things about myself that I couldn't believe. Vickie looked at me like my begging didn't mean anything to her, so I added, "Remember I saved your life?" I immediately felt bad saying that because it was extremely low to trade off a heroic act to get something you wanted, especially after what I did to Vickie in the sewers. I momentarily considered taking it back, but of course at that point there was no way I was going to make myself take it back. I decided to see what would happen and leave it instead as either a sin or a black mark, although I wasn't exactly sure which one it would be.

"You *are* a persistent little thing." She looked at me sideways with that drunken half-smile of hers, and then she pulled open her robe so that both of her breasts were out, and there were thin gold rings in both nipples, the same ones I saw down in the sewers. "You got one minute," she said.

"One minute? Why one minute?" I was hoping that this was just the beginning.

She folded her hands on her lap and leaned back into the couch. "You're wasting time."

I wasn't sure what to do in my one minute. I really wanted to see the other rings and to find out how she got the rings and why she got them, and all of that. "Why didn't I see these when I . . . uh . . . came over to collect on the IOU you gave me? How come you're wearing them now?"

"I always wear them. If I don't, the holes fill in. Once in a while I take them out. They're kind of personal—I probably wasn't wearing them before."

I pulled gently on one of the rings. "Does that hurt?" I asked.

"Not really. Sometimes it feels good, but I'm not in the mood right now. Your minute's up." Vickie pushed my hand away and closed up her robe. "I've got to go to work soon, and you've got to get out of here."

"What kind of work do you do?"

"Boy are you nosey."

"Then tell me how you got those rings in your nipples."

Vickie stood up and arched her back, tightening the belt to her robe. She looked at me for a few moments, still drunkenly, "I had a boyfriend once—a biker . . ." she sort of faded off.

"A biker?"

"Yeah. He drove Harley—a big Harley. He was into tattoos and piercings, stuff like that. He kinda got me interested."

"You have tattoos?" I couldn't remember seeing any tattoos on Vickie.

"I have two. One on each cheek." Vickie smiled broadly.

I glanced at Vickie's face and there were no tattoos. "You mean your . . . butt?"

"One on each cheek. Now get out of here. I have to take a bath and sober up."

"What kind of tattoos are they?"

"Damn are you persistent. None of your business." She was talking a little severely, but still smiling.

"Can I see them?"

Vickie grabbed me by the arm and pulled me toward the door. She stumbled a little and laughed gently. "Now, get out of here." As she pushed me out the door she said, "You're a cute guy, but you better learn to make your moves when a girl's in the right mood."

I got home and it still wasn't very late, but I told my parents I was going to bed early. In my bedroom I put a few clothes in a backpack and sat listening to the Rolling Stones, loud, but in my earphones so no one else could hear. I was charged up from Vickie and I wanted adventure in my life. I had already figured that I was back to my old self and that I couldn't pass up this weekend with Franny. I was just waiting the hour or so for my parents to go to their bedroom so I could slip out of the house.

It was past midnight when I reached the beach. I was a lot more tired than I had thought and I stood for a long time at the top of the cliff looking down at the lights and reflections of light that were the night highway, the beach and the ocean. I was becoming relaxed by my exhaustion, the peaceful night and the dark, immense ocean. Finally I walked to the small bluff out of sight below the top of the cliff and lay down to rest for a little while under the small poem tree. I used my backpack as a pillow and for a blanket I used a jacket I had brought with me.

I didn't wake until early the next morning. Around me a dense moist fog covered everything—the world seemed dissolved two feet from me in all directions. The top of the cliff above and the Pacific Coast Highway below were beyond what I could see.

The fog was too dense at the highway to expect a passing car to see me in time enough to stop, so I walked a half mile up the coast to an intersection with a traffic signal where some cars would stop and others would slow as they turned onto the highway. It wasn't long before a flatbed truck with crisscrossed wooden railings along two sides slowed to turn onto the highway. I held up my thumb as the truck approached and the driver jerked his thumb toward the back of the truck as he slowed to a stop. In the back of the truck were stacks of newspapers. The top sheets and the edges of the newspapers were dark with moisture. I tossed my backpack between two stacks of newspapers and sat on the truck so that my legs hung off the back end. We drove slowly up the coast and there were only very occasional cars on the road.

After about ten minutes the truck slowed to a stop and the driver leaned his head out of the truck. Without looking back he called to me, "I'm goin' up the coast from here."

I called back, "Fine with me. I'm trying to get up past Santa Barbara."

The truck pulled off the road onto a short, unpaved road leading to a gasoline station. I held onto the wooden railing as the truck bumped and jostled over the uneven dirt and finally stopped. The driver leaned out the window again and called back to me, "Would you mind throwin' one of those bales up by the door?"

"Sure thing," I called back and I pulled one of the stacks of newspapers bound by tough plastic ribbon off the truck and tossed it in front of the door to the station's small office. The stack of newspapers was heavier than I expected it to be. "Just one?" I asked.

"Just the one," the driver called back. "Thanks." I climbed back onto the truck and leaned against one of the railings with my legs hanging out. The truck drove pretty fast along the highway and I had to hang on to keep from getting bounced out when we hit some of the bumps in the road. We stopped every so often at a gas station or a little store and the driver told me to toss one or two stacks off at each place. The fog stayed thick and I couldn't see much beyond the edges of the highway.

I was thinking that this was a great adventure and I was looking forward to seeing Franny, but I couldn't seem to get Vickie off my mind. The more I thought about it the more I couldn't believe she ever had a boyfriend who drove a big motorcycle and that was how she got those rings. I wanted to see her tattoos and I wanted to be with her when she was in the right mood so that it felt good to pull on the rings in her nipples. I wondered how I could ever get her in that mood. And then I got to remembering how Vickie had laid her head against my shoulder after I sat beside her on the couch. I felt a little disappointed in myself because maybe she was sad or wanted to confide in me about something, and all I could think about was getting her clothes off. That was a definite sin for my list. I decided that it was also a sin, but not a black mark, that I brought up the fact that I had saved Vickie to get her to show me the rings. That was pretty low, but you could understand how someone might do it.

After a couple of hours, the truck finally slowed again and pulled onto the shoulder of the road. The driver leaned his head out the window and called back to me, "Buddy, I missed my turn. I'm turnin' around here and goin' back a few miles. And thanks for the help."

I told him, "Sure, thanks for the ride," and grabbed my backpack and slid off the back end of the truck. I watched him turn the truck around and drive back up the highway. I had no idea where I was. It was still foggy and behind me and across the highway was nothing but brush as far into the fog as I could see. I figured that the ocean lay somewhere across the highway so I waited for a break in the light traffic and ran across. Maybe there would be a beach or a store or something so I could figure out where I was.

I walked through shin-high weeds and grasses and thick, low growing, scraggy shrubs that caught at my tennis shoes and pant legs and bare ankles. After a few minutes of walking I paused to listen for the ocean, but there was too much noise from the cars passing nearby on the highway. I began walking again, stepping carefully between the shrubs. Suddenly, out of the fog and out of nowhere, emerged a bent, gnarled tree growing close to the ground.

Behind the tree stood an old man, half facing me and looking down at a small gun he held in his hand. I froze and my heart started pounding like crazy. The man was only twenty feet away. But he hadn't noticed me so I took a couple of slow, careful steps backwards into the fog, until I could see just the barest outline of the man. I figured that if he looked up I could easily disappear back into the fog. But almost immediately the man turned away. I stepped a little closer, because I was too curious not to see what was going on. The man stood still for a while, then held the gun out to his side for almost a minute before throwing it far into the fog. Then he sat on the tree, still facing away from me, and he pulled a sheet of paper from his jacket pocket. I stepped a few steps back into the fog, and the old man sat reading the paper for quite a few minutes, not noticing anything around him.

Finally the old man tore the paper into small pieces and tossed the pieces into the air over his head, maybe for the wind to carry the paper where it would. But there was only fog, so the pieces of paper fell back on the man and on the tree and on the ground and on a few nearby shrubs. The man stood and stretched his arms and walked slowly into the fog, away from me.

I stood there for a couple of minutes until I was pretty sure that the old man wouldn't return, and then I walked over to the tree. It was an old cypress tree, probably bent by the constant wind blowing in from the ocean so that it grew almost along the ground. I sat on the trunk of the tree and looked out into the fog, until I realized that not ten feet in front of me was the edge of a cliff, and I carefully stepped forward to look over the cliff. I couldn't see the bottom of the cliff through the fog, but I could clearly hear the muffled crashing of occasional waves. I wondered why the man had thrown the gun over the cliff and I worried a little that he might return, although he seemed pretty old and frail.

I went back and sat on the tree for a while. I remembered the Poet who I had seen sitting all those days on the bluff and I wondered if this was a poem tree that would give him inspiration. I thought that maybe I should try writing a poem, just to try out the tree, but I didn't have a pencil or paper. Then it occurred to me that maybe the paper that old man had torn up was a poem. The pieces of paper were all around me and I leaned over and picked up one of the pieces. It was old and yellowed, about an inch square. I turned the paper over, but it was blank on both sides. I picked up another piece that had the handwritten words "I knew t" on one side and was blank on the other. I looked all around at the pieces of paper, and finally I gathered them up and put them in my pants pocket, making sure to find every piece. Then I walked back to the highway because I was looking forward to seeing Franny.

The next ride took a long time to stop for me because I was in the middle of nowhere on the side of a highway where all the cars were speeding past. But finally the fog burned off and an old man in an old sedan stopped for me. When he pulled over I was a little nervous that he might be the old man I had watched throw the gun over the cliff, but when I got closer to him I was pretty sure that he was a different person. He took me into Santa Barbara where I ate lunch. Two rides later I was at the street about twenty miles further north that Franny's sister had written on the instructions. I walked for half an hour from the highway into a quiet residential area where the streets were lined with beautiful old trees heavy with bright green leaves and little, mostly weather-beaten houses jammed almost next to each other on tiny pieces of land. I found the address Sheryl had given me and I stopped on the sidewalk in front of the house, which looked no different than any other on the street. By then it was already mid-afternoon.

I knocked on the door and almost immediately a man opened the door. "What can I do for you?" he asked. He looked to be about thirty and had a heavy, dark beard and thick shoulder-length hair. His eyes were narrow and intense looking.

"Are you Carl?" I asked.

"What if I am?"

"I'm Ben. I'm Franny's friend. She said I could meet her here."

Carl shrugged his shoulders. "She didn't say anything to me, but come on in, I guess." I stepped into the house and Carl called, "Hey, Fran, there's someone here to see you." Carl just walked away from me through the house and I followed behind him. The house was almost like Sheryl's, with a little living room, a kitchen, a small place for a dining room table and a hallway leading probably to a couple of bedrooms and a bathroom.

As I approached the kitchen Franny walked out. She was wearing an old long dress like usual. "Ben, where did you come from?" She was obviously quite surprised.

"Didn't your sister tell you? I came by her house on Thursday to tell you I couldn't go yesterday. She gave me the directions." I was a little annoyed that Sheryl hadn't mentioned anything to Franny and I was feeling sort of insignificant here. It didn't seem right that someone who cared so much for peace and everything couldn't even care enough about me to give my message to Franny. "Is that okay?" I asked.

"Sure. I'm glad you made it."

We went into the kitchen where Franny and another woman were cooking. "Ben, this is Kitty. We're making pot brownies." Kitty looked like she was about Carl's age. She wore a pair of torn bell-bottom bluejeans and a thin white t-shirt. Around her neck hung a silver chain with a small peace sign. She wasn't particularly nice looking, but I couldn't help noticing that her breasts were pretty big with giant nipples that I could see outlined under her shirt.

"Nice to meet you, Ben," Kitty said. Her hands were covered with chocolate fudge that she was mixing in a large bowl. Franny was crushing some marijuana in a smaller bowl, also using her hands. On the counter by the bowl was a small pile of seeds and little twigs that Franny was pulling out of the marijuana. She was crushing the leaves almost into dust.

"Can I help with something?"

"You can go out in the back and help Carl and Marty finish up the shed."

"Okay." I set my backpack down and walked into the backyard. It was one of the smallest yards I had ever seen, surrounded by a wooden fence. Carl and Marty were nailing a sheet of plywood onto the frame of a small tool shed. "Carl, can I give you a hand?"

"Sure, if you know what you're doing."

Fortunately I knew a lot about building this kind of stuff because Ben Sr., who was a hotshot carpenter when he wasn't drunk, taught me when he made me finish the garage and build shelves and cabinets for his tools.

We worked for the rest of the afternoon and I built a counter and a lot of the shelves inside the shed while Marty and Carl finished the outside. Carl started to like me when he saw that I was doing so much work, and it occurred to me that maybe once again Ben Sr. had been a worthwhile influence on me. As evening approached, a woman I hadn't seen before stepped out the back door and called to us. "Come and get it. Chow's up."

We walked into the house and Carl put his arm on my shoulder and said, "Where'd you get this guy, Fran? He's a real carpenter."

Franny smiled and said to me, "I thought you were a student of the human condition, Ben."

"No wonder he's such a carpenter," Carl said, laughing. I felt pretty good, like I was part of something here. I didn't mind the work, I actually enjoyed it, especially since Carl liked me now. I was sure he wouldn't mind my staying around tonight and I figured I was in for a pretty interesting night if Franny and Kitty had already been making pot brownies in the middle of the afternoon.

I was the last to clean up in the small bathroom and when I returned Franny and Sheryl were setting the dining room table. Sheryl saw me and covered her mouth. She laughed, "I'm sorry— I forgot to tell Fran you were by."

"That's okay." I felt better that Sheryl at least apologized. A few other people showed up until there were about ten people there for dinner. Someone started lighting up marijuana cigarettes which everyone was passing around.

"Don't forget about the brownies," Kitty said. "We made them pretty dense."

We ate spaghetti with meatballs and garlic bread for dinner. I was starved anyway, not to mention the munchies from the marijuana. Kitty brought out an incredibly huge plate of spaghetti and sauce and meatballs and everyone ate a lot and drank wine and laughed. Sheryl and Kitty and Carl and the woman who had called us for dinner, Sally, were old friends who had protested together and been arrested together. They were talking about the old protests and being arrested and laughing about little incidents that happened. It was great. Kitty sat next to me on one side and Franny on the other side. Kitty kept laughing and leaning into me and a couple of times her breasts even brushed against my arm. I was sure that she was into peace and especially free love. Franny was quiet, watching her sister and the other people talk. I figured maybe she was just extra stoned from the marijuana.

It was dark by the time we finished dinner. We moved to the living room while Franny, Kitty and Sheryl cleared the table. I was still pretty stoned from the marijuana before dinner, but everyone was smoking more. Carl handed me a marijuana cigarette and said, "This is special stuff. It's opiated Thai." We sat on couches and on the floor around a small table where Sally lit a couple of candles. Kitty came out a few minutes later with a plate of the pot brownies, and I wondered how high you could get on marijuana. I was already higher than I had ever been before. Usually I could focus on only one thing at a time—now it seemed like I couldn't focus on anything at all. It also seemed like I had to concentrate just to breathe, like my lungs weren't going to keep pulling in the air on their own if I didn't go out of my way to make sure they kept at it.

The brownies were pretty bad. I ate one, but it was so full of marijuana that it was dry and crunchy to eat. Little bits of marijuana got stuck in my teeth. I was curious to know how the brownie was going to affect me, but I didn't want anyone to know that I hadn't eaten pot brownies before. I figured I'd find out sooner or later.

Finally Franny came out of the kitchen and sat next to me. She ate two of the brownies. We all talked and it was like I was one of the group. Carl asked how I got up there. "He hitch-hiked," Franny answered for me. "He doesn't believe in driving cars."

"You don't look like you're even old enough to drive a car," Kitty said.

I didn't want to get into the subject in case someone asked me for identification and fortunately Marty said, "That's only because you're so old already," and they all laughed and forgot about that topic.

I told everyone about my ride up the Pacific Coast Highway and about the old man who threw the gun into the ocean. Sally asked, "Did you pick up the pieces of paper?"

"Yeah, I did," I answered slowly, and being so stoned it seemed incredible to me that she would know that. I took the pieces of paper out of my pocket and dropped them on the table near the candles.

"Let's put them together," Sally said, excited. "Go get some tape, Kitty." When Kitty came back with the tape, she, Sally, Sheryl, Franny and I all crowded around the table to put the paper back together. There was hardly room for all of us and Kitty leaned on me with her arm around my shoulder. It took us quite a long time to put that paper together. We kept laughing and disagreeing on where the pieces went and when we laughed we blew the pieces of paper off the table and all over the place. It seemed like we were all concentrating so hard, but we just couldn't seem to get anywhere.

Finally we got the paper put together and we had every piece except for one edge piece that wasn't important. Sally grabbed the paper and leaned back against the couch and said, "I have to read this first." For some reason we all let her, and just sat there for a very long time, not saying anything but watching her read.

"It's a story," Sally said, suddenly, and it seemed as though she had just woken me up from something, although I wasn't sure what. "Sort of a story—at least there's a story in it. That old man who you saw throw the gun into the ocean was young once, living in Boston." Sally looked off into space as she spoke, and it seemed to me that she spoke with a lot of emotion. "He had an apartment on an upper floor of a building and he used to lie around his apartment a lot, watching old buildings get torn down and new ones get built, and he used to get depressed about it.

"He was watching one building in particular that started out as a bunch of small houses and ended up a twenty-story hotel.

The name of the hotel was written in large letters across the top of the hotel," Sally stretched out her hand to show the letters across the top of the hotel. "And after the building was finished it took a week to lift all the letters up and put them on. Halfway through the letters being put on, this man had a great idea. He realized that he could kill himself at any time and when he realized that, he suddenly felt much better. So that night he wrote all of this down on a sheet of paper and he planned to buy a gun the next day, which I guess he did. That was . . . about . . . almost. . . forty something . . . fifty years ago . . . or so, back on . . ." Sally looked back at the paper again, "on April 19, 1924 . . . at ten fifty-two, p.m."

"All that's on that paper?" Franny asked.

"That's right," Franny took the paper, which was obviously very old and yellowed and she read it, and then each of us read it, and Kitty passed the paper up to Carl who read it and passed it to the other guys.

"Why would he feel better because he could kill himself?" Sheryl asked. "What's so great about that?"

"Because it meant there was always a way out if things got too bad for him," Sally answered.

"That's not much of a way out—killing yourself. Let's not talk about this, it's giving me the creeps," Sheryl said, and I was disappointed to hear her say that. This was a discussion about important things like philosophy and life, and it didn't seem appropriate for her to lose interest and stop us from talking about it.

"I wonder why he wanted to throw away the gun and tear up the paper," Kitty said.

"He probably doesn't need it anymore," I answered. "He seemed pretty old—maybe he's going to die soon."

Sally said, "I'll bet he wanted the pieces of paper to settle in the wind and the gun to disintegrate in the ocean. Maybe he's going to be cremated when he dies and have his ashes tossed into the ocean and scattered into the wind."

Franny said to me, "For a student of the human condition you didn't take that into account. That poor old man thinks his ashes will be scattered in the wind with the pieces of this paper—but we have the pieces of paper taped together." Franny laughed, and I felt bad because I hadn't taken that into account. I decided to keep the letter after everyone read it. I would decide later whether or not to tear it up again and take it back to where I had found it.

"Just don't bring his ashes here," Kitty said, laughing, and she put her arm around my neck and hugged me, I guess because she could tell that I felt bad.

Carl clapped his hands loudly and said, "I don't mean to break up your philosophical discourse here, but it's time for the real party favors." Carl held up a tiny brown bottle.

"You have some coke?" Sally asked. "Why didn't you tell us."

"A surprise," Carl answered. "A cocaine surprise."

"Well, here we go," I thought, because I had no idea how to take cocaine and I had no idea what it would do to me. I wondered why Jackson had never told me anything about this.

"You like coke?" Franny asked.

"Sure, do you?"

"I love it."

Kitty ran out of the living room and came back a minute later with a mirror about a foot square with a frame around it and Carl poured the cocaine onto the mirror. The cocaine was a white powder. Carl used a razor blade to chop the cocaine, although I wasn't sure why because it was already powder. Finally he used the razor blade to stretch the cocaine into thin lines on the mirror. Someone had taken a dollar bill and rolled it into a little tube. The mirror and the dollar bill were passed around and everyone sucked up a line or two of the cocaine into their noses through the dollar bill. Fortunately I was near the last person so I got to watch everyone else. I watched them suck up the cocaine and I watched them when they were done, just to see how they were reacting to the drug. I wanted to see if any of them went crazy, but nothing unusual happened.

When it was my turn I sucked up one of the shortest lines and Franny nudged me and made me suck up a very long line. I handed the mirror to someone else and waited to see what would happen to me. "Feels good, doesn't it?" Franny asked.

"Yeah," I answered, still trying to figure out what it felt like, but I wasn't sure. I was already so stoned from all the marijuana that I didn't think I could feel anything else. Carl took out another small brown bottle and poured out more cocaine and the mirror went around again and Franny started to get in a much happier mood, and it seemed like everyone did. Then I realized that the top of my mouth and my front teeth were numb. I mentioned that to Franny, as casually as I could.

Franny smiled. "Yeah, it's good stuff," she said and I was a little relieved that this was normal with cocaine.

Kitty was still sitting next to me on the floor and she leaned forward so that her elbows were resting on the coffee table and she leaned into me. Carl went over to the record player and turned on some music that I didn't recognize, but he turned it on loud. One of the guys heard what music Carl had selected and said, "Cool, perfect." I guess because of the cocaine and maybe the music I felt like I could do anything, so I reached my hand over and put it on Kitty's breast, which was hanging down below the level of the table top where no one could see. With my finger I gently rubbed across her nipple for a while until she said, "Mmmmm," and she turned to me and leaned right up to my face.

"You're here with Franny, right?"

"Yeah."

"Well, I'm here with Carl. But maybe another time." She kissed me gently on the lips and stood up and walked over to the couch where she plopped down right next to Carl. When Kitty left I wondered how I possibly had the nerve to do that to her, and figured it must be either the cocaine or the opiated Thai or the combination. I wondered when the "another time" that Kitty mentioned might be, but I was happy that it was out there somewhere, and it occurred to me that it was almost like an IOU. Franny pulled on my arm and said, "Let's go into the bedroom." I could smell the wine and marijuana on her breath, and I was starting to like that smell. We stood up and Franny was holding onto me and we fell over each other. We were laughing and I was having a hard time getting us both to stand up, although I finally did. Then it was hard to walk because my legs were so rubbery. In fact, my whole body felt a little rubbery. Franny took my hand and pulled me into one of the bedrooms. She closed the door and dropped her clothes to the floor and pushed me onto the bed. "This cocaine really gets me going," she said, and I couldn't help remembering Vickie and thinking that I should get some cocaine for her.

We lay on her bed kissing for a minute and Franny was extremely passionate. Then out of nowhere she took one of her necklaces off her neck and put it around my neck. It was a thin leather cord with a half dozen knots tied in it at various, random places and a few silver-looking beads on it. That was the first affectionate type of thing Franny had ever done to me and I was very surprised, although she was still so stoned that she seemed almost not to know what she was doing. I gave her an affectionate sort of kiss, but she pushed me back, laughing, and said, "These things are getting pretty heavy around my neck. This can be a memento."

"Thanks," I said, and I kissed her again. I was thinking that this was maybe the best night of my life.

Franny said all of a sudden, laughing, "I've got something for us to try." She jumped off the bed and walked over to a small suitcase on the floor. She leaned down and searched for a moment and brought out a white bullet-shaped thing. It was about four inches long and an inch or so across. "It's a vibrator. My sister got it." She laughed again.

"What's it for?" I asked.

"Guess." She turned the end of the vibrator and it started buzzing. She touched the vibrator to her nipple and then between her legs. "Here, use it on me." The vibrator was vibrating very quickly so that you almost couldn't see it move. It felt strange buzzing in my hand, what with the rubbery feeling I already had. I used it on Franny's breasts and then on different parts of her body until she turned on her stomach and said, "Put it in me." I put it inside of her and then she said, "No, the other place," and

I pushed it gently an inch or so into her rear end. She just lay there for a few moments, with her arms stretched out on the bed. "Put it in further," she said, and I pushed it in further, like she said. Then, every little while she told me to put it in even further, and I pushed it in a little further each time, until it was almost all the way in and there was only a half inch nub sticking out that I could barely hold onto. "Further," she said.

"I can't . . ."

"Put it in further—as far as you can!" So I pushed the vibrator in further until it suddenly just disappeared—like it got sucked in—and from the outside you couldn't even see that it was in Franny. I was a little stunned, but I didn't know what to do or how to tell Franny. I could still hear it buzzing away in there. Then Franny flipped onto her back and pulled me onto her. I was in a dream, a happy, unfocused sort of dream, except that all the time I was also a little nervous, wondering what was going to happen with the vibrator, and wondering whether being so stoned was making me more worried than I should be. When we finished, Franny reached behind and asked, "Where's the vibrator?"

"It should be there," I said.

"It's still vibrating." Franny felt around back there for a few moments but she was still very stoned and it took her a while to figure out what was going on. Finally she said, "Jesus Christ! Get it out of me, Ben!" Franny got up on her knees and I acted as though I was trying to get the vibrator out, although I didn't have a clue as to how to go about it. I couldn't even quite focus on what I was trying to do. After a couple of minutes she went into the bathroom, but she came back out after a while and said, "I can't get it out. We have to go find a doctor or something."

Franny sat on the edge of the bed to get dressed and I could still hear the vibrator, although it sounded pretty faint from where I was. And then for some crazy reason it struck me as being pretty funny, so that I had to bite my cheek to keep from laughing. Everyone else was still in the living room and Franny walked to the doorway leading into the living room and asked if anyone knew where to find a doctor.

"Are you sick or something?" Sheryl asked. Franny was staring ahead as though she was in a daze. "No," she answered without looking at Sheryl, "I have a personal problem." Franny didn't move from the doorway, I guess because she didn't want anyone to hear the vibrator, although it was hard to hear unless you were listening for it. I felt bad that I had lost control of the thing that way and I was a little afraid that we were going to have a problem getting it out.

Sheryl asked Carl, who wouldn't call a doctor when he didn't know why. But Franny still wouldn't tell Sheryl what was going on so Sheryl sort of stumbled over to us and asked me, "What is it?"

Franny whispered to Sheryl and said, "He put a vibrator up my butt and he pushed it in too far and now it's stuck. It's still buzzing in there!" Franny started to cry, and then she started to laugh at the same time. Everyone was looking at me through the smoke haze and candlelight and I didn't have any idea what to do. Sheryl started laughing and then covered her mouth and stopped herself. She walked back to the living room and said to Carl, "Is Tom still around? We should call him. It *is* a personal problem." Sheryl started laughing again, but stopped herself. She leaned over and whispered something to Carl and then he picked up the telephone.

"I don't want him to come over here," Franny said to Sheryl as Carl was calling. "I'll go there."

Carl spoke on the telephone for a while and then said to Franny, "He's the only doctor I know and he'll come over but you can't go to his house. If he doesn't come over you'll have to go to a hospital."

Franny stomped her foot and turned to me and said, "You did it, Ben! It's your fault!"

I was a little stunned that Franny would act that way, but I figured it was the opium in the marijuana. Carl said into the phone, "Come on over, Tom." Sheryl came back over to Franny and put her arm around her and they walked together into the bedroom where Franny and I had been. I just looked at the other people in the room and didn't know whether to follow Franny or to go into the living room. After a minute I decided to follow Franny because I was pretty curious about what was going to happen. When I walked in Franny was lying on the bed staring at the ceiling and Sheryl was sitting next to her. I was afraid of what either of them might say to me, but Franny didn't say anything or even look over at me and Sheryl just smiled at me and said, "I don't think it'll be any problem." I stood by the bed and we were all silent, and I could still hear that damn vibrator. I wondered what kind of batteries could keep going for so long.

The doctor came over a lot quicker than I expected and Sheryl and I went to the front door and let him in. Everyone else was talking in the living room and seemed to have forgotten about Franny and her problem. The doctor was a younger guy with a bald head and a long, thick beard and he looked like any of the other people who might have been friends with Sheryl or Carl or lived in Topanga Canyon. He saw Sheryl and kissed her on the cheek and said, "How are you? Long time no see." He put his hand on Sheryl's shoulder and she led him toward Franny. "So what exactly is the problem?" he asked.

Sheryl turned to the doctor and whispered, "Tom, she has a vibrator stuck up her ass and I think it's turned on!"

She laughed and then quickly covered her mouth. Tom smiled and shook his head and said, "Lead the way."

Sheryl and I waited in the hall and Tom came back out after only a few minutes. In his hand he held the vibrator, which was still buzzing. "Here's the culprit," he said to Sheryl and me, and then he said to me, "I gather that you're the anxious father," and he handed the vibrator to me.

"Thanks," I said and I turned the thing off. I went back into Franny's room and set the vibrator on top of the clothes in her small suitcase. She was lying on the bed on her back. I asked, "So, how are you?"

"Stoned . . . and embarrassed." She laughed a little. I was surprised at how she had reacted to the situation. I expected her to be calm and philosophic, but I figured she was stoned and it was her rear end and not mine. I stood by the bed for a minute and Franny said, "I'm pretty tired, Ben. I think I'll go to sleep. Why don't you turn off the light."

I walked back into the living room and since Sheryl had told everyone the story they were talking about the vibrator, making jokes. "Nice aim, there, Ben," Carl said, and he laughed. Tom was sitting with everyone and I sat down, hoping to be part of the group. But they only talked for another fifteen minutes or so and everything broke up. Kitty and Carl went into the other bedroom, Sheryl and Marty went to sleep in the van and the other people left. Carl said, "It looks like Fran's booted you out, Ben, so I guess you get the couch."

I lay on the couch, still incredibly stoned. I tried to close my eyes but everything was spinning, so I just lay there, wondering how I could have let that vibrator out of my control. Then I got to thinking about Connie and I remembered my parents. I knew that Connie would be calling for me tonight and that I would have to come up with a good excuse for her. I figured I could tell her I got kidnapped or something. I thought that I should call my parents, but I couldn't do it tonight because they would come get me, and that was worse than what I did with the vibrator.

The next morning I was still stoned from the pot brownies, but I helped Carl build the shed for a couple of hours, anyway. I felt like I had just woken up and that everything wasn't in focus yet, except that I couldn't shake it. I hoped that I would eventually not be stoned anymore because I didn't really like the feeling of being stoned for so long.

Finally we left for home, Sheryl and Marty in the front seats of the van and Franny and me in the back. I hadn't had a chance to talk to Franny since the incident the night before, so once we were on our way I told her quietly, "I'm really sorry about what happened last night."

"That's okay," she answered, and she even put her hand on my arm. "I'm just still so stoned from those brownies."

Most of the trip back we were silent, both of us staring into space, until Franny said out of nowhere, "Did you see those guys last night?"

"What guys?"

"Everyone." We talked quietly, but we were at the back of the van and the noise from the road and the radio covered our conversation from Sheryl and Marty. "Everyone. Sheryl and Carl and Marty and Kitty—all of them. They're not doing anything, they're just talking about old times."

"They're getting stoned and . . ."

"And so what. Anyone can get stoned." Franny shook her head. "It's over. The hippies are just history. I think it's all over." She sighed. "I missed it and I may as well just face it. I should just go home." I couldn't believe what I was hearing. First the vibrator got stuck and now this. I wasn't sure what to say so I didn't say anything. I didn't want to make things worse, and I figured maybe being stoned all this time was making Franny depressed or something.

We got back to Sheryl's house in the early afternoon and Franny went into the house without even saying anything to me. I walked over to the canyon road and put out my thumb. I was feeling pretty disturbed about how the night before had been ruined and how depressed Franny was, and how I was a low-life with Connie and the lies I would have to tell her and how Ben Sr. was likely to kill me when I got home. But somehow, after a little while in the sun, that all sort of faded away and I didn't feel too bad. I wasn't feeling like a hippie or anything, yet. But there was all the rest of my life still out there, and at least I had my foot in the door. I got home and my mother was in the kitchen. "Where the hell have you been?" she asked when she saw me. "I've been worried sick."

"What do you mean?" I asked, sizing up the situation.

"Do you know your father was in a car wreck last night?"

"Did he die?" I asked.

"No, he didn't die. But he spent the night in the hospital. I just brought him home." My mother looked severely at me and I knew immediately how lucky I was. It turned out that Ben Sr. got in the accident on his way home. He hit a tree and spent the night in a hospital where they fixed his separated shoulder and watched him to make sure he was just drunk off his ass and not in a coma or something.

"I came in late last night and left early this morning. I went to the beach. I didn't even know about Ben Sr."

"I don't believe you came home at all last night, Ben. And I don't like it when you call your father Ben Sr." Her severe look was already fading to a tired look, and I knew I was okay.

"Sorry, Mom. I'll make sure I let you know where I am. So how is he?"

"He'll be fine."

"Did Connie call?"

"How would I know, Ben? Last night was . . ."

"That's fine. I understand. Sorry." I couldn't believe my good luck. I was actually amazed at my luck because Ben Sr. was a surprisingly good driver when he was drunk. I guess it offset a little the bad luck I had with Franny and the vibrator.

CHAPTER TEN

The first day of school Graham and I rode the school bus because neither of us had managed to get a car. I thought occasionally that maybe I should have worked over the summer to save money for a car, but how does money or a car compare with the experiences of life?

Connie wasn't on the bus and I didn't see her at school until after my first class. She took my arm and led me out of the corridor to a little patch of grass behind one of the buildings. As she took my arm she said, "We have to talk, Ben," and she didn't say anything more until we were outside alone.

"Where were you this morning?" I asked. "You didn't take the bus."

"My parents wanted to drive me—because I'm sick and all. But they know I'm pregnant. They found out last night and we had a terrible fight . . ."

"How did they find out?" I interrupted.

"I told them—I had to. There's this horrible new experimental drug that they thought I should try, so I had to tell them I couldn't because of the baby."

"What did they say?"

"They were so angry, both of them. I thought at least my mother might understand, but she wouldn't even hear what I was saying. They want me to get an abortion, but I won't get one." Connie leaned into me and hugged me.

"I know," I answered.

"And they won't let me see you anymore." Connie still hugged me. "They won't even let you come to the house."

Connie went to her next class and I went to the beach. First I stopped at Connie's house to talk to her mother. I didn't know enough about Connie's sickness to know for sure that none of the drugs would work, and I thought that Connie shouldn't die to save the baby. I wanted to find out from her parents what was really happening. I knocked on the front door and Connie's father answered. I was surprised that he was home. He seemed even more surprised to see me and he said without any emotion, "What are you doing here? Aren't you supposed to be in school?"

"I am, but I need to talk to you."

Connie's mother walked up behind her father and asked, "Who is it, Joel?" She looked past Joel, saw me and turned away. "Tell him to leave, Joel," she said. "How dare he come around here!"

"Let me just talk to you, just for a minute . . ."

Joel opened the door slowly, as though he was very tired. "Come in, Ben," he said sadly, and he turned to his wife and said, "Let's listen to him."

"Joel!" Connie's mother said, but she followed the two of us into the living room.

I sat on a chair and Connie's parents sat on the couch across from me. I had been thinking about what I wanted to say, but my mind was hazy. "I just want to ask a couple of questions and then I want to say something . . ."

"What gives you the right?" Connie's mother interrupted.

"I love Connie, too," I said, angrily, and I had to bite my cheek to keep the tears back.

I could see that I was getting Connie's mother angrier, but Joel put his hand on her arm and said gently, "Just let's let him talk, Shel. Let's just listen. Ben should understand that Connie can't have the baby."

"It's his damn fault!" Shel answered, not looking at me.

"Will any of those drugs save Connie?" I asked.

"They might," Joel answered.

"Connie says they're horrible drugs that are just experimental and have a one-in-a-million chance of working. They'll just make her sicker and won't help her any."

"We don't know that they won't help her," Joel said.

"But being perfectly honest, being *realistic*, what are the chances?"

"What difference does it make? We need a miracle, but there are miracles. If we don't try . . . Connie *has* to try." He spoke calmly and softly, without emotion. I hadn't looked closely at his face before, but as he spoke I watched him and he looked old and tired. I glanced over at Shel, who was looking away from me, and she sat moving nervously, rubbing her fingers together.

There was a lot that I wanted to say, but I didn't know how to say it. I felt tension between the three of us that could explode at any time. I sat silent for a few moments, pussy moments, and finally I said, as gently as I could, "If you were Connie, and maybe you didn't have too long to live, wouldn't you want to experience as much . . ."

Shel stood up and screamed at me, "That's my little baby you're talking about! She doesn't need to experience what you want to do to her!"

"We love each other!" I screamed back.

"How dare you! Get out of here!" I looked at Joel, who stood and put his arm around Shel.

He looked at me sadly and said, "You're just a kid. You'd better go." Shel was crying when I left. I wondered if Jackson could have explained it better to Shel and maybe avoided the crying and screaming.

I went to the beach because I didn't know what else to do. When I got to the beach it was already late afternoon and I walked across the sand past the few people who were still lying on their towels, relaxing or trying to eek out a last, imperceptibly darker shade to their tans. I sat down just above the wet sand and told myself that I would watch the sun set. But sunset was still hours away and I was much too impatient to wait for it. I considered sitting under the poem tree, but I ended up walking up the ramp on the incline, next to the wall I had walked on early in the summer. It wasn't a long time that had passed since then, and yet it seemed so far away. I walked slowly and there were only a few other people on the ramp, also walking slowly. I stopped at the top of the ramp and looked down at the highway and out at the ocean. I could have let out a scream, but I didn't say anything. Summer was over and I had missed so much of it. I had missed so many of the possibilities. I just stood there for a minute and then I went home.

Connie and I spent time together at school every day, but her parents wouldn't let me come to their house. At school we would hold hands and talk and I would put my arm around Connie when we walked, but it got a little frustrating for me because there were girls all around, and all the other good things in life, and Franny in the canyon, even if things weren't going that well with her, and Connie and I had this connection with sorrow and tragedy that we never spoke of, without romance except in some eternal way that Connie always talked about but that I wasn't all that convinced of. Even Graham could see what I was going through. We were walking together one day talking about life and Graham put his arm on my shoulder and said, "Ben, you've got it bad. You've got death and this baby stuff going on and you don't even get to screw Connie anymore." Of course that was right after Graham got thrown over by his girlfriend from camp, and maybe he was just comparing his unhappiness to mine.

I stopped in the little town in the canyon twice during the first week of school, but I couldn't find Franny either time. I had seen Franny a couple of times since that weekend I hitchhiked up north, but things were never the same between us. We had one great night when we smoked pot and Franny got really high and let me take pictures of her. But that was just sex and immediately afterwards she wanted me to leave. The sex was great, of course, but I was already starting to realize that there's something about real love and affection that, well, there's just something about it. I was frustrated because I couldn't exactly figure out what was going on. I had decided to stay away from the canyon for a while thinking maybe Franny would miss me and things would be better, but it was almost three weeks until I finally saw her again. She was sitting on the stone steps of the front porch of Sheryl's house and I saw her as I crossed the little bridge. Franny glanced up and saw me and I lifted my hand to wave, but she looked away immediately so I stopped my arm in mid-air and let it drop. I didn't say anything until I got up next to her. "Hi, Fran. How are you?" I asked, gently, trying to sound friendly.

She glanced at me and said, "Fine, I'm fine. How are you?"

"I'm fine." I sat next to Franny on the stone steps, which were tree-shaded and cool, even in the heat of the late summer afternoon. Franny didn't say anything else or even look at me, so finally I asked, "What's wrong? I stopped by a couple of times this week but I couldn't find you."

Franny let out a long sigh and said, "Look, Ben . . . I'm pregnant and I'm going home."

I was stunned. "You're pregnant?" I couldn't believe it. I looked around, thinking that it couldn't be possible. No wonder the world was so overpopulated.

Before I could say anything else, Franny said, "Don't worry, Ben, it's not yours." She still had not more than glanced at me since I sat down.

"What? How do you know?"

I thought that maybe Franny was angry with me because I hadn't seen her for a few weeks, or maybe she was still annoyed about the vibrator incident, but she answered, "It's not your baby. You had nothing to do with it. It's too far along. I can't believe it—there was just one month where I messed up with the pill."

For some reason it bothered me thinking about Franny having sex with someone else. "Were you sleeping with someone else at the same time . . ."

"That's none of your business," she interrupted, and there was anger in her voice.

I looked at Franny sitting there, pregnant with someone else's baby. She had obviously forgotten all about peace and love and all of that. Maybe she never really understood any of it. "But why are you leaving?" I asked. My voice was rising out of anger that I couldn't really control or understand, even though I was starting to think that I didn't care if Franny stayed or left. Some of the magic was gone, and for the first time I could understand how

Jackson felt about his girlfriends and how he felt that he'd picked the wrong philosophies in life, which just meant that some of his dreams and illusions were shredded over time. "I thought you wanted to live out here. You didn't like it at home."

"I wanted to live out here five years ago when everything was happening, but nothing's happening anymore. Those days are past. This place is boring. The people here are leftovers from the protesters and the people who really care . . ."

"People are still protesting and lots of people still care . . ." I interrupted and Franny interrupted me back,

"Not like before. These people are only playing at it. I guess I just missed it . . . and so did you. Maybe you don't realize that, yet. Maybe you're not the great student of the human condition that you think you are."

I couldn't believe that Franny was getting so angry at me and so sarcastic, and it was making me even angrier. Only I didn't know what to say. "I'll probably have an abortion," Franny continued. "But that's something I'll have to decide." I just looked at Franny, who was looking away. I didn't know what else to say. My anger was fading away but I was still frustrated. Not necessarily because of Franny, but because of everything. I looked around at the trees and the mountains and then at the little bridge. For some reason I wanted to say something to Franny to have the last word, but I didn't know what that should be. Before I could think of anything Franny said, "Why don't you go, Ben. I have to pack and there's nothing else for us to say, anyway."

It didn't seem right that it should end this way between Franny and me. I put my hand on Franny's shoulder and she shrugged if off, and I got angrier suddenly that she would shrug off my hand. I stared at Franny who was looking away from me. Finally I stood and said, "You're right—good luck," and I walked away without even looking back. I didn't want my memories of Franny and this place to be ruined any more than they already had been.

Connie was only in school for about a month and a half when

her parents took her out. I thought that she was starting to look even sicker, but she was also starting to look pregnant, if you knew to look pretty closely for it. No one at school but Connie, Graham and I knew that Connie was pregnant, and I was impressed with Graham that he had kept the secret.

Connie's parents couldn't convince her not to have the baby, although they fought about it all the time. I was amazed at Connie's strength. Her father even called Ben Sr. to tell him what had happened. It wasn't the best time for Ben Sr., like usual. He called me into the study, where he was having a drink. He sat down like we were going to have a real talk, and I was even hoping that I could talk to him about what was happening and that he would give me some advice or something. He started telling me about the responsibilities of life and how I was a disappointment to him and how he couldn't believe that I had done that to a sick girl, and then it sort of degenerated even more until he was screaming at me. He sat behind his desk with a glass of the scotch he always drank and I sat on a chair in front of the desk until I moved to a couch a little further away as he kept drinking. He always got angrier when he got drunker and finally he came around the desk and I knew he wanted to punch me. I could have escaped, but I let him land one on my cheek that wasn't too bad but would show a bruise, and I ran out of the house. Before he got too drunk he mentioned that Connie's father had said that with Connie being pregnant her sickness would get worse faster, and I was angry that he would say something like that, but upset that maybe it was true.

I went over to see Graham and we walked the neighborhood for a couple of hours. It was October and the nights were already chilly. We talked about life and about Connie and whether her pregnancy really made her get sick faster. Graham told me that he had decided that we had to do something in Connie's honor, only he was trying to figure out what it should be. When it got late Graham went home and I stayed out until the early morning before I finally went home to sleep for a few hours before school.

After Connie stopped going to school I couldn't see her anymore, so Graham went to her house each day after school to give her homework and to exchange letters for us. On weekends he stopped by just to talk to Connie and to exchange our letters. Every day I wrote a letter and so did Connie. After a few days Graham and I agreed that he should be able to read the letters because we were best friends and blood brothers and all, and the three of us were really sort of in this trusting relationship together. At first that didn't seem right to me, but after I thought about it I realized how good a friend Graham was and I guess I was a little relieved to bring Graham into the whole thing.

We exchanged the letters for a week and then I didn't know what to write anymore. Connie always wrote about life and dying and feeling the baby inside of her and how she missed me and wanted to hold me and talk to me. Graham started helping me with the letters and then every morning he showed up at the bus stop with an entire letter that he'd written, telling Connie how I loved her and that she should keep her spirits up and that we'd find a way for me to see her, and even a little corny philosophy about life now and then. I would rewrite the letters so they would be in my handwriting and would be my own thoughts and everything, but I did use a lot of Graham's thoughts and we basically worked on them together.

Each day while Graham visited Connie I waited down the street and when Graham came back he told me how Connie looked and how she was doing and we read Connie's letter together. At first Graham came back after just a few minutes, but as the days went by Graham took longer and longer until after a couple of weeks I found myself standing around for so long that I went home and lay under the tree in my front yard, waiting sometimes an hour or more. Graham was starting to like Connie, I could tell, and I was happy that he was. He told me that she was smart and nice and that they talked about important things, and that I was lucky that she loved me. At first he couldn't talk to Connie about her dying, but one day after he had been with her for a long time he came back and told me that he'd asked Connie if being pregnant made her get sick faster. She wouldn't give him an answer, and I could tell that it bothered Graham.

About that time I got a letter from Jackson. I didn't recognize the handwriting on the envelope and where the return address should have been was written only "G.I." Then I noticed that the letter had a Tennessee postmark and I figured it was from Jackson. I opened the letter pretty quickly because I hadn't heard anything from Jackson and I was anxious to know how he was doing. A picture dropped out that was a group of four army guys standing around together in their uniforms. They were all smiling and had short hair, and it took me a little while to figure out which one was Jackson. I laughed out loud when I recognized him. The letter read,

Dear Ben,
As you can see from the picture, they've turned me into an army man. (In case you can't tell, I'm second from the left in the picture with some "army buddies.") It's been quite an experience, but I've met some pretty good people (and a lot of real crazy ones). I've also had a pretty good share of pussy minutes the way they run things here. When I get back you and I'll have to spend some time in the old stone room and talk about all this. I'm a little scared right now because we're shipping off tomorrow (I can't say where and they censor all the mail).
As you can see, I'm not much of a letter writer, but we'll catch up on everything when I get back (whenever that is). I wouldn't mind hearing from you and finding out how everything's going. There's an address on the back of the picture.

Take care, friend,
Jackson

On the back of the picture was an address that just said United States Army with battalion and other numbers on it. I looked for a long time at the picture of Jackson and then I thumbtacked it to the small bulletin board over the desk in my bedroom.

One evening Graham returned from visiting Connie, handed me Connie's letter, which he had already opened and read, and said, "Connie and I came up with a plan. We're going to sneak you up to Connie's room tonight."

"How can we do that?"

"We'll get a ladder—we have one at my house that's big enough—and we'll lean it against the house and you can get through Connie's window. We'll do it after midnight so her parents will be asleep."

That night Graham and I walked through the hills waiting for midnight so that we could get the ladder from Graham's house and I could see Connie. It was a cold November night. Clouds were heavy overhead, although we didn't expect rain until the next morning. We talked about Connie as we walked, until I didn't want to talk about her anymore. I was looking forward to seeing Connie and all, but I was also a little afraid to see her. I was afraid that she would look real sick, and the dying business was hanging over me. Somehow Graham had the whole thing romanticized so that I think he lost track of the fact that Connie was actually dying.

I had been thinking lately that I should talk to Graham about smoking pot. In fact, I had been carrying a joint in my pocket for the last two days, trying to decide. In a way I didn't want to share it with him. I was annoyed at Franny for leaving me and Jackson was in the army with a crew cut, going to war, but I was happy about the times I had with them, that we had smoked pot together and shared things. I was afraid that if I smoked with Graham it would do something bad to those memories. But Graham was my friend, and I didn't want him to end up sad like Jackson, or worse.

I took the joint from my pocket and held it out toward Graham. It was a very thin joint. "You want to smoke some pot?"

"What is that?" Graham grabbed the joint from my hand. "That's a doobie! Is that a real doobie?" His eyes were open wide.

"It's real," I answered and gently took the joint back from

Graham before he destroyed it. "It's a pinner, but it's definitely real."

"A pinner?"

"A thin one."

"Where'd you get that?"

"Jackson gave it to me before he left. He got me stoned for my birthday, and we smoked a few times after that. He couldn't take it with him in the army, and he was afraid the rats would eat it while he was gone."

"Bullshit! You didn't smoke grass with Jackson! You smoked it all the way back on your birthday and you didn't tell me? Why didn't you tell me?"

"I don't know. I thought with your new religion and everything . . ."

"It could have just been a sin. That was no problem. I would've just confessed it away."

"Sorry."

"Did you tell Connie? Did you smoke with her?"

"I didn't tell her. If I did she'd want to smoke it with me and I don't know what happens when you mix cancer with pot. I'm not sure I'd want to take the chance."

"Hmmm. Can we smoke it?" Graham asked.

"Sure, that's why I brought it along. It's good to smoke pot and talk about life."

We walked up the street to a vacant lot and sat on the curb under an old oak tree that overhung the street. Graham watched me closely as I lit the joint and took a hit. The tip of the cigarette glowed in the dark as I breathed in.

"So what do I do?" Graham asked when I held it out to him.

"Just breathe it in like a cigarette, but not too much at once. This stuff is a little raspy so it'll burn your throat if you take too much at once. And be careful how you hold it. I rolled this thing myself and I'm not that good at it, yet."

Graham carefully took the joint between his thumb and forefinger. "You rolled this yourself? How do you know so much about this stuff?"

"It's easy to learn."

Graham took a hit and coughed a little and handed me back the joint. I took a hit and we traded until the joint was too short to hold and I had to drop it into the street. "Too bad we don't have a roach clip. There's a lot of good resin wasted in that roach."

"Do you have another one?" Graham asked.

"Not with me. But I have a little pot at home."

Graham sat silent, staring out into the night, down the street and up at the sky. "What's supposed to happen, now?" he asked.

I could feel the pot working its way in, the high building inside me, the night become a little fuzzier. "You're getting high. You just don't know it, yet. It's hard to tell the first time. Let's walk."

We walked just a few steps and Graham said, "I can feel it! I'm definitely high! Definitely!"

"It's pretty cool, isn't it."

"Very cool."

We walked slowly, wandering along to nowhere in the dark, quiet streets. We didn't see anyone in any of the houses we passed, and rarely did a car drive past us. We didn't say anything for a long time, until out of nowhere Graham said, "You know, Ben, you'll be the only person in the world who ever made love to Connie. She'll die, and you'll be the only one. You'll be the only person who even felt her up."

"How do *you* know no one else ever felt her up?" I asked.

"You told me or something. But the point is that you'll be the only one."

"So, isn't that how it is with lots of people?"

"Maybe," Graham answered, "but they have a whole lifetime to decide. They can choose whatever they want. Connie can't make any kind of choice."

"She can make a choice. Just because she doesn't have a whole lifetime doesn't mean she can't still make a choice. But I can't do anything about that, anyway."

"Would you, if you could?"

"Would I what?"

"If you could do something about it, would you?" Graham asked.

"What are you talking about?"

"Okay, Ben." Graham stopped walking and I also stopped and turned toward him. "Okay," he said again and he held up his hands with his palms toward me. "I don't want you to take this wrong . . . and it's just a thought. Just something to think about."

"What is it?"

"Remember, it's just a thought. Just something to talk about."

I started walking again and said, "You're too weird for me, Graham. I think you're even weirder stoned. Did I tell you I got a letter from Jackson? It had a picture of him with his hair cut and wearing a uniform, standing around with a bunch of other army guys."

Graham ran up beside me. "So? He's not a friend of mine. He found that woman in the sewers and I should've found her. Anyway, don't you want to hear what I have to say? Isn't Connie more important?"

"Yeah, if you'd say it."

"Okay, this is it. Remember, Ben, it's just a thought . . . something . . ."

"Jesus, Graham!" I interrupted.

"Okay, this is it . . . Maybe I should make love to Connie."

I just kept walking for a couple of seconds until my mind realized what Graham had said. My first impulse was to laugh, so that's what I did, for a long time. I couldn't help myself. Soon Graham started laughing, too.

"It's not funny," Graham said, finally.

"We're stoned," I answered, and then I was angry, but also only for a moment. "What do you mean?" I asked.

"I like her a lot, Ben. I've gotten to know her and she's really nice. When I was at her house all those days we talked about all different things and I really like her. I never thought she would be the way she is, but I've never met a girl like her. I can't believe she's going to die and then maybe I'll never meet anyone else like her." Graham was talking very fast, so that I had a hard time following him because I was thinking about what he had suggested.

"Do you love her?" I asked.

"Do you?" Graham asked.

"Yes," I answered. I had to love her.

"Well, so do I. I love her, too. And maybe it's fair if she gets to make love to more than one person before she dies. Don't you think that's fair?" I didn't answer for a while until Graham asked again, "Well, don't you think that's fair?"

"Maybe. I'm thinking." Graham started talking again, but I wasn't paying attention. I was thinking about Franny for some reason, and about the summer, and about another girl at school who I thought was cute but who I couldn't even talk to because of Connie. I didn't want to be Connie's whole life. I didn't deserve to be. I interrupted Graham, who was still talking, "We can't just decide that. I don't think Connie will want to."

"I think she will. If you tell her it's okay. If you tell her that I love her and how you and I are best friends and everything. I don't even have to make love to her, I could just hold her and kiss her. That would be fine." There was an earnestness in Graham's voice that surprised me so that I had to look closely at him. We walked on in silence, each of us thinking about the awesomeness of what we were talking about. I thought about Jackson, that I should write to him about the situation. He would recommend that we get high to talk through everything.

"And there's another thing," Graham said after a while. "This is something you don't have to help me with. It's up to you. I thought that . . ."

"Just tell me, Graham." I interrupted. I couldn't even imagine what else Graham might have in mind.

"Okay, this is it. At school, in my history class, we have to do this big project where we choose someone we admire and then look around and find ways that person helped the world or maybe find things that remind us of that person. Do you have that project?"

"Not that I know of . . . unless I missed hearing about it or something."

"You probably just don't have it. I've got this new teacher for history. She's fat, but she's young and she has these different ideas about teaching. So, anyway, she wants us to pick the person and spend like two months just thinking about everything around us . . ."

"I don't get it."

"Let's say I picked Beethoven. You know who Beethoven is, don't you?"

"No, I don't know who Beethoven is. Jesus, Graham."

"Sorry. So let's say I picked Beethoven. I'd listen for his music, like if I heard it on the radio, or if it was used for a T.V. commercial or something. But I'd also think about what Beethoven stood for. He'd see music as beauty, or maybe love. All around there might be different things that could inspire him. So I'd have to look at everything and say, 'Hey, Beethoven would love this sunset.' He'd write a symphony about it. Or maybe he'd write a symphony about some great love."

"I get it. So you're going to have Beethoven writing symphonies for you and Connie."

"No, Beethoven's not the person I picked. I haven't picked anybody, *yet*, but I have to decide on someone by next week. I'm thinking of choosing Connie."

"Connie? Why Connie? She's not famous or anything. Why would you pick her?"

"The person doesn't have to be famous, Ben, just someone you admire. I admire Connie."

"Why?" I asked. "I mean, Connie's nice and everything, but I don't see how she compares to Beethoven or someone like that."

"How can you say that, Ben? She's your girlfriend and pregnant with your kid and dying of cancer and everything. How can you say that?"

I wasn't sure how I could say that. "We're just talking now, Graham. Remember we're stoned."

"I'm not feeling very stoned anymore."

"That's because we only had the pinner and it was your first time. When you smoke more it builds up in your system and you can get higher quicker."

"Is it built up in *your* system?"

"A little."

"Damn! I want it built up in *my* system . . . Anyway, with Connie, I was thinking that I might choose her for my project."

I felt bad about it, but I still couldn't see Connie the way Graham did. "Yeah, I can see that," I answered. "So, what . . . how would Connie remind you of things? Like what you were saying about Beethoven."

"Her suffering, Ben. She's pregnant and dying. She'll never be twenty years old. She'll never see the world. She'll never hear her child say, 'Mommy.' She'll . . ."

"Yeah, I know what you mean." I didn't want to hear about all the things Connie would miss. "So suffering is going to remind you of Connie? Where are you going to find that?"

"Suffering is everywhere, Ben. Everywhere. But we can find it easiest down in the poor areas. That's what I want to do, go down to some poor area and look for suffering. It's everywhere, Ben. I want to see it etched in peoples' faces . . ."

"Etched in their faces?" I asked. I didn't know where Graham got some of this stuff.

"That's right," Graham answered. "And then I'm going to write poems about the people and their suffering."

"That sounds like fun," I answered. Graham was too bizarre for words.

"It's not fun, Ben, but it's to honor Connie."

"I understand. I bet it's past midnight already, so we can go to Connie's. What do you think?"

"I don't know. Maybe not yet. One of us should wear a watch so we'd know." We had been walking for quite a while, eventually wandering out of the hills. We found ourselves about a mile from our homes, in the alley behind the little stores on the boulevard. Graham suggested, "Let's check the barber shop." We sometimes found magazines with pictures of naked women in the trash container behind the barber shop.

Graham ran up ahead and lifted the lid of the large rectangular metal container. "Empty," he said as I stepped up next to him. "They must've picked up the trash yesterday or today." Graham lowered the lid and we continued down the alley. "There's another thing I have to tell you about Connie, about honoring her."

"What's that?" I asked.

"Well, it's . . ."

"No, what's *that*?" Next to the barber shop was the veterinarian's office and on the ground beside the vet's trash container was a cardboard cylinder about eight inches high and four or five inches across. Graham picked up the cylinder and it was cardboard with a metal screw-on cap.

"I don't know what it is," he said.

"What does that say?" I pointed to a white label that was pasted onto the cardboard.

"I can't really read it, there's not enough light." We walked closer to the building, under the single light that was attached high up on the wall. Graham read, "Here lies the remains of *Gipper*!"

"Let me see." I took the container from Graham and read the label myself.

"There's a dead animal in there," Graham said. "Gipper's in there and they threw him away."

I shook the container. "I don't feel anything in here. Who's Gipper?"

Graham said, "It's Gipper. It's old Gip and they threw him away!"

"I'm going to see what's in here," I said. I held the container at arm's length and slowly turned the cap, which wasn't even on very tightly. When I got the cap off I lowered the container and tilted it toward the light so that I could look inside. Graham leaned over and looked in, also. There was no animal inside, just powder. I brought the container close and Graham and I both looked more closely.

"They burned him," Graham said and he was shaking his head. "That's right — they cremated old Gip. They did that to my grandfather, only they threw old Gip into a trash can. I wonder where my grandfather is. Maybe they threw *him* into a trash can someplace."

"They'd have to put him in a bigger container," I said. "I guess these containers come in all different sizes."

"Well, I'm going to give Gipper a proper burial." Graham took the container from me and walked across the alley to a grape stick fence that separated someone's backyard from the alley. A little dog started barking from inside the yard as Graham approached. Graham stood on the fence's lower cross support and reached over the fence. He dumped Gipper onto the barking dog. As Gipper rained down on him the dog yelped a little and backed away from the fence. He was quiet for a short time, maybe as a sort of respect for his cremated fellow dog. But soon he was back at the fence, barking again. Graham ran back over to the trash container behind the veterinarian's office and said, "Let's see who else they threw away." But that container was also empty. "I guess Gipper must've spilled out when the trucks came for all the trash."

"I guess so. Let's get out of here. That little dog's going to wake up everyone."

We ran to the end of the alley and Graham stopped. "Okay, I have one more thing to tell you about Connie, about honoring Connie."

"I know. You're going to find suffering poor people and write poetry about them."

"No, something else," Graham answered. He opened his jacket and pulled a small stack of money out of the inside pocket. Even though it was late at night and we hadn't seen anyone for hours, Graham looked around nervously and pushed the money back into the pocket.

"What's that?" I asked.

"Six hundred fifty dollars."

"Six hundred fifty dollars? Where did you get that?"

"It's for Connie, Ben."

"What do you mean?"

"I mean this is serious stuff, Ben. This is about life. It's serious like when I came back from camp and you told me you were screwing Connie and she was pregnant and everything."

It began to rain, just an occasional drop. "Let's go," I said and started up the street. Graham followed next to me. "So, what are you talking about?" I asked. "What's the money for? Is Connie getting an abortion? Her parents wanted her to. They'll pay for it."

"No, it's nothing like that. Connie wants the baby. This money is to *honor* Connie. I stole it."

"What?" I stopped walking "You *stole* all that money?" The rain was already starting to come down more seriously so I began walking again. "Who did you steal it from?"

"From my Uncle Stan."

"Your Uncle Stan?"

"Yeah. The money was in a pot with a fake plant. He had thousands, but I just took $650. I could've taken it all."

"How did you find money in a pot?"

"My aunt was telling this story to my mother once about how their house caught on fire and Stan ran outside carrying a fake plant. It was the only thing in the house he grabbed, but it was because he had all this money stashed in the plant. Anyway, Stan is rich as hell, you know that. This is like Robin Hood, taking from the rich and giving to the poor . . ."

"Since when are *you* poor?"

"It's not *for* me, Ben. That's the point." Graham had that earnestness in his voice. "It's to honor Connie. I took the money, committed the sin, took the *stand* in life that I was going to do something. I'm going to honor Connie with it."

"How?" I asked. I had to respect Graham taking a stand that way, although I wasn't completely sure that it made any sense.

"I wasn't sure at first, before I took the money. I just wanted to do something that would be in Connie's honor since we love her and she's dying. Something more than just my school project. That's why I'm telling you. I thought you might want to be in on honoring her. What do you think?"

"Sure," I answered. It didn't seem reasonable for me not to be in on honoring Connie, considering everything. "How do we honor her with $650? And why did you take 650, instead of, I don't know, 750?"

"I didn't purposely take 650. I just took some bills—there were stacks of money—and I counted it later. It turned out to be 650."

"But he's your uncle, Graham. I don't understand. First you're a religious fanatic and the next thing I know you're stealing hundreds of dollars from your own uncle."

"I'm not a religious fanatic, Ben. I know he's my uncle, but that's the point. I know he can afford it. I'm not *hurting* anyone. So what if he has a few hundred dollars less? He can sure afford it. It won't affect him one bit. But it's a statement about life, about taking a stand."

"So what are you going to do with the money?"

"I want you to be in on it with me, Ben. We should honor Connie together. I'll take the sin for stealing the money, but you can get in on doing the honor."

"Okay, sure. So what should we do?" I wondered if this should go on my list of sins, or maybe a different list. I wasn't particularly clear on this one.

"Well, we can't build a big statue or anything, but we could do something smaller. Just something to honor her. Just the point of taking a stand, of doing something to honor someone you love, and to help your fellow man."

"You mean like give the money to some cancer research place or something? Everyone will want to know where the money came from. Unless you gave it anonymously."

"No. I want to give it to a poor person. We'd go out and find a poor person and just give him the money."

"While you're looking for the etched suffering we could also look for someone to give the money to."

"Right," Graham answered. "We can't change the world or anything, but that would be a little act of kindness or something in a world of war and repression and hunger and possible nuclear war and . . ."

"And suffering. You forgot suffering."

"And in a world of suffering. Just one little thing to make a poor person happier. We could just tell him it was from Connie, and you and I and that guy would remember what we did and we would all know it was to honor Connie."

I almost shook my head at how bizarre Graham was, except that I was sort of impressed with the idea. "Where do we find this poor person?" I remembered that old woman Jackson and I saw at Betty's Burgers, but I didn't have any idea how to find her.

"We'll just go looking for one. We'll drive down to a poor area and look around until we find the right one. I'm going down there anyway for my school project."

"Okay," I agreed. All things considered it didn't seem all that unreasonable a thing to do, especially since Connie *was* my girl-friend and pregnant with my baby.

The night had somehow dragged on and it was cold and raining hard. By the time we got back to Graham's house it was way too late to be thinking about dragging the ladder over to Connie's, but Graham and I were operating on momentum, and so we had no choice. We were soaking wet and exhausted and not at all stoned when we reached Graham's house and we crept silently through the house to Graham's room where we both changed into dry clothes. That's when I first noticed the leather cord Graham was wearing around his neck. We sat on the floor, putting our wet shoes back on and I asked Graham in a whisper about the leather cord.

"Yeah, I got that about a week ago. I forgot to tell you."

"Where did you get it?" I asked.

"At the grocery store. It's really supposed to be a leather shoe lace or something. I put these couple of knots in it, but I still have to get some beads, like yours. Where did you get those? From some head shop or something?"

For months I had wanted to tell Graham about Franny and the canyon and how I got my leather cord, and now I wanted to tell him also that a leather cord from the grocery store was meaningless, almost an insult. I had wanted to tell him about smoking mari-juana and doing cocaine and making love to Franny and about the vibrator incident and about belonging to something important. After our talk about Connie earlier that night and seeing his leather cord I wanted to tell him more than ever about all of those other things. I needed to tell someone and I thought that he might understand. But I couldn't tell him about any of it, because of Connie, and I just answered, "You can get them at a head shop."

Seeing Connie tonight was now a matter of principle for us and so we went back down to Graham's garage. Graham found a couple of thin, oversized raincoats that we put on and we quietly carried the ladder out of the garage and down the street. The ladder was ten feet long if you stood it up in an "A" and it folded out to twenty feet if you wanted to lean it against a building. It was made of some gray space-age metal and was surprisingly light to carry when we each took an end. The cold rain continued to fall and the raincoats were defective so that water leaked through in certain places, but we trudged ahead.

We were about half a block from Connie's house when the police car drove by. It slowed as it passed us and then backed up and one of the cops rolled down his window and shined a light on me and then along the ladder to Graham. The cop called to us, "Where are you boys going with that? What time do you think it is?"

Graham and I looked at each other through the rain. It might have been alright if we got arrested, but we couldn't return the ladder without seeing Connie. "It's pretty late, sir," Graham answered.

"It's nearly two o'clock in the morning. Where are you taking that ladder?"

"Over to *his* house," Graham answered, nodding his head toward me. "He has some work to do and he needs the ladder."

"At two o'clock in the morning in the rain?"

For some reason I was reminded of the other day in school when I was in my English class timing speeches. We each had ten minutes to give a speech and I was supposed to hold up a card to tell the speaker when he had one minute left to speak. Lately I was getting bored and disgusted with things in general, and I felt especially bored with this girl's particular speech, so I held up the one minute card when she still had seven minutes left. I got in trouble, but I didn't care. I said it was an accident. I smiled, thinking that I should hold up the one minute card, and then I realized that these were pussy minutes we were wasting with the cops, so I answered, "I promised my father that I'd finish it by today, uh, yesterday, Friday, and he's pretty strict about that stuff.

If I don't get it finished by the time he wakes up I probably won't get to use his car for a month, and I have this new girlfriend who I really think will put out if I can get her alone at the beach at night."

The cop sitting closest to us turned to his partner and asked, "Did you hear that?" He turned back to me and said, "I sure hope she's not my daughter."

Graham answered, "I doubt it, sir. She doesn't look at all like you. And besides, I've met her father."

The cop laughed and shook his head. Then he took our names and addresses and said, "We'll be driving back by here in a little while and I hope you two are gone."

"We will be, sir," Graham answered. "We'll be working hard to get Larry's work done." We had given the cops fake names and addresses, I guess on principle. As the cop car drove away and we started walking again Graham said, "That was a damn good line you gave him. Where did you come up with that?"

"I know it was good. I think it was just inspiration." After a moment I asked, "Do you think that was a sin?"

"Sure," Graham answered. "Lying to cops? That's definitely a sin."

I hadn't yet told Graham about my lists, but I was thinking about what I was going to add to my lists and I said, "I don't know if it's really a sin. What right did they have to ask us those questions? None. And what did we hurt by telling them lies? Nothing. We have something important to do and we have to do what's necessary to get there. No, I don't think it's a sin."

"It's definitely a sin," Graham answered. "Lying is a sin, period. You might not like it, but you have to face the fact on that. Lying is a sin, period. You can't change that."

"Well, maybe under your religion it's a sin. But in the grander scheme . . ."

"What do you mean, 'the grander scheme'?" Graham laughed. "Religion tells you what's a sin. Without religion, there aren't any sins."

"You're wrong. There's right and there's wrong . . ."

"And then there are sins," Graham interrupted. "If you believe in that religion that can't eat cows and you eat a burger, it's a sin, right? I'm sure they have sins in that religion."

"Hmmm," I answered. I didn't like it when Graham was right. And I wasn't sure if what Graham had said affected my list of sins. I decided to get stoned sometime to think about it.

We carried the ladder into Connie's back yard and set it on the grass. I looked up at Connie's bedroom window and could see a faint light through the drawn shades. "Do you think she's still up?" Graham asked.

"Maybe. With Connie you never know."

Graham stood staring at the window and he sighed. "You're lucky," he said. We unfolded the ladder on the grass so that we could hook it into the full twenty feet. In the dark with the rain still falling it was difficult to swing the ladder up, but after struggling a while we managed to stand it on end and set it gently against Connie's house. We had to pull the bottom of the ladder out a little so that the top rested just below Connie's window. "Good luck," Graham said.

"Thanks, but what are you going to do?" I was shivering from the cold and the water that had been slowly soaking me under the raincoat. In the struggle with the ladder I had gotten a lot wetter, and I assumed that Graham was as wet as I was.

"I'll go wait over in the shed." Graham nodded his head toward a little tool shed in the corner of the yard. I felt bad for Graham having to wait out in the cold, and I appreciated what a good friend he was.

"I won't take too long," I said.

"That's okay. And maybe you can think about what we talked about with Connie. Maybe you can ask her."

I climbed tentatively up the ladder, a little afraid that I would slip and fall or that Connie's parents or the police would see me. I wondered whether Connie would still be awake and how I would get into her room. When I reached the top of the ladder I could see that the screen was hanging loose and the window was open a few inches. The screen was attached at the top and I pulled the bottom away from the window and leaned it against the back of my head while I lifted the window. The drapes were closed so I pulled them apart and put my head in the room. Connie lay asleep on her bed. The light was from a small lamp on her bed stand. Connie was sleeping on her stomach and I watched the slow rise and fall of the blankets with her breathing. It seemed ridiculous for me to wake up Connie at this hour, but I glanced back at the little tool shed where Graham sat and I realized that after all Graham and I had gone through to get the ladder here I had to go in. I wasn't sure what to do because I was already dripping water into the room, but I was afraid to call out, so I climbed through the window, bringing a lot of water with me. I took off the raincoat and dropped it on the carpet under the window and walked slowly over to Connie's bed. I was short of breath from being anxious about seeing her again. I stood over the bed watching Connie, glancing at her door every once in a while. Connie lay with her face turned away from me and finally I set my hand on her cheek. I didn't realize how cold my hand was and Connie jerked her face and woke up.

She rolled onto her back, with her eyes only a little open, and she asked, "Ben?"

"Hi, Connie."

"What time is it?"

"A cop just told me it's two o'clock in the morning."

Connie was a little more awake and she said, "Close the window and take off your clothes and get in bed with me."

"I'm getting your room all wet. It's pouring out there. And what about your parents?"

"Come to bed, Ben."

I closed the window, wondering whether Graham was watching the window and could see what I was doing. Then I laid my clothes on the floor so I would be able to get them on quickly if I had to. I got into bed and Connie turned to me. "Ooooh! You're cold!" Connie leaned away from me and turned off the light. "If my parents peek in here and see the light off they'll go away." We lay there for a while, just holding each other. I could tell that Connie was exhausted and about to fall back asleep, but she wanted me to make love to her, so I carefully lifted myself on top of her. She kissed me a few times and then just lay there, but when I finished she said, "Thanks. I've missed that," and she kissed me again, lightly on the lips, and I wasn't exactly sure what she meant since she was practically asleep the whole time. She lay in my arms and after a few minutes she fell completely asleep, even snoring lightly. I lay with Connie for a while, all the time remembering Graham outside and realizing that it would soon be morning. I got too nervous to lay still any longer and looked around the room and saw that there was a lit clock on Connie's night stand that said 5:20. I figured that I must have fallen asleep for a while myself and I quickly slipped away from Connie and got dressed. It was hard to get my clothes on because they were still wet and I was thankful that Connie's parents hadn't come into the room. I kissed Connie before I left.

It was already dawn outside and it was still raining, although only lightly now. I tossed my raincoat out the window and climbed quickly down the ladder, certain that someone would see me. I was also certain that Graham had left and that I would have to try to carry the ladder myself, but Graham was sleeping in the shed, huddled in a corner. I woke him up and he stumbled sleepily out of the shed and we pulled down the ladder and carried it away from Connie's house, walking as quickly as we could, but still stumbling in our exhaustion. Neither of us said a word until we got the ladder back to Graham's garage and then I said, "Thanks, Graham. Let's get some sleep and I'll see you later . . ."

"What did Connie say?" Graham interrupted.

"She didn't say much. I'll tell you later." I was tired and cold and wet and I wanted to go home to bed, but Graham wouldn't let me.

"Just tell me what happened and what she said. I'm just curious. You were up there a long time. Did you kiss her? Did you *screw* her? You didn't screw her, did you?"

"She just wanted me to . . . to make love to her, and then she fell asleep."

"She did?" Graham looked away from me and he seemed a little sad. "How was it?" he asked, tentatively, watching me closely.

"It was good . . . it was okay. It was nice to see her."

Graham sighed. "Yeah, let's talk about it later. Did you ask her about me? What do you think about that?"

"There wasn't time for us to talk about it. She slept most of the time."

When I finally awoke late in the afternoon I looked out the window and saw that the rain had stopped, although everything outside was still wet. I rolled onto my back and lay in bed for a while, happy that it was the weekend and there was no school. I didn't think about anything although everything kept trying to run through my mind. I figured that I was getting numb to life because I wasn't going crazy with all that was happening around me.

That night when Graham and I met in front of his house we did our secret handshake and Graham told me that he had set our agenda for the night. "We'll eat, I'll see Connie and see if I can get her parents to let her go out of the house with me. And then maybe you can visit Connie tonight. We'll get the ladder again."

"You think Connie's parents will let her go out with you?"

"They like me. They think I'm a clean-cut kid, I guess because my hair is a lot shorter than yours and I didn't get their daughter pregnant." I still had not cut my hair since the beginning of summer and it had grown down to my shoulders. Graham's parents wouldn't let him grow his hair past his ears.

We walked to Betty's and Graham asked, "Did you think any more about what we talked about with Connie? We have to settle this, you know. I mean, she's dying."

I had been thinking a lot about what Graham had asked the night before, and I didn't know what to answer. I didn't know how I felt about it and I didn't know if it was right or wrong, whether I would betray Connie if I agreed. "You love Connie, right?" I asked.

"Yes, I do love her."

"Well, so do I."

Graham said, "She won't be able to have another boyfriend after you, the way most people do. She has to have them all at once."

"I know . . ."

"And after she's gone, you'll have other girlfriends," Graham interrupted. "You know you will. You won't be a monk or something for the rest of your life. But she won't have any other chances."

"I know that. But having a lot of boyfriends isn't everything. She's having a baby and that's important to her. Besides, it's better to have one real love than to screw a bunch of people."

"Then it's better to have *two* real loves."

"If she wants to."

"That's right, if she wants to."

"Okay," I said, "if we both love her, then she should decide. If she wants to have two boyfriends, then it's okay with me—if you *really* love her."

We had arrived at Betty's and Graham smiled and held out his hand for me to shake, in the regular way and not with our secret handshake. "Let's eat and then I'm going over there to talk to her. I think that *I* should talk to her first, not you the way I thought before. I have to tell her how I feel, either way. Is that okay?"

"It's okay."

While we ate Graham made me tell him in detail about the night before with Connie. I wasn't sure what to tell him and what would be a betrayal of Connie. I thought about how Graham had helped Connie and me, how he had seen all of our letters, even helped me write them, and how he loved Connie. Finally I told him, "Her boobs are bigger, definitely bigger, and I think she's sort of heavier with the baby, but it was mostly dark and I couldn't even see her well."

Graham nodded as I talked, and he sighed when I finished. "I want to hear, but I don't want to hear," he said. "Do you think Connie loves me, too?"

That seemed like a crazy question for Graham to be asking me, but I answered, "I don't know. You'll have to ask her."

For some reason Connie's parents let Connie go out with Graham, although it was only for a couple of hours. I was happy that I was going to see Connie, but I was a little irritated because

I was the baby's father, after all, and I had loved her all this time, and she couldn't go out with me. Graham got his father's car for the night and the plan was for Graham and Connie to pick me up at a corner we had selected about a half mile from our homes, where we were certain that no one would see us.

I walked to our meeting place while Graham went to Connie's. I passed the Kuchers' house and was tempted to slip into the backyard to see if Mrs. Kucher was up to anything interesting, but I decided against it, mostly because I didn't want to be late for Graham and Connie, but also because I was doubtful that there would be anything to watch. In all the times I had stopped there since watching Mrs. Kucher that first time, I had never seen anything interesting, although each time for a while I was certain I would. I even brought my camera once or twice, thinking that I might take some more pictures. But life is like that, things just seem to happen or not. It amazed me about the way life and what you get to experience in life is so much a matter of luck and timing. I wondered about all of the things I had already missed by a few minutes, or by making the wrong choice about even an insignificant thing. I put it on my list of sins each time I went to watch Mrs. Kucher, even though I didn't see anything.

The rain from last night had stopped early in the day, but the ground had still not dried completely and it was cold from the end of the storm that was passing through. I walked quickly to stay warm, kicking up the wet leaves on the sidewalk that had been strewn around by the wind and rain. When I reached the corner where I was to meet Graham and Connie they were not yet there, so I leaned for a while against a light post, then sat on the curb for a while, and then walked back and forth down the street ten or twenty yards because I was getting cold. I didn't wear a watch, but I knew they were pretty late, and I wondered what had happened. I walked back and forth until I got bored, and then I walked from one corner of the block to the other and finally, after I had waited an hour or more, I walked back home.

Graham finally came by my house later that night. When he saw me he asked, "Where were you? We looked all around for you."

"I was where we were supposed to meet. I waited for an hour."

"You were on the corner at Brooks and Whisper?"

That wasn't the corner we had agreed to and I looked at Graham for a few moments. He was squirming around so I knew he was lying. "That's not where we agreed," I said.

"Yes it was. Brooks and Whisper."

I wasn't sure what was going on with Graham. I thought that maybe he was so in love with Connie that he was stabbing his best friend in the back. But I said, "I guess we messed up. What happened with you and Connie? How is she?"

"She's fine. We had a good talk and . . ." Graham hesitated.

"What?"

Graham pursed his lips. "It's sort of complicated." It took Graham a long time to tell me what he and Connie had discussed. We walked quickly because it was late and the night was cold, and Graham explained over and over about how he loved Connie and how she should have more than one boyfriend during her life and all the other things he had been telling me before. He was agitated as he talked, moving his arms around and talking loudly. Finally I got annoyed and said, "So just tell me what happened with you and Connie. You told me all that stuff before."

"Okay. I told Connie I love her, because I do and I had to tell her. And I told her she should have another boyfriend before she dies. That's only fair. I told her that you thought it was a good idea too."

"So you two just drove around looking for me, talking about that? What did Connie say about that? Does she want another boyfriend?"

"Yes, she does."

"Instead of me?"

"No, I don't think so. I think she just wants two boyfriends. She's dying, you know."

"You don't have to keep telling me that."

"And I kissed her," Graham said. He *had* to tell me that, I could tell by the way he sort of forced it out. I didn't answer and Graham said, "I *really* kissed her, with our mouths open and everything." We were walking and Graham was looking away from me as he spoke.

"She wanted you to kiss her?" I asked, calmly, although I felt this rage of jealousy surging through me.

"She liked it," Graham answered.

"How do you know that?"

"I could just tell." Graham was looking at me, now, and I was looking at him, trying to figure out what I felt. My jealousy seemed to be dissolving a little.

"What else did you do?" I asked. "Did you feel her up or something."

"No, although I think I could have. I wanted to talk to you first."

I could feel my jealousy dissolving almost to nothing, but I was angry with Graham. "Yeah, well it's my baby in there, you know."

"I know," Graham answered. "But it's still *her* body."

"What does that mean?" I asked.

"I don't know. It's just what Connie said when I told her I felt sort of bad kissing her because she was pregnant with your baby."

"Well, I guess that's true—it is her body," I said, and I was reminded of Franny. It made me angry that I had so little control over anything. I felt like telling Graham that he could have Connie and I didn't want to see her anymore, anyway, but I couldn't say that. "Tell me one thing," I said, "and tell me the truth. Did you look for me tonight or did you just drive around with Connie and purposely go to the wrong corner."

"What . . .?" Graham began, as though he was going to protest what I said, but then he stopped himself. "Okay, that's what I did. How did you know?"

"I just figured. Why did you do it?"

Graham was watching the ground in front of him, shaking his head. "I don't know, Ben." He sighed. "I feel bad about it, in fact I was going to add it to my sin list. But I just couldn't help it—I just wanted to talk to Connie. I just *had* to."

"Did you put kissing Connie on your sin list?"

Graham looked slowly over at me, puzzled. "Kissing isn't a sin, is it? No, it can't be a sin."

"Even if you're kissing a girl who's pregnant with someone else's baby? Isn't that sort of like adultery or something?"

"I don't think so. You and Connie aren't married or anything. In fact, it's *your* sin for screwing . . . making love . . . screwing Connie in the first place."

"Yeah? So what about the part where you stabbed your best friend in the back?"

Graham sort of frowned and nodded his head. "That definitely goes on the list. Although you *did* say it was okay with you if Connie wanted it," he said.

"Jesus, Graham. You should have told me first and you shouldn't have left me waiting out there . . ."

"I'm sorry, Ben. I won't do it again, I promise."

CHAPTER ELEVEN

At first I wasn't all that sure that we would ever get around to finding the poor person. For a couple of days Graham talked about it all the time, but I figured he'd lose interest soon enough. I thought that maybe he would go to confession and feel better about having the stolen money and then decide to buy a car in Connie's honor, or something like that. But more days passed and Graham wouldn't stop talking about his love for Connie and his suffering project and finding this poor person, until finally it became a mission in our lives to do this for Connie.

Only it wasn't all that easy to find a poor area, much less a poor person. We looked up on the map for the areas that people always referred to as being the poor areas and we drove to quite a few of them. Graham and I agreed that before we decided on any particular poor area we would visit enough of them to be sure that we picked the right one. After school each day, Graham drove us in his parent's car to a poor area, parked and walked around. Graham carried a small notebook and a pen to take notes on suffering. Some of the areas didn't seem too bad—I guess they were poor because the houses were tiny and the cars were mostly old. Other areas were dirtier with trash strewn and piled in vacant lots and there were bars on peoples' windows and graffiti on a lot of the walls. But there were still plenty of average people carrying on with their lives. Graham always had at least a little luck finding suffering in peoples' faces in each area. It was finding the poor person to give the money to that was causing us a problem.

After a week we found the perfect poor area. It was different from any place we had ever been. The buildings were built right up to the sidewalk, mostly four or five stories high, old brick structures that were clearly decaying right before us. Some of the buildings were only apartments and others had small businesses on the first floor and apartments upstairs. Windows were dirty and cracked or broken out entirely and were covered only rarely by screens that were torn and dirty. Old doors with rusted locks and hinges were warped and worn. There was trash everywhere, strewn all along the street and pressed into the gutters and the ground and the corners of buildings so that it felt as though the trash was part of everything and could never be cleaned up. Old, barely running and broken-down cars were scattered along the streets. Laundry hung out of apartment windows. And there were people everywhere—old people, women with dirty little children, drunks and drug addicts—all walking along the streets, or sitting at bus stops, in doorways, on the curb, even leaning on the window sills above us. There were veterans with one leg asking for money and women we thought were prostitutes getting ready for the evening.

As we drove through the area Graham looked over at me and said, "This is the place. I can feel it. This is definitely the best poor area we've seen. There's suffering everywhere and the poor person we need is out there somewhere. I know it."

"I don't think this place is very safe," I said. "We're going to get robbed or mugged or something." I had been a little uncomfortable in some of the other areas, but I was extremely uncomfortable about this place.

"This is for Connie," Graham reminded me. "This is something we *have* to do."

I was becoming annoyed that Graham had made this whole thing into such an important mission for us. I mean, it was a good idea and everything, in a romantic sort of way, but it was starting to take a lot of time and it didn't make that much sense to be putting ourselves in danger. Graham was at least using it for school. I was just wasting time. Except that Connie was *my* girl-friend and *I* had made her pregnant and everything, so I couldn't do anything but go along with looking for this poor person. I got to thinking that it might be a good idea if Graham became another boyfriend of Connie's and he could do this on his own and I wouldn't have to feel bad because it would be Graham's own mission for being Connie's second boyfriend. Then it occurred to me that maybe Graham was doing all of this to pressure me into helping him become Connie's other boyfriend.

"Well, then let's do it," I said. "We should be able to find a good poor person around here." I figured that it would take us just a few minutes to find a poor person who we could give the money to and then Graham would be on his own as far as any remaining suffering went.

We parked the car and walked tentatively along the street. It seemed to me that people were looking at us strangely, but Graham didn't think so. "We fit in here perfectly," he said. "This is where the downtrodden masses live." He looked around and waved his arm to point out the downtrodden masses.

"We're not exactly downtrodden," I answered.

"Yes we are. At least *I* am. I'm downtrodden in love. The woman I love has cancer, is pregnant with someone else's child and I can't even kiss her, much less do anything else with her without . . ."

"Forget it, Graham," I interrupted. "You're just downtrodden in brains. Besides, these people can't go home to get away from here, like we can. How would you like to live here?"

"Great art is derived from great suffering," Graham answered.

I looked at Graham dubiously. "Where did you get that from?"

"I think from one of my teachers—but it's still true. You need to suffer to really create. All the great writers and painters suffered. That's why I don't mind suffering."

"So you're going to be a student of human suffering?" I asked and I remembered talking to Franny at the little clothing store in the canyon and telling her that I was a student of the human condition, and it made me smile. Then I was sorry I had given the idea to Graham, who immediately took it for himself.

"Maybe I am a student of human suffering. Maybe that's what true art is about."

"Are you sure you're not talking about your religion again?" I asked.

"No, I'm talking about creating. The creative spirit. The creative spirit loves to suffer. It *needs* to suffer to create."

"Well, I don't see you suffering that much. I think you're going to have to be a lawyer or something." I laughed.

"You can suffer and it doesn't necessarily show," Graham answered. "You can suffer inside—from love, for example. I'm always suffering from love."

"Then what is your creative spirit going to create?" I asked. I was going to add, "Other than lies about what you and Connie have been doing," but I decided against it.

"Time will tell. Maybe it depends on how much I suffer."

We walked slowly around the area for over an hour, but we couldn't seem to find anyone to give the money to. We approached a bent old woman bundled in an old tattered overcoat and wearing a grey, torn flannel cap pulled down over her head and almost to her eyes. She carried an overfull paper bag which she held close to her chest. She walked, stopping and starting down the street, twitching her head and talking to herself. Graham saw her and said, "Well, we found the poor person." He walked up to the woman and said, "Excuse me, ma'am," and he tapped her lightly on her shoulder. The old woman looked slowly over at Graham, just moving her head, until she was looking at his face. "Excuse me . . ." Graham began, intending to tell the woman about Connie and how this woman was about to receive six hundred-fifty dollars. But the woman went crazy. She interrupted Graham, screaming at the top of her old lungs and hitting Graham with her left hand while she still clutched tightly to the bag with her other hand. Graham jumped back, stunned, but the woman pursued him, hitting him with her hand and still screaming, until Graham had to turn and run half a block, and then the woman said something to herself and continued walking down the street.

I wasn't sure whether to laugh or run. I was afraid the police might come after Graham or that some of the local people might attack Graham and me, thinking that we were trying to hurt that old woman. But no one did anything. A few people looked over when the old woman was screaming, but once she quieted down everything was back to normal, as though nothing had happened. Graham walked slowly over to me, carefully watching the old woman walk on down the street. "Jesus Christ!" he said.

"You're not kidding," I answered. "Was she suffering, or just crazy? Are you going to write a poem about her?"

Graham didn't answer. He had never showed me his poems or told me anything about them, even when I asked. I considered telling Graham about The Poet up on the bluff, but I didn't. I kept trying to figure out the difference between Graham looking for poems in suffering peoples' faces and The Poet looking for poems by sitting under a tree. In the end it sort of bothered me that nothing seemed to be special.

Now that we had found the place to find our poor person, we kept returning each day after school. Only it turned out not to be that easy to find the *right* poor person. A number of times we saw someone who we thought would be a good poor person, but we were a little bit wary after that incident with the old woman and each time we picked out a poor person he or she somehow disappeared before we could figure out what to do. We thought of putting the money in the pocket of a needy person sleeping on the sidewalk, but we both felt pretty strongly that unless we could explain to the person about Connie we wouldn't accomplish what we needed to accomplish. And it became obvious right away that we couldn't just walk up to some person, hand over six hundred-fifty dollars and say, "This is in honor of Connie, who's dying of cancer."

After a few days I began to feel comfortable walking along those dirty, decaying streets, among all those downtrodden people, as Graham referred to them. It reminded me a little of how easily I got used to being in the sewers. We walked slowly along the streets, not even stepping over the trash anymore. We were working on momentum and were now consumed with Graham's mission. It was something that we were going to stay with it until it was finished. I don't know whether Graham's momentum was really coming from his heart, like he kept saying, or was like mine, which was that feeling where you're running a race and you're most of the way through and you know your body's suffering but it doesn't matter because at that point there's nothing left to do but finish the race. In either event, we just kept going down to that poor area, searching for that perfect poor person.

We were walking down the street and a young man stepped out of one of the buildings in front of us. He looked to be about twenty, and fairly average, except that he was dirty and all agitated. "Hey, man, what's the word?" he said to Graham and me.

"Nothing," Graham answered.

"You lookin' to buy?" he asked.

"To buy what?" I asked.

The guy twitched his head and shrugged his head. "You just call for it and I got it." He twitched his head again. "What'd you need?"

"You mean like pot or something?" I asked. Graham looked over at me.

The guy twitched again. "I got pot, I got ludes, I got white crosses, I got coke . . ."

"Cocaine?" I asked in a whisper. Graham was staring at me.

"Sure."

"How much?" I asked.

The guy shrugged his shoulders. "A Ben." I was taken aback that he would know my name and Graham was shocked. "A Ben for a gram. That's market. That stuff's hard to get, but I got the best."

"A Ben?" I asked and the guy could tell I didn't know what he was talking about.

"You don't know a Ben? A Benjamin Franklin. A 'C' note."

"A hundred dollars," Graham said to me. "That's a 'C' note."

I had been wondering for a long time how I could get some cocaine. After it got Franny so excited that time I wanted to try it on Vickie and see if it got her in the right mood. Only I was nervous about buying cocaine, especially out here. "What do you think?" I asked Graham.

"About what?"

"Okay, I'll take some," I said.

"You're going to buy some cocaine?" Graham asked in a loud whisper, and he was obviously stunned.

"He knows the best," the guy said to Graham. "I bet he has a lady that gets hot on this stuff." The guy was wearing a heavy army jacket with a peace sign sewn onto one of the pockets. He opened the jacket and out of one of the inside pockets he brought out a little bottle like the one Carl had up in Santa Barbara, except that it was clear instead of dark. "It's a full gram. I don't chince on this stuff. It's just not my style, man."

I turned to Graham and whispered to him, "I need a hundred dollars. I'll pay you back later."

"Are you crazy?"

"Just give it to me." Graham turned away from the guy and pulled a hundred dollar bill out of his pocket, which he handed to me. I gave the hundred dollars to the guy with the cocaine and he handed me the little bottle.

"Enjoy it, man," he said, and he disappeared quickly into the building.

"Let's get out of here," I said, because I was nervous having the cocaine on me, and we started down the street.

That was when we met Arthur. We didn't know at first that he was our poor person. He was blind and he stood on a corner holding out a little metal cup, begging for money. He looked incredibly poor, with the most tattered clothes you could imagine. He wore round, black, blind-man-type glasses, had a ragged beard and his dark brown hair was stringy and hung below his ears.

As we approached Arthur he said, "You got money for that pusher low-life but nothin' for a blind Vietnam vet like me that lost his eyes?"

We stopped in front of the blind man and he was staring straight ahead. "How did you know?" Graham asked.

"Maybe I don't see, but I still got my ears and they hear real good. I could get you better stuff than that low-life you were dealin' with. When you lose your eyes, you do what you have to do."

Graham and I looked at each other. After a few moments Graham took twenty dollars out of his pocket and put it in the blind man's metal cup. "That's from Connie," Graham said.

"Well tell Connie that Arthur appreciates her support."

When we were in the car Graham was all excited. "I can't believe you bought that cocaine!" he said. "What, are you a drug addict or something?"

I still couldn't tell Graham about Franny or Vickie, because of Connie, so I said, "I tried it once with Jackson. That and pot."

"You smoked pot *and* did cocaine? What else didn't you tell me about?" Graham was obviously offended.

"I was just waiting for the right time." Graham made me tell him what it was like to be on cocaine, and I had to tell him that the cocaine I just bought was for him to try with me. I figured we wouldn't use that much and there would be plenty left for Vickie.

A couple of days later was Saturday and I woke up late. As I was eating breakfast the mailman slipped the mail through the slot in our front door. I never got any mail, but I always looked through it anyway. I got up from my breakfast to pick up the mail, and there was a letter for me. I couldn't find a return address on either side of the envelope and I didn't recognize the handwriting. I thought for a moment it might be from Jackson, except that it looked like a girl's writing. I was carrying the letter back into the kitchen when I thought to look at the postmark, which said Philadelphia. I would have expected my heart to skip a beat or something, but it just kept beating away without taking notice. I put the letter in my back pocket and finished my breakfast.

I took the letter up to my bedroom and closed the door behind me, but I just stood in the middle of the room, holding the letter in my hand, looking all around the room, until I decided to go outside. I lay under the tree in my front yard when I opened the letter. It was a cold autumn day and I was a little uncomfortable, but I couldn't think of any other place to open it. If Jackson were around I could get stoned with him and open it in the stoning room, but Jackson wasn't around.

It wasn't much of a letter. It went like this:

Dear Ben,

I hope that everything is well with you. I know it's been a long time since you've heard from me and I'm sorry about that. I'm also sorry for the way I left last August. Please try to understand.

I decided not to keep the baby. I'm too young to have my life determined for me that way. I also decided to go back to school. I didn't know it, but my parents got a year extension to my acceptance and I started college in September. I'm enjoying it and I'm thinking about going to medical school. I also met someone who I really care for, a law student, and we're living together.

Please don't try to contact me. That sounds callous, but it's not meant to be. We just don't have anything in common and there would be no point in our keeping in touch. I was going through something during the past year, but that's over. If you had some good times over the summer, just remember those. Take care and the best in everything you do, and in your life.

Love,
Fran

Like I said, it wasn't much of a letter. I re-read it a few times and it didn't get any better. At least she signed it, "Love, Fran," even if she didn't mean it. I hid the letter in my bedroom and I went over to visit Graham.

On Monday I was still thinking about Franny's letter and I decided to skip school and go to the canyon to buy another bead, a silver bead for the leather cord Franny had given me that I still wore around my neck. I couldn't really afford to miss school because I was struggling already, but I just didn't have it in me to go to school.

I left for school as usual, but hid my books under a bush and hitchhiked to the beach. When I got to the beach I was feeling melancholy. It was a cold autumn morning. I stood for a long time in the park at the top of the cliff above the highway, looking both directions along the beach and out at the ocean. I stood near the top of the wall I had walked on during the summer and I glanced briefly beyond the wall at the cliff below.

I hadn't been to the beach for a month or two, but it seemed a much longer time than that. The beach was different now, and I stood for a long time wondering what had changed to make it so different, until I realized that it was only that summer was long past. There were few people on the beach and I knew that the number would not increase much as the day wore on. There would be only the few year-round beach people and the tourists and the bored people who thought they'd try the beach today, the people like myself. There was a gentle breeze blowing in from the ocean that mixed with the early morning and made me almost cold, even in my jacket. I thought that if I lay on my back on the sand, even at this early morning hour of a winter's day, that I should be warm, that the sun should still have the strength to soak some warmth into my skin. I remembered last summer and the feeling of having the sun's rays beating down on me and the breeze blowing over and around me. But I doubted that I could truly be warm lying in the sun this morning and I didn't feel like going down to the sand, anyway. I watched the few people who were down there, large insects, and I thought that I could tell a couple of women from among the men who were jogging or walking along the wet sand.

I decided to go fishing in the morning and out to the canyon in the afternoon. I didn't know what time it was so I ran the half mile or so along the park and out to the end of the pier. I got there in just enough time to rent a fishing pole and buy some hooks and weights before the boat left.

It was Monday in late November so there were few people on

the boat. The breeze that was mild and cool when we were docked was much stronger after the boat left the pier and picked up speed. I stood for a few minutes with my hands in my pockets, leaning my back against the railing, watching the waves behind the boat and catching a little spray on my face from the boat pounding through the small waves, but soon I went into the cabin to escape the cold.

The fishermen were playing poker inside the cabin and I leaned against the door jam and watched, being careful not to stand where I could see anybody's cards. Fishermen playing poker get quite annoyed if people see their cards, particularly if they happen to be losing at the time. But I wasn't much interested in the game, anyway. I was trying to stay warm and I was thinking about Franny, who I couldn't get off of my mind since her letter came. I took the letter out of my pocket and read it for the tenth or twelfth time, and it still wasn't much of a letter. I knew that life carried on and I was learning how it worked with love and all of that. But I kept thinking that there was one thing that sort of bothered me about everything that had happened with Franny.

What bothered me was that when I got back to the canyon the day after Franny told me she was pregnant, she was already gone. She hadn't left a message for me or anything, and she had even told Sheryl not to give me her address or phone number in Philadelphia. That's what bothered me. The letter made up for it a little, but not enough.

I stepped out of the boat's cabin into the cold, misty breeze. There was one thing that made it easier about Franny. That was the pictures I had of her—I sort of felt that if I had the pictures I still had a little of Franny. Maybe she didn't love me or even care for me, and so in a way I really didn't have anything, but I had the memory of her and I had the pictures, and so in a way I did have something, and I could live with that.

I'm not exactly sure how it came about that I got the pictures. I was just lucky that I had my camera with me at the right time. It was a night when we were stoned at Sheryl's house. I had brought my camera to take some pictures of Franny and the house and the little bridge—just the usual pictures of Franny sitting around and that kind of thing. I took a few pictures while we were in the living room and then Franny wanted me to follow her into her bedroom. I closed the door and Franny stood in the middle of her small room and dropped off her dress and said, "Why don't you take some more pictures?" She was only wearing underpants.

"Okay, sure," I said, and I couldn't believe it, except that we were both stoned and at the time I still figured anything could happen when you're stoned. I thought that I was lucky I had brought my camera, the way it was lucky I had my camera when I saw Mrs. Kucher that time, and it sort of evened up for the time I forgot to bring extra film when I went back to get Vickie in the sewers. I took a picture of Franny standing with her hands above her head, and as the flash disappeared from the room Franny ran into the bathroom, still wearing only her underpants. She returned a couple of minutes later and her hair was brushed out and I could tell that she had washed her face because her forehead wasn't at all greasy and her hair was a little wet around the sides of her face. I finished the roll of film that was in the camera, took another full roll of thirty-six pictures and then half of another roll. Franny took off her underpants and I took pictures like you'd never dream you would get a chance to take. Franny kept getting more and more excited as I took the pictures and she kept making up better and better poses, doing things I wouldn't have had the nerve to ask her to do. Only she sobered up a little before I left and she made me destroy the film. So I took the film out of the camera and exposed it. Franny knew that I had changed the film, but she only remembered one of the changes, so I exposed the first roll with the pictures we had taken in the living room and only a few pictures in the bedroom, and she didn't know the difference.

Unfortunately, after taking the pictures of Franny I ran into a small problem. When I got home that afternoon after Franny told me she was pregnant, I went straight up to my room to get the roll of film with her pictures. I was pretty angry at Franny and had decided that I would have the film developed. I didn't care if someone else happened to see the pictures—Franny had let me take the pictures of her own free will and now she was leaving me. But when I looked on my bookcase, where I had put the film, I found that the three rolls of film—of Franny and Vickie and Mrs. Kucher—were mixed together. They were the same kind of film with the same number of pictures and I couldn't tell which roll was which. One of the rolls had a scratch on the metal casing and I thought that it might be the roll with the pictures of Vickie in the sewers. Another roll had a very slight dent in the casing and I thought that I remembered seeing that dent when I put the film away that night after the incident with Mrs. Kucher. But I wasn't completely sure and I couldn't take the chance. I looked at those three rolls of film quite a lot on and off all afternoon and during the next couple of days, but I got less and less sure. Finally I gave it up.

In the end it didn't really bother me that the film was all mixed up. I figured that some day I would get all the photo equipment I would need to develop all three rolls of film myself, and I would have the pictures. Of course by then Franny would probably be an old married woman with children and she wouldn't have any idea that I was looking for the first time at pictures of her naked back in the canyon.

It wasn't much of a day for fishing. I caught a couple of mackerel, a sculpin and a small bass and I gave the fish away to someone on the boat who wanted to eat them. I think I was still on the boat when I got the idea of visiting Franny in Philadelphia, but it wasn't until I got into the canyon that I actually decided to go. I was standing in front of the old house that used to be the Fifth Quatrain, the shop where I had sat in the black light room and listened to music and dreamed of meeting a girl and living in the canyon, and where I had bought my beads. The shop was out of business and once again it was an old house, overgrown with bushes and weeds. There was a "For Sale" sign among the weeds. I just stood there in front of that old house. I was angry and I was sad. I had missed the whole goddamn thing, just like Franny said.

So I couldn't buy the silver bead and I couldn't believe that so much could change in a few months. That's when I decided that I would definitely visit Franny. I wasn't really sure when I'd go, what with Connie and all, but I figured the right time would come.

In the meantime I went to visit Vickie. I had a tendency to do that when I had the time and nothing else to do, which wasn't all that often anymore. Only I could never seem to find Vickie at home. It was driving me crazy, especially since I finally had the cocaine. I was dying to get back to Vickie's on a Friday night, which was the night when I found her drunk and she showed me the rings on her nipples. But with school and Graham and Connie keeping track of me, I just couldn't manage it.

Today I brought the cocaine along, just in case. I knocked on Vickie's door for a long time and there was no answer. I turned the doorknob, just curious, and I was surprised that the door was unlocked.

A voice behind me said, "Aren't you a little young to be visiting *her*?" I turned and an older man was leaning up against the railing, watching me.

"What do you mean?" I asked.

"How old are you?"

"Seventeen," I lied.

"That's bullshit. Anyway, she's gone. Left two days ago. You a . . . client?"

"No . . . what do you mean?"

The man sniggered and shook his head. "Don't bullshit me. You can't bullshit a bullshitter."

"Vickie left?" I asked. "She moved out?"

"That's what I said."

I couldn't believe that Vickie had moved. "Where did she go?"

"You tell me."

My hand was just a few inches from the doorknob and I wanted like crazy to push the door open and look inside, to see if Vickie really had moved. I watched the man for a few moments and he just stood there. "Who are you?" I asked.

"Who are you to ask me questions?" he answered, squinting

his eyes. He was an older guy and he didn't move, so I wasn't worried, but I figured I'd just leave him alone.

I shrugged my shoulders and answered, "Just curious. Well, see you."

I walked out of the building and down the street. I sat on a curb and counted seven minutes to myself and then went back. I was getting agitated thinking about Vickie having moved and her apartment being open up there.

When I got back to Vickie's building I slipped around to a back entrance where I could look up at her apartment. The man wasn't anywhere in sight so I crept quietly up the stairs and over to the apartment. I stepped inside and closed the door quietly behind me. I stood with my back against the door for at least a minute, looking around the living room, expecting someone to have seen me and come knocking. But nothing happened so I locked the door.

I walked slowly into the room. Vickie had definitely moved out. The apartment was empty except for a broken kitchen chair and a lot of trash that was strewn around. You could see the dust and dirt on the carpet and walls where the couch and heavy chairs had been, and impressions in the carpet where the tables had stood. I walked into the bedroom and it was just as empty. I pictured Vickie lying on her bed, which was now only an outline of dust and trash. I stood where the bed had been. There were a couple of empty condom wrappers by my foot. They were covered with dust and had obviously been under the bed for a long time. For some reason that sort of bothered me. I kicked them with my foot.

I searched the apartment for clues. Except that I wasn't really sure what I was looking for. I found 57 cents in change on the floor. At first I didn't want it, because I didn't want to take any of Vickie's money. I finally picked it up and put it in my front left pocket where it wouldn't get mixed up with any other money.

I looked carefully through everything, but there wasn't much of anything but trash, except for one drawer in the kitchen that Vickie must have forgotten to pack where there were some forks and knives. I took one last quick look through the apartment, but it was the same. I paused at the front door, sad that all the traces of Vickie would be cleaned out soon. Someone else would live here, maybe an old man, who would sit around in his torn t-shirt and watch T.V., and have no idea he was plodding through a little shred of life where people had danced and gotten drunk and made love.

CHAPTER TWELVE

I was becoming a little annoyed at Connie. I knew that she was sick and all, and so I understood that she might not be happy all the time, but it was beginning to bother me. Late every night Graham and I would carry the ladder over to Connie's house and I would climb up to visit her, and Graham and I were both walking around exhausted all the time because of it. Connie was less affectionate and more distracted and generally seemed not to be that interested in me, and even though she was sick I couldn't figure out what was going on with her. I also couldn't figure out what was going on with Graham. He came with me every night and waited for me in the little shed and asked me how Connie was, and never complained about being out so late or being tired or anything. During the days he still visited Connie and a couple of times he took her out at night and the three of us drove around and I sat with my arm around Connie and we all three talked. Connie hadn't said anything for a long time about how she loved me and sometimes she made me leave right after I got to her bedroom because she was tired. I would climb up the ladder, talk to her for just a minute and climb back down, and Graham and I would carry the ladder back to Graham's house.

I think Connie was the one who actually brought up the idea of having Graham as another boyfriend. It was late one night and we sat whispering on her bed. Connie didn't want to make love or anything, she just wanted to talk. She asked, whispering, "Do you believe in God, Ben?"

"I don't know," I answered, "do you?" I knew what she would answer because people who are dying always believe in God.

"Yes, I do. How can you *not* believe in God? Graham believes in God."

"I didn't say I don't believe in God. I just don't know if I do."

"Don't you believe there's some meaning to everything?"

"Yes, there's definitely some meaning."

"Well?" Connie shrugged her shoulders. "What other meaning could there be?" There was irritation in her voice.

"What other meaning?" I looked around the room, looking for the other meaning, I guess. I wanted it to be last summer, hot and sunny and before everything got so difficult. Vickie and the little gold rings she wore on her nipples and between her legs crossed through my mind, the way she did now and then, at the least appropriate times, however much I tried to keep her out of my mind. "Maybe you're right," I said, finally, because it didn't seem right to talk to a person who was dying about the beauty of the bits of life that happened every day, about the excitement of discovering those wonderful little things that are hidden and have to be discovered, about the hope of making the world a little better tomorrow, that kind of thing. "No, you're definitely right." Guilt from thinking about Vickie pushed me a little further. I wondered briefly whether thinking about Vickie was a sin for my list, only because it made me feel guilty enough to lie to Connie. But I decided it wasn't.

I guess I took a little steam out of Connie when I agreed with her and we sat in silence until Connie asked, "Did Graham talk to you?"

"Talk to me about what?"

"Did he tell you that he loves me?"

I sighed to myself. Graham hadn't said much to me lately about being Connie's other boyfriend and I had been wondering a little what was going on. "Yeah, he told me."

"You didn't say anything to me about it. Why didn't you?"

"I thought that you and Graham needed to talk about it first."

Connie was silent for a few moments and then she said, "Well, I care for him also, Ben."

"I know. Graham told me," I answered and suddenly it was

slipping away between Connie and me, the way it had with Franny, and it made me a little frightened. I had been thinking for a while that maybe it was a good idea for Graham to be another boyfriend of Connie's, but I had just put off making the decision. At this moment, though, I wanted Connie to be mine alone, to love me and no one else. For a few moments I wanted desperately to change Connie's feelings about Graham, but only for a few moments. I was already becoming wise about love, and I knew that no amount of begging or whining or asking what I did wrong would change her feelings. I had thought a lot about this since Franny left me and it wasn't something I was necessarily happy about, but I knew that it was good, because it leaves real love as the one thing you can't change with words or politics or whatever. And I think that, underneath, I had been waiting for this and was a little relieved that Graham would share the responsibility for Connie.

"Okay," I said, calmly. "So what do you want to do? Do you not want to see me anymore?"

"No, I still care for you also."

"Do you want to make love with Graham? Is that what you want to do?"

My voice was getting a little louder and Connie raised her finger to her lips and said, "Shhhh." She hesitated, then asked, "Graham didn't tell you?"

"Didn't tell me . . . what?" I was afraid that I already knew what she was going to say.

"We made love already." I fell back on the bed. "Ben . . ." Connie began, but I interrupted her.

"When?"

"Graham came back a few times after you left . . ."

"With the ladder? He brought the ladder back by himself?"

"That's right. We thought of trying to sneak him through the front door, but I was too afraid because we'd have to walk past my parents' bedroom and they sleep with their door open in case I need them. And if they came in to check on me or something there wouldn't be any way to escape."

"Graham brought the ladder all the way back here by himself after I left?"

"That's right. He did it a few times."

"Jesus Christ!" I couldn't believe it, but I was also impressed with Graham's fortitude that he could drag the ladder all the way back by himself and then take it home again.

"Don't be mad at Graham, Ben. It's just that he loves me."

"Jesus Christ," I said again and I sat up. "So, what do you want? Just to see Graham? Just to make love to him?"

"Can I make love to both of you?" Connie asked.

"Jesus Christ!"

When I saw Graham outside I didn't know if I should punch him or what. It wasn't until we took the ladder down from the side of Connie's house that I asked, "You sure you don't want to just leave the ladder here so you don't have to carry it back later."

Graham frowned. "Connie told you?"

"Why didn't *you* tell me? Why did you *do* it?" I was very calm, I guess because it seemed almost impossible that Graham would have done what he did with Connie, and without my having any idea that he was doing it.

Graham started walking with the ladder, pulling me along. When we were on the sidewalk, away from Connie's house, he answered, "I don't know why I did it—but Connie wanted it, too. I guess it's just love, Ben. It's just love."

"It's not just love, Graham. What about friendship and loyalty? What about that?" I was starting to get angry and I could hear my voice rising. "I thought you were my best friend. Did you do this just to have another sin? You couldn't think of something else?"

"It wasn't so I could have another sin. There are lots of other things I could do if I wanted to sin. It was because I love Connie . . . and she loves me, too."

"Jesus Christ!" We walked in silence for a while, at either end of the ladder, through the cold of the late night. "Does she still love me?" I asked, finally.

"Yes, she does, I think. I'm sure she does. It's your baby she has."

"So what are we going to do? Connie said she wants to screw both of us."

"What's wrong with that? She's dying, you know."

"I know, I know. You always remind me."

"But it's important in this whole thing," Graham said.

"Well, maybe it is, but maybe it isn't. I'm not really sure. How do *you* feel about her screwing both of us."

"It's okay with me."

"It doesn't bother you to know that I'm up there screwing her?"

"It did before I was . . . you know, before, but now it doesn't. Does it bother you?"

"Yeah it does! Well, I think so . . . maybe not. I have to think about it."

"I'm supposed to take Connie out tomorrow night," Graham said. "I think we should all talk about it, then."

The next night Graham picked up Connie and then me, and the three of us ate dinner at Betty's and then drove around and talked about what we should do. We decided that Graham and I would alternate seeing Connie, but we would see her only every other night because it was too tiring for her and for us, so I would see Connie every fourth night. After we resolved everything Connie, who sat in the front seat between us, kissed me and then Graham, and she seemed very happy, especially for someone who was going to die. Then she told us that she could feel the baby move a little. I looked out the window and wondered about life. I decided that maybe this was free love the way it was with Franny and the other people in the canyon, except that it seemed to be working the wrong direction for me. I wondered whether Graham was really any friend at all and I thought about Jackson and wondered where he was right now, whether it was night or day, whether he was in battle someplace, whether he was being killed at that very moment. I thought that I should send him a letter about all of this and maybe he would write me back because I hadn't heard from him since that first letter, even though I had written him a couple of times. I looked forward to the two of us smoking marijuana in the stoning room and trying to figure it all out.

After we came to our agreement, my turn was first, and Connie was happier and more passionate with me than she had been for a while. She kissed me as I left and said, "I love you, Ben," and I said I loved her, too, and I didn't feel bad at all because I knew that Graham was coming in two days and everything didn't depend on me. A couple of nights later it was Graham's turn and I sat in the little shed waiting for him. I dressed warmly, knowing that I would be in the cold. Graham climbed the ladder and my heart started to pound and my breath got short, so that I thought I would have one of those attacks, but nothing happened. Instead I watched Graham climb through the window and I walked back to the shed and my heart slowed down and I got calm. I sat in the corner where I had found Graham sitting all those nights when I came down from Connie's room, and after a few minutes I felt a sense of peace. The night around me was cold and clear and dark and quiet. The moon was only a sliver over the hills and there were more stars in the sky than I could remember seeing. I could see Connie's window from where I sat and I knew that the faint light was from the lamp on Connie's bed stand. I leaned back into the corner and pulled up my legs to stay warm. I thought about last summer, about Franny and Jackson, and some of the other people I had met in the canyon. I thought about the beach and the girl who had danced on the table, whose breast had popped loose from her bikini as she danced, and I wondered a little where they all were right now. It seemed strange to me that I should be sitting where I was, waiting for Graham to come down from Connie's bedroom, and I wondered what the convolutions of life had done to the lives of some of those other people. Finally Graham came down and we carried the ladder back to his house, and we didn't say much of anything.

After that Connie seemed a little different to me. I knew that she was happy about having two boyfriends and all, but it seemed to be something more. Maybe it was that she seemed too happy and energetic for a person dying from cancer. I asked Graham a couple of times what he thought, but all he did was shrug his shoulders.

Graham and Connie and I worked our arrangement pretty

well for a while and I didn't really complain. It bothered me a little that I could be so callous about a girl who was dying and had my kid and who loved me, but I think I was more bothered by the betrayal than by losing Connie. I wanted life to move on and I didn't want to get bogged down with death.

Every other night about midnight Graham and I carried the ladder to Connie's and leaned it against her house and one or the other of us climbed the ladder to Connie's room. It was amazing that we could carry that huge ladder down quiet streets with houses all around, in the middle of the night, and never get stopped, except for that first night when the police stopped us in the rain.

One night Graham picked Connie up from her house and the two of them met me around the block in Graham's father's car. Connie sat with her arm around Graham's shoulders in the front seat and when I got in she kissed me and put her other arm around my shoulders. She was in a happy mood and she looked back and forth between the two of us and said, "My men."

"That's us," Graham answered, and I was relieved that Graham always seemed to be so enthusiastic with Connie because I was frankly getting a little tired of Connie and this whole relationship. It was on my list of sins that I felt that way about Connie with her being pregnant and dying of cancer and all, but I couldn't help the feelings. There was too much of the rest of life out there and Connie seemed to be holding me back from it. And, anyway, I was starting to feel like the odd man out the way Graham and Connie were getting so attached. Or maybe life just wasn't moving fast enough for me right now. Or maybe I was worrying myself too much about Vickie, who I couldn't get off my mind. Graham patted Connie's stomach, which was noticeable by now and asked, "So, how's the little one?"

"Good," Connie answered. Graham was getting pretty attached to the little baby in there and he told me once that he thought Connie would name it Graham, after him, since I had the honor of being the baby's real father and he needed some honor for being whatever he was in this whole thing.

"You know, I was thinking," Connie continued. "I love both of you and I get to make love to each of you . . . I was just thinking that it would be wonderful to make love to both of you at the same time." I didn't have to glance over because I could feel Graham look over at me.

"Where did you come up with that idea?" Graham asked.

"I don't know. Maybe from Ben." Connie looked at me. "You were always talking about the people in the canyon and free love and everything . . ."

"You came up with this idea?" Graham asked me.

"Not exactly," I answered. I guess that was free love, but it was definitely working in the wrong direction once again.

"You can think about it," Connie said. "I just thought that it would be something wonderful for all of us to share . . . I don't know for sure how long I might have and, like Graham said, I might not have that much opportunity to experience life." I could just imagine what Connie's mother would say if she found out about *this*.

"We'll think about it," Graham said, sounding a little encouraging, but I just shook my head to myself. That was one thing that was definitely *not* going to happen. I wasn't even sure how the process would work with the three of us.

The next day I got another letter from Jackson. It read:

Dear Ben,
Here I am, in the thick of it. They made me a medic and it's pretty cool, helping people and all, except that there are friends dying. Don't tell my old man, but if I get through this I may become a doc or something. Meantime I'm catching up like crazy. Poontang on every corner and I'm getting my share of it. No pussy minutes here. Hope you don't have any there. Much to discuss in the old stone room when I return.

Take care, friend
Jackson

I didn't know what poontang was, but I figured it had to do with either drugs or sex if Jackson was catching up. Jackson didn't make any mention of my letters and I wondered if he ever got any of them. I was looking forward to having Jackson back some day. There really was much for us to discuss in his stoning room. I hoped that being in the army wouldn't make him so straight that he wouldn't want to smoke marijuana anymore.

Connie was in the hospital a week or so later, just a few days after Christmas. No one told Graham or me and it was my turn that night, so I climbed through Connie's window and the room was empty. Connie's bed was made and there was no sign of her anywhere. I waited for half an hour or so in the closet, in case Connie's parents came into the bedroom with Connie, and then I climbed back down the ladder because Connie never arrived. Graham didn't believe she wasn't up there and had to climb up the ladder to see for himself.

The next day Graham stopped to visit Connie and that's when we learned that Connie was in the hospital. Connie's mother said that she had been taken in a couple of days before, but she wouldn't tell Graham anything about what had happened. Connie hadn't said a word to us about going in for tests or anything, so I assumed the worst. As soon as Graham could get his mother's car we drove over to the hospital. "I guess this is it for Connie," I said on our way.

Graham sighed. "And I thought that maybe she was getting better."

"Why would you think that?" I asked, surprised because recently it had seemed that way to me, too, and I had asked Graham before but he hadn't said anything. Graham looked over at me with a disgusted look on his face that I knew well. "Okay, so what did you lie to me about this time?"

"I didn't exactly lie."

"So, just tell me."

"Well, I heard Connie's mother talking . . ."

"When was this?" I interrupted.

"Oh, maybe a few weeks ago. I was waiting for Connie to come downstairs and her mother was on the phone talking to someone and she was pretty excited and happy. And Connie's mother is *never* happy. And I could only hear her side of the conversation, but she seemed to be saying that Connie was well or something. It sounded like that to me, but I figured she was just saying that Connie was getting better. And she said something about the baby being too far along or something."

"Why didn't you tell me about that?" I asked. "I don't understand why you wouldn't tell me."

"I didn't really know what she was saying. I didn't want to get your hopes up."

"Okay," I answered, realizing that Graham hadn't told me because if Connie were getting better there wouldn't be any reason for her to have two boyfriends. But I didn't care. I was happy that she had two boyfriends. I could see Graham making a mental note to add this lie to his list of sins. Then it occurred to me and I asked Graham, "What if she gets better? Do I have to marry her?"

"I wouldn't worry about it. If they had to rush her to the hospital she probably took a turn for the worse."

We found Connie alone in a small room at the hospital. Graham went in first because I was afraid to run into her parents, who still hated me. Connie was lying comfortably on a hospital bed and she was very happy to see us. Graham kissed her and then I kissed her. "What happened?" Graham asked, and he stood next to Connie holding her hand. He looked very sad and serious, expecting the worst.

"Nothing, just tests. They're just running tests."

"Why didn't you tell us, then?" I asked.

"I don't know. I guess I just forgot to tell you."

"How long will you be here?" Graham asked.

"For a few more days, I think. I'm not really sure why they want to keep me here all that time." Graham and I looked at each other and we both knew that there was something serious going on.

New Year's Eve was two days later. Graham had been bothering me to try the cocaine ever since we bought it and I had been putting him off because I wanted to save the cocaine for Vickie, just in case I miraculously found her one day. But tonight he was extra persistent, even for him. I guess it was because Connie was in the hospital and it was New Year's Eve and all. I had told Graham how Jackson liked to get stoned and talk about important things because he thought you got a different perspective when you were stoned. Graham kept saying, "We should do the cocaine and talk about Connie. And don't forget we bought the cocaine with Uncle Stan's money that was supposed to go to honor Connie. It's really both of our cocaine and it has to go to honor Connie."

So after Graham's parents went out I brought the cocaine over to his house. We found a small mirror and a razor blade and I poured out the cocaine and chopped it up the way I had seen Carl do it. Then I spread out some lines and rolled up a dollar bill. Graham said, "Jesus, Ben, where'd you learn all this stuff? I never should've gone to camp."

I leaned over the mirror and sucked a couple of lines into my nose. Then I handed the rolled up dollar bill to Graham, who did exactly what I had done. He sat up and asked, "Now what? I don't feel anything, yet."

"It's hard to explain. You feel good, and the top of your mouth and your front teeth get numb."

Graham sat staring at the floor, feeling around his mouth with his tongue. "I think I need more," he said. "I don't feel anything. Do you?"

"Not yet."

We each did three or four more lines but still didn't feel anything. "Damn! This stuff is fake," I said. "We were ripped off!"

"How do you know? Maybe it just takes longer," Graham suggested.

"No, we should feel it already. I'm sure of it. We were ripped off."

We did some more lines until Graham was convinced. "Damn," he repeated, then asked, "Don't you have any of that pot that you got from Jackson? We could do that."

"I don't have any more. All I had was a little and I smoked it."

"Without me?"

"I just had a little. It barely got me stoned. It was when I had to think about what was happening with you and Connie."

"Well, we should get some more pot and some real coke. It isn't fair that you've done both of them and I haven't."

"Okay," I agreed. I was beginning to see that it was a lot easier than I had thought to end up like Jackson. I figured that I'd probably end up like him in some areas. There was just so much of life and it took so much luck to find out about it.

Finally I took a bottle of brandy from my house and Graham and I split it. We walked up into the hills and sat under a pine tree and passed the bottle back and forth.

Graham said, "It's another year, Ben, another year."

"In a few hours," I answered. "What do you think we'll be doing on New Year's Eve in ten years?"

"If we're still around," Graham answered. "I saw this T.V. program where they were saying that everybody's having so many babies that there won't be enough food, so there'll be starvation and disease . . ."

"Yeah, and nuclear war," I interrupted. "Don't forget nuclear war."

"That's what I was going to say—we could have nuclear war by then."

"Well, I'm not worried," I said, and I leaned back against the hillside where we sat. I looked up into the night sky. "Screw nuclear war."

"I might build a bomb shelter by then, if we're still around," Graham said. "I'll be twenty-six, with my own house and my own family, and maybe we'll be sitting in my bomb shelter on New Year's Eve while they're having a nuclear war."

"Maybe," I said. "But I think I'll be doing cooler things than that."

We were silent for a while, passing the bottle back and forth. We had been invited to a couple of parties, but it seemed more appropriate for us to sit alone and get drunk, what with Connie dying in the hospital and everything. I had never really been drunk before, even with my family tradition. At first it was a little like getting stoned, but as we worked our way through the bottle it changed. Graham was talkative at first, then loud, then sort of morose and quiet, and finally he started to throw up. I didn't drink as much so I fortunately only made it to the quiet stage, which wasn't very morose for me. I expected that we would talk a lot about Connie, but we hardly talked about her at all. We discussed a little about life and we remembered some of the things we'd done together during our lives. When we were just a little drunk we started our remembering and out of nowhere Graham pulled three or four sheets of paper from his pocket and handed them to me. "Here, read this," he said.

I thought it was a list of Graham's sins, which he used to give me to review when he first started collecting sins. "Jesus Christ!" I said when Graham handed me the papers. "This is a goddamn thick list of sins!"

"It's not a list of sins, it's a story from when we were kids. It's also a little bit of a story about life."

"Yeah? Why are you carrying it around?"

"I was going to show it to Connie—she wanted to see it— only I didn't get a chance because she went into the hospital."

"Why did she want to see it?"

"Because I told her I wrote it. She wanted to see it because I wrote it. But you can read it."

"I didn't know you wrote this kind of thing—I mean stories and stuff. I thought you only wrote sins and poems about suffering."

"No, I also write stories." It was too dark for me to read the story where we sat, so we walked half a block to a street lamp and I stood under the lamp and read the story, which went like this:

You might argue that the children were caught up in every- thing around them—the thousand little details of the crowded street, the gentle breeze of the warm spring day, the million other tiny bits of life all around, or you might just say that there was some small purpose to one of them, the brown-eyed, brown-haired ten year old boy who looked like a thousand other boys, bumping into the man as the man stepped back from the store window. The boy was startled, though just for a moment, when the man raised his hand, and the boy took a step back. But before the invisible rock left the man's hand the boy already understood, and he managed just in time to have an invisible stick appear in his hand and to tap away the rock with the stick.

The man looked for a moment at the boy who looked for a moment also at the man. An invisible bat replaced the boy's invisible stick and he began tapping the bat on an invisible home plate. The man pulled an invisible baseball from his jacket pocket, inspected it, tossed it into the invisible air a few times, then walked out to the invisible pitchers' mound. The other two children, the catcher and the umpire, took their places. The people walking along the street did not understand and stayed off the playing field.

The man stood confidently on the pitchers' mound surveying the plate and the batter. He straightened his body, brought the ball and his mitt up to his chest, and threw a fastball: chest high, right on the inside corner of the plate.

"Ball one," announced the umpire.

The catcher tossed the ball back to the pitcher. The man was angry. He turned his back to the plate and walked a few steps back out to the mound. His next pitch was a curve, low and outside, obviously a ball.

"Ball two," he heard the catcher say.

Already the man was behind, two and zero, but he was far from worried. He signaled the umpire for a new ball, which he caught and inspected. He then took off his cap, wiped his forehead with his shirt sleeve and walked back up onto the mound. With his right foot on the rubber and his left foot toward home plate he stood for a long while, considering his next pitch and relaxing. He took a slow wind-up, followed it with a perfect release, and watched his change-up sail over the plate about waist high: a perfect strike.

"Ball three," cried the umpire and the man stared in disbelief. He took two steps toward the plate, then changed his mind. He had often found himself in this position, down three and zero. It was difficult to beat, but he was confident that today he would do it.

The man signaled the catcher to return the ball. He took off his mitt and walked out beyond the mound where he bent over and picked up his resin bag. He rubbed the bag between his hands, dropped the bag, put his mitt back on, and took his position on the mound. He stood deep in concentration, ignoring the signs from his catcher. He felt anxious, but still confident that he was in control of the situation. It was all up to him and he could handle it. His wind-up, release, and follow-through were flawless. A perfect slider approached the plate. The man released a sigh of relief and contentment as he watched the pitch—his best, just when he needed it. He turned slowly, away from the plate . . .

"Ball four!" screamed the umpire. "You stink!"

The man whirled again, quickly enough to see the three children running down the street, but too slowly to hit them with the invisible rock he held in his hand.

I read the story slowly, and I thought it was a good story. I was learning that Graham had a lot of interesting aspects to him that I didn't even know about. "Why didn't you ever tell me you write stories like this?" I asked Graham. "I've known you all these years and you never told me. And you start screwing Connie for a couple of weeks and all of a sudden you tell her everything."

"I don't tell her everything," Graham answered. "I didn't think you'd understand about the stories. You could hardly stand to read my list of sins when I used to give it to you."

"That's not true. In fact, I helped you with half of what was on your list. Just think about your early sins—probably half of them came from me. What about the sewers? What about throwing things at cars? And what about all the sins coming out of this thing with Connie? I'll bet you're getting hundreds, maybe thousands, and that all started with me. It's just that you wanted me to read your list constantly, so that I got sick of reading the same thing over and over again."

"Yeah, I guess so." We walked down the street and back up the hillside to the pine tree where we had left the bottle of brandy. "So you liked my story? Do you remember when that happened?"

"Of course I do." I remembered the Poet on the bluff from last summer and the poem he had given me. It seemed that everywhere people were writing stuff. "I like the story—it's history." I wondered if Graham was going to write about Connie some day.

"That's right. This is my first story that I finished." Graham folded the story and put it back in his pocket. "But I'm going to write lots more, about all the different things that happen to me in my life. I'm even going to keep my list of sins going until I'm fifty or so, and then I'll turn it into a book."

"You could call it 'Fifty Years of Sinning' . . . or 'My First Fifty Years of Sinning,'" I suggested.

"That's a good title—the second one especially—because I could write another book when I'm seventy-five, and then another when I'm a hundred. I could call the last one . . ."

"'A Hundred and Still Sinning Strong,'" I interrupted, and we both laughed. I said, "That's a pretty neat idea—to save a list of all your sins for fifty years. You could sit down once in a while and remember all the good things you did during your life."

"You're being sacrilegious," Graham said.

"Maybe for you, but not for me. I didn't tell you, but I've been keeping a list of my sins also."

"You are? For what? You didn't become Catholic or something, did you?"

"No, it's not for confession or anything. I'm just collecting them for myself, to keep a hold on how I'm living my life. But I'm keeping lists of other things, also." I explained my other lists to Graham and he listened intently.

"What do you have on all your lists?" Graham asked.

I wanted to tell him about a lot of the things on my lists, but I answered, "I'll tell you another time. I'll show you my lists sometime." I wasn't ready to tell Graham about Franny or about what happened with Vickie in the sewers or even about taking the pictures of Mrs. Kucher and so it wasn't worth telling him anything.

Chapter Thirteen

The next day was a new year and that's when we found out about the miracle. I'm not exactly sure when the miracle occurred. It might have been happening bit by bit for a long while, like most things in life.

Graham and I were both pretty sick from drinking the night before, so we didn't visit Connie at the hospital until late in the afternoon. "I'm glad you came," Connie said when we walked into her room. "I have something to tell you—I'm going home today. I'm cured!"

"What?" we both asked.

"That's right, I'm not sick anymore. The cancer's gone. It might come back sometime, there's always that chance, but it's gone now."

"How?" I asked. "I thought you weren't taking any drugs or anything because of the baby."

"It's just a miracle, that's all it is. Sometimes the cancer just goes away—hardly ever, but sometimes."

"They brought you in for tests to figure that out?" Graham asked.

"Well, not exactly. See, it's been going away for a while—the tests have been reversing or something, but they didn't know for sure. The tests were looking better and better until last week it looked like I was fine. They brought me in here to make sure and to try to figure out how it happened . . ."

"Why didn't you tell us?" Graham asked, before I could say it.

"Because I didn't know for sure. I wanted to know for sure before I told you. I didn't want you to get your hopes up." I looked over at Graham, remembering that he had said the same thing to me and I wondered if he remembered. Graham glanced back at me, with a little of that disappointed look on his face. We were both happy about the miracle, but somehow it didn't seem right that Connie hadn't told us she was getting better, and somehow it changed everything.

"Jesus Christ!" I said.

On our way out of the hospital Graham said, "I guess that at least takes care of doing that three-way thing with Connie. I can't believe she asked us to do that when she knew she was getting well."

"I can believe it. If I had two girlfriends I'd sure try to get them to both have sex with me at the same time—if I could."

After a moment Graham said, "Yeah, I guess I would, too. Only I didn't think girls would do the same thing."

"Me neither. But why shouldn't they? It just goes to show you what we don't know about girls."

That night we went back to look for a poor person. We had sort of put our search on hold because of everything that had been going on. We drove out to the poor area and on the way Graham handed me the money to count. I counted the money twice. "Is this everything?" I asked.

"That's all of it. Why?"

"There's only about $300 left. I can't believe we spent hundreds of dollars already. Did we spend all that just on food and gas?"

"Don't forget the fake cocaine."

"Oh, yeah," I remembered.

"We're going to spend all of it before we find the right poor person," Graham said.

"Yeah, except that we probably don't even have to find a poor person anymore since Connie isn't going to die." We hadn't spoken of Connie since we left the hospital hours earlier.

"That's true . . ."

"But we should," I interrupted, knowing that was what Graham was going to say. "Just because Connie isn't going to die doesn't mean we shouldn't give the money to a poor person. After all, we . . . *you* got it from your uncle to do that great thing in life."

Graham nodded. "Yeah, that's true. It just seems a little

different now that Connie's okay." He added immediately, "I'm glad she's okay, it just seems different."

"Aren't you a little pissed that you're doing that school project on Connie?" I asked.

Graham frowned. "Yeah. I'm a dumb ass."

"A suffering dumb ass," I offered. "You might get some good suffering out of this."

"Yeah, I guess it *is* suffering when you walk around knowing you're a dumb ass." Graham stood shaking his head. Finally he said, "We can still do it in Connie's honor, you know. I mean, for other people *like* Connie, who don't get better. There's still plenty of suffering. And Connie inspired us to do this."

"Sure," I answered. I didn't really care, I just wanted to be done with the poor person. We were silent for a few moments, and then I said, "What about that blind guy?"

"The blind guy? You mean Arthur?"

"Yeah, Arthur—we should give it to Arthur."

Graham shrugged. "Okay," he answered. "He's plenty poor enough, and blind to boot. We should've given it to him in the first place, right after we found him."

"And then we'll be done with it," I said. "We won't be looking around for poor people anymore, and life can just go on. And you can have Connie for your girlfriend, by yourself."

"What?" I was driving and looking forward, but I could feel Graham stare at me.

"I just said you could have Connie as your girlfriend. She's not dying anymore, so it doesn't make any sense for her to have two boyfriends."

Graham was silent for a few moments. "Maybe she should be *your* girlfriend. It's *your* baby. Anyway, I thought you were going to marry her."

"I'm not *planning* to marry her. I was just wondering before if I might *have* to marry her. But she didn't say anything about it, so I probably don't have to. That's all I was saying. So what's wrong with her being *your* girlfriend? You don't want her? I thought you loved her and that's why we both had to be screwing her and everything."

"I do love her . . . okay, she'll be my girlfriend."

Graham and I drove to where we found Arthur before, holding his metal cup. The evening sky was full of dark, ominous rain clouds. I love the rain and would have liked to walk slowly around or sit on a porch in front of one of these buildings waiting for the first drops, but we had to hurry because Arthur would probably leave once the rain started.

Arthur was leaning against a building. We parked and got out of the car and I said to Graham, "I wonder why he stands in that same place. Everyone around here is too poor to give him any money."

"Maybe he doesn't know how poor the area is because he's blind. He can't see it."

"He can tell if he's not getting any money."

"Where can he go if he's blind? He can't drive anywhere. And he wouldn't know where he was going."

"Yeah, I guess."

We reached Arthur and Graham said, "Hi, Arthur. Remember us?"

Arthur turned his head toward us. "Sure I remember. You're Connie's friends. You have something for me today?"

"Actually we do," Graham said slowly, and we looked at each other. "You have a good memory."

"For a blind vet. So, what do you have?"

Graham looked over at me again and I nodded my head. "Hold out your hand." Arthur held his hand out toward Graham, who looked up and down the street, then took a stack of bills out of his pocket. Arthur stood perfectly still, doing a blind-man stare at Graham. "Now, there's $311." Graham put the money in Arthur's hand. "Stick it in your pocket or something so no one will steal it from you. But just know there's a hundred, ten twenties, a ten and a one, in case anyone tries to cheat you.

"And one other thing you have to know, and remember. This is for Connie."

Arthur took the money and shoved it in his pocket. "You two are crazy. Who is this Connie?"

Graham and I looked at each other. I guess we didn't really know how to answer. Finally Graham said, "She's pregnant and she inspired us."

Arthur nodded his head. "You have any more money for me?" he asked.

"That's all we have," I said.

"Just remember it's for Connie," Graham said again. "You promise you'll remember that?"

"Sure I will."

We left Arthur and I was a little relieved that we were through with this place. But when we were half a block away Graham said, "You know, we should make sure he doesn't get robbed. Someone might have been watching us that we didn't know about. We should just watch him for a little while to make sure."

We looked back and Arthur was already walking away, tapping down the street with his white cane. We ran back and followed a hundred feet behind him. "How far do you want to keep an eye on him?" I asked.

"Just a few more blocks, until we're sure no one else is following him."

Arthur turned down a couple of streets, tapping wildly with his stick and walking pretty fast for a blind man, and then down an alley between an old building and a vacant lot. There he took off his glasses and put them in his jacket pocket, and then he started walking normally, with his cane tucked under his arm. He took the money out of his pocket and counted it as he walked. Graham and I looked at each other. "He's not even blind!" Graham said, and he was as stunned as I was.

"We were ripped off again," I said.

"I don't believe it! Jesus, we're dumb asses! First the fake cocaine and now the fake blind person. Jesus! Well, I want to follow him, just to find out where he's going. Maybe he's not even poor. In fact, I bet he sells drugs! That's why he stands at that same place. Remember he said he could get us the cocaine? I want to follow him."

Arthur cut across the lot to a large building that looked like an abandoned factory. The wall of the building that we could see was covered by layers of graffiti and had a number of windows that were protected by heavy metal bars bolted onto the building. Many of the windows were broken despite the bars, and in places paint was peeling from the building in large sheets. There was an old wooden door at the corner of the building and Arthur pushed open the door and walked in.

"Well, that's it. There goes our money . . . my uncle's money," Graham said.

"So much for doing that great thing," I said.

"Damn!" Graham answered.

"I wonder what he's doing in that building."

"Maybe he lives in there. He probably *is* poor, even if he sells drugs and isn't blind. Lots of bums live in places like that."

After a few moments I asked, "Do you want to go in and see?"

"Are you crazy? Who knows what's in there." I felt the first drops of rain on my face. "And it's starting to rain. Let's just get out of here."

"I think we should go in there."

"Why?" Graham asked.

I didn't know why, exactly. Maybe because it scared me to go in there. I answered, "It doesn't feel right. We can't leave it like this. We have to know a little more about the person we gave the money to . . . for Connie . . . or maybe because it's stolen money and you have to do right by it." I figured Graham couldn't object to that since he was the one who stole the money.

Graham sighed, "Alright, Ben. I just hope he doesn't murder us or something."

We ran across the vacant lot and carefully opened the door Arthur had walked through. Inside was a large empty room, littered with trash and a few pieces of old, broken machinery. The early evening light filtered through the dirty, broken windows. Outside was chilly and wet, but inside was colder and it made me shudder. There was an open door across the room and I said, "He probably went through there."

We walked across the room and as we approached the door

Graham said, "Maybe he knows we're following him and he's leading us some place to kill us. Maybe he thinks we have a lot more money."

I hadn't thought of that, but I answered, "I don't think so." We walked into another room, this one much smaller and completely dark except for some light coming from another door at the other end of this room. Graham and I looked at each other. "What do you think?" I asked.

"I don't know. Because we're dumb asses?" Graham answered.

I shrugged my shoulders. "Because we're dumb asses," I agreed. That was a good enough reason for me.

Through the other door was a small landing and a flight of metal stairs. The light was from a small fixture on the wall. "I guess we keep going," I said. Graham didn't answer, so I started down the stairs, which were steep and very long.

When I got to the bottom of the stairs I was in a long tunnel, about ten feet on each side. Metal pipes of different sizes, held into place by metal brackets every few yards, ran along the roof and along wall, into the distance. There were light fixtures like the one at the top of the stairs every twenty feet or so along one of the walls. I thought I saw someone, who I figured was Arthur, disappear far down the tunnel.

We walked a long ways, but there were never any doors to turn in. Finally I started to get kind of unnerved by being so deep in this tunnel. I asked Graham, "You think we can find our way out of here?"

"I was just thinking the same thing. Maybe we should give it up. I think we've gone far enough."

I was ready to agree until I saw what looked like an opening a ways further up the tunnel. "Okay, let's just check up there where it looks like there's a door, and then we'll go back."

We walked further down the tunnel and began to hear voices that got louder until we reached an opening in the wall, which was a metal door that was solid except for a rectangular hole in the middle of the door about two feet by three feet. The hole was covered by a wire mesh that was like a piece of chainlink fencing.

As we reached the door I could hear a man say, "Twenty dollars and the panties come off. I just cut 'em off."

Another man said, "You got twenty."

Graham and I looked at each other and then leaned over so we could look through the opening. We were looking into a large, empty room that looked like a storage room or something. Just a few feet to our left were a dozen chairs and to the right, about twenty feet or so, was a large, thin mattress on the floor. Men were sitting on most of the chairs and some of the men had cameras around their necks or on their laps. Arthur sat on one of the chairs, partly hidden by a man sitting in front of him. The men were watching a woman who lay on the mattress. She lay on her back with her head propped up on a thick pillow, facing away from us and her legs were spread wide apart. She was wearing only a pair of white underpants and a bright spotlight shined on her.

After a little while I noticed that around the woman's wrists and knees were ropes that were tied on the other ends to the handles on the sides of the mattress. A man sitting in one of the chairs held out a bill and another man walked over from next to the mattress and took it from him. Then another man, who was also standing beside the mattress, unsnapped a knife case on his belt and took a large folded knife out of the case. The man opened the knife and walked over to the woman, leaned down and took hold of the crotch of the woman's underpants and pulled it away from her body. He was bald except for a thin rim of greasy black hair and his head shined in the spotlight when he leaned over. He quickly cut the underpants across the crotch and once more across the elastic and pulled the underpants off of the woman. A number of the men took pictures. The woman shook her head back and forth a couple of times, struggling, and I could see her face briefly for a few moments. The woman didn't seem particularly attractive, but there was something about her face that was sort of familiar, although I couldn't say why, and it troubled me a little. The man holding the underpants tossed them on the bed next to the woman, then stepped back. The man looked like he was about forty years old and he wore a pair of black slacks, a white t-shirt and a pair of black dress shoes and his belly hung over the front of his pants. I could see the man's eyes as he stood up after cutting off the woman's underpants, and they were beady with a crazed look that made me nervous.

The man who had taken the money walked back over to the side of the mattress. He was thin and wiry, but muscular, and younger than the bald man, and he wore a patch over one of his eyes. He leaned over and slapped the woman's thigh, hard enough that it made me wince, although the woman didn't say anything. I wanted to say something to Graham, but I was afraid the men would hear me. Then the wiry man pulled a thick four inch needle out of his pocket and said, "Who wants to see this go through her nipple?" That's when it hit me, but I thought that it couldn't be. It couldn't possibly be.

"How much?" one of the men asked.

"Forty."

Another man said, "Forty dollars! Damn! This is costing way too much! She's an ugly bag!"

I was watching the woman intently, waiting to get a better look at her face. The wiry man glanced at the bald man on the other side of the mattress then looked back at the men in the chairs. "Look—it's forty or forget it. For forty we put one in both nipples, and then we work our way down." He leaned down and slapped the woman on her thigh again. The woman shook her head again, and again I got only a brief look at her face, and I still wasn't sure. But my heart was pounding so hard it was almost like I couldn't breathe! "Look down here. We can tie her open down here." The men in the chairs talked among themselves and then came up with forty dollars, part of it from Arthur. After the wiry man took the money he said, "Look. You came here for something different. For five bucks you could go anywhere. Where you gonna get this?"

One of the men said, "Let's see what we get. All I see is some ugly bitch on her back."

The wiry man lowered himself to his knees on the mattress beside the woman and took one of the woman's nipples between his thumb and forefinger. The woman struggled, moving her head from side to side, until the man brought the needle close to her nipple, and then she lay still, her head turned toward me, and I couldn't believe it! I just couldn't believe it. I just couldn't fucking believe it! I almost didn't recognize her because it didn't seem possible—but there was Vickie, with all those guys watching her and that slimy guy getting ready to put needles through the holes where she wore her little gold rings.

It must have hit me pretty hard because my knees got weak, just like you hear people say, and I thought I was going to slump to the floor. But only for a few moments because I had to watch what was going to happen. I looked over at Graham, who was still watching intently, with his mouth hung open. It bothered me that Graham and all these other men were watching Vickie that way. I thought of Jackson and knew how disappointed he'd be when I told him about this because, even though we had already cashed them in, this somehow it made our IOUs a lot less valuable, at least on Jackson's scale.

After the needle was all the way through Vickie's nipple, she screamed, and when the man was finished he stood up and Vickie moaned loudly and struggled against the ropes. The wiry man walked around the mattress and leaned down on his knees and took Vickie's other nipple between his thumb and forefinger, and when he was finished Vickie screamed again. Even though I knew she had the holes there already and I figured that the needles didn't hurt her at all, it still made me wince when the man put the needles in.

Over the next hour the two men pushed needles and rings through Vickie's lips down below and tied them open with thin chains wrapped around her legs and around the needles through her nipples, at each move getting more money from the men who watched and got more excited and walked around taking pictures. Arthur was walking around, looking at Vickie from all different angles and pitching in a lot of money to keep the men doing those things to her. I tried to keep track of how much of Graham's uncle's money he was spending, but there was no way

I could tell. After I recovered from the first shock, I was irritated and uncomfortable, and then I guess I got curious, and after a while I was sort of thankful that the men had enough money to keep getting Vickie doing all those things, although something in me really wished it was some woman other than Vickie. I kept wondering how Jackson was going to react when I told him about this. I was also a little worried about what some of those men might do to Vickie, but the two men running the show were amazingly good at making sure that the other men stayed at least a few feet from the mattress while they looked or took pictures. The few men without cameras became quieter and more sullen.

Vickie screamed frequently and moaned and pulled against the ropes. I watched her face to try to be sure that she wasn't really in pain, but from the angle we were watching I couldn't see much of her face except when she struggled and turned her head from side to side. Finally Vickie had chains holding her open and criss-crossing her body, and the wiry man said, "That's as far as it goes, gentlemen. Hank, let's go."

Hank pulled out his knife and quickly cut the four ropes that tied Vickie to the bed and he helped Vickie to her feet. Then he put a large overcoat, which I hadn't noticed before but which had been on the floor beside the mattress, around Vickie's shoulders, and the two of them walked away. Vickie walked slowly, with her legs far apart. "Another time, gentlemen, we can show you some more specialties," the wiry man said. "We can show you all kinds of things." The wiry man kept talking and glancing at Hank and Vickie, until a few seconds after the two of them walked through a door, and then he said, "Well, so long, gentlemen," and he backed away from the men until he got to the door and then he quickly disappeared through the door.

One of the men still in the room said, "Jesus Christ! How much did that cost us?"

Graham had no idea that it was Vickie we were watching, but he seemed to be in even greater shock than I was. I grabbed his arm and pulled him toward me. "Let's get out of here before they come through this door!" I whispered, and then I started running, with Graham right behind me. We ran full speed down the long tunnel and bounded up the stairs. The room upstairs was dark because it was night already and I tripped over trash of some sort as we ran across the room to the faint outline of the door we had come in through.

Outside it was raining hard. It always seemed to be raining lately. We were immediately soaked and cold, but we kept running until we were blocks away from the building. As soon as I caught my breath enough to talk I said to Graham, "That was Vickie."

"Who was Vickie? Who's Vickie?"

"The woman we were just watching, who was tied to the mattress—that was Vickie. She's the same woman we found in the sewers, that Jackson and I saved."

Graham stopped walking. "Bullshit," he said.

"I swear it. I completely swear it. That was Vickie."

"How do you know?"

"I just know . . . I saw her in the hospital, remember? I went there a lot of times, just to check on how she was. That was her, one hundred percent for sure."

Graham stared at me for a few moments, but it didn't seem to be all that significant to him, maybe because he wasn't in on saving her. "No wonder she ended up in the sewers," he said, finally, and continued walking. Then he remembered the IOU. "Jesus, Ben! You have an IOU from her! Jesus!"

"Yeah, but there's Connie to remember," I answered. I still hadn't told Graham that I'd already cashed in my IOU.

"That's true."

Once we were in Graham's car he said, "That was unbelievable! . . . I didn't know people did things like that! That was unbelievable!"

"There's a lot that people do that you and I don't know anything about. A lot. Believe me."

Graham was silent for a while, and then he looked over at me. "Maybe she would give *me* an IOU, too," he suggested. "If we tell her how I was the first one to see her. I bet she would. She didn't care that all those guys were watching her—what's one more

IOU to her? If it wasn't for me no one would have found her."

I couldn't believe Graham was asking me that, after everything that happened with Connie. I was thinking of asking if he wanted to get his hands on every woman I ever met in my life, but I didn't say anything. I actually didn't care if he got an IOU or not, so I said, "Sure. If we ever see her again we'll ask her."

We sat in silence for a long time before Graham said, "You know what I just realized? Arthur was paying that woman . . . Vickie?"

"Yeah, Vickie."

"Arthur was paying for what Vickie was doing with my uncle's money. The money we gave him to honor Connie."

"I know that," I answered.

"What should we do about Arthur? We have to do something about it."

"Forget it, Graham. We can't tell the police because you stole the money to begin with, and I'm not going to try to take it back from Arthur. He went to Vietnam, remember? Maybe he was a Green Beret or something and could kill us with one blow. Just forget it, Graham. We were ripped off again, and that's life. That's the risk you take when you take a stand and try to do some great thing in life."

Graham sighed. "Yeah, I guess so. We should've just kept the money and paid Vickie to do that stuff for *us*. I mean, Connie isn't even going to die anymore."

"Maybe you can talk Vickie into an IOU and she'll do that stuff for you when you cash in the IOU," I suggested. I knew that she wouldn't, but I figured Graham deserved to get a little crazy about it for being so bizarre.

Graham didn't answer for a long time, and then out of nowhere he said, "Well, one thing I know—we're spending way too much time in places like that tunnel. Remember the sewers and now this. That isn't normal."

"It's adventure, Graham. It's normal if you like adventure. If we didn't follow Arthur into that place we never would've seen what they were doing to Vickie. We might never in our whole lives know that stuff existed. Never."

"Well, we don't have to find out by crawling through the sewers and places like that. This is just a phase or something. Someday I'll travel around the world and do great things, and that'll be adventure for me." I had been turning the channels on the radio to find a good song, but I stopped at static when Graham said that. I couldn't help myself. It was getting so that nothing about me was different from anyone else.

"What's wrong?" Graham asked. "Why don't you put on a station?"

"Nothing." I turned to the next station. "It's just that you shouldn't even say that. You can think it, I guess, but don't say it."

"I shouldn't say what?"

"About traveling around the world and doing great things—stuff like that."

"Why shouldn't I say that?"

"Because you'll end up like my father. You'll turn around one day and find out that you're getting sort of old and you did hardly any of those things that you thought you'd do, and you'll know that you'll never do them, and then you'll sit around all day watching television and yelling at your kid because he doesn't do all the great things you didn't do."

"You think that's true?"

"I think it's true. I think it's like saying that a pitcher has a no-hitter going into the ninth inning—it just ruins it. Jackson told that to me once, only he was talking about *his* father, and it turns out it's just like *my* father, too."

Graham was silent for a short while and then he said, "I think that might be like my father, too."

Chapter Fourteen

After Graham and I visited Connie in the hospital and found out about the miracle of her getting better, everything happened with Connie in a way that was very strange. And it didn't seem right after how Connie and I loved each other and she was pregnant with my baby and all of that. Graham was at her house waiting for Connie to come home from the hospital. Only she wasn't especially happy to see him and didn't even want to talk for more than a few minutes. She told Graham that neither of us could climb the ladder up to her room anymore, but she wouldn't say much more than that. At least that's what Graham said. Of course it's possible that Graham was lying about what Connie said and that he actually carried the ladder to Connie's house himself those few nights before she left, but that's one of those things I may never know. Unless I get a chance to see Graham's complete list of sins someday.

It was in the morning of the coldest day of the year, two days later, and I was sitting on my front porch waiting for Graham to come back from visiting Connie. He was going to find out more about the mystery of what was happening with Connie, and maybe when I could see her again.

Graham came running up to me, exhausted and out of breath. He had run all the way from Connie's house. "Come, quick!" he yelled as he approached.

"Why? What's going on?"

"Just come! Now! Run!" I ran after Graham, not having any idea what was going on. We ran two blocks and stopped at a corner.

"What is it?" I asked again.

"Just watch," Graham said, between breaths.

A few moments later Connie's father's car drove slowly toward us down the street. When the car got close I could see Connie in the back seat and her window was down. She saw us and waved and blew two kisses, and then the car passed and after a few more moments it turned and disappeared down another street. "What's happening?" I asked.

"That was Connie. She's leaving with her mother." Graham was still breathing hard from running. "They're going to the airport to Toledo or someplace where Connie's aunt lives so that Connie can have the baby away from here. She's too pregnant to get an abortion now."

I looked down the street in the direction Connie had disappeared. "That's it? She just waved and blew me a kiss?"

"She just told me, Ben. I think she was surprised. Her parents figured this all out while she was in the hospital." Graham shrugged his shoulders. "That's what she told me. She just wanted to see you before she left. She said she'd write you a letter when she gets to Toledo, or wherever she's going."

"Jesus Christ!" I couldn't believe it. I didn't particularly want another letter.

"At least you're definitely off the hook for marrying her," Graham said.

"Yeah, I guess so." I figured that Connie was going to live and if she wanted to disappear then I could live with it, even if she did have my kid. Someday I would find my kid and I'd figure out what to do then. Connie never did send me a letter, but called instead. In fact she called an hour later from the airport. I was getting ready to leave with Graham to check Vickie's apartment again when my mother told me that Connie was on the telephone.

"Connie?" I asked.

"Hi, Ben. How are you?"

"Fine. How are you? Where are you?"

"I'm fine. I'm at the airport. I thought it would be better for me to call you here so it wouldn't show up on my aunt's phone bill. My parents still don't want me to talk to you."

"I understand," I said.

"Ben, I'm sorry I didn't get a chance to talk to you in person before I left. I didn't even know I was leaving—my mother planned it all. She thought it would be better if I have the baby out there—it's too late for an abortion, it would be too dangerous for me—and then I can carry on my life, maybe back here, except that I think my dad's going to sell the house." I didn't know what to say and so there was silence until Connie continued, "Ben, I just want to thank you for everything—for loving me and everything. I'm sure you'll get over me . . ."

"I'll never see you again?" I interrupted, and there was more emotion in my voice than I wanted. Just the other day I was ready to give Connie to Graham, and here I was getting upset that she was leaving.

"Not *never*—but maybe someday. You should just think that everything's over, that we're friends forever. You'll get over me, I know you will. You're young and good looking . . ."

"What about my IOU?" I asked, because I had thought about that after Connie left.

"Your IOU?" Connie hesitated for a few moments. "Oh, that." She laughed a little and said, "I guess you still have that and I still have half your sun. Maybe we'll trade back someday."

"Maybe I can cash in the IOU sometime."

"Maybe," Connie answered, but she didn't say it the way I would have wanted her to. I was being thrown over again and I didn't like the feeling. I wanted all the women to always be in love with me and it just wasn't working that way.

"I'm happy that you're well, Connie."

I didn't know what else to say and Connie said, "Thanks, Ben. I knew you'd understand—that's just how you are. I've got to go. I told my mother I was going to the bathroom." As soon as I hung up I wished I had asked about the baby and about ten other things. And then I wished I had told Connie how angry I was with her and how unfair it was that she had treated me the way she did.

Of course it didn't matter, anyway, because I found out that afternoon that Jackson got killed. It was a goddamn son-of-a-bitch. He was killed a week ago and no one even told me. Maybe he died while Graham and I were watching Vickie. Jackson was the best friend that I ever had and the best person I ever knew. Never mind that he stole the watermelon and picked the wrong philosophy in life.

His funeral was the next day. It was what you'd expect, except that it was real military with people in uniforms and everything and there was an American flag on the casket. Some priest or minister or someone gave a speech about Jackson and then his father gave a speech, but neither speech really said anything about Jackson. It was just a Jackson they wanted to invent and remember because he was dead. I waited through the whole ceremony, even though they were pussy minutes, most of them. They didn't open the casket, but when I passed by I put my hand on the cold, polished wood and said, "Good-bye, friend," and I guess I was crying a little, and people looked at me in a strange way because my hair was down to my shoulders and they were burying a soldier.

After the funeral I didn't know what else to do but go to the beach. I walked to the freeway on-ramp and stuck out my thumb. I ended up at the top of the cliff overlooking the ocean, next to the incline where I had walked up the wall last summer. I stood looking out at the ocean for a long while, thinking of oceans all over the world, and of large and small boats sailing or powering from port to port, city to city, places that someday I would see. It was cold, but I took off my shoes and set them on the ground at the base of the wall, and then I hopped up onto the wall. I looked out over the ocean and at the highway below. I was thinking how nice it would be to go back to last summer. I took a step along the wall, and then another and I wasn't giving a thought to walking down the wall, until one step led to another and I walked all the way down the wall. There was no one watching me and no pressure—it was just something I did. The cement felt rough and cold to the bottom of my feet, until my feet became almost numb by the time I jumped off the wall at the bottom of the incline. When I reached the bottom of the incline it wasn't last summer but was still that cold January Saturday, and everything else was still the same. That's when I decided that I would hitchhike to Philadelphia to visit Franny. I would leave tomorrow. It seemed like the only thing for me to do. I walked back up the incline on the sidewalk and put on my shoes and went back home.

That evening I told Graham about my call from Connie and about Jackson's funeral. "Yeah, she threw me over, too, before she left," he said. "I just didn't want to mention it before. Do you still love her?"

"I don't know," I answered.

"Me, neither," Graham said.

"She pisses me off."

"You're not kidding." Graham didn't say anything about Jackson. Nothing.

Then I told Graham all about Franny. He didn't deserve to hear and I don't know why I told him, except that I don't always do the noblest things. That's one of my flaws.

At first Graham didn't believe me about Franny, until I told him details, including the vibrator incident. I was going to tell him how I cashed in my IOU with Vickie, but for some reason I didn't. I could tell him someday, if I felt like it. It was nice to be able to tell Graham about Franny and, in a way, it was nice that Connie had thrown me over. Then I told Graham that I was going to Philadelphia to visit Franny. "I'm going to hitchhike. I'm going to have adventures on the open road, see the country, all of that."

"I'm going," Graham said. "Connie threw me over, too, you know, and I'd like to have those adventures."

"Fine, but I'm leaving tomorrow morning, at five o'clock. I like to leave early, and anyway, I have to get out of here as soon as I can."

"Fine, I'll be there."

We decided to have dinner at Betty's to talk about Connie and our trip and maybe just life in general. As we approached the door to Betty's there was an old man sitting on a bench by one of the tables. He was about sixty or so and he had a couple of days' growth of beard on his face. He wore a tweed sports coat and didn't seem to be a bum or anything, though his left arm hung limp at his side. He tried to catch my attention, only I ignored him and kept walking. But Graham walked over to the old man. Graham stood in front of him for a few moments and the old man mumbled some words that were hard to understand and motioned with his head so that Graham and I both looked down and saw that the man's shoe was off his foot. "You want me to help you with that?" Graham asked.

The man nodded his head and mumbled something else we couldn't understand and Graham bent down on his knee and put the man's shoe on and tied it. The man smiled at Graham and mumbled something else and Graham and I walked into Betty's to eat dinner.

"That was a nice thing to do," I said.

"I think he had a stroke or something so he couldn't get his shoe on," Graham answered. I was angry at myself for ignoring that old man. It wasn't much, but it was an act of kindness that Graham did and that I'll probably always remember and it pissed me off that I missed one more opportunity.

At five o'clock the next morning I was waiting with my backpack in front of Graham's house. It was still dark, without even a hint of day anywhere, and so foggy that the grass and bushes and even the sidewalks were wet. I was a few minutes early so I paced back and forth along the sidewalk. I was a bit agitated, but I was excited about leaving. I was thinking about how Franny would react when she saw me. I would probably be a little dirty and sunburned from being on the road, even though it was January. At first she would be shocked, but after a minute she would admire me for making the journey, and then she would realize how much she loved me and how sorry she was for leaving me. I hadn't yet decided whether I would take her back or just look at her and say something like, "I was passing through on my way to Tibet, so I thought I'd drop by for a minute," and then leave.

Graham came out of his house, but he was barefoot and wearing a bathrobe. I figured that he must have overslept and that he was coming out to tell me to wait a little while for him. At first he was walking and then he started trotting awkwardly toward me, holding his robe. "What's wrong?" I asked.

"I can't go," Graham answered.

"What? What do you mean?"

"Just that I can't go. I've almost got my dad talked into getting me a car—you know that. If I take off like this I'll never get the car. After I have the car we can drive to Philadelphia. There won't be any reason I can't go once I have my car." Graham was stepping from one foot to the other and holding his robe tightly around him because of the cold.

I watched Graham for a few moments and said, "You'd give up all that adventure, that experience of life, for a car?" "I don't know why you want to go see her, anyway. That's a long trip just to see *her*. Didn't you say she's already living with some guy? I mean, why don't you find another girlfriend around here? You can have plenty of adventure and experience of life right here. Didn't we have plenty already?"

"Maybe," I answered.

Graham went back into his house and I dropped my backpack at home and wandered through the streets, which were quiet and peaceful. I wasn't disappointed and I wasn't quite relieved, although I couldn't believe that I had been so sure about leaving and then given it up so easily. I wondered what kind of character I had. After a little while lights started going on in houses and the streets got peopled, and I went home and back to sleep.

I stopped to see Graham that afternoon and the first thing he said when he saw me was, "You're not mad about this morning, are you?" He didn't even seem surprised that I hadn't gone without him.

"No," I answered, and I really meant it. Graham was cutting up a watermelon in his kitchen and he offered me some of it.

I asked, "Is it stolen?"

Graham looked over at me like I was crazy and answered, "No, of course not. Why would it be stolen?"

"I don't know. I was just wondering." I wasn't hungry but I agreed to eat a piece of the watermelon because it was out of season and Graham told me that this was probably the only watermelon I'd get a chance to eat before next summer. We took the watermelon into the den and ate on a coffee table while we watched television. After we sat down Graham lit a cigarette. I had never seen him smoke before.

"What're you doing?" I asked.

"I don't usually smoke . . ."

"I know," I interrupted.

"Just when I eat watermelon. I learned it from a guy at camp. Watermelon tastes better this way." Graham took one or two puffs on a cigarette for each bite of watermelon. He was eating a full cross-section piece so it took him an entire cigarette to eat all of the watermelon. Graham asked if I wanted to try a cigarette with my watermelon, but I told him I wasn't that crazy. I ate a few bites of the watermelon, but it didn't compare with the stolen one I had shared with Jackson.

Graham spit a pile of seeds into his hand and said, "We both lost our true love—just like that. Can you believe it?"

"You mean Connie?"

"Who else would I mean?"

"Maybe she wasn't really our true love. If she cared that much about me, do you think she would've screwed you, too? Especially after she found out that she was getting better?"

"She might have. She might have decided she loved me more, but just didn't want to hurt your feelings . . ."

"So she let me keep screwing her?"

"Why not?"

I just shook my head. "It doesn't sound like true love to me. I think it sucks."

"We've both been thrown over twice since summer," Graham said. "But you can't let that ruin your whole view of love and humanity."

I looked slowly over at Graham and shook my head again. It was another of his bizarre lines. "I don't know where you get all that bullshit or how you can fit it all in your head."

"It's not bullshit—it's philosophy."

The next weekend we were at Graham's house with nothing to do, thinking how boring this week had been and how boring in general it was now that Connie was gone. It reminded me of what Jackson had once told me: that life was just a series of adventures with dead space in between. Graham suggested, "I think we should get drunk tonight, in honor of Connie . . ."

"In honor of Connie," I agreed.

"And Janie," Graham added. "My girlfriend from camp."

"Okay, in honor of her, too . . ."

"And Vickie."

"Okay . . ."

"And all our old girlfriends . . ."

"Which there aren't very many." I thought of throwing Franny into the pile, but decided against it.

"Then in honor of our future ones, too," Graham suggested, and we agreed to it. "And I know a party we can go to after we get drunk."

My parents and sister were out for the evening, so Graham came over to my house. We made an agreement that we would each take a drink from every bottle of liquor that we found and then we would go to the party. Graham didn't understand why I came up with that idea until we started looking for bottles. The bottles were mostly the thin, dark, bent-type, and they were everywhere. I was used to always finding them around my house, but Graham couldn't believe it. The bottles were in drawers, in closets and in cupboards all over the house. I knew where to find them from years of experience, but Graham picked up on it pretty quick.

Graham took the first drink from every bottle and he seemed to take large mouthfuls. I reminded him of how he threw up the last time, but he didn't seem to care. After Graham took a drink

I lifted each bottle like I was drinking a lot, but I drank just a little, I guess because I knew how many bottles we were going to find. I lost track of the number of bottles we actually found, but it was more than ten. We would probably have found more if we hadn't lost interest and stopped looking. I was drunk by then and Graham was past drunk. He was laughing and he wanted to go to the party right away. The party was about a half mile from my house and it took us about fifteen minutes to walk there.

It was long past dark because the days were so short this time of year. And it was cold, so I held my hands in my coat pockets and my arms close to my sides. I felt as though I were walking in a dark dream. Graham wasn't cold at all. He walked with his jacket open and he talked constantly as we walked, mostly about Connie and that it wasn't fair that she treated us the way she did, particularly me. The party was at the house of a girl from school who I knew only by name. I wasn't invited to the party and I don't think that Graham was either, but according to Graham it was a party open to anyone who wanted to go. When we got to the house Graham rang the doorbell and the door was opened immediately by a girl who I didn't know. Before we could say anything the girl said, "Come on in."

There were about thirty or forty people in the house and a few more in the backyard. I recognized a lot of the people from school, and I knew a lot of their names, but I didn't really know most of them well enough to talk to them. Graham started walking around and I pretty much followed next to him. He walked up to a few guys that he didn't know very well and he patted them on their backs. Then he went over to the bar where there were glasses and ice and open bottles of liquor. I didn't see any adults around and there were a lot of other people holding drinks. Graham filled one of those short glasses with scotch and drank it down without catching his breath, and then he drank down another glass—or at least half of the glass before he spit up some of the scotch.

That was when he started vomiting. First he stood perfectly still, took two steps, and then vomited half on a couch and half on the floor. All at once people everywhere were saying, "Shit!" so that the word was echoing through the house and sort of hanging in the air. I was thinking that the couch was wasted because it was white and brown, but it was lucky that the carpet was orangish-red because the vomit color might mix right in. No one wanted to touch Graham because he had vomit on his arm and he might vomit on them, but somehow he was directed into the bathroom and he vomited only once more in the hall on the way there. I couldn't believe the quantity that came out of Graham's stomach.

I followed Graham into the bathroom where he went straight for the toilet, ending up on his knees on the floor. The bathroom door was open and people were standing three or four deep watching him. It was pretty undignified for Graham so I said in general to the audience, "Don't you have any respect for other people?" and I closed the bathroom door. I guess the alcohol had made me a little depressed or something because I sat on the floor with my back against the wall, watching Graham, who was throwing up. It didn't seem to matter about Graham. He'd be better later or tomorrow. I was just sitting there thinking about everything that had happened to me lately. Connie was gone, Franny was gone, Vickie was gone, Jackson was gone, the summer was long gone, my hitchhiking trip to Philadelphia was gone. I had found out what poontang was and I was happy that Jackson got to do some catching up before he was killed. It struck me as odd that he had to go to war to catch up when there was supposed to be so much free love around here. Of course, like everything else, I guess that was only for some people.

The floor was made of small green tiles and slightly larger white tiles. I tried to find a pattern to the way they were placed on the floor, but there wasn't one. Then I tried to find a route from one wall to the other traveling only on the white tiles, and I couldn't find one of those, either. I sat there for quite a while, all pussy minutes. Graham had stopped throwing up and lay on the floor with one hand on the toilet seat.

The bathroom door opened part way and I was ready to yell

at whoever was behind it. But a girl stuck her head around the door and asked, "Can I come in?" I knew the girl by sight from school, and I knew that her name was Donna. She was short and slender with long dark hair and she had a very pretty face. I had seen her in the room where Graham first got sick. Before I could figure out anything to say, she came into the bathroom and closed the door behind her. She asked, "How is he?"

I looked over at Graham lying on the floor and I answered, "Fine. He just drank too much—it's been a pretty tough week for him."

"Why is that?" Donna asked.

"He got thrown over by his girlfriend."

"I'm sorry. It looks like he took it pretty hard." Donna stood at the door without saying anything more and I didn't say anything either. Graham moved and raised himself up to the toilet rim, but he didn't vomit again. I was uncomfortable with Donna standing there, but I didn't know what else to say. Graham looked over at her and then he curled into a ball on the floor. I was watching Graham, but he didn't move and he didn't say anything, so I looked over at Donna. "I'm Donna," she said, softly, and she leaned over and held out her hand like she wanted to shake mine.

"I know," I answered, and I slowly held out my hand. "I've seen you at school."

Donna took my hand and she said, "You're Ben, right? I've seen you at school, also." Her hand was soft and warm. She didn't try to pull her hand away, but I let it go because I felt as though I was holding on too long. Donna squatted down against the wall across from me. The room was small, so she was only a couple of feet from me. Graham was still curled up on the floor. He hadn't moved at all for a while.

"You don't usually come to these parties," Donna said, softly.

"No, I guess I don't," I answered. We whispered some bullshit for a while, and someplace during the bullshit Donna gave me one of those twenty pound looks with her eyes, the kind that weigh right down to your heart. I don't know exactly how it came about. It was stronger even than the one I got from Franny, which was the strongest one I'd had before. I just couldn't look away from Donna's eyes. I almost couldn't move. And I couldn't believe it was happening again so soon after Connie, so I said, "I better take Graham home. He's in pretty bad shape."

"Good idea," Donna said. "I'll give you a hand."

But Graham didn't want to move, much less walk half a mile home. He wasn't sick anymore so he was happy to lie motionless on the floor, curled into a loose ball on his side. I didn't want to sit in the bathroom all night, especially with the smell of vomit in the air and Donna sitting across from me. I said to Graham, who I knew wasn't listening, "I'll be back later." To Donna I said, "I need to get some fresh air." I said it quickly and stood up so that my eyes wouldn't get caught on hers again.

Someone had cleaned up after Graham, but there was still a faint odor throughout the house. We were standing in the living room and Donna said, "Why don't we go outside? I can still smell it in here, too." I agreed, although I wasn't sure what was going on. Those twenty pound looks don't necessarily mean anything. That's one of the things you learn in life.

Outside it was cold and I felt more comfortable. I started walking and Donna walked with me. We walked for quite a long time and we talked about a lot of things that weren't just bullshit. Donna told me that she was lonely sometimes and that she didn't like parties particularly and quite a few other things that you wouldn't think she would talk about. I got to like her a lot in the hour or two that we walked together. It got to the point where we stopped under a streetlight and I looked at her face and my heart picked up its pace all of its own.

We ended up at our school even though we were walking aimlessly. Donna said, "I've never been here this late. Let's walk around and then I have to get home—it's probably pretty late." We walked past the administration building, past the building where I had my English class and then Donna slipped her hand into mine. I looked over and smiled at Donna and she was looking up at me. Even in the scant light from the few bare light bulbs on the corners of buildings I could see a little panic in her face, and

I loved her for that. "You don't mind . . ." she began.

"I don't mind," I interrupted and I put both of our hands in my coat pocket.

We walked to the far end of the school to a large old tree with benches under it. We sat on a bench and Donna said, "I've never been under this tree. I always see people sitting out here . . . kissing." Then I kissed her and we hugged each other tightly. "I'd better get home because my father will kill me," she said.

I put my arm around Donna's shoulders as we walked and she leaned up against me. We walked for a long time without saying anything until we turned the corner onto the street where she lived and she said, "I'm glad that I talked to you at the party tonight. I didn't know I had the nerve to do that—to just walk up and start talking to you. I always see you at school and I kept thinking of talking to you there."

I was quite surprised by that. "Why didn't you?"

"I don't know, I just didn't." My hand was cold and stiff so I let go of Donna's shoulder and took hold of her hand. "I just always see you at school and you're always so tan, especially around summer. You're a surfer, aren't you?"

"Yeah, I am," I answered, before I could think about what I was saying.

"I thought you were."

We reached Donna's house and she said, "I have to go," and she gave me a light kiss on the cheek. "I don't want my parents to see anything. My phone number's in the phone book. I have my own phone so you can call anytime."

"I'll call you."

"Promise?"

"I promise."

Donna ran up to her front door. I watched her and I remembered Graham and walked the few blocks to the house where I had left him. I had no idea what time it was, but the party was clearly over. The house was quiet and dark except for a light on the front porch. I figured that someone had helped Graham get home.

Then I realized that it was quite late. The streets and houses were silent and motionless. Even the cold was heavy and still. There was only the barking of a single dog in the distance, and the imperceptible rising of a narrow crescent moon low in the sky. I walked slowly past the house and breathed deeply the night air. I was walking generally in the direction of my house, but I didn't want to go home. I wasn't sure what I wanted, and finally I decided to go to the beach.

I walked to the freeway on-ramp where I usually hitchhiked to the beach. There was a street lamp directly over the ramp and I stood in a vague spotlight. All around me the world was asleep. I waited at the on-ramp for five or ten minutes without a single car passing by, so I sat on the curb, gazing into the darkness beyond the light that surrounded me. Franny was on my mind and so was Connie and so was Donna. Peace was on my mind, and love, and Jackson was up there. Somewhere in my mind was Mrs. Kucher and somewhere was Arthur and somewhere was Vickie. There were more things in my mind than I could get hold of. They floated in the darkness, just outside the light, except for Donna, who all of a sudden was stuck firmly in my mind, who all of a sudden was crowding out everything else. A little of my heart was with Franny, and a little with Connie, and a little with my baby that would be born soon, but for now my mind was on Donna. I couldn't believe how life could just keep going on that way. I guess it's good and all, but I still couldn't believe it. I decided to walk to another on-ramp where I might have a chance of getting a ride.

After I reached the other on-ramp I got a ride almost immediately. The car was a plain middle class car and the man wore a green shirt. A plaid sports coat hung along the door in the back seat. As I got in the car the man looked at his watch and asked, "Where are you going at two-thirty in the morning, if you don't mind my asking?"

"I'm heading home. I live down by the beach," I lied, because it was easier than telling the truth. Anyway, I didn't feel like talking about it and I had the feeling that this guy was going to talk during the entire ride. But he didn't say anything else—he just turned the radio to one of those stations that plays elevator music.

I was already feeling tired during the ride, and when I was dropped off I was too tired to stand still or to sit down, so I started walking in the direction of the beach, which was still miles away. For a while I stopped and turned around and held out my thumb when cars passed. Then I kept walking but held out my arm when I heard cars or saw light from their headlights as they approached me from behind. Finally I just walked, not bothering to try to get a ride.

It occurred to me that if I had left for Philadelphia that morning, right now I might be asleep in any of a million places. It would have been a full day on the open road and I might be asleep in a boxcar or a flea-bag motel or in a field under the same sky that was over my head right now. My face would take its place among the myriad others, alive and long dead, that were weathered along those same roads, in that same desert by that same sun. It struck me that Graham shouldn't be out there with me, and I decided that when I went, and I *would* go someday, I would go alone.

I looked around at the quiet houses I passed and I imagined that I was in a place far from here, where I had never been before; that I didn't know what was around the next corner, what was to happen in the next ten minutes. And in a way I didn't. I looked carefully at a house across the street that had a single light burning in an upstairs room. I wondered if there was someone awake up there. I remembered hearing about a woman who lived a century ago who was studying to be a lawyer. At night she would tie her arm to a bed post while she studied so that if she fell asleep the pain would wake her up. I thought that maybe there was someone like that woman working up in that room. Or maybe someone just forgot to turn the light off.

I walked and I walked. I wandered back and around along streets I had never taken before. At each juncture I took the street I felt less inclined to take, so long as it took me toward the beach. It was cold all around me, but I was warm, even a little sweaty, and occasionally I dropped my coat off my shoulders. I felt drunk, but I was only tired and hungry. I had to pee in someone's bushes along the way.

As I got closer to the beach the fog began, and then I was walking in a dream world of darkness, silence and thick fog. I felt carried along, slowly, painstakingly through the narrow streets. I was trying to think how important it was to have peace all over the world, and love, and no nuclear bombs. I wanted to feel strongly about those things, even if Franny and other people left them behind. But my mind kept wandering until even Donna wasn't on my mind anymore.

Very gradually for a while and then much more quickly the world came to life around me. It was still dark, but I could feel tomorrow coming on, creeping up behind me as I walked. By the time I reached the park that overlooked the beach and the ocean, the new day was breaking behind me. But so far, just the barest trickle of sunlight had managed to work its way through the dense fog.

I was weary and I wanted to lie down. I had already decided to rest for a while under the poem tree. It was the only place I knew around here where I was sure that I wouldn't be disturbed. I climbed down the path on the side of the cliff, largely feeling my way in the early morning light that was still no more than a faint glow to the fog. I looked for a long time, but I couldn't find the path that led to the poem tree. I guess that you can't expect one person's path to stand up to even five months of rain and wind and growing brush. Finally I just pushed through the brush and worked my way to the tree. The tree looked the same as the last time I saw it and the small clearing under the tree was still there. I lay down under the tree and looked down at the highway and the beach. Through the fog the highway was just occasional headlights of early Sunday morning traffic and the faint outline of the few small buildings that were lined up along the highway. Beyond the buildings I saw the beach quite clearly, only it was summer in Atlantic City and my grandparents, who were long dead, were there, wearing those funny old-time bathing suits. I blinked my eyes and there was only the highway through the fog, so I blinked my eyes again to see what would happen, but nothing happened. Then I laughed right out loud because it occurred to me that all the world was carrying on around me and I just lay there in the fog, a little crazy, maybe, awash in pussy minutes and collecting sins. But I was too exhausted to deal with all of that right then, so I closed my eyes to go to sleep.

BOOKS AVAILABLE FROM SANTA MONICA PRESS